RESOUNDING PRAISE FOR
THE AWARD-WINNING NOVELS OF
ROBIN BURCELL

"[Burcell] grips like a pair of police-issue handcuffs . . . [with] total authenticity, high stakes, and extreme suspense."
Lee Child, *New York Times* **bestselling author**

"Great authors only get better over time. [Burcell is] pushing to new heights of storytelling . . . [with] intrigue and cutting-edge forensic science."
James Rollins, *New York Times* **bestselling author**

"Excellent . . . [Burcell] scores big. . . . A real winner."
John Lescroart, *New York Times* **bestselling author**

"Terrific."
Library Journal **(★Starred Review★)**

"Smart and sexy . . . [Burcell] kept me up all night."
Janet Evanovich, *New York Times* **bestselling author**

"Riveting . . . I couldn't put it down."
William Heffernan, Edgar® Award-winning author

"Smart, tough, and right on the mark."
Catherine Coulter, *New York Times* **bestselling author**

"Robin Burcell is among the best writers of crime fiction."
Jan Burke, Edgar® Award-winning author

By Robin Burcell

ROBIN BURCELL

THE KILL ORDER

HARPER

An Imprint of HarperCollinsPublishers

"The Last Second" was first published as an e-book novella December 2013 by Harper Impulse, an Imprint of HarperCollins Publishers.

This is a work of fiction. Names, characters, places, and incidents are products of the author's imagination or are used fictitiously and are not to be construed as real. Any resemblance to actual events, locales, organizations, or persons, living or dead, is entirely coincidental.

HARPER

An Imprint of HarperCollins*Publishers*
10 East 53rd Street
New York, New York 10022-5299

Copyright © 2014 by Robin Burcell
"The Last Second" copyright © 2013 by Robin Burcell
ISBN 978-0-06-227371-0

First Harper mass market printing: January 2014

HarperCollins ® and Harper ® are registered trademarks of Harper-Collins Publishers.

Printed in the United States of America

Visit Harper paperbacks on the World Wide Web at
www.harpercollins.com

10 9 8 7 6 5 4 3 2 1

To my mother, Francesca,
who always encouraged imagination and dreaming.

Acknowledgments

I owe a debt of gratitude to the usual suspects who have helped me with some of the details that bring the best out in a story. Sometimes I have to stretch reality to fit my plot. Any factual errors are mine. Come to think of it, any fictional errors are mine, as well. To (retired) supervising Special Agent George Fong, FBI, who always ensures that my FBI elements are based on reality. To (retired) Sergeant Dale Miller, LPD, my expert on explosive devices, who has helped me through several books and short stories to ensure that anything that explodes does so with a semblance of believability. To author Susan Crosby, my friend who has faithfully read each of my books all these years, offering the best of advice that has added to the story. To my mother, Francesca Santoro, who has helped me with all the various European locations, those we visited together, and those with which she had personal experience. To my friend Paolo Magnanimi, of Rome, Italy, the owner of the wonderful restaurant Hostaria Antica Roma (who asked to be an assassin in this book! Your wish has been granted!), who kindly helped me with some Italian translations. Thank you all.

Of course a book wouldn't be published without those who work behind the scenes. To my agent, Jane Chelius, for being there for me. To everyone at HarperCollins for all the hard work. And to my editor, Lyssa Keusch, (who always manages to make me laugh with some of her comments in the side margins), my books are always better because of you.

The only secure computer is one that's unplugged, locked in a safe, and buried twenty feet under the ground in a secret location . . . and I'm not even too sure about that one.

Dennis Hughes, FBI

One should rather die than be betrayed. There is no deceit in death. It delivers precisely what it has promised. Betrayal, though . . . betrayal is the willful slaughter of hope.

Steven Deitz

1

South San Francisco, California

Piper Lawrence eyed the cigarettes in the pocket of the man sitting next to her on the bus. She'd given up smoking a year ago, because she couldn't afford it *and* community college. Or anything else for that matter. Books cost a fortune. Food wasn't exactly cheap, either. But sometimes people tucked money in their packs—she used to. Besides, pickpocketing kept her skills sharp, and in this case it wasn't really going to harm anyone.

Her stop was coming up, and she waited for the bounce that always occurred as the bus crossed this particular intersection . . . Then, "Sorry," she said, accidentally bumping into the man as she rose from her seat. She moved toward the front, holding on to the handrail. As the bus slowed, then stopped, she hurried down the steps, and the door swished closed behind her, sending a slight gust of air at her back as the bus took off.

The cigarette pack felt slightly heavier than it should, and she was curious, but figured it wasn't wise to open it there, in case the guy discovered it missing too soon. She quickened her pace, turned the corner, and walked the two blocks to her destination, a small business park filled with warehouses, most subdivided into small shops. It was located in the city of South San Francisco, on the east side of Highway 101. Her friend's shop wasn't in the nicest of areas, but this time of night it was quiet.

About to open the pack, she hesitated when she saw a black sedan parked near the corner. The streetlamp cast just enough light for her to see two men sitting in the front seat, and a third man with gray hair standing at their open window. Apparently the conversation had concluded, and he started to walk away, but the driver called him back, saying, "Hey, Brooks." The man returned to the car.

The vehicle faced the direction she was headed, and she couldn't see the two men he was talking to, or hear what they were saying. For a moment, though, she thought this Brooks guy was the gray-haired man from the bus, waiting with undercover detectives to arrest her for pickpocketing. Then again, she'd been in the back of a few cop cars. Around here they drove those big Fords, she thought as the gray-haired man turned, looked right at her. She realized then that he was not the same person at all, and she chided herself.

How stupid to think they'd send out detectives over a pack of smokes, and she wondered why these men were here at all. This time of night, everything in the area was closed.

Drugs? Probably not. They didn't look the type.

Since none of them seemed interested in her, she ignored them, crossed the street, and opened the cigarette pack, thereby discovering it contained a few cigarettes and a lighter, which was probably why it felt heavy.

Waste of talent, she thought, then pushed open the door of her friend Bo Brewer's shop. Bo fixed things for a living. Today it was copy machines. Tomorrow it would be something else, depending on what he bought from the government surplus auctions. In the most recent lot, he'd purchased seven copy machines, all the same model, all in various states of repair. The fact he was able to buy perfectly good office equipment for so cheap was, in his opinion, why the government was broke. He'd quickly fixed two machines by swapping out parts, estimating that he could sell the pair for what he'd paid for the lot, which meant that he'd already recouped his investment.

Bo looked up as she walked in. "Hey," he said, then bent back down over his keyboard, typing something into his computer.

"You realize there's two guys sitting in a car out there? Some guy talking to them. Kind of strange, don't you think?"

"Saw it there earlier. Probably the cops. I think the auto repair shop next door is dealing in stolen car parts."

"Doesn't look like a cop car."

"If they're undercover, it wouldn't."

"I brought you something." She set the cigarettes and lighter on his desk.

"Who'd you steal that from?"

"Some guy on the bus."

He went back to work.

After a long stretch of silence, she said, "Let's go somewhere. A movie."

He didn't answer. It wasn't that Bo was ignoring her. It was more that he was intent on what he was doing. A week ago after he'd finished breaking down the remaining machines, determining which could be used for parts and which would be repaired, he made the unfortunate-for-her discovery that the federal government had left the hard drives in the copy machines. The moment he tapped into a few, he'd become obsessed with reading what was on them. Especially one machine from the San Francisco FBI office because it had something on it besides the usual reports on bank robberies and white-collar crimes. A page filled with nothing but a list of numbers. Bo figured it was a code of some sort. Because he was a semidecent computer geek, it was now his mission in life to learn what it was, and he'd searched every which way on the Internet, even running it past one of his geekier friends.

He balked when the guy wanted to see the whole thing. He was paranoid. Nothing was safe on the Internet in his opinion, and so he never showed the entire list.

He did, however, give it to her to read, but it meant nothing to her. Numbers just sat in her head, literally and figuratively like dead weights, refusing to go away.

And tonight, he was still at it. Piper watched him for a few minutes, bored to tears, hoping he would have moved on. She liked him, a lot, but he didn't seem to notice the attraction. In fact, the only time he seemed to pay attention was when he needed her to memorize a list. Like the stupid numbers.

Piper had an eidetic memory for anything she read, including long strings of useless numbers, the result of an injury to her left hemisphere at the age of twelve. Unfortunately all it did was turn her into a novelty when anyone found out, especially at parties. Bo was the only one who seemed not to be fazed. Until he'd found this list.

"Bo, you promised we'd do something tonight," she said.

"We will. Soon."

She sat on the edge of his file cabinet, eyeing the computer monitor. "Why are you still working on those things?"

"I think it's some sort of program code. Why would they have copied it, unless it was something important?"

"At least take a break." He started typing, and she wondered if he even knew she was there. Hell. Did he even know she was a woman? "You want to have sex?"

He stared at the computer, not hearing a word.

"We could do it right here. On the desk."

"Wait a sec," he said, typing fast.

"Isn't that stuff supposed to be classified or something? It's from the freaking FBI. What if they catch you?"

"This from the girl with the sticky fingers? They shouldn't be leaving this stuff on hard drives if they don't want someone reading it. Lucky for them it's only me and not some terrorist, right? Besides, I erased the hard drive so I could reinstall it in the copy machine after I fix it."

She hopped off the file cabinet and moved to the window, peering out the slats of the vinyl blinds. The car was still there, the two men sitting in it, but the third man was gone. "Maybe those guys waiting outside are the FBI. Coming to arrest you."

"Yeah. Right. Besides, one touch of the button, this thing's erased. They'll have a hard time proving their case."

"Can you play with this later? I'm hungry."

"I called in for pizza right before you got here." He held up his car keys. "I'll share if you go pick it up . . . ?"

She took the keys, gave an exaggerated sigh of discontent—not that he paid the least bit of attention—then said, "Money?"

"Upstairs. And don't take all of it!"

"Have a little faith, Bo. I don't steal from my friends."

She walked through the dark shop, then on up the stairs. Bo lived in the loft above the warehouse shop, even though the area wasn't zoned for residential. Maybe not the nicest view out the second story window, unless you liked to watch cars on the freeway, but the neighborhood was quiet. And since the commercial warehouses closed at night, Bo had considerable privacy, something Piper cherished, since her own apartment complex had paper-thin walls and nosy neighbors to the extreme. She turned on the light, found his wallet on a mirrored tray at the kitchen counter, took out enough money for the pizza, then stopped. The strangest feeling swept over her, and she looked around, not sure what was wrong. And then it occurred to her that the window was open.

Strange, since Bo wasn't the fresh-air sort, especially in winter, when he was paying for the heat. And it definitely was cold in here.

Shrugging it off, she turned out the light, and was just starting down the stairs when she heard the swish of the shop door opening.

She stopped in her tracks. Looked down the stairs, and though from up here she could see only their legs as they both headed straight for Bo's office, she knew without a doubt they were the two men from the car. It didn't take a rocket scientist to realize they weren't there for a late night sale of used copier parts.

"Bo Brewer?" one said.

"Who's asking?"

"You got something of ours. We traced it to your computer."

"Are you the police?"

"We're much bigger."

Piper's heart started a slow thud, and she stepped back in the shadows. *Please don't let him get in trouble . . .*

"The numbers you were running? Where'd you get them? And what are you trying to do with them?"

"I—I found them. I don't even know what they are."

"That right? From where?"

"A hard drive. I wasn't doing anything with them. I just wanted to know what they were."

"Where is it? The hard drive?"

She imagined him pointing to the bin on his desk as he said, "But it's erased."

"Listen real careful. I need to know *every* copy you made."

"Just there. On the computer. But it's erased. I swear."

They were going to arrest him. Would they arrest her, too? She stuffed Bo's keys in her pocket so they wouldn't rattle, then backed up the stairs.

"Does anyone else know about this?"

"No. I swear."

"What about the girl we saw? What does she know?"

"She's, uh, upstairs. She looked at them, but that's all," Bo said.

Piper's heart constricted. Why had Bo implicated her in this? She had at least two stolen credit cards in her apartment, and she wondered if they'd go there and search it.

"Get the computer."

"Hey— Look. I'm erasing it. See? You don't need to take that."

"What the— Get that computer. Shut it off."

Suddenly a hand clamped down on Piper's mouth. Someone pulled back, hard. She waited for her neck to snap, wondered if she'd feel it. Her pulse thundered in her ears as he clamped tighter.

A gunshot echoed through the warehouse.

And before she could even grasp that Bo had been shot, that she was next, her captor put his mouth next to her ear, whispering, "I'd like for us to get out alive. So *don't* make a sound." He lowered his hand.

She was almost afraid to turn, but her would-be rescuer took her by the hand, pulled her to the kitchen area. She caught a glimpse of someone tall and broad-shouldered, in black clothing. "On the counter," he whispered.

This didn't make sense. She eyed him, and he pointed up. She looked, realized he was going to lift her into the rafters. Her gaze swung to the open window, and suddenly things started to make sense. And here she thought she was the cool thief. He'd climbed in the window, had hidden in the rafters, and had probably watched her when she'd walked upstairs to get the money.

He took her by the waist, lifted her onto the counter, followed, then hoisted her so that she could grasp on to the lower crossbeam in the rafters.

What she couldn't do was pull herself up beyond hanging there with the beam beneath her armpits, and then she heard that voice from the office. "Look for the girl upstairs. I'll look down here."

"Right."

Her rescuer was unfazed. He gave a hop, grasped the lower beam, pulled himself up, swung one leg over so that he was straddling it, reached down and pulled her up the rest of the way. And then, as if he did this all the time, he stood, held on to the rafter, and reached out to help her to her feet.

She looked down, her heart racing as she heard the heavy footfalls of someone on the stairs. A moment later, the gunman was there in the loft, a flashlight beam bouncing around as he searched the walls. She kept waiting for it to aim upward, reveal them, and she glanced at her rescuer, surprised to see a gun in his hand. Was he a cop? The two men who shot Bo obviously weren't. Or if they were, they sure as hell weren't on the side of the law.

What had Bo gotten into?

The gunman's flashlight swung up and she gripped the wood tighter, certain he was going to shoot them, but then heard a soft click as he turned on the light in the main living area.

He shoved the flashlight in his pocket, and gun in one hand, he walked toward the kitchen. She glanced down, saw her reflection in the mirrored tray right beneath her where Bo's wallet sat, and she prayed the intruder wouldn't notice.

"Find anything?" the other called from below.

"Nope."

"You see any computers up there?"

The man stopped, looked around. "Not a one. The window's open. She musta gotten out that way."

"Let's go. We've spent enough time here."

He moved to the window, looked out, then returned the way he came, shutting off the light before heading downstairs. She didn't dare move, barely dared to breathe, until she heard the swoosh of the warehouse door as the intruders left.

Suddenly she felt sick, the adrenaline starting to flush from her system, and she barely had the strength to hang on to the rafter. She looked at the man standing in the shadows across from her, his gun still pointed toward the stairwell.

"Who are you?" she asked softly.

He held up a finger, waited several seconds before answering, as though listening for something. "Let's get down from here."

She wasn't sure if she could, her knees were starting to shake.

"Sit on the crossbeam, then turn," he instructed her. She did, and he holstered his gun, hopped down first, his agility confirming in her mind that he was used to this. She was not, and her effort would have been comical, if not for the circumstances. Once they were on the floor, he held out his hand, saying, "Griffin. Department of Justice."

"Why didn't you shoot them, Griffin, Department of Justice? And how do I know you're really who you say you are?"

"First, I'm here by myself, and I don't know if there were only two. I didn't like the odds. Second, you're going to have to trust me on this, since I'm all that stands between you and probable death."

"But they're gone."

"For now. What's your name?"

"Piper."

He motioned her to follow him to the stairs, and as they descended, he asked, "Do you know anything about this list of numbers those men were asking about?"

She stopped, crossed her arms. "Maybe trust is too big a first step. Do you have ID?"

He gave her a slightly annoyed look over his shoulder, dug

a billfold out of his back pocket, then handed it to her as he continued down the stairs.

She opened it, could just make out the seal of the United States Department of Justice, and then his photo and name, Zachary Griffin. It seemed legit—and unfortunately devoid of money and credit cards. "Your wallet."

He took it from her, and returned it to his pocket. "About those numbers?"

"He found them on a hard drive."

"Where'd he get the computer?"

"Not a computer. A copy machine."

"A what?"

She pointed into the depths of the darkened warehouse, where just visible in the light spilling out of the office sat the copy machines Bo was in the process of rebuilding. "He bought them at a government auction. The one with the numbers came from the San Francisco FBI office."

He stopped suddenly, turned toward her. "You're sure?"

"Very. There were other reports on it. But he didn't look at those. I swear."

He glanced toward the machines, then started toward the exit once more. But as they approached the office, he said, "Wait here."

He walked into the open door, was gone no longer than thirty seconds before stepping out and walking back to her. "Was he a friend of yours?"

People didn't say "was" unless the outcome was death, and she nodded. Tears clouded her vision.

He took her hand, saying, "When we walk past, try not to look in. Maybe even close your eyes. You don't want that to be the way you remember him."

"Okay." It came out more of a croak, her throat having closed up, and she was grateful when he didn't let go. As they approached the office, she caught a glimpse of black and white on the floor before she looked away. Bo's Converse tennis shoes, she realized, then squeezed her eyes shut, not opening them again until he led her outside and the cold misty air hit her face. Only then did she say, "Shouldn't we call the police?"

"No."

"But—"

"The last thing you want is your name in that report. The men who killed your friend? They won't think twice about coming back for you. They have his computer, which means if your friend communicated with you through it, you're at risk anyway."

"What am I supposed to do?"

He looked toward the end of the drive, saw a vehicle slowly cruising toward them. Headlights suddenly turned on, blinded them, and the vehicle sped up. "Right now?" he said, grasping her hand tight and pulling her in the opposite direction. "We run."

2

Several days earlier, Special Agent Zachary Griffin received an alert that a partial match from a list of numbers code named the Devil's Key—stolen by a former military agent and hidden away at a villa in Ensenada, Mexico—had popped up from an IP address in the Bay Area. It had taken his team that long to track the computer to this warehouse, and he'd prayed that the FBI connection he'd suspected wasn't a factor. What he didn't expect was that someone else was tracking it, too. That meant that someone other than an authorized U.S. agent—and as far as he knew, the agents on his team were the only ones authorized—had tapped into a secure database.

In other words, a simple operation to plant a few bugs and find out where the info originated had gone downhill fast. And as much as he'd hoped there was no connection to the San Francisco FBI field office, or Sydney Fitzpatrick, the FBI agent he was currently dating, tonight's mission had confirmed his worst fears.

Now he had one civilian dead and was left babysitting an-other one who looked like she'd just stepped out of some mosh pit from an underground concert, with her black and pink spiky hair and facial piercings.

So much for getting in and out without a body count, he thought, hitting the button on his Bluetooth to call his partner, James "Tex" Dalton, who was supposed to be checking the other source of the numbers, a friend of this Bo Brewer's at an apartment about two miles away. The two had used computers to send the numbers back and forth. He and Tex had decided a divide-and-conquer approach would be faster. Now Griffin wished they'd stuck together.

"Where are you?" Griffin asked, when Tex answered.

"Just hitting the freeway. The source on this end? Bo Brewer's friend? Dead. And they took his computer."

Two deaths. "They're here now. Same result. Except they're looking for us."

"Us?"

"Picked up someone. We could use a ride."

"On my way."

Griffin heard the beep as Tex disconnected, then looked over at the girl. At least she wasn't prone to hysterics. And she was dressed in black. He led her to the rear of the building, just as the car pulled to a stop out front. A chain-link gate blocked the vehicle from following them, and he heard the engine shut off and two car doors closing. Only two. He could deal with those odds if necessary, but he'd rather avoid any shooting. In this area, if anyone heard the earlier shot, it might be dismissed as a backfire. Multiple shots were likely to be called in, and if he could, he'd like to get out before the police arrived.

Looking around, he saw the yard belonged to an auto repair shop, and he noticed a stack of old tire rims near the wall that separated the area from the freeway. Counting on the road noise to help mask any sounds, he leaned close so she could hear. "Do you have a cell phone?"

"Of course."

"Turn the ringer off. Don't use it. Unless I'm dead, dying, or bleeding. Your number will come up on the police switchboard, which means a trail directly to you. Very bad," he said, then directed her behind the rims, not having time to explain why that would be less than desirable. He drew his gun, then watched as the two men came down the side of the building.

He looked over, saw a hole in the fence between the auto repair yard and the warehouse yard next door. "If I can create a distraction, we're going to move to that fence, then go under."

"Distraction?" She dug into her pocket. Pulled out a set of keys with a remote, then pointed it up the drive toward the two men who were heading their way. The pair walked past a dark SUV parked alongside the building. "That's Bo's car," she said, then pressed the button. The car alarm beeped. The suspects stopped, swung around toward the vehicle, pointing their guns.

"Get ready," Piper whispered, then pressed another button.

The SUV's engine started and the headlights turned on, silhouetting both men, who started firing at the vehicle as they advanced.

Impressed, Griffin pulled Piper toward the fence. Piper scrambled under and Griffin followed suit. They raced around the building toward the front.

"That's their car," she said, pointing to a mid-sized Chevy.

There were several cars parked in the lot, and since he'd come around from the other side when he'd made entry, he had no idea if that one had been there earlier. "How do you know?"

"License plate's the same."

Not a lot of people went around memorizing license plates. An oddity for sure, but he wasn't about to stop and ask her why. He nodded toward the corner. "End of the street, turn right. My partner, Tex, should be arriving any minute in a dark blue Ford Fusion. I'll be right behind you."

She hesitated the barest of instances, and he pushed her in that direction. "Go!"

She ran.

Griffin kept close to the building, making his way to where the gunmen's car was parked. He peered around the corner, saw them looking into Bo's SUV. One of them started swearing, as the other yelled, "Idiot! It's a remote start. They're still back there." Both men lumbered down the drive toward the rear of the auto repair shop.

Perfect, he thought, then pulled a knife from the sheath in his belt, aimed, and threw it at the car's left front tire. The moment he heard the hiss of air as it hit, he raced toward the end of the street. As he rounded the corner, he saw Tex waiting in the car, but Piper was nowhere in sight. He didn't have time to hunt for her and try to convince her that, for a while, her life was no longer her own. But she popped up from behind a hedge, and when he pulled open the back door, she slipped in without him asking.

"Buckle up," he said, then got into the front seat. And just as Tex hit the gas, then sped forward, he caught a glimpse of one of the gunmen in the side mirror running around the corner. "Get down," he told Piper.

Tex kept it floored until the first right that led over the freeway. He didn't slow until he was certain they weren't being followed, then worked his way around until he found the freeway onramp.

"Where are we going?" Piper asked Griffin.

"As far from here as we can get."

Piper was quiet a moment, then asked, "What do the numbers belong to?"

Tex glanced at Griffin, then back at the road. Griffin wasn't about to divulge anything to her, but he still needed to know what she knew. "What'd your friend tell you?"

"He thought they were some sort of computer code."

"Any idea what sort?"

She shook her head. "He said they might be out of order. He changed them around because it made more sense."

Griffin noticed Tex's grip tightening on the steering wheel, undoubtedly wondering what exactly her friend had just delivered to the enemy before he was killed . . . "In what way?" Griffin asked, trying to keep his voice neutral, as though none of this was of any importance.

Piper shrugged. "Trust me. I had no idea what he was talking about. Besides, he erased them. They got nothing."

"Any chance he made a copy they don't know about?"

"He didn't need to. He had me."

Tex checked his rearview mirror, then signaled and moved to the slow lane. "Maybe we should find a place to stop," he said, taking the next exit. Eventually he drove into a grocery store lot, parking so that he had a view of the cars coming in and out.

Griffin shifted in his seat so that he could see Piper. "He had you? What exactly are you talking about?"

"Numbers. Lists," she said. "If I see it, I remember it. It's sort of a curse. I can't shut it off."

"You remember numbers?" From the corner of his eye, he saw Tex's eyebrows go up. "As in the list your friend changed?"

"As in I can re-create it to a T."

"The new list."

"The new list. The old list. Any list."

Assuming she was telling the truth, not exaggerating, this was big. This code she'd allegedly seen had been stolen twenty years ago, and the government had been searching for it ever since. They'd thought it lost until just a few months ago, when an FBI agent, Sydney Fitzpatrick—the woman he was currently dating—had recovered it while investigating the murder of her father, who had been involved in the theft of the code.

The implications hit Griffin and he took a breath, telling himself that they needed to take this slow. Sydney was supposed to have turned over the only known copy of this code to her superiors at the FBI, who had then turned it over to his agency, ATLAS. The obvious explanation for it suddenly appearing here on a copy machine hard drive was that *Sydney* had made a copy.

And now, because of that, someone was dead—and this girl's life endangered.

Then again, maybe he'd misunderstood what this punk rock kid was saying. "Can you explain it a little more?" he asked.

"About this list or my memory?"

"Both. Start with the memory."

"When I was twelve, my foster dad took me to spring training for the Giants. I was hit in the head with a baseball. A line drive. It knocked me out, and I ended up in a coma for two days. When I woke up, this, well, thing happens. I have a precise memory of whatever I read. I can show you if you like."

"How?"

"Maybe the license plates in this lot? You have pen and paper?" Tex pulled a pen and small notebook from the center console. When he tried to hand them back to her, she said, "Drive through the lot first."

"How fast?"

"Normal speed. I just need to be able to read the plates."

Tex shrugged, then pulled out, cruising the lot. There were about twenty cars in all. When he finished, he parked in the same spot, then handed her the pen and paper.

She immediately started jotting down the plate numbers. Without hesitation, Griffin noted. When she finished, she handed Griffin the list, then instructed Tex to drive past the cars to check it.

Tex drove through again, while Griffin compared the list to the plates.

She wasn't even looking at it when she said, "Ignore the fourth one down. The white Lexus left."

And it had. "She didn't miss one," Griffin said.

Tex returned to their original parking spot, then looked back at her. "How much can you read at one time and still retain what you see?"

"I don't know. Whole books' worth. The thing is, I'm not like a math genius or anything. I didn't understand this computer code stuff that Bo was working on. I can't do formulas or computations. I just memorize what I read."

"But you remember the code Bo was looking at?" Tex asked.

"Because he *made* me read it. I think he was afraid of getting in trouble, because the machine belonged to the FBI. He was curious, that's all. He just wanted to make sure there was a copy to look at again after he erased the stuff . . ."

Griffin asked, "How many people know about this talent of yours?"

"I don't know. Most of my friends just think it's, well, like a game."

A deadly game should the wrong person discover what she was keeping in her head.

"Where do you live?" Tex asked.

"A couple miles from Bo's place. I took the bus."

"Anything you can't live without?"

She shook her head, looking scared, as though it was finally hitting her. And Griffin saw tears welling in her eyes.

"We need to call McNiel," Tex said, referring to their boss. He pulled out his phone.

Griffin stopped him from calling, then told Piper, "Can you excuse us for a moment?"

He got out.

Tex followed, and both men moved a few feet away. Griffin wasn't even sure how to break it to Tex.

"What," Tex asked, "aren't you telling me?"

"Where the numbers came from."

"Which would be . . . ?"

"A hard drive from a copy machine that used to sit in the San Francisco FBI field office."

"As in Sydney Fitzpatrick's former office? The same Sydney you're currently dating?"

"As in *someone* in that office made a copy. We don't know for sure it was her."

"Does it really matter? It means there's *still* a copy floating around out there. And we need to find it. Before someone else does."

Griffin's stomach knotted. Tex had warned him—on more than one occasion—that he needed to have a frank talk with Sydney about this list she'd recovered. "Do *not* say I told you so."

"Wasn't even thinking it."

"Like hell."

"Okay, maybe I was. So what're you going to do?"

"About telling McNiel?"

"About telling Sydney," Tex said. "If what you're saying is true, she's unwittingly responsible for *two* deaths tonight, if you count this guy's friend in the other apartment. I won't even go into the national security issues, what with the evidence being pretty strong that *Sydney's* got a copy of the Devil's Key in her possession, which we're now going to have to recover. For God's sake, Griff. They didn't put out a kill order for anyone in possession of that thing for no reason. How long you think it's going to take for her to start putting two and two together?"

"And what am I supposed to tell her?"

"I don't know," Tex said, his voice dripping with well-deserved sarcasm. "Something along the lines of, you know that case in Rome? The one where you did the drawing of the skull for us? Well, we sort of met you several weeks before that. Covertly. In Mexico when you were looking into your father's murder and recovered that list of numbers. Oh. And, in case you were wondering which government agent was shooting at you—?"

"I get it. Anything else you want to throw at me?"

"I think that should do it. Unless of course you want *me* to call McNiel?"

"No thanks. I prefer to tighten my own noose," he said, taking out his phone. He hit the speed dial for his boss, heard it ring several times, while Tex got back in the car.

It was after one A.M. in Washington, a fact McNiel felt it important to emphasize by saying, "At this hour? I'm not going to like this. Am I?"

"No, sir." And then Griffin proceeded to tell him a condensed version of events, starting with the few facts he might have neglected to mention about the mission in Mexico, that Sydney probably had a copy of those numbers, and the recent murders—along with Piper and her eidetic memory.

"First," McNiel said, "address the matter of the witness you picked up. I'm sending Lisette out. I don't even want that girl going to the bathroom by herself. Understood?"

"Yes, sir."

"I'm sending the jet out for the girl. When Lisette gets there, one of the two of you will be with her the entire time. Tex can go out to Carillo's place to make sure *he* doesn't have a copy." Tony Carillo was Sydney's partner at the time, which meant he very well could have one.

"And Sydney?" Griffin asked. "What do I do about her?"

"Once you get the girl back here, and Marc arrives to relieve you, *you* can deal with Sydney Fitzpatrick."

"How?"

"I couldn't say. I've never slept with someone I was supposed to kill."

"For what it's worth, we're only dating. I haven't slept with her."

"O for two, Griffin. Because you didn't kill her, either."

3

Griffin spent the night tossing about on the sofa in their hotel room, and by the time morning came, he was exhausted. Over the last few months, he'd worked several cases with Sydney Fitzpatrick, an FBI agent now assigned out of Quantico. Though they'd spent a considerable amount of time together on those investigations, it was only recently, these past few weeks, in fact, that they'd actually started to date. When he'd told McNiel that he hadn't slept with her, it was the truth. It wasn't that he didn't want to; God knew he did. And when Sydney assumed his reticence to take their relationship any further had more to do with his not quite letting go of his feelings over his late wife, he had let her think that's what it was.

It wasn't like he could just blurt out the truth: *Oh, by the way, I was supposed to kill you in Mexico, while working a case which I'm not at liberty to discuss. But since I didn't go through with it, any chance you still want to sleep with me?*

Right.

Still, in light of recent events and with everything that was likely to be coming down on her, he had to give her some sort of warning. The fact these numbers had shown up meant that certain things were going to start happening in short order, and Sydney would soon find herself in the thick of it, wondering what the hell hit her.

He called her phone, got her voice mail, thought about leaving a message, except there was a knock at their hotel room door. Since he wasn't even sure what he'd say to Sydney at this point, considering most of the information was classified—never mind it wasn't really a conversation that one could have on the phone—he disconnected, then got up to answer the door. They were expecting Lisette Perrault. Like Griffin and Tex she worked for ATLAS, a covert government agency that very few people even knew existed. He looked through the peephole, saw it was she, then opened the door. "You made good time. How was the flight?"

"Not sure. Slept the whole way."

"At least somebody did," he replied, stepping aside to let her in.

She took stock of the room, gave an amused look at Tex, reading the paper, sprawled out on one bed, Piper on the other. And then she eyed the couch where Griffin had spent the night. "Drew the short straw?"

"Something like that."

"So," Lisette said, walking over to the bed where Piper sat propped up on the pillows, working the television remote. "You must be Piper?"

The girl glanced over, then back at the TV and the reality show she was watching. "Good guess." Her red-rimmed eyes gave evidence that she'd spent the night crying—quietly, but Griffin had still heard, and it bothered him to think that he was indirectly involved with her pain. She'd lost her friend, was being yanked from her home and shipped off across the country for who knew how long.

"Well," Lisette said, holding up one of two shopping bags. "New clothes. You'll need to change before we leave."

Piper slid off the bed, took the bag, looking inside as she walked into the bathroom. "Pink and blue. So . . . not me."

When she disappeared into the bathroom, Lisette whispered, "Not taking it so well?"

Tex scoffed. "Taking advantage of the situation is what I think."

"How so?"

"Stole my wallet. So watch your things on the flight back is all I can say."

"Apparently you got it back."

"Damned good thing, too. Imagine if I *hadn't* noticed it missing until after the three of you left. Quite the thief, that one," he said, turning the page of the newspaper. "She also stole some candy from the gift shop. That we didn't discover until after she started eating it."

Griffin eyed the other bag Lisette was holding. "What's in there?"

"Hat for the hair. I'd like to get her into D.C. without too much notice."

Tex rattled the paper, straightening out the pages. "Then keep her the hell away from anything not glued down."

"Sore, are we?" she said to Tex.

"We saved her life," Tex said. "You'd think she'd be grateful."

"Have you told her where she's going?"

Griffin and Tex looked at each other, but didn't answer.

"I take it that means no?"

"Time never seemed right," Griffin said.

Lisette shook her head, then walked to the bathroom door, giving a light knock. "Everything okay in there?"

The door opened, and Piper poked her head out. "You sure I can't go in my old clothes?"

"Positive. And you need to remove the lip, eyebrow, and tongue piercings."

"Why?"

"Because they clash with pink and blue."

The girl's eyes teared up, and Lisette turned toward Griffin and Tex, giving them an accusing stare. A moment later, Piper stuck her head out again. "Well I'm gonna need help. The eyebrow ring always gets stuck. I don't understand why I have to take them off. Everybody has them."

Lisette slipped into the bathroom. "It's too noticeable. I'm sorry," she said, then closed the door. He heard them talking, then heard Piper crying.

A few minutes later, Lisette emerged. Alone. She walked over to the table and sat.

"Is she okay?" Griffin asked.

"Hardly. Her world's just been turned upside down, her best friend was just murdered, and she thinks he betrayed her at the end."

Tex looked up from the newspaper. "Betrayed her? How?"

"Told the gunmen she was there."

Griffin rubbed at his stiff neck, trying to remember the sequence of events from last night. "They probably had a gun shoved in his face. Surely she realizes that."

"Someday maybe. Now? She's a bit raw."

Griffin's head was starting to hurt. He got up, dug a bottle of ibuprofen from his carry-on. "Did you tell her where she's going to be staying?" he asked, referring to the witness protection they'd be placing her in.

"Me? I am not going to be the bad guy. I told her we'd be staying at my apartment until we decide what to do next."

He popped open the bottle, shook two pills into his hand, then looked around for something to drink. The only thing available was his cup of cold coffee from breakfast. He swallowed the pills, then the stale coffee.

"And you?" Lisette asked Tex. "I'm assuming you must have something going on, or you'd be flying with us back to D.C.?"

"I don't want to talk about it," Tex said.

The aspirin felt like it was stuck in his throat, and he took another swig of coffee. "He's paying a visit to Carillo tonight."

"Not a social visit?"

"Since Carillo was Sydney's partner in San Francisco at the time she found those numbers in Mexico? Not social." He finished the coffee, then tossed the cup in the trash.

"You think he might have a copy?"

"We have to assume so until we find out otherwise."

"Then why not ask him?"

Tex tossed the paper down, clearly frustrated. "That's exactly what we should do. But McNiel says no. Carillo doesn't have the clearance."

And Griffin said, "If we're lucky, he'll never find out."

"If the two of you are lucky," Lisette countered, "he'll forgive you when he does."

The possibility existed with Carillo. Of forgiveness, that was. He was the pragmatic sort. Sydney was not, he thought, ignoring the pointed stare Lisette had turned his way.

"So," she said, getting up to sit on the edge of Tex's bed, her look one of cynical amusement. "How are you planning to recover this alleged info?"

"He hasn't decided," Griffin replied.

Tex looked over the top of the paper. "More like I've been avoiding the issue, because both options suck."

"And they are . . . ?" Lisette asked him.

"One, I leave now and go in while he's at work. Two, I wait for dark, call to say I'm in the area, get his ass drunk, then search while he's passed out."

She crossed her arms. "You're right. They both suck. But the first plan is far less slimy than buttering up your friend with alcohol and pretending to be all buddy-buddy as you're shoving a dagger in his back."

"Like I wasn't feeling crappy enough," Tex said. The shower stopped, and they all looked at the bathroom. Tex turned his attention back to the paper, clearly done with the conversation, and they sat there in silence, even after the blow dryer started.

Unfortunately it gave Griffin far too long to think about everything that had resulted, the lives touched—the lives lost—because of a decision *he'd* made before he even knew Sydney or Carillo. His mission had been to recover the Devil's Key—and failing that, to kill anyone in possession of it. Those numbers Sydney had found were that important, that dangerous to national security. And yet when it came right down to it, Griffin ignored the kill order, deciding instead that Sydney, who was known for being a rule follower, would turn them over to the agents as instructed.

Who could have foreseen this?

Right now, he was actually glad his pounding headache made it difficult to concentrate on any one thing. He leaned his head back, closed his eyes, trying not to think about the implications of his actions. And when he'd almost succeeded, Piper stepped out, the piercings in her face no longer present. Although she still had the black and pink hair, gone was the tough, goth, punk rocker. In her place stood a young, vulnerable girl, reminding him once again that there were consequences for his actions—and his inactions.

Lisette smiled at her, holding up the shopping bag. "A hat. This way, you can at least keep your hair for a while."

The girl took it, pulled out the fleece cap, and put it on.

The moment her hair was covered, hiding the vivid pink tufts, the effect was complete. She looked like any other young girl.

Tex eyed the two of them. "She could pass for your younger sister, Lisette."

Piper looked over at her, her expression one of curiosity as she examined Lisette's face. And then Piper gave a hint of a smile. "You're pretty."

Lisette walked her over to the mirror, then touched her on

the chin. "And so are you." She stood there, looking at their reflection a moment. "Perhaps you are my long-lost cousin? Yes? Clearly we both have good genes."

The girl smiled again, and Griffin was grateful for Lisette's ability to bond so quickly. It would make the process much easier when they finally had to inform her that she'd be going into witness protection. Nothing like telling a girl barely twenty years old that she was going to have to give up everything she ever knew and start over again.

Then again, with her history, maybe a fresh start was just what she needed—even if she didn't realize it. From what he and Tex had learned after talking to the girl last night, she was alone in the world. She'd been raised in foster care, but when her foster father died just after her thirteenth birthday, and her foster mother's health had failed, she'd been shuffled around through the system, some places better than others. Once the physical abuse turned to sexual, Piper ran away. The authorities picked her up, placed her in a new home, where the foster parent only cared about the money, not where the kids were or who they were with. Unfortunately the woman also didn't care about feeding them, and so the kids found other means to acquire food. Stealing, Piper decided, was the only option she was willing to resort to. After a couple of arrests, however, a probation officer assured her that she'd end up in prison if she continued down such a path and didn't make an effort to straighten out her life.

A lot of good that did her, Griffin thought, as he looked at his watch, then walked over and picked up his overnight bag. "We should get going."

Lisette turned to Tex, and just before they left, said, "Be careful."

He gave her a dark look. "What can possibly go wrong?"

In their business, Griffin thought, plenty, and he hoped like hell Tex was successful.

FBI Academy
Quantico, Virginia

"Gun!"

Special Agent Sydney Fitzpatrick drew her weapon, fired twice, then scanned her surroundings. The agent next to her did the same.

"Holster!" the range master called out, then walked down the line, making sure everyone had complied. When he reached Sydney's side, he eyed her target, saw a tight pattern that would have been excellent—had it not been to the right and slightly below the ten X. "You're pulling."

"Trigger's a lot stiffer than my normal weapon," she explained. Her issued weapon had been secured after a recent on-duty shooting, and this, her temporary replacement, same make and model, Glock 22, was brand-new out of the box.

"Until you get yours back, this is what you're working with. Take it up to the armorer. Have him lighten that trigger pull, see if we can't move that pattern back over."

She did as told and was standing by while the armorer stripped down the weapon, adjusted the trigger pull, and was putting it all back together when her cell phone rang. It was Tony Carillo, her former partner, calling from the San Francisco field office.

"Any chance you have a few minutes to talk?" Tony asked.

The sharp crack of gunfire echoed in the distance, as she said, "In the middle of qualifications. Why?"

"Call me as soon as you can."

He disconnected before she could ask what was going on.

"Here you go, Fitzpatrick," the gunsmith said, wiping the excess oil from the empty weapon, then handing it back to her. "See if that works a little better."

"Thanks."

She carried it to the range, put on her shooting glasses, and waited for the range master to give the okay to reload and fire. This time the pattern was mostly in the center. The moment he signed her off, she cleaned the weapon, then hurried off to her basement office in the academy building, calling Carillo from the landline phone. "What's going on?" she asked.

"Trivia question. Guess what office item besides your computer has a hard drive?"

Even though she thought the question absurd, her gaze flicked around her office. "A printer?"

"Besides that," he said.

"No clue."

"Copy machine."

"And your point?"

"There was a murder in South San Francisco that was connected to the machine from our San Francisco office."

"What makes you think that?"

"We recently had ours replaced after it went kaput, along with several others. Only someone forgot to remove the hard drives from said machines prior to their being auctioned off at the surplus warehouse. Apparently, this was an oversight, as the tech folks are aware of the hard drives, and they're *supposed* to remove them before the machines leave the premises."

"How do you know all this?"

"It's in the policy and procedures manual."

"Not about the copy machine hard drive. About the murder being related?"

"Because the South San Francisco PD has spent the last several hours collecting evidence on a murder victim's place of business, and they apparently found a number of machines to which they ran the serial numbers, which led to our office. They also found most of the hard drives to the machines still intact."

Sydney leaned back in her chair, not sure where Carillo was heading with this. "What do you mean *most* of the hard drives?"

"Because the one that's missing? It was from the machine in *this* office. This floor. The one you and I made a certain copy on. And in case you're forgetting *exactly* what that copy is of, maybe a certain trip you took to Mexico to investigate your father's murder might help to refresh your memory."

A sick feeling started in the pit of her stomach. "Someone was killed?"

"Yeah. Shot in the head. Point-blank."

"Oh my God . . ."

She closed her eyes and leaned back in her chair. Shot . . . Because of her.

She'd been the one to track down Robert Orozco, all because she'd wanted answers about who had killed her father. She'd used every FBI resource at her disposal to find Orozco, who'd apparently spent the last two decades in hiding for some crime that he and her father had committed. Orozco had been certain that once he turned over the list of numbers to her, he and his family would be safe . . .

It simply never occurred to her that someone completely uninvolved with the case could be targeted.

"How do you think they found him?"

"The copy machine guy? You know how Doc warned us not to run the numbers on the computer?" he said, referring to his current partner, and the only other person who was aware of how she'd acquired that list of numbers. "He thinks the kid did just that. Ran them on his computer."

She thought about that trip to Mexico. Someone had tried to kill her, and she'd had no doubt it was a government agent. She'd barely escaped . . . "You think the government did this, too? Murdered this kid because he found the numbers?"

"Can't say. But if there were any doubts that someone's watching our every electronic move, this should erase them."

"What about Orozco? Someone needs to warn him."

"Not to worry. I'll call Agent Venegas as soon as I get off the phone with you. I just figured you should know."

"Thanks."

"I'll get back to you once I find out more. I'm on my way to South San Francisco now."

She hung up, stared at her phone while the news sank in. And then she unlocked her desk drawer, saw the envelope with her name on the front. Carillo had figured her office in Quantico was probably the most secure location for what it contained, Orozco's list of numbers, and she picked it up, weighed it in her hands. Hard to believe something so seemingly insignificant—just a page filled with indecipherable numbers—could be the means to such a deadly end. Then again, maybe not. Hard to overlook that *she'd* almost been killed retrieving the envelope from Orozco in Mexico.

Had someone murdered this kid for the same reason, because they thought he had the numbers? She'd turned over the original list to the U.S. government. And until now, this copy she held was, she thought, unknown by all except her and Carillo.

Footsteps echoed down the corridor toward her office, and she shoved the envelope in the drawer, closed and locked it. This was not the place to be waving around something that she was not supposed to have in her possession. Her boss, Terrance Harcourt, stopped in her doorway, carrying a manila folder. The gray-haired man eyed the keys in her hand. "On your way out?"

"I just got back, actually. Qualifications."

"How'd the new gun work out?"

"Fine after a few adjustments."

"I hate new guns." He took a step in, held out the manila folder. "Letter of commendation for your work on the terrorist explosion," he said, handing it to her, then turning on his heel.

"Thanks. I appreciate it," she replied, even though he was halfway down the hall. Harcourt wasn't the social type. Just as well, since she had a few things on her mind at the moment. She flipped open the folder. Her name was typed at the top of the letter, and it was signed by Brad Pearson, the director of the Foreign Counterintelligence unit. Pearson was someone who probably knew what those numbers in her desk meant—never mind he was one of the *last* people she'd want to show them to. A bit hard having to explain why it was that she and Carillo had a copy, when they'd been ordered by Pearson to turn them over to the government agents to begin with.

She let the folder drop shut, not caring about any letter of commendation. She'd brought those numbers into this country, having no idea what they belonged to, except that Orozco told her they were important and the government wanted them back. If this young man was killed because someone thought those numbers were in his possession, then she damned well wanted to know what they were for and who was looking for them.

Her father had been murdered because of his connection

to Orozco and this list of numbers. And even though at the time of her own investigation into his death, she'd felt certain that she knew all the facts surrounding the case, her ex-boyfriend, Special Agent Scott Ryan, had recently mentioned that what she'd discovered, her father's and Orozco's involvement, was only the tip of the iceberg. Apparently Scotty had some old files on the case that she had not yet seen.

To her, her father's case was closed and she had no interest in reliving the nightmare of his murder.

With the news about the recent killing in South San Francisco, perhaps she needed to reassess her conclusion. Not about who killed her father—that she knew—but about the circumstances that led up to his death.

Clearly it was time to pay Scotty a visit and see if he had something of value, or if he was using this so-called mystery file as a way to maintain a connection with her, now that she was dating someone else. Hoping for the former, not the latter, she grabbed her keys and headed out the door.

Sydney drove straight to FBI headquarters in Washington, D.C., where her ex-boyfriend Scotty worked. It was the perfect locale for him, since it kept him close to the movers and shakers. When they'd first started dating, Sydney had admired his determination to promote himself to get ahead, and had even harbored similar aspirations. Now, however, she preferred her basement office at the academy in Quantico, where she taught forensic art to law enforcement officials—when she wasn't working actual cases. Far removed from the political scene, it offered solitude, something she found herself seeking more often of late. Being involved in several high-profile cases that had nearly cost her and her family their lives will do that to an agent.

And yet, here she was, about to involve herself in yet another one?

Not another one. A continuation of one, she amended. She

thought of her young sister, her mother and stepfather . . .
If it meant keeping them safe, she told herself, she'd go to
the ends of the world. She paused, reaffirming in her mind
that she was doing the right thing, then knocked on Scotty's
door.

He was typing a report when she entered.

"Sorry to disturb you."

"You're not," he said, his focus on the computer screen.
"Just finishing a few last details. What'd you want to talk
about?"

"I came to see the file you promised." He continued
typing, and she had a feeling he was only half listening.
She closed the door behind her. "The W2 files," she said,
referring to the law firm being investigated in secret by
the Department of Justice, Wingman and Wingman—aka
Wingman Squared or W2.

Scotty's fingers stilled on the keyboard at the name and he
looked up at her.

He was listening now. "Why?"

"You told me there were things about my father's death I
didn't know, and that Wingman Squared was somehow involved."

"Jesus." He got up, opened his door, looked out, then
closed it again. "Look, Syd," he said, keeping his voice low.
"The only reason I told you about the Wingman Squared
files was because I thought it might shed some light on the
questions you had about that law firm and the link to your
father's case. I didn't intend for you to actually start investigating it yourself."

Scotty's sudden reluctance to turn over the promised files
confirmed in her mind that he'd only been using them as a
way to maintain his connection to her. He, apparently, had
known about them from the beginning, when she'd first
started looking into her father's murder. And yet the moment
she started dating another government agent, Zachary Grif-

fin, Scotty suddenly decided to reveal their existence? "You only dangled that case in front of me because I was about to walk off with another man. And now that he and I are a couple—"

"News flash, Sydney. *I've* moved on. Or did you forget about Amanda? In fact, she and I are going away next weekend. Together. Overnight."

"Why promise the files, then change your mind?"

"Because I've had time to think about it."

"What's there to think about?"

"You might not like what you find."

"Because it involves my father? Could it be any worse than what I've already discovered about him?"

"That all depends on your perspective."

He was talking in circles, and she wasn't sure why. "How about you let me see it so that I can decide for myself?"

Scotty stared at her for what seemed several seconds, then moved to his desk, pulled a handful of pens from an FBI Academy mug, and dug out a USB flash drive from the bottom. He returned the pens, then held the drive out to her. When she took it, he closed his fingers tight around hers. "Do *not*," he said, keeping his voice low, but firm, "let anyone know I gave this to you."

"I won't."

"And for God's sake, Syd, don't open it on any work computers, or anything connected to the Internet."

"I get it."

"I don't think you do." There was a knock at the door, and Scotty gave her a pointed look, then sat on the edge of his desk, as though they'd been shooting the breeze, not having some conversation that could get either one of them in trouble. "Come in."

Brad Pearson, the director of the Foreign Counterintelligence squad, opened the door. Tall, thin, with military-short graying hair, he pinned his gaze right on Sydney as though he'd come here looking for her, and she gripped the flash drive tight, keeping it out of sight. "Isn't Quantico a bit farther south?" he asked.

"I *knew* I took the wrong exit," she said. "Freeway signs. So confusing."

"GPS. So convenient." He eyed Scotty, saying, "You have that report for me?"

"Just finishing it up," Scotty said, and she relaxed once she realized she wasn't the focus of Pearson's attention.

"Get it to me before lunch. I'd like to read it over before my meeting this afternoon." He started out, then stopped, turned back to Scotty. "Almost forgot. The class I need you to take over for me? It's next weekend. I had the date wrong."

"*Next* weekend? I—"

"If you're free that is."

"No, it's fine."

"I'll let them know you'll be there."

Scotty nodded in return. Pearson barely glanced at her on his way out. The moment he closed the door behind him, Scotty turned the force of his stare on her, clearly unhappy about her presence, especially with Pearson so nearby. At least that's what she thought, until he said, "I don't suppose you'd like to take your new boyfriend to a bed-and-breakfast next weekend? It's not like I can use it now, so it's just going to go to waste."

So he really had been planning a getaway with Amanda. She, for one, was glad. "Why not tell Pearson you have plans?"

"Amanda won't mind. She's sort of a homebody," he said, then picked up an envelope from his desk, handing it to her. "Take it."

She opened it, saw the certificate for two nights at a secluded bed-and-breakfast just across the Potomac in McLean, Virginia. "Pretty nice place . . ." Certainly one she could never afford.

"I won it in a drawing."

She handed it back. "Let me think about it? Griffin never knows his schedule from one day to the next anyway."

"You start looking into those files," he said, placing the envelope on his desk, "you're going to need it way more than me." Scotty had warned her back when he'd originally divulged his knowledge of this W2 file, that if Pearson so much as found out that she was looking into the case, he'd transfer her in a heartbeat to some godforsaken outpost where she wouldn't see the light of day.

Her cell phone vibrated in her pocket, and she pulled it out, looked at the caller ID. Speak of the devil. Zachary Griffin, the covert government agent she was currently dating.

"Gotta go," she said, even though she wasn't about to answer Griffin's call. Not here. She had too much to think about, and he had an uncanny knack for knowing when she was getting into something she shouldn't.

If Scotty thought Pearson would have objections about her seeing that file, it was nothing to what Griffin would do should he find out. Griffin's boss had also warned her off of looking into the W2 case, as had Griffin—and this presented a whole new set of problems. Pearson had a direct pipeline to Griffin's boss, who had a direct pipeline to Griffin.

The things she didn't think about when she decided to start dating the guy.

She walked out, tucking the flash drive into her pocket.

Time to find out what everyone was keeping so hush-hush.

5

San Mateo, California

Tex had no doubts about his ability to get in and out of Carillo's condominium without being discovered. He'd called to say he might be in the area and would there be a good time to stop by—which was how he found out Carillo would be gone for a couple of hours. So why then was he hesitating? Guilt over past activities that were best left buried? Or Fitzpatrick's reaction should she learn his part in it?

He always knew there'd be trouble, once Griffin started dating her. Especially with their mutual background, of which only *half* the party knew about. The Griffin half. Not exactly an auspicious beginning.

Still, guilt came with the territory, so it wasn't that. Not entirely. Reality was that working with Carillo on the last two cases had complicated things, because they'd become friends.

Like it or not, Tex would have to deal with the fallout. He was doing the right thing by taking this on himself, even when Griffin had offered. He'd almost convinced himself until he saw that he wasn't the only one interested in Carillo's residence, a corner unit of a Mediterranean-style complex with tiled roof and sand-colored stucco siding.

A man was walking along the far side of the building, his attention fixed on Carillo's unit.

The wind gusted hard enough to shake Tex's car, spattering large raindrops across his windshield, obscuring his vision. Whoever said it never rained in California was an idiot. As was the agent who neglected to pack rain gear. Then again, he hadn't arrived in California expecting to be here when the rain started.

He was supposed to be home by now, *not* breaking into a friend's house.

Or watching someone else try to.

He got out, walked toward the complex. A newspaper in plastic wrap sat on the sidewalk in front of the courtyard entrance, and he picked it up before walking toward the arched entryway as though he lived there. From his peripheral vision, he saw the man glance over at him, then continue toward Carillo's enclosed patio. There was no gate to the patio, the front doors to all the condos happened to be inside the courtyard, therefore no reason for someone to be loitering in the area outside. Tex tossed the paper onto the closest front porch, stepped back out, knowing without a doubt the only place the man could have been heading for was over the six-foot stucco wall surrounding Carillo's patio.

Unless of course he'd misread the entire scenario, and it was just some poor schmuck out for a walk in the beginning of a rainstorm.

Fat drops slapped at Tex's face as he walked to the corner, looked down the street. Not a soul in sight, which meant the suspect had to have gone over the wall. The perfect place to break in without being seen—since Tex had intended on using the same point of entry.

Nothing like being last to the party.

Tex reentered the condominium courtyard standing to one side of the stuccoed arched entry, out of the rain, hoping to approach Carillo's unit without being seen. The security lights cast long shadows across the terra-cotta pavers, the perfect concealment as long as he stayed to the dark side of the columns.

How could he even tell Carillo that someone was breaking in without implicating ATLAS? Carillo wasn't expecting him to be there for several hours.

He thought about going in after the guy. Except if someone was breaking in for the same reason as Tex, it was bound to turn deadly and Carillo would *definitely* notice if Tex killed the suspect in his condo.

Keep it simple, he decided, adjusting the Bluetooth in his ear. Call the police and let them do the work. Then, when the police were on their way, Tex would simply wait for the suspect to emerge and follow him. He took out his phone, and punched in 911. When the dispatcher answered, he said, "Someone's breaking into an FBI agent's apartment. He climbed in through the back patio and is inside now."

"The address?" she asked. He gave it, and she followed with "Any weapons seen?"

"Unknown."

"Your name, sir?"

"Anonymous. I need to contact the FBI agent. I'll have him call you." He pressed the button on the Bluetooth to disconnect, not having time to deal with the cumbersome details the local police needed, and then he called Carillo. "It's Tex."

"How's it going?"

"It's been better," he said, eyeing Carillo's unit. "I decided to swing by your place since I got done early, just to see if you'd left yet."

"Guess you found out I had."

"Which is why I'm calling. There's a man inside your condo. Saw him go over the back wall."

"The back wall? The alarm didn't go off?"

"No. But I called the police and I'll be standing by until they get here."

"Son of a bitch. I'm on my way. Be about five."

"I'll wait."

"Appreciate it."

Tex disconnected, then phoned Griffin next, keeping his eye on Carillo's front windows. "I take it the three of you made it back to D.C. with no problems?"

"We did. How's your, uh, thing going."

"Slight problem," Tex said, then informed him of the break-in.

"Maybe your garden-variety burglar?"

"Ever the optimist. What I'd like to know is—assuming whoever is breaking in is part of the affair last night—how'd they make the connection to Carillo so fast?"

"Clearly someone knew he was involved with Sydney in the case. This isn't good. You can't tell Carillo why you're there."

"Not to worry. The cops are en route. I'm just playing the part of the concerned citizen."

"You see anything?"

"A light inside . . . Wait. It just went dark."

"How likely is it that Carillo kept a copy of the list?"

"We're talking Carillo. If he thought something was up, highly likely."

"Let's hope you're wrong."

To say the least. He turned his attention to the condo. If the suspect came out the front door, Tex had him . . . But he wasn't coming out the front. And the cops weren't surrounding the place as fast as he'd hoped. Which meant the suspect had a chance at escaping via the point of entry. Tex turned to exit the courtyard, intending to follow.

"Police! Show me your hands!"

White light flooded the area, blinding him.

"What the hell's going on, Tex?" Griffin asked.

Tex squinted, raised his hands, palms out, and two officers approached, both with their guns pointed at his chest. One cop ordered him to turn around slowly, interlace his fingers at the back of his neck, then kneel to the ground. "A slight flaw with my plan, Griff."

6

The police were walking Tex to his car just as Carillo arrived. If Carillo was surprised by the arrest, Tex couldn't tell, but he took out his credentials, identifying himself to the officers.

"Congratulations, boys," Carillo said. "You've just arrested the reporting party. He works with me."

The female officer had Tex by the elbow. "He's an FBI agent? He didn't say so. Even after we found a gun."

"His branch of the government is . . . a little more obscure." Carillo's smile was more sarcastic than amused. "For some reason, those handcuffs look very appropriate on you." Then, after a thoughtful glance toward his apartment, he said to the officers, "What we have here is a bit of miscommunication. The condo's mine. He's working with me on a local case, and I'm sure if you look in his wallet, you'll see an identification card from DOJ there."

She removed Tex's wallet from his back pocket, found the identification card as stated. "Sorry about that." To Carillo, she added, "We saw him running out of the main entrance and he matched the description."

Carillo eyed Tex while the other officer removed the handcuffs, then returned his gun. "He does have that shady look. Even so, I appreciate you coming out. Maybe you two can run an area check and see if the guy's still around? He and I will check the condo. Make sure it's clear."

"Sure thing," the officer said.

He and Tex entered the courtyard to the condo. "Point of entry through the back?" Carillo asked Tex.

"If he left, out the back, too. Can't imagine he'd stick around once the cops showed up." Tex put his hand on Carillo's shoulder as Carillo took out his keys to unlock the door. "Assuming he *did* get out. I never got past the courtyard."

Carillo nodded, and both men drew their pistols, standing one on each side of the door. Carillo turned the key in the lock, then pushed the door open with his foot. He entered, Tex right behind him. They cleared each room, determined that the place was empty. The back slider stood open a few inches. The window in the kitchen that also overlooked the patio was open and the screen nowhere in sight. Smeared gritty dirt, still wet, marred the otherwise clean white tiles on the counter, confirming it was the point of entry. "What're the chances he left prints?" Carillo asked.

Tex didn't answer. He knew there'd be none. Instead, he asked, "Anything missing?"

"Not that I can see . . . Stereo and TV are still here. Definitely not after big-ticket items . . ." Carillo walked to his bedroom, checked the wooden box on his dresser. "Wedding ring and dress watch still here. I don't own any other jewelry, so what were they after?"

"You have a safe or anything?"

Carillo made a beeline to his office. Tex followed.

A large gun safe stood against the wall, and Carillo spun the dial, then turned the combination until it opened. "Guns are still here. Deed to the house is still here, which means my won't-be-soon-enough-ex wasn't the culprit."

"It definitely wasn't Sheila I saw."

"Coulda been one of her low-life friends?"

"Thought you two had sort of patched things as far as the house custody."

"Well, we have. I just can't figure out what anyone would want in here if not the guns or money."

Carillo stood there looking around, and when his gaze lit on Tex, it was filled with suspicion.

He knew.

But instead of saying anything, he closed and locked the safe, left the room, walked to the kitchen. He slid the window shut, used a towel to wipe off the footprints on the counter, closed and locked the slider, then double-checked his alarm to make sure it was working.

That done, he went to the refrigerator, opened it, and pulled out two bottles of Sierra Nevada Pale Ale, then the opener from the drawer, popped off the tops, and handed one to Tex. "I find that when my constitutional rights are being violated, alcohol helps dull the need to call an attorney."

"We would have told you if we could," Tex said.

"Yeah. Right. But breaking in seemed the better option?"

"Something like that."

"Did you find what you were looking for?"

"I didn't do it."

"You mean I just wiped off valuable evidence and you *let* me?"

"I doubt these guys would leave any. You're probably fine."

"If not you, then who broke in?"

"If I had to guess, the guys responsible for the homicides in your town last night."

"The kid from the warehouse?"

"And his friend at another apartment."

Carillo took a sip of his beer. Apparently mulling things

over. Then, "This over the hard drive from the copy machine from our office?"

"It is," Tex said, not too surprised that Carillo knew.

"Which means those numbers Sydney brought back from Mexico don't belong to some offshore bank accounts like we thought?"

"Correct."

"Guess I lost that bet. So what *do* they belong to?" he asked.

"Can't say," Tex replied.

"What *can* you tell me?"

"Not much," Tex said. "Except that if you have a copy, or know where it is, we need it."

"Don't *you* already have a copy? Fitzpatrick turned it over right after we made ours."

"So she does have a copy?"

"She does. The *only* one. Unless you count the hard drive. I gave it to her. So what do you need with hers?"

"You saw what happened to the last person to run them. Ergo, we need to recover it and destroy it."

"Ergo? Sounds like something in a French restaurant. And I don't do French. What I do do is make logical deductions. One. Someone knew Sydney's every move back when she was looking into her father's murder. Two. She dodged a lot of bullets when that list of numbers hit her hands. Three. The moment she got back here to the office, someone swooped in and grabbed said list from us before we could even look into what it was for, hence the reason we made the copy. Four. You're here without a search warrant, looking for something you probably wouldn't even dare to articulate in open court, except someone beat you to the punch. Conclusion? You, or someone from your branch, were the guys shooting at Sydney in Mexico. How close am I?"

Tex refused to answer.

Carillo leaned back against the kitchen counter, eyeing

him. "You know how many bullets she dodged *getting* that list? She's not going to like finding out after the fact that you were involved. Hell. That *Griffin* was involved. Because if I'm not mistaken, *they're* involved."

"I'd appreciate it if you let us tell her when the time is right. Him, actually."

"And when will that be?"

"When we recover the list from her, and when we know it will be safe to say something."

"The honor," Carillo said, pointing his beer bottle at Tex, "is all *yours*. But be aware she knows about this mess here in South San Francisco, because I called her the moment I learned of the murder at the warehouse."

"What about you?" Tex asked Carillo.

"You mean how am I taking the fact you went spy versus spy on me? Keeping secrets? Breaking into my place without a warrant? Or attempting to? I'm pragmatic enough to realize if one plays with a scorpion, expect to get stung. I also know if the roles were reversed, and it was *my* case, we'd be having this conversation in *your* kitchen, not mine." He took another sip of his beer, then set the bottle on the counter, his expression turning dark. "And before you go blaming Fitzpatrick, because she smuggled the numbers from Mexico, *I'm* the one who made the copy, not her. So *I* have to bear the guilt of this kid's death."

"It's not your fault," Tex said.

And then Carillo looked right at him. "My conscience tells me otherwise. I also know there's enough guilt to go around. Which is why I'm cutting you some slack, so drink your goddamned beer. But a word of advice. When Griffin finally gets around to telling her about your and his involvement? I'd highly recommend he wears body armor. I can almost guarantee she's going to go ballistic."

7

Washington, D.C.

Trenton Stiles sat back in his seat, listening to the strains of Tchaikovsky's *Sleeping Beauty*, while his driver maneuvered the streets of Washington, D.C., then pulled up in front of the offices of Wingman and Wingman, the law firm where he'd worked as a lobbyist ever since he'd left Congress more than twenty years ago.

Even though the firm was currently being investigated by the Department of Justice, Stiles wasn't worried. They'd weathered the storm in the past, and they would again. Once he got his hands on the remaining copy of the Devil's Key that was stolen more than twenty years ago, the entire DOJ investigation would take a new turn—one of his choosing.

This time, however, it was going to take a little more finesse, especially now that this latest threat had popped up in California, he thought as his phone rang. He looked at the number on the caller ID. Finally. He answered it. "Mr. B. This better be good news."

"Depends. The hard drive we recovered from Bo Brewer

was erased. But we found out *where* the information originated. A copy machine taken from the FBI's office in San Francisco."

"How did the FBI get it?"

"We think from Orozco."

"Orozco?" he said, stepping out of the car, as the driver opened the door. Robert Orozco had been a former army black ops man, who had brazenly orchestrated the theft of the Devil's Key from a safe at Wingman and Wingman more than twenty years ago. Their mistake had been hiring Orozco and his men to steal the thing from the government to begin with. Orozco must have guessed that his knowledge of the key's existence meant his days were numbered, and so after Orozco turned it over to Stiles, he stole it a second time, then simply disappeared off the face of the earth.

Stiles had been searching for him and the key for the last twenty years with little luck.

Until now.

The morning was cold, crisp, with a clear blue sky overhead. He could see his breath as he talked. "How did you find him?"

"Surprisingly easy, which makes me wonder at the timing. We tapped into the military database. He decided to finally start withdrawing his pension. The only reason we can assume is because, one, he figured statute of limitations. Two, he no longer had the key. Three, maybe he was never aware of the kill order for possession of the thing, or now that he didn't have it, no one would care."

Stiles waved off his driver, but didn't move from the sidewalk. There was more privacy out here. With the DOJ nosing around all the time, hoping to tie Wingman and Wingman into the theft of the key code, one was never sure if there were any bugs inside, even though Stiles made sure his men continually swept the offices. "And the FBI? Why would they have it?"

"Remember that FBI agent asking about W2 a few weeks ago?"

"Of course." According to several sources, someone named Sydney Fitzpatrick had been making unofficial inquiries about the firm. "What about her?"

"She's the daughter of one of Orozco's partners. We think she might have been in Mexico back in October."

"And you think this is how she got the key? How it came to be on their copy machine?"

"It fits. She worked in San Francisco at the time."

"So Orozco gave *her* the list?"

"So it would seem."

"Why would he do that? He knew how valuable it was."

"Only valuable if you knew what to do with it, and he didn't exactly get that part. Then again, it's possible he still has the original."

Stiles looked up at the door of the building, seeing the Wingman and Wingman sign in gold-leafed lettering. The firm had been on life support when they approached him for help more than twenty years ago. He'd worked hard to ensure its continued success, getting into bed with almost every White House administration since, facilitating those candidates who would best serve his purposes, all while keeping the DOJ wolves from getting past the gates.

This matter with Orozco didn't help. If he had his way, he'd kill the man right now. "Find this FBI agent. If she's got a copy, I want it."

"And if she doesn't have it? Because we know her partner didn't have it. We already checked."

"*Someone* made a copy or those numbers wouldn't have ended up on a copier machine hard drive and popped up in the search. We start going down the list of who knew. In fact, since your men are on the West Coast, have them drop by for a chat with Mr. Orozco. Find out what he knows about the code he's been holding on to for two decades, and what he told this FBI agent. And don't leave any loose ends." He took a frustrated breath, not happy that his morning routine had been interrupted. "Anything else?"

"One of those so-called loose ends might be an issue. A girl was at the scene. She may have seen me."

"What the hell were *you* doing there?"

"If the Devil's Key was there, you think I was about to entrust it to anyone else to bring it back?"

"Where is she?"

"Not sure. She disappeared right after my men made contact with her friend. They went looking for her, but she had help."

"Government help?"

"Possibly. We have to assume they've been monitoring the Internet as well. And it fits, since the girl simply disappeared."

"Disappeared? We may not have the key yet, but with the database you have access to, people do *not* just disappear."

"Put it this way. She never returned to her apartment."

"Find her. Make sure that she never does. When the time comes, we'll take care of anyone else who had access to the code."

Stiles disconnected, then dropped his phone into his pocket. He hadn't lasted this long by being careless, and when it came to loose ends, his philosophy was to eliminate them. Unfortunately, it was becoming more difficult to eliminate anyone who posed a risk to his plans without drawing undue attention.

Certain people would have to be killed. The girl, for one. Others . . . ? This would definitely take some creativity on his part to make sure they didn't get in his way.

8

The following morning

Although Sydney had wanted to begin her investiga-tion of the files Scotty had given her the moment she got home, she didn't want to open them on a computer that she used to connect to the Internet. Unfortunately, finding her old laptop proved harder than she expected. She spent her time looking through several boxes in her spare bedroom, digging through things she hadn't yet needed, therefore hadn't bothered to unpack. In fact, she only ventured into this room on the rare occasion she did need to search for some long-missing item. Thinking that the laptop would be in the one marked "Old Office Equip," she shuffled the boxes, pulling it out from the bottom. It wasn't there.

Her eleven-year-old sister, Angie, had helped her pack when she'd made the move from San Francisco to Washington, D.C. Maybe she'd be able to remember which box it might be in. It was nine-thirty here, six-thirty back home. Angie would be up, getting ready for school, and Sydney called, figuring it would be faster to ask her sister, rather than emptying every single box.

Her mother answered. "Is everything okay?"

"It's fine, Mom. I was just sort of hoping Angie might remember which box she packed something in."

"*Angela . . .*" Sydney heard Angie's footsteps as she bounded down the stairs. "Your sister's on the phone."

"Sydney?"

"Hey. You remember which box you packed my old laptop in?"

"Yeah. The one marked 'Doodads.' Why?"

Sydney glanced at the box marked in her sister's writing at the very bottom of all the others. Apparently Angie considered a half-working laptop as odd. "I just need a backup computer."

"But the wi-fi's broken, and— *Oh . . .*" she said, her voice taking on a conspiratorial tone. Angie was all about mystery, and wanted nothing more than to grow up and follow in Sydney's footsteps, much to their mother's regret. "You don't *want* to connect to the Internet. I get it. What kind of case are you working?"

"None of your business, squirt. And what makes you think it's related to any case I'm working?"

"Because you wouldn't have called home first off, and second you wouldn't have said it's none of my business."

"It just so happens I need an extra laptop. That's all."

"Yeah, right, because—"

"Angie . . ."

"Your secret's safe with me. Here's Mom."

"What secret?" her mother asked.

"Nothing, Mom. Angie's just being her usual silly self."

"I can't believe you haven't finished unpacking. I could fly out there some weekend to help—"

"Gosh, look at the time, Mom. Don't you have to get Angie to school?"

"She's fine."

"But I'm running late. Have to go. Love you, bye!"

She hung up before her mother had the chance to pin her down for some visit she wasn't ready for. Not in the midst of this can of worms. She turned to the closet, saw the box on which Angie had scrawled, "Doodads, Odd Items."

Most of what was in the box was junk, she realized, after hauling it to the bed, opening it, finding the laptop, then digging around for the power cord. Hating any sort of mess, even in a room she didn't use, she repacked all the boxes, returned them to the closet, then finally carried the bulky laptop to her kitchen table. The thing was as slow as molasses, the battery had long since given out, and, as Angie had mentioned, it was not wi-fi capable. That, however, meant no one was going to tap into this machine unless it was hardwired to the Internet via Ethernet. And since she wasn't about to do that, it was probably the safest machine she had to look at the files Scotty had given her.

She only hoped it still worked. She plugged it in, then made herself a cup of tea while the thing booted up.

There was only one folder on the thumb drive and she double clicked.

A list of case files. Or rather the face sheets, which included names and a few lines stating what was in the original report, which was not attached. She read the first one, an anonymous report that the lobbyists at Wingman and Wingman were paying off lawmakers to curry favor for certain bills.

Nothing new there. Wasn't every lobbyist and lawmaker guilty of that? In fact most of the older reports were of a similar type, she found, after quickly scanning several.

Her stomach knotted as she read the next report's synopsis. Even though Scotty had warned her, she hadn't expected that seeing her father's name as a suspect on an actual case file would still hurt.

He and Robert Orozco were accused of breaking into a travel agency in Washington, D.C., that was suspected of being a front company for Wingman and Wingman's lobbyists. Apparently the FBI had been investigating the company, because they'd received a tip that the travel agency was giving congressmen bribes and gifts of stays at exotic locations, all expenses paid. The company closed down shortly thereafter, and the matter was dropped after they inexplicably declined to press charges.

Her father was implicated with Orozco in a second burglary, this one being at Wingman and Wingman.

This was six months before her father was killed. That knot in her stomach tightened, and she felt nauseous.

Scotty was right. She didn't like seeing it.

Reading her father's name on that type of case made her feel as if he'd somehow betrayed her by pretending to be someone other than the man she thought he was.

This was *not* the father she had loved her whole life.

And even though this wasn't the first time she'd been faced with this fact, she knew that if she let it, the knowledge would tear her apart. She couldn't let that happen again, not after the emotional toll it took when she'd first looked into his decades-old murder, and she told herself that the man listed on these FBI files was what her father did when he went to work. It was *not* who he was when he came home at the end of the day.

That man had truly loved her, and after all, wasn't that what counted in the end?

Exactly what counted, she told herself. When she finally managed to look at this with clinical detachment, she realized Scotty was right. Her father *was* connected to Wingman and Wingman.

The list of numbers she had locked in her desk drawer were the numbers her father and Orozco had stolen from Wingman Squared.

And all these reports were somehow connected.

But apparently not enough to have made a case to go after Wingman.

Somehow there was a thread in here that connected them . . .

Brilliant thought. Of course there was a thread. Her father had also been involved in the theft of money from a bank called BICTT. The acronym stood for Bank of International Commerce Trade and Trust but was better known in the intelligence world as the Bank of International Crooks, Terrorists, and Thieves. It was operated by a group called the Black Network, a cabal of criminals, politicians, and businessmen involved in a number of enterprises such as arms trafficking, drug money laundering, even terrorist funding if it furthered their own ends.

Everything she knew about the Network was from working with Griffin and ATLAS, and they had also implicated the Network with the BICTT scandal. What she knew very little about was Wingman Squared.

Her father, she was sure, had somehow been involved with both. Which, in her mind, at least, meant they were connected.

So why was Wingman and Wingman still up and running if it was a Network firm?

Unfortunately, she couldn't tell from reading the face sheets of these cases.

But then, at the end of the file was a list of names with no explanation. Some were listed as witnesses on the cases she'd just read, others not listed at all. Curious, she wrote the names down on a sheet of yellow legal paper, tore it from the pad, then set it by her purse, wondering how to research this without using the Internet or her work computers.

A knock at her door startled her, and she glanced out the peephole to see Scotty and two other FBI agents she recognized as working for Pearson standing beside him.

She opened the door, noticed the tense expression on Scotty's face. "What's going on?" she asked him.

"Pearson needs you down at the office."

Her heart started a slow thud. She knew what for, and she was acutely aware of the laptop sitting behind her, along with the flash drive connected to it. Scotty's flash drive. No wonder he looked upset. "Why?"

"Is it okay if we come in?"

Sydney didn't move. "For what?"

Scotty took a deep breath. "Permissive search for the list of numbers you recovered from Mexico."

She told herself to remain calm. "I can save you the trouble of searching. They're locked in my desk drawer in my office at Quantico. Have at it."

"Pearson would like to search your apartment, as well."

"Do I need an attorney?"

He looked her right in the eye and lowered his voice. "You know I'd tell you if you did. It's . . . more a matter of national security. And your safety. Pearson will explain when we get to his office. He's asked that I escort you."

Still she didn't move. It wasn't because she didn't believe him. She knew Scotty enough to realize he wouldn't lie about something that important. If he said they were searching as a precaution, she believed him. Her concern, at this point, was for the laptop with the files on it. Actually not the laptop, which could only be traced to her. If, however, they were to discover a flash drive in its port that might very well have Scotty's fingerprints on it?

"Fine. Let me get my phone and my keys. I'll drive myself. You can follow me."

She turned around, knowing they'd be watching her like a hawk. She walked straight to the kitchen table, keeping her back to them, hoping she could palm the flash drive without them seeing.

"Don't touch the computer," one of them said.

"You need the flash drive?" She pulled it from the port, smeared her thumb and forefinger across it to smudge any prints, then held it out.

The dark-haired agent closest to her reached over, took it from her. She eyed the notes she'd made from the flash drive files, wondering if they'd take that, too. Maybe they wouldn't connect it to the flash drive. Losing the laptop, she could handle. Losing the notes?

Unfortunately one of the investigators looked at it at the same time, then picked it up along with the laptop.

She wondered if her day could get any worse.

9

Sydney had been holed up in Pearson's office ever since she and Scotty left her apartment. He did allow her to make one stop, to her across-the-hall neighbor, Tina, so that she could explain that a couple of her coworkers were going to be doing some work at her place and not to be alarmed if she saw them removing any property. Once at HQ, Pearson explained their position, his concern being only for her safety—look what had happened to the young man in South San Francisco who'd found the numbers on the copy machine and been shot as a result.

That she understood. Even so, she paced the room, feeling like a criminal. Pearson eventually left, had been gone for a couple of hours, and Scotty had been assigned the job of babysitter. And for what? To make sure she didn't run off? They undoubtedly had the list by now. So what the hell was taking them so long? she wondered, looking at the clock. It was almost five P.M.

"This is utter bullshit," she said, yet again. "Why are they searching my apartment? What are they expecting to find, when the list they want is—was—locked up in my desk drawer at Quantico?"

Scotty was seated in one of the chairs in front of Pearson's desk. "You heard what he said. They've just got to be sure. Protocol and all."

"What's there to be sure of? I wouldn't lie to him."

Scotty got up out of his seat, looked through the partially open blinds out to the main floor, then turned back to her. Up until now, he'd been fairly quiet, not commenting on the case. Probably because he was worried about what they might find that could lead to him. Not that she was about to say anything. Not here. Not when she didn't know if there were any listening devices.

"You made a copy when you *knew* it was a classified document," he said, his look almost pleading with her to shut up. "That's not exactly telling the truth."

In this case, truth was subjective. The last thing she wanted to do was get Carillo in trouble over this, so she wasn't about to mention that he'd made the copy, not her. "An oversight on my part. How was I supposed to know the thing was some national security document?"

"Because I told you so."

"No, what you *told* me was a bunch of mumbo-jumbo about once those documents were recovered, the objective changed, and it was all about damage control. What the hell does that mean? You *knew* I thought those documents had something to do with my father's murder. You also knew I thought they were offshore bank account numbers from BICTT," she said, referring to the international CIA bank scandal that had also been connected to her father's case. "Anyone who asked knew exactly what I thought, so thinking I *wouldn't* make a copy was probably stupid on their part, don't you think?"

Scotty threw her a dark look. "Are you serious? That's

your weak excuse?" He stalked back to his seat and dropped into it, clearly upset with her.

She didn't care. Right now she had bigger issues, and, looking out the window, she saw one of them was about to hit. Pearson approached, carrying her old laptop.

Scotty happened to look up at the same time, saw it, then turned an accusing glance her way. "Please tell me he's not going to find anything incriminating on there?"

When she didn't answer, he closed his eyes, took a deep breath, then wiped all emotion from his face before Pearson walked in and deposited the laptop on his desk.

"Is this yours?" he asked Sydney.

"Yes."

"The files on it?"

"What about them?"

"You put them on there?"

"I did. I don't recall seeing any marks showing them as classified."

"Except they all pertain to a classified investigation we've been running for years."

"The only thing I was aware of was that they pertain to my father's murder."

"How did you acquire them?" Pearson asked.

She could feel Scotty's gaze burning a hole in her back and she didn't dare turn his direction. "Lots of digging over the years."

"The files are dated a few months ago."

Which was interesting, since she'd only downloaded them today. But then she remembered which computer she was dealing with. The date was probably set wrong, never mind the battery had been dead forever. Apparently he thought the laptop date was correct, not the flash drive date. So be it. "*If* you recall, a few months ago, I was actively pursuing my father's case. These are the files I felt were somehow connected."

"And what was the connection?"

"Honestly? I haven't a clue. Which is why they're still sitting there. It's hours of research over the years that finally led me to believe that my father's case was possibly tied into other cases, some of which are still going on today. That and the bits and pieces I was able to gather after talking with Robert Orozco down in Mexico," she added, since she damned well knew he'd have a hard time checking into that. "But what does this have to do with the list of numbers you were looking for?"

He didn't answer.

Not a good sign, she decided. "You did find it? In my desk drawer, where I said it was?"

"Yes."

"Am I under arrest?"

"No."

"Am I being investigated?"

"No. As I'm sure Scotty explained, this is about national security *and* your safety. The only reason we asked to search your apartment and office—which we thank you for your cooperation—is because of the last few missions you've worked. You've been exposed to things beyond your clearance level. Things that, when you started looking into them, you could never have realized the implications."

She stood there a moment, trying to think of what to say, what might help her case, but nothing came to mind. "Can I go?"

"Yes."

She glanced at Scotty. Normally she had no trouble reading him. He was mad, she knew that. She just wasn't sure where that anger was directed. At the Bureau or at her? Probably her, she decided, and walked to the door, opened it.

"Fitzpatrick?"

She stopped, waiting for whatever it was Pearson was going to throw at her. She did not, however, turn around.

"I know it doesn't seem like it right now. But I'm on your side."

He was right. It didn't seem like it. Not that she was foolish enough to say so out loud. "Thank you, sir."

She left, and headed down the corridor, and it was everything she could do to keep calm. She jabbed the elevator button, then lost the effort, fuming as she waited.

Scotty ran up just as the doors opened, and they rode it down in silence. It wasn't until they reached the parking garage that he said, "We need to talk."

"Ya think?"

"Come back to my place."

"Why would I do that?"

"Moral support? Company? Someone to vent to?"

"Thanks. But right now, I just need to be by myself. Think things through."

He studied her face for a moment, as though making sure she really should be alone. "Call if you need anything."

Both turned toward their respective cars, but after a few steps, Sydney stopped, called out to him. "That offer of taking the weekend at the B&B? Is that still on the table?"

"Of course. I can't use it. And Amanda doesn't want to go without me."

"The prospect of sitting in the middle of the forest completely alone is suddenly very appealing, even if I do have to wait until next weekend."

"It's on my desk. We can go back up and get it."

"If it's all the same . . . ?" Running into Pearson was not high on her priority list right now.

"Back in a few."

She waited at the elevator, glad for a moment to just regroup. She could deal with being under the microscope. Nothing new for her. The fact they'd found the files Scotty had given her on her laptop had shaken her, though. The last thing she wanted to do was jeopardize his career.

When he returned, handed her the envelope, she reached up, hugged him. "Thanks."

"I should be thanking you," he said quietly. "For not throwing me under the bus."

She looked down at the envelope, fingered the edges. "I'd never do that. Not after . . . you know. I'm only sorry I dragged you into it as far as I did. I never meant—"

Scotty reached out, lifted her face so that she was looking right at him. "I'm not sure I would have done any different. If I were you, that is." He smiled at her.

"But you're glad you're not me?"

"Pretty much."

She smiled back, relieved that they had come to an easy truce after all this time. "I'll call you."

He nodded, then walked to his car, leaving her to hers. The moment she got in, slammed the door shut, she checked her cell phone, saw she had missed a call from Griffin and three from Carillo. She ignored Griffin's call and phoned Carillo instead. "You'll never guess who just searched my apartment and office. Pearson," she said, before he could even get a word in edgewise. "They were after the numbers."

"Tex was at my place earlier, so I figured it was a matter of time. Had you answered your phone, I would've mentioned it, right along with his request that I let *Griffin* tell you about his involvement."

"Let's just say I drew a logical conclusion."

"Hard not to. I assume he's back in D.C., since he wasn't here with Tex last night. Have you talked to him yet?"

"No. But I can't wait to hear his explanation for all this."

"So what now?"

"Regroup. I'll call you when I come up with a plan."

"Stay safe."

"Likewise."

She left, navigated through commuter traffic, and eventually pulled onto the freeway, trying to decide what her next

step should be. It was then she looked into her rearview
mirror, noticing a dark-colored vehicle that twice changed
lanes when she did.

Her phone vibrated in the cup holder, and she glanced
down, saw it was Griffin.

Maybe she didn't know his full involvement in all this.
Plenty of time to find out later. Right now she had more
important things to focus on. Like whether the black sedan
trailing two cars behind was actually following her, or
whether she was merely being paranoid.

10

Sydney took the long way home, after several eva-sive maneuvers. Maybe she was, maybe she wasn't being followed, but she wouldn't put it past Pearson to assign a couple of agents to keep track of her whereabouts. What'd he think she was going to do? Materialize some nonexistent copies of this list and post them on the Internet?

She should have listened to her mother and become a kindergarten teacher. Right now, the thought of facing a room full of five-year-olds, their eyes filled with admiration while she taught them their ABCs, was eminently appealing. And by the time she pulled in her driveway, she'd almost convinced herself it was time to give up this job, go back to school, and get that teaching credential.

But then her phone rang. Griffin. Again.

After a deep, calming breath, she realized she was not ready to discuss this with him. She shut the thing off, tossed it into the center console, and stared out the window, feeling the weight of the world crushing down on her.

How had she been so blind? How could she not have known that he'd been involved that whole time?

A knock at her window startled her, and she looked over, saw her neighbor, Tina, with her black Labrador, Storm. The dog jumped up on the car door, whining, as though sensing the struggle she was going through at that moment.

"You okay?" Tina asked.

Sydney nodded, but didn't move.

Neither did Tina, apparently not convinced. And when Storm pawed at the window, Sydney smiled, opened the door, and patted her lap. "Good boy."

He pushed his nose into her, and she scratched him behind his ears.

Tina stood there, bundled against the cold, watching. They'd undoubtedly just come back from their evening outing at the dog park.

"How was the walk today, Storm?" Sydney asked, hoping Tina wouldn't feel it necessary to delve into her personal life.

Like any true dog owner, Tina was happy to discuss her pet's activities. "For him? He can chase a tennis ball for*ever*. For me? Nothing like spending an hour in near-freezing temperature to get that blood pumping. I can't wait to get into a hot shower."

Sydney attempted a smile. "Same here." She got out, locked the car, and the two of them walked to the elevator together.

For a moment she was almost able to pretend that nothing was wrong. That feeling lasted until they reached their floor and Tina said, "Those guys from your work? They sure were around a long time. They even came back a couple hours ago."

Sydney gave a sigh. "Glad they're gone. I'm looking forward to a little downtime."

Downtime was not what was waiting for her when she walked into her door and discovered the mess the agents had made during their search.

She stood there a moment, at first disbelieving what she saw, then, as it sank in, felt the blood rushing to her head in anger.

"Goddamned sons of . . ."

Cereal had been dumped into the sink. Every cupboard was open, every drawer. In her bedroom, her dresser had been completely emptied, the drawers out, turned upside-down. The closet was ravaged, the shelves emptied. Same in the spare bedroom, where the boxes she'd carefully dug through to find her computer were dumped on the floor.

Even the bathroom had been searched in similar fashion.

The entire place looked like narcotics officers had gone through it looking for drugs and evidence of dealing.

They'd treated her like a common criminal.

She grabbed her phone and called Scotty. "You goddamned bastards! How could you do this?"

"Syd. We discussed this. I thought—"

"No. What we discussed was that the list was in my office drawer. Not this. *This* is way over the top. You can tell Pearson that he can kiss my—"

"Syd! What the hell is wrong with you?"

"Wrong? Either Pearson sent a couple overzealous agents, or they were looking for evidence that doesn't exist. What part of 'it's in my desk drawer' did they not believe?"

He didn't answer.

She looked around, walking from room to room, feeling like a tornado had swept through. "I don't believe this. Pearson *said* he was on my side. You heard him. And *this*? What the hell?"

"What are you talking about?"

"The *goddamned mess in my apartment. That's what.*"

"Calm down—"

"Calm down? Did you know about this? That they were going to toss my apartment like I'm some goddamned drug dealer?"

"Of course not."

"Well. Glad we got *that* cleared up." She disconnected, threw the phone on the counter, then stood there, feeling the urge to drop a match to everything and let it all burn. This was Griffin's fault.

Everything was his fault.

Well screw him. And everyone who worked with him.

It took her several minutes before she could even think about what to do. She had two choices, she figured. Pack a suitcase and stay in a hotel, or start cleaning.

She was too mad to get behind the wheel, so she chose the latter, and began in the kitchen, scooping the dry cereal into the garbage, along with the empty boxes. Every dish they touched, she put in the dishwasher or stacked in the sink, feeling as though all of it was contaminated. By the time she had the kitchen nearly cleaned, the dishwasher running, there was a knock at the door.

She stalked over, looked out the peephole, saw it was Scotty, and opened it. "I can't believe you even have the nerve to come over here."

"Nerve? No one tossed your apartment, Syd. They simply went through your computer, making sure there was nothing on it. I swear."

"Really?" She held the door wide, motioned him to enter. "See for yourself. Oh, and FYI? The kitchen didn't look this good when I got here. I only just now finished cleaning it."

He walked in, glanced over, then continued on into the living room, where there wasn't much to mess up, other than couch cushions and pillows, and where the furniture clearly had been moved, as though someone had been looking beneath it.

"The bedrooms and bathroom," she said, then stood there, waiting, while he looked.

He returned a moment later. "Sydney. I swear I didn't know."

"Yeah? Well that makes me feel a hell of a lot better. *Not*."

He took out his phone, made a call. "It's Ryan," he said. "What the hell did you do at Sydney's place . . . ? That right? It's completely tossed. As in *every* room . . ."

And as she listened, she realized he was telling the truth. He had *not* been aware they were going to toss the place. In fact, the look on his face when he ended the call confirmed it. What he said next, however, completely unnerved her.

"They swear the only thing they did was a cursory search after they looked at your computers."

"Then who did this?"

"That's just it. They don't know."

11

ATLAS (Alliance for Threat Level
Assessment and Security)
U.S. Headquarters, Washington, D.C.

It was well after six P.M. by the time Griffin left for his
office—once Marc finally relieved him at Lisette's apartment where they were keeping Piper. They'd soon be making
plans to place her in witness protection, but until then, Lisette and Marc were her babysitters.

McNiel wasn't in, and Griffin hoped he'd left for the day,
knowing that anything his boss would have to say to him
was not going to be good. He checked his voice mail, hoping
that Sydney had finally returned one of his calls. There were
no messages from her. After one more try on her cell phone,
he telephoned Tex, needing to hear at least *one* friendly
voice that evening.

Tex was still in California, waiting on evidence in the
South San Francisco killing that might lead to who had gone
after the hard drive. "Hate to break it to you, Griff. It's possible she's not picking up because Carillo may have already

called her. At least that's the only reason I can think of. Let's just say he wasn't real happy when I left him."

"You told him what was going on?"

"He guessed. He did, however, promise not to say anything directly about Mexico, at least not until you had a chance to talk with her yourself. But we *are* talking about Carillo, here. He beats to his own drummer, so hard to say if he did or didn't tell her anything."

"Looks like he has, otherwise why wouldn't she call me back?" He stared out the window, thinking things had been much easier when he'd only known Sydney from afar. Unfortunately he hadn't counted on the circumstances that had thrown them together on that Rome operation, or the growing attraction the longer they'd worked together. After that, it had been all too easy to ignore what had taken place in Mexico. Ignore? No, definitely not ignore. Avoid. "Makes me wish I'd come up with a better cover story."

"Spies are supposed to be good at lying. Sort of a requisite. Except when it comes to the girl you're sleeping with."

"I'm taking things slow."

"What part?" Tex asked. "Telling her the truth or sleeping with her?"

Griffin leaned back in his chair, resisting the urge to hang up on Tex. It was none of his business whether Griffin and Sydney had actually slept together, but he couldn't ignore the dig. "And what? You didn't sleep with Genevieve after your night out in Paris?" he said, referring to the CIA agent Tex was now dating, one whom he'd met on their last mission. "You've known her less time than I've known Sydney."

"That's different."

"Why?"

"Because we pretty much know all there is to know about each other. At least the important stuff. Like where we *met* the *first* time, even if we didn't know what each other did for a living. I wouldn't want to be you if Sydney's figured all this out before you tell her."

"Well it's looking like she knows," he said, picking up a pen from the desktop, then drawing concentric circles on his blotter.

"She's smart, Griff. And right now you're digging yourself into a really deep hole that's gonna bury you."

"Thank you for your philosophical analysis." He jammed the pen tip into the blotter paper, causing a tear. "If I admit I'm an ass, do I get to skip the lecture when you get back to D.C.?"

"Don't ask me, ask Sydney."

Griffin tossed the pen aside. "Have to go. Duty calls."

He disconnected, then glanced up at the clock. Nearly six-thirty. He wasn't even sure why he'd bothered to come in. He might as well go home, he thought, then heard the elevator open on the floor. A moment later, McNiel stopped at his door. "My office. Now."

Definitely a bad sign.

"Where's the report on Quindlen?" was all McNiel said as Griffin walked in.

He was referring to a drug and gunrunning case down in Pocito, Arizona near the border, allegedly run by an ex-CIA agent, Garrett Quindlen. They'd recently learned that Quindlen was connected to a man known only as Brooks, who was the reported mastermind behind the ring. The high-priority case had moved down on the list once this current case was brought to their attention. "For the most part, done. I wasn't able to follow up on the last lead, since this came up."

"Once Tex finishes up in California, have him follow it up. If there's any connection between Brooks and Quindlen, I want it. And the update on South San Francisco?"

"The girl is with Marc and Lisette. They're following protocol and she won't be left alone. As for Tex, he met with

Carillo," Griffin said. "He did not have a copy. He said he gave it to Sydney."

"Tex *discussed* this with Carillo?"

"Actually, the other way around. Apparently Carillo was the one who made the copy and gave it to Sydney. After the murder in South San Francisco, and the connection to the copy machine, it didn't take much for him to deduce that our presence was related."

"How much does he know?"

"Enough," Griffin said, "to make a very educated guess about our involvement in Mexico."

"And what has he told Fitzpatrick?"

He thought about what Tex said. "As far as I know, just about the murder in South San Francisco. He's allowing us to tighten our own noose."

"*Your* noose," McNiel corrected. "One that wouldn't be there if you'd dealt with this correctly in the beginning. You failed your mission, ignored the kill order, and Fitzpatrick has the list. You've endangered countless lives as a result."

"What was I supposed to do? Kill an FBI agent?"

"Had it been Orozco in that boat, you would have killed him."

"I didn't know him, and *he* was a criminal."

"You didn't know her, either. Not then."

"But I followed her for long enough to get a feeling. She's on our side. If I ask her for the list, she'll give it to me."

"She was *supposed* to have turned it over back in October, when we sent a team to San Francisco. How high does that body count have to reach before you put aside your personal feelings and realize that she's demonstrated on more than one occasion that she has her own agenda?"

"If I can—"

"The last thing we need is a rogue FBI agent putting this country in danger because she can't follow orders."

"At least let me talk to her."

"Too late. The search has been done."

Griffin stared in disbelief.

"After what happened in South San Francisco, my hand was forced. I contacted Pearson to do the search. Can you imagine what would have happened if Fitzpatrick had run those numbers?"

Griffin didn't want to imagine. He didn't want to think at all. "Where is she?"

"She left Pearson's office. Probably home by now."

Griffin was out the door before McNiel even finished talking. The moment he was in the parking lot, and able to make a cell phone connection, he tried calling again. It rang several times, then went to voice mail. "Syd. Call me. Please. It's important."

He tried again once he was on the road, but this time, it went straight to voice mail, telling him that she had probably seen his call, and was choosing to ignore him. He drove straight to her apartment, the speed laws be damned. And once he was there, he called her house phone, telling her he was in the parking lot, asking her to at least meet him outside.

He waited, even though she didn't answer. A few minutes later, she came down, and Griffin saw her walk out the lobby doors, then over to his car.

"Why are you here?" she asked.

"Because we need to talk."

"Apparently we needed to talk a long time ago. I heard you were in California. You were there to investigate the numbers I made copies of. You *knew* about them, and you never told me."

He took a deep breath, not even sure what to say, and could almost hear Tex's voice in his head, telling him to start at the beginning. "It was classified or I would have. The case in Mexico. Your father's friend. Robert Orozco."

He could see her tensing, and realized that Carillo had *not* told her everything. "What about him?" she asked.

"When you were down there . . . When he gave you the list of numbers—"

"You're *admitting* that ATLAS was involved with my father's case?"

"Then and now. I was there in Mexico when you were. Tex and I were both there."

He wasn't sure, but it seemed she stopped breathing momentarily. It was several seconds before she responded, the longest several seconds of his life. "What do you mean *you* were there?"

"In the helicopter. After you left Orozco's house."

Her mouth dropped open. She stared at him in silence, tried to speak, then turned away. He stepped toward her, and she held up her hand, warning him off.

He didn't dare move closer.

"I need to think about this," she said.

Finally she looked at him. He saw the confusion, the hurt, the betrayal on her face. All directed at him. And then, as if it hit her at once, she turned the full force of her gaze on him. "Oh my God . . . *You* shot at me . . . *You* were up in that helicopter, firing at my boat. *I could have been killed.*"

"I know."

His response seemed to surprise her, as if maybe she'd expected him to deny it. "You mean you were supposed to . . . ?"

He refused to answer. There were so many variables, so many things he couldn't even begin to explain right now.

"I asked you a question. Were you supposed to kill me?"

"It's not as cut and dried as 'supposed to.' "

"I can't believe I'm hearing this. A kill order? Why would you keep something like that from me?"

"I'm sorry. I—"

"No." She shook her head and backed away. "You *don't* get to apologize like it's some minor transgression. You shot at *me. And* you kept it a secret. How the hell am I supposed to believe that anything we have together—*had*—is even real?"

"It is—"

She closed her eyes, wrapping her arms around herself. "Why are you even telling me now? Here? In the middle of a parking lot? It's not like there weren't plenty of opportunities."

"You wouldn't answer your phone."

"Oh. You were going to tell me on the phone? That's rich. Because I have nothing to say to you. It's January. Or did that escape your notice? And this happened when? Last October?"

"Syd . . ."

"I don't want to hear it right now." The bottom of her eyelids glistened and he knew she was having a difficult time keeping it together.

She turned away, started to walk off.

"Syd."

She stopped, rounded on him, an anger like he'd never seen lighting her eyes. "No. I knew you were involved. That ATLAS was involved. I guessed that much, after Carillo called. The whole timing thing with the murder over there and Tex showing up at his place. But not this. *This* I *never* expected."

"At least let me explain."

"I think the time for that is long past." She looked like she might walk off, but stopped, suddenly. "Are *you* responsible for tearing up my apartment? Couldn't find the list at Carillo's place?"

"What? No. I—"

"Go to hell."

She turned away, walked toward the apartment building. When she stopped at the doors, hesitated, he thought she might return, talk to him. But she merely reached up, brushed at her eyes, apparently composing herself before entering. She never looked back.

12

The meeting at ATLAS the following morning dragged on for far longer than Griffin had hoped. As McNiel spoke, going over possible actions they needed to take, Griffin's attention wandered. He'd had little sleep, his mind turning over every possibility of how to straighten out this matter with Sydney. A thousand what-ifs, and not one would have solved the problem. It didn't matter that Tex had warned him, for weeks in fact, because in every scenario in which he informed her of their shared past, her reaction was always going to be the same.

Hurt and betrayal.

He hadn't wanted to inflict either on her. Surely that should count for something?

Deep down, though, he was very much aware that the reason he hadn't told her was completely self-serving. He knew she'd leave, walk away, and never look back.

Just as she had yesterday.

And he didn't know how to fix this. In fact, he was fairly certain he couldn't. Not without some divine intervention, something he had little faith in these days.

"I'm assuming that's what you still believe?"

McNiel looked directly at him, waiting for an answer.

"Still believe?" Griffin echoed. He had totally lost track of the conversation.

McNiel's gaze hardened. "That the Black Network's involved. Wingman and Wingman has never been implicated in any of the Network's activities. Or in any illegal activities. At least not enough to be charged."

Donovan Archer got up to pour himself another cup of coffee. He was a relatively new agent, and hadn't worked the number of cases that Griffin had. "In my book," Donovan said, "that makes them a bigger candidate." Which was exactly what Griffin was thinking. The Network specialized in politics—handpicking their own candidates or bribing public officials already in office, be it in the U.S. or on foreign soil—the better to set domestic and foreign policy that furthered their own agendas and lined their pockets. The problem with keeping such an organization viable was that it took vast amounts of money, and the Network had no qualms about lining their coffers with drug and arms trafficking, or selling of technology, or any other means that they saw fit.

"Why do you think that?" McNiel asked Donovan.

"Are you telling me that an organization like the Network that's infiltrated the U.S. government, doesn't have tentacles reaching into the intelligence arena? How else are they always one step ahead?"

How indeed? Griffin thought. "Whether W2 is part of the Network or not," he said, "it has no bearing on the bigger question. Someone's been monitoring electronic data, or they wouldn't have been at that warehouse looking for something they shouldn't have even known about."

"The Devil's Key? Agreed," McNiel said. "The timing is far too close to ignore. So whoever it is, they had to have knowledge of the program's capacity to begin with, or they wouldn't have known what to even look for."

Which didn't bode well. The Devil's Key exploited a back door into a data mining program developed more than twenty years ago by a software company. The Strategic Integrated Network Case Management System, better known as SINS, was marketed as cutting-edge case management and sold to a number of foreign countries around the world. Of course, it was also stolen—they suspected by someone at Wingman and Wingman—and sold on the black market to even more countries. Once the NSA discovered the back door's existence—and the very real threat of it possibly being used *against* the U.S.—they started on damage control. What the intelligence communities didn't know was who proposed, then implemented the spyware into the program. McNiel believed it was a Network operation from the start, and Griffin tended to agree.

"Maybe I'm missing something," Donovan said, returning to his seat. "Devil's Key? This is about what Sydney Fitzpatrick found in Mexico?" Donovan had not worked the BICTT case when Sydney had found the key in Mexico, and since it had been on a need-to-know basis, he hadn't been included in the intel.

"Yes," McNiel said, and Griffin could see the stress in his face.

"So it's true?" Donovan asked. "There really is a back door built into the SINS program?"

"Not just built into the program," McNiel replied. "But into the millions of computer chips throughout the world. They can infiltrate any system."

Donovan was just taking a sip of coffee and nearly choked on it. "Uh, did I hear that right?"

"You did."

Unbeknownst to all but a few select individuals, because of the chips used, the program allowed for a back door into *any* computer that contained one and was running it—providing one had the code to get in.

It was not only a political nightmare, it was a national security disaster waiting to happen. Once this backdoor vulnerability on the chips had been discovered, the U.S. government, realizing the devastation, the potential for evil, took the unprecedented step of destroying every known copy of the code that allowed entry. There were ten codes in all, aptly named the Devil's Keys.

Nine were destroyed. The tenth was stolen by a former government operative, Robert Orozco, about to be arrested along with Sydney's father for their involvement in the BICTT banking scandal. The theft of the code was Orozco's insurance policy. Leave him alone. If they came after him, he'd make sure the code was delivered to enemy hands, and reveal what the U.S. had allowed to slip through their fingers.

For twenty years Orozco had been the most hunted man in the world, successfully dropping out of sight until one FBI agent did what the entire CIA failed to do. Find him. Sydney Fitzpatrick had wanted answers about why her father was murdered, and Orozco had been a friend of her father's. Based on some childhood memory of a fishing trip her father had taken her on down near Ensenada, she located Orozco, who gave her the last known key code, apparently thinking he'd be safer without it.

And he was right—to some extent. When, after several years, the CIA failed to locate him or the code, ATLAS had been given the task—along with the kill order.

Donovan was clearly trying to wrap his head around what he'd just learned, and McNiel said, "Welcome to our national security nightmare, should the Devil's Key fall into the wrong hands."

"You mean, what this girl in South San Francisco has sitting in her head? *That's* the Devil's Key?"

"The same."

And Griffin said, "We have to assume the Network's

involved, and they're probably one and the same as W2. They've certainly had the capabilities to run a program like this. And for them to show up at some obscure repair shop in South San Francisco of all places . . . That copy machine was sold in a batch of dozens, and the guy who bought it was running the numbers from it on his computer."

"Right now," McNiel said, "we'd be remiss in thinking the Network isn't doing the same. Who knows where their tentacles reach."

"If that's the case, we're in bigger trouble than we thought."

"If that's the case," Donovan said, "stay off the god-damned Internet."

McNiel's phone rang. He answered it, listened, clearly disturbed. "Of course not. The only search I knew of is the one you did . . ." He closed his eyes, then rubbed the bridge of his nose. "No, Brad. We're *not* running some rogue operation here. I would have informed you if that were the case . . . Exactly *what* is she saying happened . . . ? Yes, I'll hold."

He covered the mouthpiece of the phone. "It's Pearson. Apparently someone was in Sydney's apartment. Ripped through the whole place, probably looking for the list."

"List?" Donovan echoed. "As in *the* list, key, whatever the hell it is?"

Griffin's gut twisted. "She mentioned it last night."

"Why didn't you say something?" McNiel asked.

"I had other things on my mind."

Apparently Pearson came back on the line, because McNiel uncovered the phone. "I assure you, Brad. We aren't in the habit of breaking into FBI agents' homes . . . Yes, a lapse of judgment at Carillo's condo, but my agents were worried about the classified nature of the . . . Of course. I'll see you there."

He hung up. "Hard to deny our involvement when we've already conducted *one* illegal search."

"Not quite," Griffin said.

"In Carillo's case, it's the thought that counts. Lucky for us Pearson's more worried about the fact someone else is searching."

"That's three," Donovan said. "The warehouse where Piper was found, Carillo's before Tex could get there, *and* Sydney's. Hard to overlook."

"Hers," McNiel said, "was apparently searched *after* Pearson had already been there and confiscated her computers. They're clearly looking for the Devil's Key—the only place they haven't hit yet is Mexico." He picked up the phone and called Tex. "New mission. Contact Robert Orozco and verify that he does or does not have a copy of that key. He may be in danger," he said, then explained about the search on Sydney's apartment.

There was a knock at his door, and his secretary opened it, looked in. "Sir? Lisette's on your other line. She says it's urgent."

"Thanks." Then, after telling Tex to call him the moment he made contact with Orozco, he disconnected, and picked up the second line. "Lisette . . . ? He's here now . . . I'll tell him." Then to Griffin, "Your witness said she heard a name mentioned when she was at the scene. Brooks."

"If we were looking for a connection to the Network," Donovan said, "we just found it."

That was, unfortunately, all they knew about the man they believed to be instrumental in the creation and theft of the Devil's Key—just the one name—even after the recent intel on the gunrunning operation with Garrett Quindlen in Pocito, Arizona. "When was this?" Griffin asked. "I didn't hear it mentioned."

He pressed a button so that they were on speakerphone, and Griffin repeated the question to Lisette.

"Apparently it happened just outside the building, before she entered. And before she realized what was happening.

The two men who came into the warehouse were talking *to* him."

"As in she *saw* him?"

"Definitely. I think she could do a sketch of the man."

"If so," McNiel said, "it might be our first glimpse of a face that has eluded us for a couple decades." He looked at Griffin. "Call Fitzpatrick. This takes priority."

"Somehow I doubt Sydney's going to want to help us with this. In fact, I'm probably the last person she's going to want to talk to."

"Notice I'm not asking. So fix it. Whatever it takes."

Not wanting to be overheard, Griffin went to his office and closed the door before calling Sydney. He left a message, asking her to get back to him. When he tried again, it went straight to voice mail.

Resisting the urge to hurl his own phone across the room, especially since it was tethered to the wall by the cord, he leaned back in his chair and stared out the window, trying to think how McNiel expected him to fix something that was undoubtedly broken beyond repair.

And that was where Donovan found him several minutes later. Still seated, just staring out at the leaden sky.

"We should talk," Donovan said.

"About?"

"Sydney."

"There's nothing to discuss."

"Shouldn't you at least call her?"

Griffin grabbed his keys, then his coat and started toward the door. "I have. Several times. She's not answering."

"Thought about driving over there?" Donovan asked, following him onto the elevator.

"So she can slam the door in my face? Yeah. I thought about it. For all of ten seconds."

"Then she slams the door. At least you tried. But if you don't go? What's she supposed to think?"

"That she dodged a bullet—no pun intended."

"FYI? There comes a point when the hole you dig is so deep, there's no climbing out. And you're getting to that point."

Griffin jabbed at the Down button. "I take it you've been talking to Tex?"

"As a matter of fact, yes. He's worried about you," Donovan said, placing his foot in the elevator door so it wouldn't shut on him. "Because you're having a real hard time seeing what's right in front of your face."

Donovan removed his foot; the elevator closed, leaving Griffin alone as it descended.

He looked at the keys in his hand, knowing that Donovan was right. So what if she slammed the door in his face?

Any reaction from her was better than not knowing what she was thinking.

He drove to her apartment, managed to enter the lobby when someone was walking out, and took the elevator up. He knocked on the door, and when no one answered, he called out her name.

The door behind him opened.

"Sydney's not home."

He recognized her neighbor, Tina, and her black Lab, Storm, both standing there watching him.

"Any idea where she is?"

"No. She took off a while ago."

"If she comes back, can you tell her to call me? It's important."

"Sure thing."

He left, sat in his car, and tried to think where she might go. And then it occurred to him that she usually kept in close touch with Carillo. He called.

Carillo didn't answer, either, and so he left a message. "It's

Griffin. If by some chance you know where Sydney is, can you call me? It's an emergency. And I'm not the one asking. McNiel is." As if that would make a difference.

He disconnected. His phone rang a few minutes later. Carillo. "You've got a lot of nerve calling her after everything that's gone on."

"I know," Griffin said. "I don't know how to make this right. I don't even know where to begin."

"Can't help you there. Except to say that trying to contact her right now is probably *not* in your best interest."

"We need a sketch from our witness in the South San Francisco murder."

"She figured if you were going to contact her, it'd be for that. So in anticipation, she asked me to pass on a message. Something to the effect of go screw yourself. Only four letters. Beginning with an F."

"Ever helpful, Carillo."

"For what it's worth? I really *don't* know where she is, but depending on how important this is . . ."

"Very."

"I did hear Scotty's voice in the background. Just thought I'd throw that out there."

"Thanks."

Not about to chance that she'd leave if he called, he drove straight to Scotty's. Somehow he was going to have to make Sydney understand that this was far bigger than the two of them.

Scotty looked less than pleased to find him at his door. He didn't invite Griffin in.

"I'm looking for Sydney."

"That right?"

Scotty didn't budge from the threshold.

"I wouldn't be here if it weren't a matter of the utmost importance. *National* importance." Scotty of all people could identify with that. Or so he thought.

But Scotty glanced back into the room, toward a blond woman sitting on the couch. Amanda. Then he turned back to Griffin, lowering his voice, saying, "She's not here. That's all I can tell you."

So much for Scotty recognizing the importance of it all. Not that Griffin could fault his loyalty. "Thanks for your time," he said, and was about to leave, when Amanda looked up, saw him, and smiled.

"You're Sydney's friend," she said. "I remember you from the bar that night."

"I am."

"You just missed her," she said.

"She was here?"

"Well, until we dropped her off at the airport."

Scotty closed his eyes in frustration. "She's so going to kill me," he whispered.

"Get in line," Griffin told him. "Because I'm pretty sure I'm first in her sights. Where's she going?"

"Dulles. Flying home for a few days." He looked at his watch. "But you better hurry. Her plane leaves in less than an hour."

Sydney didn't notice Griffin until he sat down in the seat next to hers in the waiting area near her gate. She glanced up from the magazine she was reading, then turned her attention back to the article.

He saw it was about the making of *Doctor Who*. "I wasn't aware you were a fan," he said, hoping, if nothing else, she would at least discuss that.

"Time travel. You should try it."

"You're not even going to say anything?"

She flipped the page. "Will it make you go away?"

"No."

"Waste of breath, then."

"At least talk to me about this."

She turned another page. "Nothing to say."

"There are reasons I couldn't tell you about my involvement."

"Why? Because it's easier to start a relationship with someone if they don't know you were trying to—"

"My orders were to make sure that information didn't make it out of Orozco's hands."

"Guess you screwed up. And now look where we are."

Like he needed a reminder of the ripple effect.

Sydney looked away, watched the travelers walking through the terminal, some meandering, others in a rush to make their connections. When she turned back to him, her eyes were cold, hard. She fixed her gaze on the magazine. "You should probably leave. I'm engrossed in this article."

"Sydney, we need to talk."

"No. We don't." The flight attendant at the gate announced that they'd be boarding in five minutes. She got up, tossed the magazine onto the chair she'd just vacated, grabbed her overnight bag from the floor, then started walking toward the gate.

He followed. "I need a sketch from the woman we picked up in South San Francisco. One of her friends was murdered because of what was found on the copy machine."

Sydney's footsteps faltered, and then she stopped, turned, and faced him. "Why are you telling me this?" she asked, keeping her voice low. "I'm done with you and your whole crew. I want *nothing* to do with any of you."

"Like it or not, your actions are partly responsible."

"And what? You're blameless?"

"No. But you can help me put this right. One drawing, that's all I ask."

"One? It's always just one. And every time I do a sketch for you, someone's getting shot. Even when I'm not doing one for you, someone's getting shot."

"Which is why we call you and not someone else."

"I don't even know how to take that."

"As a compliment. You can handle yourself."

"Woe be to the artist who ever hooks up with your crew."

"This will be the last one if that's what you want. And then I'll be out of your life for good."

She stared at him for several seconds, as though weighing the decision in her mind. "Fine. That's a deal I can live with. And you can pay for my missed flight, too."

13

North of Ensenada, Mexico

The early morning sun rose over the red tile roof of the villa perched on the hilltop overlooking the Pacific Ocean. Robert Orozco watched his almost three-year-old granddaughter, Rosa, running down the beach, her little feet barely making an impression in the hard, wet sand. She stopped suddenly, bent down, her brown curly hair falling in her face as she examined whatever it was she'd found.

He was about to call her back, worried she might wander too far, when he noticed two men exiting a black sedan parked up on the side of the road. This was a stretch of beach not quite on the beaten path, never mind that neither man was dressed for a casual stroll. Both wore dark suits and were walking in his direction, their strides sure, purposeful. His first thought was that they were government agents, but his instincts told him that even if they were, something was amiss.

His gaze flicked to Rosa, who stood there, wriggling her

toes in the bubbles from the seawater that skimmed across the sand. Farther up the beach he saw a couple walking a dog, the woman's long blond hair making him hope she might be American. He could use a break right now, and he took out his cell phone, texted a message, even though there was no signal. At least there would be a record of it, and he bent down toward his granddaughter, his knee aching from a recently healed gunshot wound.

"*Mija*," he said. She ran over to him. "Let's play a new game."

"*Sí*, Poppy."

He wrapped her chubby fingers around the phone, then changed his mind, and wedged it in the tiny pocket of her jeans, hoping it wouldn't fall out. "Do you see those people, *mija*? The man and the woman?"

She nodded.

"How fast can you run to them?"

"Why?"

"Please, *mija*. But you must be very fast. Faster than the waves."

"Why?"

"Because I have to go to work. Okay?"

She didn't move, instead putting her thumb into her mouth, staring at him with her large black eyes.

"The pretty lady with the yellow hair. She might have candy for you."

Her gaze widened.

"But only if you run very fast."

She took off. He stood, his breath catching from the pain in his knee, the limp he'd almost overcome returning as he hurried across the sand toward the two men. The moment Robert reached them, one man shoved the barrel of a semi-auto into Robert's side, and he prayed that no one else would see it, that Rosa wouldn't change her mind and come running back, running toward him.

"Your nine lives are up, Orozco," the gunman told Robert. "In the car."

The other man nodded toward the coastline. "What about the girl?"

Robert's heart pounded as he waited to hear the answer. *Not Rosa . . .*

The gunman pulled the door open, glanced in that direction, then said, "You want to go get her?"

"No."

"Then who cares. She's too little to know what's going on."

Relief flooded through Robert, and he looked toward the water, caught a glimpse of his beloved granddaughter, saw her stop, distracted once again by something in the sand. He smiled to himself, closed his eyes, burning the image into his mind, then prayed for a miracle that might spare the rest of his family.

The low rumble of tires on the paving stones carried in with the breeze through the open veranda door as a car drove beneath the arch into the villa's courtyard, stirring Maria from her early nap. Five months along, she thought she'd have far more energy, but this pregnancy was so much different than when she'd carried Rosa. A car door slammed, and she raised herself up on one elbow, glanced through the partially open slats of the second story window, catching a glimpse of a black sedan parked in the courtyard next to the fountain.

Curious, she stood, walked to the window as the driver exited, opened the back door, allowing her father to slide out. Her first thought was that Rosa should be with him. And when she realized that her daughter wasn't there, Maria was about to call out, ask what happened.

But then she saw the gun.

Her heart clenched.

She turned on her heel, ran from the room and was stopped by her mother in the hallway.

"Mama. They have Papa. I don't know where Rosa is."

"Hush, *mija*. Don't make a sound. We haven't much time."

"Time? I have to find her."

A woman's scream shattered the quiet, then a gunshot rang out, echoing up the stairwell. The young woman they'd recently hired to help out around the house. Had someone shot her?

Maria's pulse thundered as her mother reached up, put a finger to her lips, warning her to silence. And then she drew her to the back of the house, the master bedroom, closing the door. "Listen, *mija*. Those are the men your father warned us about. They are here to kill us."

"Mama—"

Her mother shoved a business card in her hand, then closed her fingers around it. "They are looking for something we do not have. Hurry. Out the back, the way you used to when you went to meet Jorge. Rosita is safe. I feel it in my heart. Your father must have left her on the beach for that reason. He would not want her harmed. If you hope to ever see her again, you must go." She pushed Maria toward the veranda. "Hurry. And don't look back, *mija*."

"This is all Papa's fault. If he hadn't hid out here—"

"If? I would never have met him. Would never have had you." She reached up, touched her daughter's cheek, and tears stung Maria's eyes at the sight of her mother's pain. "Go."

Maria hesitated, up until she felt the baby move in her belly. "I love you . . ." She hugged her mother, then hurried out to the balcony, quickly climbing over the balustrade, trying not to think of her family as she climbed down the trellis. Everyone she loved was downstairs. Her husband, her father, her uncle. And soon, her mother.

Tears clouded her vision, but she shook them off, knew she had to get away. She glanced down the side of the house, made certain no one was waiting. And then she darted across the back lawn toward the bougainvillea. In the corner, there was just enough space to slip behind the thorny vines, between the stucco wall and the trellis that allowed the vines to grow up and over the wall, a space that hid a gate from the casual observer.

The sharp thorns scraped her arms as she shimmied toward the gate. It was dark behind the vines, smelling of greenery and dampness, and she blindly reached out, felt for the gate's latch. As her fingers found it, she heard a gunshot, then several more. Her heart jumped, then thundered double-time in her chest, and she pressed her hand against her mouth, stifled the sobs. Tears blinded her as she subconsciously counted the shots, and with it the deaths of each person in that house.

She was truly alone, and she couldn't move. Didn't dare move, certain her legs would give out beneath her. She leaned against the gate for what seemed an eternity as she heard things in the house crashing. They were searching her home for whatever this thing was, this thing her mother said they didn't have, and then she heard footsteps echoing across the courtyard, the sound of two car doors slamming shut, followed by the screech of tires as the vehicle sped from the villa, then down the street.

But she didn't return to the house. She knew better. They would come back for her if they knew she was alive, knew she had escaped. She waited, forcing herself to take deep breaths. Finally, after what seemed an eternity, she opened the gate, stepped out, wondering where she'd go next. And then she looked at the business card in her hand, damp with sweat from clutching it so tight.

She needed to go to the beach, find her daughter, Rosa. Her Rosita. Tears blurred her vision, and she brushed them away, then focused on the card her mother had given her, reading the name.

Sydney Fitzpatrick, FBI.

This was the woman who had come down to visit her father several months ago, she realized. The U.S. government had followed this FBI agent straight to Maria's father, and they had shot at him as he had helped this woman flee.

The name burned into her memory.

Why on earth would her mother tell her to find this person? The woman who had brought death to her family?

But then she turned the card over and realized there was something else written on it. And suddenly she understood.

14

Sydney hefted her overnight bag on her shoulder as she and Griffin walked through the terminal. "Since I didn't bring a car," she told him, "you can pay for my taxi. When am I doing this sketch?"

"The sooner we have it, the safer she'll be. So I hope you don't mind if we forgo the taxi and I take you straight there?"

As much as she didn't want to ride back with him, she agreed. The faster she did the sketch, the faster she could wash her hands of him. They walked out of the terminal and to the parking lot in silence.

"Where is she?" Sydney asked, once they were in the car and on the freeway.

"With Lisette. She'll remain there until she goes into witness protection."

"All because of those numbers?"

"And who she saw."

"Who is this person?"

"We believe one of the key figures of the Network. Someone we've only heard about, but have never been able to trace."

"How long have you been looking?"

"Over twenty years."

"So before you even started. Is he part of this W2 investigation?"

"I have no idea. We have every reason to believe W2 and the Network are connected. And if he's as important as some of our sources have led us to believe, he may be at the heart of it."

Sydney glanced over at Griffin, who was watching the road. Suddenly she was very interested in who this person was, what he looked like. Especially if he was connected to the W2 case. And if it took doing a drawing for Griffin to get more answers, she was willing to suffer his presence.

"Do me a favor," Griffin said, when they arrived at Lisette's apartment. "Don't mention the witness protection angle. We haven't told the girl yet, and I'd rather not leave Lisette with the fallout."

"I won't say a word."

"And watch your belongings. She has a habit of taking things that don't belong to her."

"Seriously?"

"I seem to be a few dollars short after having spent a couple of nights with her. She ripped off Tex as well."

"I'll keep it in mind."

Lisette's Washington, D.C., apartment was typical government fare for government agents who didn't spend a lot of time in the area. A prefurnished abode with no personality whatsoever. In fact Sydney had lived in one very similar when she'd first moved here. She'd hated it. The apartment didn't seem to bother Lisette, who welcomed Sydney, kissed her on both cheeks, then drew her into the room to introduce her to Piper, who was watching TV.

The girl was not what Sydney had expected. Although her clothing seemed normal, blue pants and a pale pink shirt, her hairstyle had more of a punk rock look, short black hair with pink spiked tips. She also noted the slight mark on her eyebrow and lip, which had apparently once sported piercings. It seemed to Sydney a façade that did little to hide the vulnerable young girl beneath. "Hi. I'm Sydney. I'll be doing the sketch with you."

"Hi." Piper rose, then stood there awkwardly for a few seconds.

Not sure what to say to the girl, Sydney walked to the dinette area. "Okay if I set up here on the kitchen table?"

"Probably the best place," Lisette said, then glanced at Griffin. "Since you're here, it'll give me a chance to run a few errands. Marc's taking a nap."

"Have at it."

"Make yourself at home," Lisette told Sydney. "Fresh coffee's in the pot and there are a few odds and ends in the refrigerator."

After she left, Griffin pulled up a chair. "You don't mind if I sit in, do you?"

"Feel free," she replied, even though she did mind. It wasn't her case, so it wasn't like she had a say. Besides, if she wanted to find out who it was that was allegedly behind the whole W2 affair, probably best to mind her manners. He did not sit at the table, however, but pulled up his chair behind Piper so that she couldn't see him while they worked. As Sydney had mentioned to Griffin in past sketches she'd done for him, there was less chance of outside influence when it came to recalling faces if the witness was not looking at one directly. To the same end, Sydney had Piper face her chair toward the wall, then explained the process, how long it would take, usually several hours, adding, "I will, however, have you go over things that happened well before the crime, as it'll help bring out the more salient details you might miss otherwise."

"Cognitive interview techniques," Piper said.

Sydney, in the middle of arranging her pencils, eraser,

and sketchbook on the table, looked up. "Yes. How did you know?"

"I remember things exceptionally well. It's from a book I read on investigation techniques in college."

"Not quite what I'd expect from someone of your age."

"I like to read. So, where would you like me to begin?"

She was, Sydney realized, remarkably calm, although Sydney sensed a fragileness about her, as though it were all a façade that would crack at any moment. For that reason alone, she didn't want to say the word *murder*, and so simply replied, "An hour before . . ." and let her fill in the blank.

"I was getting dressed, getting ready to visit my friend Bo. I sort of had a crush on him, so I put on my best black jeans." Her face relaxed, as though the memory was pleasant, and, in comparison, it probably was. And without Sydney even directing her, she supplied the necessary details that Sydney would normally ask about. "It was around eight in the evening, and the weather was cold outside, in the upper forties. I remember thinking I should have brought a coat, but once I got on the bus, I wasn't cold anymore." She detailed the remainder of her activities, how she stole a pack of cigarettes, and then believed the man had called the police on her, adding that "I thought I saw him—the guy from the bus—talking to two men as I walked down the street toward Bo's. It wasn't him, though. I—I walked past them, not thinking that, well, anything was off. I mean, something was, but not anything like this. And then I went inside the shop where Bo works. He lives over it. That's where I was when he was shot. I didn't see that."

"At what point did you see this man's face? Brooks?"

"Right after the driver called him back to the car. He looked over at me just before I crossed the street."

"That's the moment I want you to remember."

She nodded.

And so it began, much like every other drawing Sydney

had done; she asked the basics, height, weight, general description, then on to the shape of the man's face, his eyes, nose, mouth, and she took notes, jotting them down in the upper right corner, so that she could refer back as she worked. He was, according to Piper, about six feet tall, mid to late fifties, gray hair. The next step Sydney took was to draw an outline of the man's face on the paper. She turned it toward Piper, who examined it, then looked quickly up and to the side, then back, saying, "His jawline is narrower, the face itself shorter. He was handsome. For a guy with gray hair."

Sydney hid her surprise at the speed with which the drawing progressed. The process was usually much slower, quite often more generic, as her witnesses, even the most articulate of them, had difficulty describing what they saw. Sydney had her own theory on someone who was too helpful, too exact, but she tucked that thought away, as Piper proceeded to describe his eyes, nose, and mouth with equal precision. Sydney dutifully sketched, turned the sketchbook for Piper to see after finishing each step, then taking the directions on what needed to be changed. And she wondered what Griffin might be thinking at this point. Even he must surely realize that something wasn't quite right. This was too easy, she decided, once again turning the sketchbook toward Piper, who shook her head. "The nose is wrong."

At last, some changes, a mistake, she thought, then asked, "What would you do to change this?"

Piper clasped her hands in her lap, indicating her reluctance to comment.

"You won't hurt my feelings," Sydney told her. "I assure you. The drawing is only as good as the witness."

"The nose should be longer, the bridge of it narrower." She pointed to the paper. "Here," she said, indicating with her fingertip where she thought the nose should end.

And Sydney drew. They finished in less than an hour, a

record in her experience, since the average drawing took three.

She held up the completed sketch, asking, "Is there any final change you'd make to this that might help?"

"No."

"On a scale of one to ten . . ."

"Eight-ish? It's probably as close as I can describe, without actually drawing it myself—one thing I am not good at." Piper paused, as though trying to decide what she should say next.

"I think we're done, then. Thanks for your time."

The young woman looked at Griffin. "Is there anything else you need me for? I was thinking about taking a nap."

"If there is, I'll let you know. Thanks, Piper."

She gave one last look at the sketch, then left.

When Sydney heard the door close, she turned to Griffin. "Something's not right."

He picked up the sketchpad, examining the drawing. "How so?"

"In my entire career, the few sketches I've done that were finished that fast, they turned out to be lies. The witnesses had made up the details in their heads."

"I don't believe that to be the case here."

"Why not?"

"She has special talents."

"Her exceptional memory that she mentioned?"

"Not exceptional. Eidetic." He handed the sketchbook back to her.

"Eidetic? As in she recalls everything she reads?"

"Everything."

"And what is it she's read that has you so worried?"

"The numbers you copied."

"Does that mean they're not numbers to offshore bank accounts?"

"They are not."

"Then what are they for?"

"I can't tell you. It's classified."

"Why am I not surprised?"

"I can tell you this. If anyone knows she has this skill and what she saw? She's in a lot more danger than just being a witness to a murder."

15

The White House
Washington, D.C.

In hindsight, McNiel wished he'd never informed them of Piper's existence, or turned in his report on her. But then who could have foretold that she might very well be instrumental in bringing down one of the most sought-after espionage agents in recent history? Or that she'd be the link to a code they'd worked so hard to keep out of anyone's hands ever since they'd learned of its existence? All he could do now was damage control. And pray their only concern was for how this latest incident affected national security—not that ATLAS was indirectly the cause of her being placed in this position to begin with. He glanced over at the president, trying to read his expression, but the man's face was a blank slate.

McNiel finished detailing what the girl had seen on the computer, but nothing about *who* she had seen, or that they were doing a sketch of the suspect. He had his reasons for that, and his search for Brooks wasn't necessary for the purposes of *this* meeting. What was important was the girl's eidetic memory, and he explained why he'd left it off the written report. "In light of what she may have seen on that computer," he explained, "I firmly believe that what we know about her and what she is now carrying in her head needs to stay in this room."

"Worst case scenario," Roy Santiago, the assistant deputy director of national intelligence, said, when McNiel finished. "If this girl falls into enemy hands?"

"She won't," McNiel said. "We're placing her in witness protection. The arrangements have already been made. They'll be picking her up this afternoon."

President Evanston looked directly at McNiel. "But if she does?"

"Worst case?" General Woodson said, before McNiel could answer. "She could start World War Three."

"An exaggeration, don't you think?" McNiel said.

"Hardly," Woodson replied. "Let's say you're one of our allies, and you find out that we've been looking at every national secret that's ever passed through your country's databanks these last couple decades—"

"Seriously?" Santiago said. "Everyone's spying on everyone else. I don't see our allies suddenly turning this into an issue worthy of declaring war."

"Nor do I," McNiel said, somewhat surprised to see Santiago siding with him.

General Woodson, however, was a different matter. He dumped a packet of sweetener into his coffee cup. "I'm talking about our *declared* enemies, and the countries that are *un*declared, the wobbler countries who are just waiting for a reason to turn on us. What about when *they* find out we've been spying on them for X number of years? Watching their every digital move? And what about when the news gets out and the good voting citizens start figuring out how many times we've had to look the other way on certain attacks, all to keep these other countries from knowing what we know without letting on that we've been monitoring the lot of them for years?"

"What attacks did we know about?" Santiago asked.

"That's not important," Woodson continued. "What is, is that for the last two decades we've managed to convince the world that us having a backdoor entry into the world's computer banks is one big conspiracy theory. A *theory* right up there with Washington, D.C., being built on a giant pentagram, directly atop a Masonic treasure. And now this girl could blow it wide open."

"How?" McNiel asked. "She doesn't even know what she's seen."

"Doesn't matter. We might be the only ones who know what's in her head, but others are probably thinking she could have a *copy* of this thing tucked away. They may be after her right now."

Truer words were never spoken. Not that McNiel was about to admit to it. "*Nobody* besides us knows about her."

"Nobody? *Somebody* was running a half-functional version of that program, or they wouldn't have discovered her friend to begin with. They don't call that thing the Devil's Key for nothing. You want to chance that they'll pick her up and put it together?"

McNiel didn't like the direction this conversation was taking. "Of course not."

"Then you have one choice," General Woodson said. "Make sure she never reveals what she knows. Standing kill order."

"Kill her? She's barely an adult."

"And what?" Woodson said. "You've suddenly grown a conscience?"

"Unlike you, I never lost mine."

"No. Which is why I'm able to make the tough decisions that don't allow our country to be placed in danger. Or are you forgetting what put us in this position to begin with?"

"Enough!" President Evanston said. "We're not going to run around assassinating girls who are barely old enough to vote."

"She's the equivalent of a suicide bomber," Woodson said. "One life versus how many? We can keep her contained, and we're fully prepared to take action, should the unthinkable occur."

The president looked right at McNiel. "He's right. I think the military *is* better equipped to handle this sort of thing. Turn her over to them."

"Sir—"

"That's an order." He turned to Woodson. "I'm counting on you to keep her safely contained."

"We won't let you down. But should the unthinkable happen?"

"I do not want her in the hands of our enemies. Not with what she's carrying in her head. If that should happen—and I expect you to make sure it does not—you have the kill order."

"Sir," McNiel said. "She's a girl. A victim of a crime, in fact. Witness protection is far better suited than a military prison."

"Witness protection? We're talking about a threat to national security. You, of all people should realize that such a program is fine for the usual criminal. It is *not* suitable in this instance."

McNiel gathered up his papers. "We've used it successfully in the past," he argued. "Why should this case be any different?"

The president was quiet a moment, then looked at Woodson. "Your opinion?"

"I know I argued otherwise . . ." Woodson eyed McNiel.

"As much as this goes against my better judgment, she is, as Director McNiel said, practically a kid. God knows she'd be better off in a more normal environment."

President Evanston leaned back in his seat as he contemplated the matter. "McNiel. If *anything* happens to her, it's not only your head that will roll. It may very well be the end of ATLAS. There's already a report being circulated about what agencies we can eliminate over the budget crisis, and ATLAS was one of them."

Which moved the rumors that they were trying to shut down ATLAS to near-confirmation. Still, he couldn't just hand the girl over, not when her life was at stake. "Understood."

At the conclusion of the meeting, McNiel left without stopping to talk to anyone, and had just exited the building when he heard someone calling him. "McNiel!"

He turned to see Parker Kane hurrying down the hallway. Kane worked for the CIA, but he had not been in the meeting. His classification wasn't high enough, though McNiel had heard that was likely to change. Kane headed up a unit at the CIA that was similar to ATLAS, though not as far-reaching. It was the sort of experience the president was looking for, and he was considering Kane for appointment as the next deputy national security adviser. Probably a good choice, even though McNiel didn't necessarily like the man.

"You have a minute?" Kane asked.

"Sure," he said, wondering what on earth Kane wanted.

"I read the report from South San Francisco."

"I wasn't aware you had a copy."

"I'm sure it was forwarded to me because of, well . . ."

"Right. Congratulations, by the way." So the rumor of the appointment was true. It just wasn't formally announced yet.

Kane looked at his watch. "I have to run. Before I go, I just wanted to say that if you need any help, I'll make my office available to you."

"I appreciate it."

McNiel hailed a cab, glad for the unexpected support, from at least one person, but unable to ignore the feeling that he had not walked out of that meeting with the upper hand.

For Piper's sake, and his team's sake, he hoped he was wrong.

16

Griffin had spent the night at Lisette's, because Marc and Donovan were out on a surveillance that took most of the night. He drew the second watch, slept in late, and when he awoke, showered, and went in search of coffee, Lisette was sitting at the kitchen table, looking at Sydney's sketch. The TV was on, but the sound off. Piper was still asleep.

He poured himself a fresh cup. "Marc's not back yet?"

"Should be here any time." She held up her mug. "And yes, I'd love a refill."

He took her mug, topped it off, then brought it back to her.

"No eggs with my coffee?"

"How do you take them?"

"I was kidding. I'm not expecting you to cook me something."

"Well, I'm fixing myself some anyway."

"Scrambled, then." She slid the rubber band off that morning's newspaper, shook it open, then made a scoffing noise as she perused the front page. "I'll bet this ruins McNiel's weekend."

"What does?"

"The president's announcement to appoint Parker Kane as the deputy national security adviser."

"He's a firm believer in not only knowing your enemy, but also knowing what part of the government they're working in at any given time."

"Who would have guessed that Manuel Torrance would have to step down after being caught in an extramarital affair while on the job?"

Griffin walked over, looked at the paper. "Talk about conspiracy theory. I heard that Parker Kane introduced the two of them. Torrance and his flame."

"You think he did it on purpose? Set Torrance up?"

"This is Washington. Would you put it past him? What I can't understand is why someone in Torrance's position would ever compromise himself to begin with, so that the Parker Kanes of the world can swoop in and take advantage of it."

"They can't help themselves," she said, handing him the newspaper. "Position of power, and suddenly women are throwing themselves at their feet? They're not used to being . . . what's the term you American men are so fond of? Chick magnets. It goes to the wrong head."

Piper's bedroom door opened, and Griffin bit back the sarcastic retort, saying instead, "Too bad. He wasn't a bad adviser. Let's hope that Kane makes his peace with McNiel once he is appointed."

Griffin tossed the paper onto the kitchen table, as Piper walked in. "Making some scrambled eggs. You want some?"

She shook her head. "Lisette said there was cornflakes. I'd rather have that if it's okay?"

"Cornflakes it is." He handed the box to her, as well as a bowl, spoon, and then the milk from the refrigerator. "Coffee?" he asked.

"Yeah." She took everything over to the table, sitting next to Lisette where she could see the TV. Suddenly she stood, knocking over the cereal box in her haste. "That's him!"

"Him who?" Griffin asked, momentarily confused. Her gaze was riveted on the television screen.

"That Brooks guy you're looking for."

Griffin eyed the television, saw a short film clip of Parker Kane standing with a bevy of other political hotshots in the background while the newscaster announced that he was most likely next in line to take Torrance's spot as deputy national security adviser.

When Griffin glanced at Lisette, she sat there, looking as stunned as he felt.

The girl had to be mistaken, and he watched her closely, looking for some sign that she was lying, making this up. "Why do you say that?"

"Because I know who I saw. And I saw him." She got up, walked toward the television. "Who is he? Why is he on TV?"

There was a knock at the door, and Lisette said, "That's got to be Marc. I'll get it."

Griffin glanced toward the door, then back at Piper. "It is very, very important that you don't discuss with *anyone* what you saw at your friend's shop or on the TV just now, do you understand?"

She didn't answer.

He walked up to her and leaned over. "We are going to investigate this thing, but what you *think* you saw complicates things."

"How? Why can't you just arrest him?"

"If this is the man you saw, we're all in danger. We can't protect you if you don't do exactly as we say, and right now I need you *not* to say anything to anyone. Until I say so. Do you understand?"

"Yes."

Lisette gave Marc a kiss when he walked in.

"Sorry about the delay," he told her. Then to Griffin, "Thanks for covering."

"Actually it worked out for the best. Lisette? Hope you don't mind if I skip making the eggs?"

"I'll get over it."

"Why the rush?" Marc asked.

Griffin grabbed his things on his way to the door. "Because we are now in way deeper than we ever thought."

"How so?"

Griffin showed him the photo on the front page.

"What about him?"

"Brooks."

"*The* Brooks?"

"That's who Piper thinks he is. Saw him on TV."

"She has to be wrong."

"We'll obviously have to verify that. Sydney did a drawing. Before any of us saw the news." He pulled the sketchbook from his bag and showed it to Marc. Sure, there was a resemblance. But who would ever suspect a man like Parker Kane?

Marc whistled softly. "That is what you call a game changer, no?"

"Definitely. I'm on my way to inform McNiel."

"Better you than me."

Griffin called McNiel the moment he drove out of the parking garage. "I need to see you at the office."

"Is there some reason whatever this is can't be dealt with over the phone? I'm just leaving the White House and I have a couple of stops I need to make first."

"You're going to want to see this."

"Give me half an hour."

ATLAS Headquarters

McNiel was waiting in his office when Griffin arrived. "The least you could do is bring me coffee," he told Griffin. "Tex does."

"Do I look like Tex?"

"Not even close. It's been a bad morning. So what do you have?"

"Sydney's sketch." Griffin pulled out the book, flipped the cover up, then turned the pad so McNiel could see it.

"This is who the girl saw?"

"Yes."

"Brooks?"

"Allegedly."

"And do we have someone in mind as a suspect, because I'm not seeing anything pop out."

"Parker Kane."

McNiel stared in disbelief. When the momentary shock apparently wore off, he said, "Okay, it *resembles* him, but it also resembles any number of gray-haired men in their early fifties."

"The girl has no idea who he is. She saw *him* on TV. She might be a liar and a thief, but I don't think she could fake a reaction like that."

"She's young, impressionable, and you know as well as I that you throw faces at someone, memory is fragile."

"Top right corner. Read Sydney's notes. She described him to a T."

McNiel took the pad from him, read the notes, then set it down on his desk. "*If* this is Kane, and trust me, I'd like nothing better than to bring him down, I don't think we have a snowball's chance in hell of proving our case before he's appointed." He stared at the drawing for several more seconds. "Thank God we didn't have this conversation before my meeting this morning. I ran into Kane when I was leaving the building."

"He knows about her?"

"Someone forwarded the report. He knows about her, but *not* about her eidetic memory."

"What if someone tells him?"

McNiel paused as though considering the matter. "I don't think they will. And definitely not before his appointment is made."

"So what should we do about the sketch?"

"We can't let anyone see this. Most of all Kane. If it is him, if he *was* there, last thing we need is to spook him, because *he's* going to see himself even if no one else does. As for the rest of the intelligence world, this does us no good. We need a solid case with irrefutable evidence. He has a lot of powerful friends in the government who wouldn't think twice about shutting us down if they thought we were stepping out of line. We're already close enough to the brink as it is."

"You think they'd go that far?"

"Much farther," McNiel said. "For over twenty years I've been searching for this man, and he's been right in front of us. No wonder he's slipped through our fingers every time we've gotten close. He's been here. Watching us. Safe and secure that we were clueless, while he monitored our every step." He took a breath, his gaze fixed on the sketch. "Our only saving grace these last several years was that the right hand doesn't talk to the left, so we've actually managed to keep a few secrets."

"And we now are holding on to the one person who can ID Kane in the vicinity of a crime connected to him."

"Her life's not worth a damn if he thinks she'll be able to place him at the scene." McNiel picked up the sketch. "If it is him, we've been searching for Brooks because *that's* the name we've heard. His middle name is Bruxton. "

"B-R-U-X?" Griffin doubted he would have ever made the

connection if not for the sketch. "I'm guessing we don't want that spelling of Brooks mentioned outside this room."

"Definitely not. We have a very small and fragile window to investigate this." He tossed the sketchbook onto his desk. "General Woodson's right. This girl you picked up is a walking time bomb. Just not in the way we expected."

"One advantage. Kane doesn't know that we have the sketch. *Or* that she identified him."

"If he has any idea that we have this . . . she's dead."

"And what happens if he discovers she has a head full of numbers that he probably wants? Especially if he finds out what she's capable of?"

"Good point," McNiel said. "Either way, *we're* dead."

Donovan walked in at that moment, Griffin having called him in right after he phoned McNiel. "Pretty serious in here. Something happen while I was gone?"

McNiel showed him the sketch. "It's Kane."

"*Parker* Kane? Holy . . ." He sat, stared at the drawing, shaking his head. "I'm having a hard time wrapping my brain around this." They all were, and the three of them studied the sketch for several seconds, until Donovan broke the silence. "Okay . . . so, what's the plan of action?"

McNiel let out a slow breath, as though trying for some sense of calm. "This couldn't be any worse. Here I was worried about Thorndike, when I took the lot of you from the CIA. Kane was just a pompous ass. I always thought it was a grudge thing. Sour grapes on Kane's part, because I was given ATLAS and he wasn't. Apparently I was wrong."

Griffin thought about the implications of such an appointment. ATLAS, being an entirely covert group, had a certain autonomy not afforded to other government agencies. "Imagine if Kane *had* been appointed instead."

Donovan gave a cynical laugh. "And here we thought keeping the right hand from knowing what the left is doing was a bad way of running the government."

"Exactly what I said," McNiel replied. "Now that I've had time to think about it, what about those times when we *have* shared? How many operations has he managed to sabotage? We have no idea what he's been privy to."

"So we assume he's been privy to a lot," Griffin said.

McNiel eyed the drawing. "He's had twenty years to gain the upper hand. Twenty years of watching our every move in the investigation of W2. What better way to stop us than shut us down?"

"You think he'll try that?" Donovan asked.

"It's not only a matter of when, but how. Budget cuts? Merger? Sudden plane crash with all of us aboard? Piper saw him, and he knows we have her. He's been threatened in a big way. His advantage is that he knows we won't say a thing until we have proof, and the word of a twenty-year-old girl with a police record is not going to cut it. I can tell you this. Once he's appointed, our days are numbered."

"Then we get to him before he gets to us."

"I wish it were that easy. God help us if anyone who is working with him learns we are looking into this," McNiel said. "Therein lies our biggest problem. We don't know who we can even bring in."

"We can trust Pearson."

"If this goes south, Pearson's greatest advantage will be staying well away from us."

"Hell," Donovan said. "We have to go public. This drawing goes out to everyone. We state who we think it is—not that it's Parker Kane—that it's Brooks."

"No," McNiel said. "I've already thought of and dismissed that idea."

"Why? At least if something happens to us, it's on record."

"He's had the president's ear over the last three years, never mind where he's worked. You're talking decades of having a spy in the midst. What administration is going to want that to come out?"

Donovan gave a sarcastic laugh. "Which administration *hasn't* had a spy in their midst? What about Miles Cavanaugh? He was actually advising the president in security matters."

"Not for very long. *And* he's conveniently dead, which makes it easy for the president's office to close the book with none the wiser. This . . ." McNiel shook his head.

"How's this different from any other intelligence agency?" Donovan said. "There's the FBI. They've had a few. Robert Hanssen. You can't ask for a bigger intelligence disaster than that."

"Hanssen wasn't bending the president's ear. Kane is. Couple that with the Devil's Key and the nightmare if that gets out, that we've had the capability to spy on every country who's running that software. Even worse, that it's not the SINS program at all, but the chips, which makes us *all* vulnerable—"

"Maybe," Griffin said, "we can buy some time."

"How?"

"We have Sydney do a second sketch. A fake one that looks like anyone but the real suspect. If nothing else, Kane won't know we're looking his direction."

"She's already on their radar," McNiel replied. "I don't think we want to draw any more attention to her. Like I said, if that is Kane in the sketch, and everything points to it being him, he knows we have Piper. He knows she saw him, and that there's every chance she's already told us. And he knows that's all we've got, which isn't enough. You can't convict a man of twenty years of espionage based on the testimony of one girl unless you have twenty years of proof. And if he manages to get a copy of the Devil's Key, he'll have the means to eradicate twenty years of evidence no matter how condemning, and re-create enough evidence to exonerate himself."

"It's that powerful?" Donovan asked.

"So I've been told. Why do you think we've worked so hard to destroy every known copy?"

"We're batting zero, boss," Donovan said. "There's got to be something we can do."

"Right now our best bet is to get this girl into witness protection. Get her out of here, somewhere safe, so we can regroup. As a matter of fact, call them and verify that they're on their way. The sooner we get her where we won't have to worry, and free up Marc and Lisette, the sooner we can go after the real threat."

17

"*Witness protection?*" Piper suddenly lost her appe-
tite for the pizza on her plate and stared in disbelief at Lisette.

They were seated at the kitchen table in Lisette's apartment. All Piper had mentioned was that she wanted a job
similar to Lisette's, so she could see Europe, maybe eat real
pizza made in Italy, not the frozen stuff, and Lisette just
sprang it on her.

"Like on TV?" Piper asked. "Where they change your
name and make you live in some small town without any of
your friends?"

"The key word being *live*."

"Why can't you just find the people who did this and take
care of it? Isn't that what you guys do?" she said, looking
from Lisette to Marc. "You're secret agents. You're supposed to be able to stop people like them."

"It's not as simple as that."

"It seems pretty simple to me. If your friend had called
the police when I told him to, they'd probably have those
guys by now."

"They might," Lisette said, getting up to take her empty plate to the sink. "But the people who are after you will simply send two more. And then two more after that."

"I don't believe that. I didn't even see their faces. I saw that other guy. And he left before the murder. Why would they want me?"

"For what's in your head," Marc said. "They have one goal in mind, and that is to get you to tell them, number for number, what you saw. They've even been known to torture—"

Lisette took a frustrated breath. "Marc . . ."

"She needs to know what the dangers are."

"Don't you have a report to type?" she replied, then gave him a pointed look.

"This is not something to sugarcoat."

"I am sure McNiel asked for that report to be finished."

Piper pushed her plate to the center of the table. "How? How are they going to find out about me if there's no one there to tell them?"

"Your prints," Lisette said, "are all over your friend's warehouse. The moment they learn your name—and they will if they access the police department's records—you will be on their radar. Even if they don't yet know about you, it's only a matter of time before they do, and from there all too easy to discover your ability to retain entire documents in your head. Unless you can guarantee that no one knows. That no one has ever mentioned this anywhere electronically . . ." Lisette looked over at her, her brows raised. "Facebook? Twitter?"

"This is stupid."

"It is what it is. Are you done? I'll rinse your plate."

Piper handed it to her, then stalked over to the couch, throwing herself onto the cushions and crossing her arms. "How long will I have to stay in hiding for?"

"We don't know. But you won't be alone. I promise."

Alone . . . Piper reached over, picked up the remote control and turned on the TV, done talking about this. Her whole life had gone wrong ever since her parents' divorce, her mother's spiral into drugs, her father's heart attack that sent her and her brother into foster care. And then there was that stupid accident, when her foster father took her to see a baseball game at spring training where the line drive hit her in the head and caused this stupid eidetic memory thing to happen. Everything had sucked, all because of some stupid baseball game.

And now this. She stared at the TV through a blur of tears, trying her hardest not to cry.

Marc took one look at her face and said, "I should go work on that report now . . ." He grabbed his laptop from the table and carried it to the bedroom.

Lisette eyed Piper. "You okay?"

Piper scoffed. "Perfect," she said, then switched the channels on the TV, finally settling on *SpongeBob SquarePants*.

Lisette stood there a moment longer as if deciding whether Piper was about to do anything stupid, like run outside when she knew there were potential killers after her—*right*. Finally she walked toward the bathroom, saying, "Shout if you need anything."

A few minutes later, Piper heard the water turning on in the bathroom. The moment the steady sound changed pitch, indicating Lisette was actually in the shower, Piper glanced at the front door, wishing she had the guts to leave. The memory of Bo's black and white Converse shoes just visible as she walked past his office that night was enough to convince her that taking off was the wrong move, even if she did know the alarm code. Whoever these people were, they wouldn't hesitate to kill anyone who got in their way, and she wondered what they would do to her once she rattled off those stupid numbers everyone was so hot to get.

What was so damned important about them that someone was running around and killing people?

Had to be money, she decided, getting up and walking to the window, peering out the blinds to the street below. Millions, probably. Otherwise why would anyone care? She looked around Lisette's apartment, wondering what it would be like to live somewhere this nice, and if wherever they were going to take her would be anything similar. Well, hopefully not too similar. Judging from the lack of anything personal in the place, at least in the way of photos and the like, she had the feeling that Lisette wasn't here much.

Her stomach rumbled, and deciding she'd have that pizza after all, she walked over to the kitchen, then noticed Lisette's purse and cell phone. She glanced back, saw Marc's door closed, and heard the shower running.

She liked Lisette. And one thing she didn't do was steal from someone she liked. She was curious, however, and only meant to look inside the purse. There was no gun, not that Piper expected one. Lisette wore her weapon on a holster, and as long as Piper had been there, she never left it unattended.

The wallet was nice, soft burgundy leather, not like anything she'd ever seen in a store, and she opened it, surprised when she saw a passport. She recalled Lisette saying she was French. Piper had never been out of the country herself, and flipped through the pages, noting the different stamps. Just about every country she could think of was on there. And some she wouldn't have thought of. A lot of visits to Italy, she noted, and the thought made her smile. She had seen the looks Marc gave Lisette when he thought Piper wasn't looking. Different from the looks that Zachary Griffin had given the sketch artist.

There was a sadness about that man, she thought. One that hadn't been there before they left California. Something had changed in him. Something between him and that sketch artist, she thought, and wondered what had happened to cause it.

She turned to the last page of the passport book, running her fingers around the edge, wondering if she'd ever be able to travel like that. See places she'd only read about in books . . .

It wasn't fair that because of an accident that had happened through no fault of her own—that she'd seen documents that meant nothing to her—she'd never have the chance to go anywhere. She'd be stuck in some stupid little town, where everyone dressed in stupid pastel colors, living in some stupid state she probably wouldn't even want to visit anyway.

Life sucked, she thought, as she slid the passport back into the wallet, then, because habits were hard to break, examined the credit cards as well as the bit of cash. Life had always sucked starting long before she'd been hit in the head with that damned baseball. That accident had only made it worse. Bo had been her first friend who didn't look at her like a freak, and yet, when it came right down to it, *he* told those gunmen where to find her. And now these government agents wanted to hide her out for the rest of her life?

A knock at the door startled her, and she shoved the items into her sweatshirt pocket, then swiveled around, fully expecting Lisette to emerge from the bathroom and Marc the bedroom. When they didn't, she realized they probably hadn't heard the knock. In a moment of indecision turned to action, Piper walked up to the door, peered out the peephole.

She saw two men in dark suits standing there.

"Who are you?" she called through the door.

"We're here for the pickup." One of them held up a badge.

She took a deep breath. This was it. She didn't even have a chance to say good-bye to her brother, and she was going to be whisked away, given a new name, a new identity . . .

It wasn't like she'd had the best life in the world. They were going to pay for her to get a house and a job. How bad could that be?

"Piper! Get back!"

She swiveled around, saw Marc standing there.

"I think it's the witness protection guys."

"I'll check. Just get back from the door."

"I wasn't going to open it." But she moved away, and Marc looked out, just as Lisette rushed from the bathroom, her gun drawn as Marc disarmed the alarm and opened the door.

Apparently they weren't taking any chances.

"It's okay, ma'am," one of the men said, eyeing the gun pointed at him, and he held up both hands, one empty, one with the badge. "Palmer and Ramsay. We're here to take the girl to WitSec."

"ID," Lisette demanded, not lowering her gun.

He handed it to Marc, who looked it over, then took his phone and called the U.S. marshal's office. "Di Luca, DOJ," Marc said. "Just confirming you sent two . . . ?"

He glanced at the second man. "Your ID?" He looked at it as well. "They're here." He listened, then said to Lisette, "It's them. Names match."

Lisette holstered her gun, while giving Piper a bittersweet smile. "You'll be fine."

What they always told her before every new foster home. And here she thought the feeling of being torn from her roots would be over and done with once she'd aged out of the system. "Sure."

Lisette looked around as though forgetting something. "We didn't even get a chance to buy her any additional clothing."

"It's okay," one of the men said. "We'll take care of all that."

She went for her purse. "You need money?"

"No," Piper said, worried Lisette would discover the wallet missing, and think Piper was trying to steal from her. If she was lucky, she could slip it somewhere where Lisette might find it. She hadn't expected such generosity. "You've done enough."

"We should go," the dark-haired guy said.

Lisette nodded, and then with an awkward smile, walked up to Piper and gave her a hug. "Be good."

"I will."

One of the men held out his hand, indicating Piper should precede him through the door. They walked down the hall-way. And as she stepped on the elevator, followed by the two men, the door whooshing shut, she wondered what on earth she could do with Lisette's wallet. Maybe she should ask the men if they could go back up, pretend that she had to use the bathroom, and she could leave it there. But one look at the man's face, and she nixed that idea. He didn't look friendly at all.

18

Funny, but Lisette didn't really think she'd miss the
girl, and yet the whole scenario reminded her of sending
one's kid off to college for the first time. That feeling that
they were going to a safe place, but they were still out of
your control. Wild parties in the dormitories, getting drunk,
getting pregnant . . .

At least that's what she assumed it was like, since she
didn't have kids of her own. And she wasn't sure she ever
wanted them. Not in this world, she thought, eyeing the dirty
dishes on the counter. She picked up the tray with the half-
eaten pizza and dumped the remainder into the trash, then
started rinsing the dishes.

Marc watched her a few moments. "She'll be fine."

"I know. I guess I just didn't realize— It's silly, I know,
but I miss her."

She looked around the apartment, thinking how quiet it
was, then noticed her purse was not how she left it. And
then she recalled how quickly Piper turned down the offer
of money. "Oh no . . ."

"What?"

She rushed over, looked in her purse, discovered her wallet missing. "I can't believe I fell for that." She picked up the leather bag, slammed it on the counter. "All my money."

"How much?"

"I don't know. Sixty, seventy dollars. And my credit cards. *And* my passport."

"Better call up and cancel the credit card at least."

"The hell with that. Bring her little butt back here and have her give it to me with an apology. And to think I was feeling sorry for her."

"Seriously?"

"Yes. Did you see how quick she was to turn down my offer to give her some money? Little thief. Call."

"What are you going to do? Have her arrested?" he said, taking out his phone. He called the marshal's office again, and said, "Marc di Luca. Two of your men just picked up one of our witnesses. Yes. I talked to them earlier. I know this is a bit unusual, but the witness took something from one of our agents and we'd like to get it back. Any way you could contact them and have them return . . . ? Probably left here about five minutes ago . . . Yes. I'll hold."

He waited and Lisette took the moment to look around, see if anything else was missing. Fortunately there was very little to take, a few clothes and personal items, since she used the apartment only on the rare occasion when she was staying in town.

"You're sure?"

"Sure about what?" Lisette asked, alarmed by his tone, never mind the look on his face.

"She says they're still en route. Palmer and Ramsay. They had to stop for gas and ended up with a flat tire."

"What do you mean still en route? They just left."

"As in they never arrived."

"But you called."

"They verified the names. They didn't realize they weren't here until they called them just now about your wallet."

"Oh my God . . ." Lisette felt as if someone had punched her in the stomach. That girl had depended on them. On her. "They showed us IDs. The names were the same."

Marc held up his finger, signaling for her to be quiet, while he listened to whatever the person was saying. "Thank you. Yes." He disconnected. "Apparently they're on their way now. They'll help in the search."

"What do we do?"

"I'll call McNiel. You call Griffin."

She grabbed her cell phone, hit Griffin's number, and the moment he answered, she said, "I lost her. I'm sorry. I—I don't know how it happened. I—"

"Lisette. Wait. Slow down. What do you mean you lost her?"

"She was here, and two men who said they were from WitSec picked her up."

"They had IDs?"

"Yes. We checked. They were legit. The IDs, I mean. Professional. The names matched."

"How long have they been gone?"

She glanced at the clock. "Ten minutes."

"Get me a description, everything you can remember about them."

And that feeling she'd had about sending her kid off to college suddenly turned into a nightmare. She was so never having kids.

19

By the time they were in the car and on the freeway,
Piper had nearly convinced herself that any misgivings were
based on the fact she was the one getting screwed in this
deal. How was it that some people she'd never met in Washington could make a decision about her life? Like it even
mattered to them? What if she didn't want to go to Indiana,
or wherever-the-hell, USA? "Where *are* we going?"

"To the airport," one of the men said.

"Yeah, I get that. I mean where from there? Why can't I
just go home?"

"It'll be like your new home."

"Probably better," the other one said, as he slid off his
overcoat and tossed it on the backseat beside her.

Jerks, she thought, then eyed the tan coat, wondering if
there was any money in the pockets. She reached her hand
out, moving it closer, then surreptitiously patted the pockets,
feeling stiff paper, about the size that a plane ticket might
be, in the inside breast pocket. So they already had it. Time
to find out if it was anywhere *she* wanted to go. Watching
the two men up front, she slid her hand between the fabric

and pulled out a rental car folder. So not a plane ticket, but better than money, she decided, since she was pretty sure one needed a credit card to rent a vehicle. She moved the folder to her other side, so they wouldn't see, unfolded it, and was slightly dismayed to discover that only the last four digits were on the receipt stapled to the top of the document.

That was a waste, she thought, then stopped at the sight of the city on the rental contract.

South San Francisco. The date was five days ago.

Her heart started a slow thud. What were the chances that they were in the Bay Area on the very day Bo was murdered . . . ? She found the license number and recognized it as the car she saw parked outside Bo's shop. It was not the car they were in now, but they certainly could have flown back here, picked up this car, and somehow found her. She folded up the receipt and shoved it into her back pocket, then stared out the window, trying to think. And that was when she noticed they were not driving in the direction of the airport—something she knew only because she'd read the road signs when Lisette had first brought her to D.C. Piper hadn't seen these particular street names before. "I don't feel so good," she said.

"You'll be fine."

"No. I think I'm going to throw up." She tried to roll down the window. It didn't budge. A bad omen, she figured, and had a feeling that if she tried to open the door, it wouldn't work, either.

The driver craned his neck around to look at her. "What do you need?"

"A little fresh air."

He lowered the window about two inches.

She took a deep breath. "I think I need crackers. Or something to eat."

"Gum?"

"Crackers. I think I need crackers." She leaned forward,

then grasped the headrest in front of her. "We need to stop or I'm gonna throw up all over your car."

"Son of a . . ." He pulled off the freeway.

The blond guy pointed. "There's a mini-mart."

She looked. "Do you think they have saltines? That's the only thing that works."

"Saltines? Probably." The dark-haired guy signaled, then got into the left turn lane, waiting for the light to change. He parked, then nodded to his partner. "Go get her some crackers."

"Can I go in?" Piper asked. "I need to use the bathroom."

"No. It's not safe."

"Okay if I lie down back here?"

"Sure."

She glanced into the store, saw there was a long line at the counter, then lay across the seat so that her head was behind the driver's side. "Can you roll down this other window, too?"

He did.

"A little more? The cold air feels good."

She heard the window's roller, looked up, saw he'd rolled it about five inches total, she hoped low enough to reach outside and open the damned door.

What she needed was to get him out of the car, and she took a deep breath, then gave a loud sigh. "You think I could have a Coke?"

"A Coke?"

"Or ginger ale. You think they have ginger ale?"

"I don't know." He took out his phone, made a call. "Come on . . . pick up . . . Hey . . . grab some Coke or something."

And her heart sank. Didn't do her any good if he didn't leave the car. She grabbed her midsection, curled into a fetal position, and added a few moans that she'd perfected back when she was still living in foster care.

"What the hell now?" he asked.

"Cramps. That's why I don't feel good."

He leaned over the seat, looked at her. "Cramps?"

"I always get sick to my stomach when I start my period. I really need to use the bathroom."

"Yeah, well you're gonna have to wait."

"Fine. But it's your backseat and I need some tampons."

"Shit . . ." He called his partner again. "She needs you to buy tampons . . . What? You're afraid of cooties, you pick up a box? Goddamn it. I gotta do everything myself around here." He threw the door open and stomped across the parking lot, setting the alarm as he left.

She watched, saw him enter the store, then pushed the door lock and pulled the handle. As expected, it didn't open. She slid up, reached out the open window, the glass digging into her underarm as she strained to reach the handle on the outside of the door. Her fingers touched it, and she was worried she wouldn't be able to grasp it. "Please . . ." She shoved herself as close to the window as she could get, putting her weight against it, trying to get that extra inch, and then she had it, pulling the handle and it opened.

The alarm went off. She raced toward the gas pumps, yelled at the man closest to her.

He had just stepped out of a pickup truck, the door open, as he pulled his wallet from his pocket and stepped toward the gas pump.

"Call the cops. Those guys kidnapped me!"

He looked up, shocked.

The two men yelled as they burst from the store.

Piper dove into the pickup truck, slammed the door shut, locked it, and prayed there was a cell phone.

Instead she saw the keys in the ignition.

She turned the key, sped out of the parking lot, caught a glimpse in her rearview mirror of the men stopping in their tracks, then racing back to their car.

The light was green as she sped toward the intersection,

but she turned right instead, then right again, pulling into a busy shopping center parking lot that had at least fifty cars in it. She parked, threw the keys under the seat, then got out, trying to decide if she should steal another car or go into the store for help, when she saw a poster in the window of a travel agency advertising winter flight specials to Europe.

She had a feeling that that would be the last place *anyone* would be looking for her.

20

"Have you heard anything?" Griffin asked once he reached Lisette's.

"Nothing. Marc's doing a search of the area for any business with a video camera to see if we can't find one with a license plate of the vehicle. They had to have been lying in wait at the gas station where the two agents suddenly had a flat tire."

"They were followed?"

"Either that or it was the biggest sort of coincidence, them ending up with a flat."

"And the suspects knew to come here to your apartment looking for her?"

"That's what worries me. How would they know that? Or the names of the WitSec guys, then have IDs to match?"

"They wouldn't," Griffin said. "Unless somehow they had access to the information beforehand. I think McNiel's right, that they have a partial SINS program running and they've been able to access the databases that way. How else could they have shown up in South San Francisco?"

"The same men or the same crew, either way, anything we access electronically, they could be monitoring."

"They'll be one step ahead of us. We'll have to keep our search for her off the grid as much as possible."

"What do we do?"

"Not sure. Yet. But she's a resourceful girl," he said, recalling the way she'd maneuvered their escape in South San Francisco.

"You're assuming she'll figure out they're not legit."

"Hoping. Knowing her, she will definitely cause issues, even if she does think they're legit. Check with the police. Maybe something will pop out there."

"In D.C.? Seriously?"

"Like I said, she's resourceful. Give it a shot."

He left, drove out of the parking lot, trying to imagine which route he'd take if he were the kidnappers, trying to smuggle a girl out. He didn't think they'd kill her right off. She went with them willingly, and they'd probably use that cooperation to get her far from the area as soon as possible. He headed toward the freeway, and was about to get on in the direction of the airport when Lisette called him back.

"You were right. There was a stolen vehicle not too far from here. The victim states the suspect claimed she was being kidnapped and asked him to call the police. And the girl had black hair with pink spikes." She gave him the address.

"En route. Let me know if there are further updates."

The police were still there when he arrived, as was the victim whose truck was stolen. Griffin identified himself as a DOJ agent, stating only that they were looking for the girl in question. "Has anyone gotten surveillance video yet?"

"Working on it," the officer said. "The clerk said he'd burn a copy."

Griffin entered the store, found the clerk in a back room,

no bigger than a closet, where a computer sat on a desk. "You have video?"

The man turned. "It's almost done."

"Can you show me?"

"Sure." He accessed the footage, then pushed his chair to one side so Griffin could see.

A dark-colored sedan was parked in the lot on the side of the store, and one man got out and entered the building, followed shortly by the second man. He didn't recognize either. And then he saw Piper reach out the back window, open the door, then race across the parking lot to the gas pumps. She jumped into a white pickup, then drove out of the parking lot.

The men in the store ran out, got into their car, and gave chase.

He copied the plate down, asked the police to run it. They did. It came back as no record on file. He figured as much. At least he had the license of the truck Piper stole. But then, so did everyone else.

With nothing left he could do there, he drove in the same direction he saw the vehicles take off. Not that he expected to find either. And after several unfruitful minutes, he returned to Lisette's. "Good news and bad. She escaped and stole a truck."

"Any idea where she might have taken off to?"

"As young and inexperienced as she is? I'd say California. Going back home, where she's familiar."

That evening, after they'd exhausted all leads, Lisette posed the question that had been bothering Griffin the most. "How are we going to find her if we can't use our normal contacts?"

"The police will be searching," Griffin said. "At least they have a physical description and the vehicle she stole."

"But they won't have her name, since I doubt that her would-be kidnappers stopped to report it. What we need is a way to tap into the stolen vehicle database without anyone knowing it's us. What if someone runs that license plate? How will we know where she is or where she abandoned the vehicle if we can't run it ourselves if someone is monitoring our electronic moves?"

She was right. Their best advantage was in letting the enemy think they were not aware of Piper's connection to the stolen vehicle. "Sydney has contacts," he said. "If anyone can get information from them on the QT, she can."

"This should be interesting, considering she won't even return your calls."

"Any chance *you* can call?"

"For Piper, yes. But at some point you're going to have to man up and talk to her."

Lisette used the speakerphone feature so that Griffin could listen in. She did not, however, mention that Griffin was present, but judging from the tone of Sydney's voice, there was no doubt in Griffin's mind that she probably guessed.

"What is it you want from me?"

"Your contact at the local PD," Lisette said. "If that vehicle's recovered, and Piper's in it, we need to know before it's broadcast. Her only chance may be if we get to her first."

"I'll phone Lieutenant Sanchez, then get back to you when I hear something," she said.

"Thanks. I appreciate it," Lisette said. But by the time Lisette heard back from Sydney, then called Griffin to report it, it was three in the morning.

"They found the car," Lisette told him. "Dulles International."

It took a moment for him to wake up. He'd been searching for Piper straight through, and didn't get home until a little after midnight. "Dulles?" he echoed, not quite taking it in.

"The airport."

"I don't suppose there was any indication on *where* she went from there?"

"None," Lisette replied. "But the moment her name pops up on any passenger list, they'll find her."

"If we're lucky, she hasn't taken off yet."

"That long ago? She could very well be back in California by now. I have a contact at Homeland Security. He can run a check if we want to chance the electronic search."

"I don't think we have a choice. Call him."

He leaned back against the pillows on his bed, closing his eyes, telling himself there was nothing they could do until they knew where Piper was. Even so, it did little to relax him. Surprisingly, he dozed off, though fitfully, waking again when Lisette called about a half hour later. "I just heard back from Homeland Security. The good news? There's no record of Piper getting on any flights. The bad news? *I* am on my way to Italy. Apparently she put my passport to good use. She'll be landing at Marco Polo around noon."

"Venice?" he asked, wondering if this operation could get any worse. "Why there?"

"Maybe she likes spaghetti. Does it matter?"

"How the hell could she fly there on *your* passport?"

"Similar height, weight, and coloring. Slap a hat on her head to hide that god-awful hair, and shove that passport under some overworked, underpaid TSA agent?"

"Good point. I'll call McNiel and brief him."

McNiel was not happy to hear the news. "How did she get to Italy?"

"She stole Lisette's passport. If I had to guess, it was probably the most recent stamp."

McNiel gave a ragged sigh. "This couldn't come at a worse time. They're expecting me to give a full report in the morning on how it is we lost her to begin with."

"What do you want us to do?"

"Have Lisette and Marc get on the very next flight out. If we found her this easy, then Kane will have no difficulty. In fact, we should assume he has somebody en route or will soon, and act accordingly."

"I'll call Giustino to have her pulled from the flight the moment it lands." Giustino, a *carabinieri* officer based out of Rome, also worked as an ATLAS agent. He would have the means to get aboard that flight before the passengers disembarked.

"Good. But stress to Giustino that this girl needs to be *off* the grid. Tell him to hide her in the last place they'd look. I'm not sure how long we can protect her otherwise."

"Anything else?"

"Just keep your eyes and ears open."

And what else could he do? Except hope that when Piper arrived in Venice, it was Giustino who met her and not someone else.

21

At one time Parker Bruxton Kane had been in line to run the U.S. arm of ATLAS. In fact, the idea for the organization came from him, from an elite unit he ran out of the Central Intelligence Agency. It wasn't as broad as ATLAS, as far-reaching, because it did not have the oversight, something he'd hoped to change when he'd actually proposed the idea of ATLAS to the last president. But his smaller version was certainly efficient, and this room was the heart of his operation, the place where the most sensitive of cases took place, where the finest analysts and agents worked. The elite of the elite, they'd been with him for as long as he'd held the number two position, each one handpicked—loyal to the government, they would lie down their lives for their president—but more importantly, loyal to him. They didn't question his needs. Every one of them had a military background, knew how to follow orders, and knew that sometimes for a job to be done right, one didn't need to know why, only what to do.

It was the perfect mix, and he hadn't yet quite decided what to do with the team once he was appointed as the deputy national security adviser. Decisions on that, however, could wait. The more pressing matter was this Piper Lawrence.

"Listen up," he said, holding a copy of the report Ron McNiel had written for ATLAS. "This girl we are now searching for is a potential threat to national security. She was last seen at a convenience store here in D.C., and may have viewed a secure document. She may even have a copy. I want to know everything there is about her. Where she went to school. Who she hung out with. What car she drove. *Every*thing. Understood?"

They looked at him, and for a moment, their expressions were blank.

"Get to it!" he yelled.

They jumped to work, turning to their respective computers to search for the information needed.

A half hour later, he walked in to see what progress they'd made.

Her identification photo was on the computer screen and one of the analysts, Alan Madison, nodded toward it. "That's her."

"And?"

"Arrested on a felony grand theft charge, dropped to a misdemeanor, in addition to several misdemeanor convictions for petty theft. Aged out of the foster care system. Currently attends community college. License valid, but no vehicles. Known associates are . . ." He pressed another button, bringing up a different screen. "Bo Brewer, owner of the shop where the first number sighting turned up. And that's about the extent of any official records."

Parker Kane walked up, eyed her photo, the dark makeup, facial piercings, and spiky black hair with pink . . . tufts? Whatever they were called, they'd sure as hell make her easy to spot, as he well knew. "Good start, but not enough. I want cell phone records, landline records. Every call she's ever made. And once you have those numbers? I want them monitored to see what comes in or out. People do *not* just disappear, folks. They leave a trail, and you sure as hell better find it. This girl needs to be in a body bag before this thing turns into a national security nightmare."

He heard the clicking of keyboards as he started to walk out. He was late for a meeting with the president, and he was *not* going to let this thing ruin his appointment.

Or the president's campaign. Marginal presidents had a difficult enough time winning a second term. Any sort of scandal could ruin it, and there was a long year of campaigning to get through.

He started to walk out when Madison said, "There is one other thing."

Kane stopped in his tracks. He hated when anyone said that. Something horrible inevitably followed. He turned, faced Madison. "I'm very late. What is it?"

"The girl. Piper Lawrence. According to several social network pages, she seems to have a special talent. Big at parties, apparently. Kids, sex, you know how it is. We, uh, saw some videos on the Internet that backed it up."

"Videos? Tell me she's giving head to some politician we *don't* want elected or save it for the report."

"Sir. She, uh, has eidetic memory."

"Eidetic memory? Sex? What the *hell* are you talking about?"

Madison shrugged, then moved his chair aside. "See for yourself."

A video of some party, the sort with kegs of beers and drunk college-age kids drinking out of red plastic cups. And there in the center of the group of drunk kids was Piper Lawrence with her black and pink hair, and someone shoving a book in front of her, while she protested. Then, under multiple drunkards chanting, "Do it! Do it!" he watched as she silently read the page of some book, handed it back, then recited the passage apparently word for word. Sex scenes from some vampire novel.

He failed to see the importance. "So she's read it so many times, she knows it by heart."

"Watch, sir."

He brought up another video, this one of the girl and several young men in a library. One of them pulled a book from the shelf, flashed the cover for the camera. *Quantum Physics*. Then he opened it to what appeared to be a random page, and handed it to her. She read it, then handed it back. This time, however, they blindfolded her before she recited what she'd read. And just in case the viewer thought it might be some joke, that it was faked, whoever put the video together had divided the frame in two, showing the page being recited so that the viewer could see.

"Play that again."

Madison did.

Kane watched the video, his thoughts racing. They'd struck out on finding the Devil's Key in every place they possibly could have found it. South San Francisco, where that idiot's laptop was wiped clean. They'd struck out with the FBI agents, and Mexico had been a bust.

But as he watched this girl reciting something only a scientist could understand, he realized that there was a very real possibility that she had seen the document. She was a walking, living, breathing copy machine.

And about to become the most hunted woman in America.

22

National Counterterrorism Center

It was everything McNiel could do to keep his face neutral, his voice calm, while he was being grilled over the incident with Piper, and then, as he'd suspected and feared, about the viability of ATLAS as a working agency. The only positive sign at the moment was that Parker Kane was not present. More importantly, McNiel trusted everyone in this room. Not that it changed the seriousness of the matter.

General Woodson shook his head. "Is there some reason we're even discussing this like there's some democratic vote to be taken? ATLAS has served its purpose. There's no need to divide resources when money and manpower are already tight. This is no way to protect our national security."

"General Woodson is right," Roy Santiago said. "I recommend we either dissolve it or absorb it. Or move it back to the CIA." Had this come from anyone other than the assistant deputy director of national intelligence, McNiel might not have been as concerned. Santiago, however, was undoubtedly acting on the president's orders.

"ATLAS," McNiel said, "is still a viable organization. But if you fall prey to the machinations of outside influences, then we're all victims here."

"What outside influences?" Woodson asked, looking around the room. "The only fact I'm seeing is that ATLAS continues to make grave mistakes that have nearly cost this country its national security. How is it that the FBI had a copy of this thing to begin with? This girl—"

"Has passed on no information and will not," McNiel said. "Not as long as she is in our charge."

"The problem," Woodson said, "is that you don't have charge of her. We no longer have the luxury of hoping you can keep a tight rein on her. If she escapes again—"

"I didn't realize she was a prisoner," McNiel told him.

"She might as well be. And that's assuming we even find her. It's not like we can let her run around. If your operatives can't keep her in control, what makes you think a program like witness protection can? There's even less oversight there."

"Woodson is right," Santiago said. "That is no longer a viable option."

"Then what do you suggest?" McNiel asked, wishing he could somehow slip his cell phone from his pocket and phone Griffin's number, somehow warn him about what was about to occur. "That we take out a gun and put a bullet through her head?"

"Obviously," Woodson said, "that would be a last resort. Protective custody. Plain and simple. And under the guidance of someone who isn't emotionally involved, because of past mistakes. The military is better equipped to handle a special case like this."

"Pissing match aside," Santiago said, "the president has asked that I get to the bottom of what went wrong. How is it that one of your agents allowed her to be kidnapped? What sort of training or lack thereof is going on in your agency?"

The beginning of the end, McNiel thought. They were going to attempt to use this case to shut down ATLAS. He only hoped they weren't so blinded that they couldn't see that someone on the inside was manipulating all of them. "The men who arrived showed Agent Perrault the proper identification. That tells me that we're dealing with someone who has access to official federal documents and identification cards. She doesn't believe they were forgeries."

"Are you saying two federal marshals kidnapped this girl?"

"No, I'm saying two men with official marshal identification cards kidnapped her."

"And where is she now?"

"She escaped. According to the police reports, she fled at a convenience store and then stole a car."

"And have you followed up on these leads? You know where she is?"

"We have. At the moment, I can't exactly say."

"But you have knowledge of where she might be?"

"She's safe. I can tell you that much."

"That's not what I asked."

McNiel looked Santiago in the eye, suspecting that this line of questioning had originated from Kane. He didn't suspect Santiago of working with him, but he was certainly being influenced by him. They all were. "Why do you want to know?"

"In light of recent events, and those leading up to them, it's my belief that you are no longer able to handle the duties to which you were assigned."

"My unit is sound."

"Is it?" Santiago replied. "ATLAS is the reason this girl, or rather what she is carrying in her head, is now a national security threat. *Your* team had the opportunity to neutralize this threat before it even started by removing these numbers from circulation and eliminating the people responsible.

Your men under *your* direction allowed the asset in Mexico to slip right beneath them. Then, when the code key was recovered last October, we discover a copy was made, one that you should have foreseen. And now you are telling us that you have a handle on this? That your operatives can be trusted, when they can't even keep a twenty-year-old girl under their protection?"

"The girl is not the threat. A mistake was made. It was corrected."

"However briefly," Woodson said, "she *was* in custody of the enemy. We have no idea what she did or did not tell them."

"Enough!" Santiago said. "McNiel. If you have knowledge of this girl, I want to know now."

"With all due respect, sir, I can't tell you."

"You're forcing my hand, you realize that?" He took an exasperated breath, his expression one of frustration and regret. "You'll report to General Woodson with the girl where she'll be taken into protective custody, until such time as we deem it to be safe for her release. If you do not, then the president has ordered me to relieve you from duty."

McNiel had not anticipated things would happen this quickly. "My apologies, Mr. Santiago. Even so, I can't do that. It's a matter of safety."

"Then I have no choice. You will be escorted back to your building, where you will make arrangements to turn over your files on any active cases, including the current case in question."

McNiel knew better than to show any outward sign of anger. "So we are being shut down?"

"Perhaps your agents will see reason if someone else is at the helm. The president needs some assurances that his trust is not misplaced."

"It isn't," McNiel said, his mind racing with how he was going to salvage this so his team could accomplish what they needed to do. He stood. "Will there be anything else?"

"Unless you plan on changing your mind and bringing her in?"

"I do not. Now if you'll excuse me, gentlemen. I have to break it to my men that they're no longer working for me. I'd like to tell them personally." He walked out, and the moment he cleared the door, he called Griffin, and, unfortunately, got his voice mail. "That tenuous thread we're operating on just broke." He was just about to disconnect, when he heard footsteps behind him. He turned to see Curt Ellis, the federal police officer, approaching, and knew right away that this couldn't be good news.

"Director McNiel?"

"Yes," he said, holding the phone in hopes it would pick up Ellis's statement. He waited.

Ellis had the grace to look embarrassed. "I apologize, but Mr. Santiago has asked that I accompany you back to your office to stand by."

"Stand by for what?"

"They, uh, intend to meet us there once they finish, to have you brief them on any open cases. I know you wouldn't do anything to jeopardize their trust, but . . ."

The stranglehold they now had him in was official. The way he saw it, Parker Kane was running scared, desperate to get his hands on their investigation of W2 as well as the code key Piper had seen. "Let me finish this call," he said. "And you can follow me there."

"I appreciate your understanding."

"I'm on my way to the office," McNiel said into the phone. "Apparently they're going to be going through the cases now, not later. I need to make sure they have access to everything."

He disconnected, then holding his phone so that Ellis couldn't see the screen, texted the combination to his safe, hoping like hell Griffin checked his voice mail and got there before he did.

If that sketch got out, more than the girl's life was at risk. His whole team and anyone who had knowledge of it were in danger.

The federal police officer was behind McNiel as they pulled out of the parking garage. This was going to take some finesse. At least they hadn't insisted on taking him into custody for contempt—probably an oversight, he thought, calling his secretary.

No answer.

Great. Last thing he wanted was for Parker to get his hands on the notes he'd compiled on the W2 case. Nothing like telling the enemy exactly what you knew about them, he thought, calling the reception area downstairs, and asking them to page her. Which was when he found out she had a doctor's appointment, but was due back any moment.

What a time for people to have a real life. When his world was falling apart. How the hell was he going to get that sketch and those files out of his safe to keep Parker from seeing it? The light at the intersection turned yellow, and as he slowed for the impending red light, he realized in that one moment, he had a choice. Change to the right lane, which was open and go through it, and hope his escort wasn't brazen enough to follow, or be the dutiful director and do as was expected, which was let Ellis accompany him into the building. Choice? No choice. He palmed the wheel, moved to the outside lane, and without accelerating, glided through the intersection, the light turning red as he passed beneath it.

He kept his car at a steady speed, exactly with the traffic, so as not to spook Ellis into chasing after him.

It worked.

If he was lucky, that bought him three minutes, he thought, making the right turn toward his office. The moment he was out of sight, he hit the gas, hoping to squeeze a few more precious seconds that might allow him to get into his safe before the federal police officer arrived to put a halt to all activities.

He had to make some quick decisions. Griffin and Donovan were more than capable of handling matters without his leadership, he thought, surveying the parking lot of the *Washington Recorder*, the cover paper for ATLAS operations, noting the usual cars parked within. It would be empty soon, everyone dismissed to go home, because once he was relieved of duty, all operations would freeze. That was ATLAS protocol, a necessary one due to the sensitive nature of their business, and it would be followed. No one would be allowed in the building, but more importantly, nothing could be removed, including the sketch and files.

It never occurred to him when the protocol was put in place that *he'd* be the focus of it.

He pulled into his slot, got out, and strode into the building, running into his secretary in the lobby.

"I just heard you called," she said, removing her gloves as she walked with him to the elevator.

"We have an issue," he said, pressing the up button. The door opened, and he punched in his code to access the secure floors. "In about three to five minutes, I'm going to be relieved of duty by the Senate's federal police officer."

"What do you need me to do?"

"What you're supposed to do. Inform the staff to follow protocol procedures. Then stall him."

She nodded, then stayed in the lobby, while he went up to his office. The staff on the lower floors, who wrote for the *Recorder*, would not be affected as much as the upper secure floors, since no one on the ground floor had access to classified material. Nor were they privy to the sensitive investigations McNiel's team conducted, although they were more than aware of the nature of said investigations. They were, after all, his employees. But the upper floors were different.

McNiel's team and IT above him were very much involved
in their casework. Should anyone try to access those computers without the proper password, it would automatically
initiate a program that would wipe the hard drives. Any classified documents were cross-shredded before they ever left
the floor.

In fact, the only thing of a sensitive nature readily available was sitting in McNiel's safe, which was against the
wall behind his desk. He entered the combination, placed
his finger on the print reader, then opened it. Inside was the
sketch as well as several file folders. He emptied the safe,
putting everything on the desk so that he could sort through
it. In his mind, there were no secure computers, no matter
how many safeguards one built into them. These files were
the bones of cases that he'd ensured remained off any electronic database.

As he flipped through the folders, he had to make quick
decisions.

W2 . . .

Kane would be expecting to find something on it. Everyone knew they'd been looking into it, even though techni-
cally not since last October, after Sydney had recovered the
list during her father's murder investigation in Mexico. And
then again when the numbers surfaced on that copy machine
found in South San Francisco.

And now, suddenly, Kane was hell-bent on shutting down
ATLAS, or at the very least hobbling it so that it was virtu-
ally useless.

This would be one file Kane would expect to find. So what
in it, besides the sketch, would he not want Kane to see?

He quickly scanned through the pages, pulling out all he
thought he could get away with and leaving only a shell of
the case behind.

Throwing everything including Sydney's sketch into a
slim accordion folder, then securing it closed with the string

tie, he shoved the remaining files back into the safe, locked it, then walked out, intending to give the packet to his secretary to shred. He hadn't taken two steps when he realized that the biggest threat might not be the handful of files after all. He stopped, turned, stared at the copy machine down at the end of the hall.

Every copy they'd ever made the last few years was on that machine. ATLAS ran covert ops, and more often than not, unsanctioned black ops. Every one of those cases could be turned against them, not only to shut down ATLAS, but to prosecute each and every one of them. And the sad thing was that prosecution was the lesser of the evils. If what was on that machine got into the hands of Kane or the Network . . .

Hell . . .

He set the files on top of the machine and opened the side panel, wondering how difficult it would be to remove the hard drive. He stared at the plate covering it. His kingdom for a screwdriver . . .

The elevator dinged.

"I'm sure Director McNiel is up here," he heard his secretary say in a louder than normal voice when the elevator doors opened.

He eyed the folder, then the open panel of the copy machine. He was trapped, with nowhere to go as he heard their footsteps behind him.

Sliding the folder toward the back of the machine, he pushed it between the wall and heard it drop to the floor. Then he kicked the access door shut with his foot, hiding the cover of the hard drive, then opened one of the drawers with paper.

He turned around, held up his hands. "Sorry," he said as she and Ellis walked down the hallway toward him. "I thought I could fix it for you. I have *no* idea what's wrong with the thing. How long has it been acting up?"

She glanced at the copy machine, then him. "Since this

morning," she said. "And I have all those time sheets due tomorrow."

He pushed the paper drawer shut, hoping that Ellis wasn't aware the time sheets were all computerized. "They can wait. As you can see," he said, nodding to the man standing next to her, "we have company. Put in a work order tomorrow." He gave her a neutral smile. "Weren't you on your way to the doctor's?"

"Uh, I—"

"Since I won't be here, you should follow protocol. Go take care of it. Your health is more important."

"I'll just get my keys from my office and be on my way."

The moment she left, the federal police officer said, "Director McNiel, I'm sorry to inform you of this, but my orders have changed. They've asked that I relieve you of duty immediately. And, uh, not allow you to access your office. You're to report to the Senate Intelligence Committee at once."

He wasn't surprised. At least now, if they were inclined to go through his safe, he could live with what they found.

As long as they didn't look too closely at the copy machine before he could get someone in there to retrieve what was left behind.

23

Capitol Building
Washington, D.C.

McNiel leaned his head back against the wall, listen-ing to the footsteps echoing down the hallway outside the room he was sitting in, while he waited to hear what the outcome of the hearing would be. No wonder Parker Kane hadn't been at the earlier meeting. He'd been here, pleading his case to absorb ATLAS into his domain. And what was McNiel supposed to do? Show his hand too soon, by announcing that he suspected Kane of espionage? That the entire government was being set up? He'd look like a fool making a desperate bid to save his place in the kingdom. They'd castrate him.

Hell, they'd already castrated him. He was now without a job. The only reason he was here was because they wanted to find the girl.

What he needed to do was bide his time. McNiel had faith that his team could survive without him temporarily or otherwise. Still, it was damned unnerving.

There had been warning signs, of course. He should have seen them. Hell, he had seen them. Like a goddamned avalanche sliding down the mountain, bringing ATLAS with it, starting with the debacle in Mexico last October. And as much as he wanted to blame Sydney Fitzpatrick for starting that avalanche, he couldn't. He'd have done the same thing if he were she. Everyone on his team would have. They were not automatons. They were human, and that was why he'd handpicked each one of them. The human element might get in the way at times, but it was the very thing that kept them centered, and he wouldn't have it any other way.

The difference between him and Sydney was that he wouldn't have gotten caught. The advantage of being better trained in countersurveillance.

In a way he should probably be grateful for her sticking her nose where it didn't belong. She'd turned up a couple of choice items that had been missing from his investigation all these years. Like Parker Kane. And the location of the damned Devil's Key that was now sitting in some poor college kid's head, turning her into the most wanted woman in America.

Who could have foreseen *that* lapse in security?

"Hindsight," he whispered, as he heard the footsteps of someone walking down the corridor outside his room. When he'd sent a team to the San Francisco FBI office to recover the bank bag Sydney had found in Mexico, it never occurred to any of them that she'd have made a copy.

And that was their downfall.

A simple oversight in allowing that copy machine out of the building without removing the hard drive had turned into the pebble that started the avalanche.

The footsteps stopped and he realized someone was standing outside the door. Waiting.

Several thoughts went through his head. He didn't think anyone would be brazen enough to kill him in here. That would raise too many questions. Not when there were so many better ways to do it. Suicide—the covert favorite assassination method—only worked when there were no witnesses to discover it wasn't suicide at all. He glanced up at the lens that was focused on him at the moment, thinking that even if it did stop working due to a malfunction, manmade or otherwise, his team would raise too many questions. As long as they were around to do so, that was.

That ATLAS had been effectively disenfranchised made things a bit . . . trickier.

The lock to his door clicked open, and he tensed.

A guard entered. Different from the last one.

"Your attorney's here to see you," the guard said.

"I didn't call him."

"Regardless. He's here. Take it or leave it."

McNiel focused on the man's posture, the expression on his face. Relaxed. Unconcerned.

"Where is he?" he asked, that suspicion rising to the forefront again.

"They're bringing him up now."

McNiel nodded, then took a seat at the table so that it was between him and the closed door. And anyone who might walk through it.

A few minutes later, it opened.

Zachary Griffin stood there. A sight for sore eyes.

"Heard you could use some legal advice?"

McNiel smiled, waited for the guard to close the door. "How's my case looking?"

"Might take a little work, but nothing's insurmountable." He put what looked like a small digital recorder on the table, then clicked the button. It was not recording. It was a pocketsized jammer that would mask any listening devices in the area. "I don't have long," Griffin said. "We've got a lot on our plate. Tex is still in Mexico. He's called Carillo in to help. I haven't yet heard back from him."

"What about Piper?"

"There's actually some good news on that front." He leaned forward and lowered his voice. "I just got off the phone with Giustino. I suppose you could say it's one of the more unusual witness protection programs. A convent in Venice."

"Come again?"

"I know it's unorthodox, but it can work."

"A convent? When I said the last place they'd look, that wasn't exactly what I had in mind."

"I'm not sure he had a lot of choices. Once they left the airport, he was informed by one of his men that inquiries were being made about the passenger Lisette Perrault. He's also worried someone's monitoring any electronic movement. On the positive side, she won't have access to computers, credit cards, or stolen vehicles. And as long as everyone follows protocol, it is as secure as any safe house we have used."

"You're sure about this?"

"He's used this particular location before. Dumas made the arrangements, and Lisette and Marc should be there by morning."

Father Emile Dumas was what could be described as a covert operative for the Vatican, if one could get past the notion that the Vatican could even have spies. He didn't carry a weapon, but he did investigate matters of security and terrorism against the church, and there were times when his cases and those of ATLAS overlapped.

While Griffin and Dumas did not always see eye to eye, there was no doubt in McNiel's mind that Dumas would do everything in his power to protect the girl. And really, could it be any worse than keeping her here in a military facility against her will? "At least that's one less thing to worry about. What about ATLAS?"

"We're locked from the building. Guard posted inside and out."

"Anyone else being questioned?"

"Not sure. I didn't get close enough to see. It looked pretty empty, though, so I'd guess everyone was following protocol."

Apparently his secretary was able to get out the word, which meant the entire staff would shut everything down, wipe computers, then make themselves scarce, until they were notified otherwise.

The fewer people around for questioning, the better. "Good. Next step, I want Parker's head before he gets mine."

"Except you're here under surveillance. That makes him one up on you."

"And if you're not careful, you're going to be joining me. I cleared the safe, but there was a slight glitch on my way out the door. The sketch and my files got stuffed behind the copy machine. I definitely don't want that sketch getting out. The files are on the W2 case. You're going to have to break in to get them."

"Just out of curiosity, how'd they get behind the copy machine?"

"I wanted to recover the machine's hard drive before they took over the building."

Griffin let out a breath. "I hate to think what's on there."

McNiel felt the same. Between their various investigations into the Black Network's activities to the detailed op plans of missions that wouldn't pass muster should they be put in front of the wrong people, anyone who worked for ATLAS was in a world of hurt if that hard drive was looked at. "The short time I've been confined to this room is enough to convince me I don't want to be here any longer than I have to. And if I'm not careful, they're likely to take me into custody for contempt."

"When have they ever done that?"

"You want to test them? I don't." McNiel glanced toward the door. "We have to assume that Kane is waiting to see what my next move is. When I get out of here, I intend to take a long drive up the coast. If they want to follow me, they're in for a long ride. And while they're tailing me, I'd suggest that if you have any intention of preserving your career, you take action at the first opportunity."

"This would have been a hell of a lot easier getting past the armed guards if we hadn't just enhanced our building's security."

"Find a way around it. Because the security's the least of your concerns. If they get what's on that hard drive, you and I will be sharing a cell in the federal penitentiary along with the rest of our team."

"Cheery thought."

"Not as cheery as the fact that *no one's* supposed to be in that building. Which means no one's going to think twice if you're killed after having been caught breaking and entering."

24

North of Ensenada, Mexico

The offshore breeze swept through the courtyard of the Orozco Villa, bringing with it a faint and refreshing tang of salt. Tex breathed in deep. After the cloying scent of death still evident inside the house, he was grateful to be standing outside.

When McNiel had ordered Tex to Mexico, he thought it was going to be a short trip. Fly in, advise Pedro Venegas of the Federal Ministerial Police that he'd be in the area, talk to Orozco about the possibility of his still having a copy of the Devil's Key, recover it if he did, then fly out the next day. No one said anything about walking into a mass murder scene. Or that a witness might have survived.

Apparently this last fact was being kept off the record. In light of the sensitive nature of the investigation, Venegas felt it best to let everyone assume that Orozco's entire family had been killed. Once Venegas had informed him that it was possible Orozco's daughter might have escaped, he couldn't just leave.

It was also why he'd called in Tony Carillo to help. For one, Carillo was familiar with Venegas, apparently having dealt with him in the past. Two, Carillo had experience working homicides, whereas Tex did not. Being a spy and investigating espionage was not the same thing as working a murder case. Three, even though Carillo had every reason to hold a grudge about the debacle with his condo being searched, Carillo owed him big-time, and he was calling in his marker. Of course, he also sweetened the deal by adding that it was, after all, Mexico in January, and on the government's dime, so to speak. At least until someone got wise and cut off his credit card, and judging by what was going on back at the office, that was likely to happen any time. He only hoped Carillo's credit card still worked, because Carillo was expecting a lobster dinner with margaritas at the conclusion.

Carillo stood a few feet away, talking to Venegas about his preliminary findings, both men with their backs to a wall covered with bougainvillea vines, the bright pink flowers shimmering in the breeze. The petals were so bright, they could be seen from the beach below, something Tex noticed when he'd first arrived.

While the two men went over the particulars of the case, Tex walked across the brick pavers out the drive to take a look. The villa property held a clear view of the coast from its perch on top of the hill. It was too far away to hear the break of the waves, or see anyone on the beach. Earlier this morning, Tex had gone down there to see if he could find anything. Tire tracks were visible where a vehicle had pulled onto the shoulder of the road, but nothing detailed enough to figure out what sort of tires or provide any useful leads, because it could have been a tourist, stopping to snap a photo. And since the beach had been empty, and he wasn't sure what, if anything, he'd hoped to find, he'd returned.

Carillo walked over, interrupting his thoughts. "You ready to go back in?"

"Not really. I don't think anything prepares you to see an entire family slaughtered. Not even in my business."

"Not in mine, either. But you never know when you might have missed something the first time around, now that they've gotten the bodies out. Venegas says the locals are insistent on it being a cartel hit."

"Highly unlikely, considering the reason we were coming here. Unless you believe in coincidence."

"Which I do not." Carillo looked out over the wall toward the beach. "What we need to do is determine if Orozco's daughter really did escape. Orozco, apparently, wasn't big on permanent identification, and they don't have a positive ID on the girl who was killed. Right now it's only a suspicion on Venegas's part." They stood there in silence, watching the ocean, though, at least in Tex's mind, not really seeing it. Eventually Carillo put his hand on Tex's shoulder. "Let's go."

Tex nodded, then followed him into the villa. Venegas walked in after them. The windows had all been opened, to allow the breeze to air out the scent of dried blood. The main living area was where two of the bodies had been found. The young woman who was believed to have been Orozco's daughter, and the man believed to be her husband. The third and fourth, Orozco and his wife, were in what was clearly his office, a room with a view of the courtyard, a large desk, and a wall safe, which stood open, and was now empty.

"How much cash did the officers find in there?" Carillo asked Venegas.

"Several thousand dollars, American."

"Anything else?"

"Nothing. If this thing they were searching for was in there, it was not when the officers arrived. It was, however, standing open."

"That's an awful lot of money to leave lying around."

"Agreed. So we know that is not what they were after."

Carillo said nothing, just looked at Tex, who eyed the open desk drawers, as well as the rooms beyond that were in similar disarray. "I'd have to guess it wasn't in there, and they hoped to find it elsewhere. Assuming it was here at all."

They finished walking the downstairs, where the fifth body had been found, Orozco's brother-in-law, in a hallway just off the kitchen leading to a back door, undoubtedly as he tried to flee. Carillo directed Tex and Venegas to the upper floor, going from room to room. It was clear that someone had searched this part of the house, especially the master bedroom, which opened up to a wide veranda. Carillo made a cursory search, then walked outside, though what he was looking for, Tex had no idea.

Tex was flipping through an address book he found on the floor that had probably landed there when someone pulled the drawer out of the nightstand, when Carillo called him over. The veranda opened up to the backyard, and beyond it and the bougainvillea-covered wall, the ocean.

"Find something?" he asked, walking over to where Carillo stood at the balcony's edge.

"Look there." He pointed to the terra-cotta tiles on the balcony's floor. Muddy footprints.

Tex noted they pointed toward the house, but had originated from the wrought-iron balcony's edge, where he could see the heart-shaped, leathery leaves of some vine that had twisted its way up a trellis from the garden below.

He walked over to look into the backyard that could grace the cover of any gardening magazine, with its meandering paths of crushed rock and well-tended flower beds. Stone benches inset with brightly colored Mexican tiles were interspersed throughout, giving one any number of places to sit and enjoy the view. At the far end of the yard stood a child's swing set, the empty swings moving as the breeze swept in from the coast and across the stretch of lawn, a reminder that a very young child had lost the only family she'd known.

Tex forced his gaze from the swing set to the ground below the climbing vines, noting the area appeared to have been disturbed, probably when someone climbed up the trellis. "Undoubtedly a point of entry, but by whom? We have the witnesses on the beach who picked up the little girl, saw a man who matched Orozco's description get into a car with two men. Who was this, then?"

Carillo put his foot next to one of the prints. "Pretty small for a guy. Could be a child, but I'm thinking a woman." Then, careful not to disturb the prints, he stepped over them and to the bedroom, calling out to Venegas, who was going through a box he'd found up in the closet. "Can I see those crime scene photos again?"

"Of course." They were in his portfolio, which he'd set on the bed, one of the few clean surfaces that didn't have finger-print powder upon it. He opened it, then handed the photos to Carillo, who looked at each in turn.

Carillo pulled out one photo and held it up. "Anyone see footprints there?"

Tex took it from him, saw it was of the master bedroom veranda. Other than a few yellowed leaves from the vine scattered about, the tiles looked clean, he thought, handing the photo to Venegas. No footprints anywhere.

"Someone," Carillo said, "entered *after* this place was processed."

Tex picked up the rest of the photos, looking at each one. "If the entire family was killed, who was here and why? Someone searching for whatever the killers were searching for? Or Orozco's daughter?"

"The latter," Venegas said. "At least a good case for it. There were armed officers out front, protecting the prem-ises. Whoever came in knew the ins and outs."

Carillo examined the photos again, one by one. He paused

on a shot of the main living area, the young woman's body by the front door. "The girl lying there. Does she look pregnant to you?" He handed the photo to Venegas.

"She was allegedly not very far along. Four-five months. A girl slightly overweight, how can you tell?"

"I'm not the expert," Tex said, "but I think you'd be showing, at least a little."

"The girl," Venegas said, "has no prints on file. But this is a small village and that's to be expected. So we cannot disprove it until the autopsy is done."

"No time to wait," Carillo said, then walked through each of the bedrooms again, this time going through the closets. "The clothes tell me that the girl in the photo is not the girl who wore these clothes, which are definitely too small."

"You think it's possible the daughter survived?" Tex asked. That would be a break they truly needed.

"Why not?" Carillo said. "Either she wasn't here at all, or she got an early warning of what was taking place. Her window overlooks the courtyard." He nodded in that direction, then walked over, looked out. "Let's say she sees her father being brought in at gunpoint. She's not very likely to go running down there. You've got someone killed right there at the front door, and someone at the back. So maybe she hears the shots and escapes down the trellis. Or she wasn't here at all. One way to possibly tell . . ." He walked over, picked up a shoe from the closet floor, then carried it out to the veranda off the master bedroom. The sizes matched.

Tex walked over to the balcony's edge, and eyed the garden wall and the thick vines covering it. "We might want to have a closer look at the perimeter."

They found the hidden gate beneath the bougainvillea leading to the chaparral-covered hillside beyond, like stepping from a lush oasis into a different world, this one brown and dull. The dirt was dry on the outside of the wall, the footprints almost nonexistent. But it seemed there was a worn path through the low shrubs, the gritty soil freshly disturbed as though someone had recently walked upon it.

They followed the trail and as they crested the hill into a shallow valley, they saw a ranch house with a few donkeys in the yard behind a barbed-wire fence. Venegas nodded at it as they walked down the hill. "Perhaps she came here for help."

"You'd think they'd call the police," Carillo said.

A sharp crack echoed across the valley as dirt sprayed up beside them.

Tex dove to the side where a few small boulders offered some cover. Carillo followed, but Venegas stood there, pulled out his badge, holding it up, trying to flash it in the sunlight. "*Policía!*" he yelled.

He was a braver man than Tex—or far more foolish—because he didn't move. Nor did he draw his own weapon.

Several tense moments passed, and the only thing Tex heard was a donkey braying, then Venegas saying, "*Por favor. Debemos aquí ayudar—*"

"I know who you are. It's the other two I'm worried about. Keep your hands where I can see them!" A female voice. Speaking English with a faint Mexican accent.

Venegas kept his hands up. "They are friends. Here to help."

"You tell those other two I want to see their hands up in the air."

Tex peered between the boulders and saw a woman on the porch, pointing a long gun at them. She was dressed in blue jeans and a plaid shirt and wore a baseball cap.

"Now!" she ordered.

Tex rolled to his side, put up his hands. Carillo waited a heartbeat. When no shots were forthcoming, he rose, keeping his hands up about shoulder level.

"The three of you walk up here. Nice and slow."

They walked down the hill toward the house, and as they neared, Tex saw she was in her late fifties or early sixties. Hard to say, since her skin was tanned and leathery, her arms muscled, as though she did a lot of the ranch work herself. Her light brown hair, flecked with gray, was pulled back in a ponytail beneath the cap, and he could see her eyes following their movements, her gaze fixed on their hands, not their faces.

When they reached the ranch house, she lowered the barrel to about their knees and Tex felt infinitely better. Until a curtain moved at the front window, and he wondered if someone inside had a gun on them, as well.

"Who are you two?" she asked.

And Tex said, "James Dalton, reporter with the *Washington Recorder*."

"Newspaper? That's a new one. You?" she said, pointing her gun at Carillo.

"Tony Carillo, ma'am. Special agent, FBI."

The front door flew open, and a young woman with dark hair and blue eyes, and a slightly rounded stomach, stepped out, pointing a gun right at Carillo, saying, "You know an agent named Sydney Fitzpatrick?"

"I do."

"Give me one good reason why I shouldn't shoot you right where you stand."

Clearly they'd found Robert Orozco's daughter.

And she apparently was nursing one hell of a grudge against Sydney.

"Maria!" the older woman said. "Put the gun down before you hurt someone."

"But she is the reason my parents are dead. And the reason my daughter is missing. If she had not come here, seeking my father—"

Venegas said, "Your daughter is safe. And in good hands."

Her eyes welled with tears, and she leaned against the side

of the house as though suddenly losing the strength to even stand.

"The gun, Maria."

She lowered her weapon.

Her guardian did not. "You," she said, raising her rifle at Carillo. "You never answered Maria's question. Why shouldn't we shoot you?"

Tex realized he needed to defuse this fast. "He came here to warn her father that he might be in danger."

The weapon came down slightly. "Why?"

Carillo looked directly at Maria. "Someone is killing everyone who saw this list your father gave to Sydney Fitzpatrick. They're after Sydney, and we knew they'd be after your father."

"But my father didn't have this list," Maria said. "He gave it to this Sydney Fitzpatrick."

"Maybe they thought he had a copy."

The girl looked at the older woman, her mouth parting as though she wanted to say something, but the woman shook her head, saying, "Senor Venegas. Maria's daughter . . ."

"Senora. I do not yet know your name."

"Lucia."

"Lucia. As I said, safe. A couple found her on the beach. The child had a cell phone in her pocket belonging to Senor Orozco with a text telling whoever found her to contact me. That is how I was notified."

"Why would he ask that you be contacted? As I understood it, he had an eminent distrust of law enforcement."

"Because I had called to warn him of the danger, after Senor Carillo called to let me know. So you see, we *are* here to help. That has always been our intent."

"I remember the call," Maria said. "He thought there would be more time . . . When can I see her? My Rosa. When can I get her back?"

"Soon," Venegas said. "As soon as we know it is safe for

you and for her. But if you could, *por favor*, help us in this, our questions. Do you know who they were? These men who killed your family?"

Maria shook her head. "But I remember after the FBI agent came. I heard my father talking to my mother once about *la llave del diablo*. He said it was the key to banks, to corporations, to everything, but one had to know the secret."

"What secret?"

"I don't know. He never said. But what he wrote on the back of the card, my mother said was important." She slipped her hand in her pocket, and pulled out a worn business card, then, turning it over read, "The Devil's Key. RC has 112."

25

Venice, Italy

A few days ago, if anyone had told Piper that she'd be staying in a convent called the Piccole Ancelle del Rio near the Academia in Venice, she would have said they were high on drugs. And yet here she was, minus the body piercings and pink hair, dressed like a novitiate, and very much enjoying her work in the kitchen, helping the sisters clean up and then prepare the mother superior's late night tea. Although it was her first day, the good sisters had willingly taken her in and put her right to work. Life here was so different from anything she'd ever known, and she was excited about learning all she could of the order. She couldn't wait for morning, if only because Sister Anna promised her that there was nothing more beautiful than the daylight pouring in through the pointed Moorish arches of the tall, fourteenth-century windows.

Peace had surrounded her when she first heard the pealing of the bells from Santa Maria della Salute, the white-domed basilica that she'd caught a glimpse of on her boat ride into

Venice. She'd closed her eyes, listening to the mournful cries of the terns, and the endless lapping of the water against the ancient bricks of the convent, which was located behind high walls, well off the beaten tourist track. And although Piper wished she could stay longer, perhaps see something more of Venice, she was told that Lisette and Marc were already on their way to pick her up.

Tonight, though, she could pretend for a short while that she'd always lived here, and nothing bad had ever happened. At least that's what she thought until she looked out the window at the mists rising from the blackened waters of the *rio*. The shadowed kitchen became a less pleasant refuge, and she turned away from the darkened windows, hoping to find comfort in the story Sister Anna was relating about her trip this evening with Sister Teresa. But Sister Anna's story caught her off guard, and she wrapped her mind around the details, becoming more disturbed.

Something about a strange man asking Sister Teresa for directions to the nearest church so he could light a candle. "It was certainly odd," Sister Anna said, wiping the tea tray with a linen towel.

Piper told herself there was nothing to worry about. She was safe here. With the exception of the mother superior, no one knew why she was here, not even the sisters. Sister Anna had misunderstood the situation, she thought, as she pulled the kettle from the burner, then poured the boiling water into the warmed teapot, the scent of chamomile rising up with the steam. "Why would a man asking directions to the church be odd?"

"Because of where we were when the conversation took place. Our church is . . . How do you say it in your country? Off the beaten path?"

The wail of a cat about to fight startled Piper. She glanced toward the door that led into the courtyard, relaxing when she saw it securely locked. Giustino had assured her that he'd hidden other witnesses here, and they'd been perfectly safe.

"If you ask me," Sister Anna continued, unfazed by the disturbance, "he did not look like someone who seemed concerned about lighting a candle in any church. In fact, the only thing remotely religious about him was on one of his work boots. A cross-shaped cut in the toe. You could see the reinforced steel right through it. I noticed it when he dropped his map."

"Cross-shaped?" Piper thought about what Mother Superior would expect her to say, since she was supposed to be devoting her life to the church—at least as far as the sisters knew. "God works in mysterious ways." Replacing the kettle on top of the large, black, old-fashioned stove, she watched while Sister Anna dusted off a teacup and saucer with a tea towel, adding them to the tray. "Did Sister Teresa say anything to him?"

"She directed him to a different church closer to the *vaporetto* stop. But something made me turn around, and when I did, I saw him going the exact opposite direction. And then Sister Teresa saw him again later, talking with someone else."

"Do you think he was looking for anyone here?" Piper asked, that knot of fear returning.

"I don't know why he would be. Our order is not very well-known." Sister Anna placed a cloth napkin on the tray, then looked up at Piper. "Even so, I should probably mention this to Mother Superior. I'm only hesitant because she's been on edge these days, ever since the Vatican sent notice that they intend to close the convent. It's the only home she's known for at least five decades, and the tension I see in her face concerns me."

Sister Anna picked up the tray, and Piper held the door for her, trying not to worry. Together they walked out, their footsteps echoing across the marble paving stones down the dark hall, their only guiding light that which spilled out of Mother Superior's open office door at the far end. Everyone else had retired for the night, and the convent was quiet, still peaceful. Not that the late hour mattered to Piper. If not for the mother superior agreeing to take her in, who knew where Piper would be staying, and she shivered at the thought, only then realizing as they neared her office just how cold it was. Far colder than the drafty convent should be, she thought, stepping across the threshold.

The first thing Piper noticed was the open window, and then Mother Superior standing to one side of her desk, instead of seated behind it. The elderly nun looked over at her, her voice sharp as she spoke to Sister Anna, surprisingly in Italian. "*Cosa state facendo qui? Non voglio essere disturbata.*"

Piper hesitated, suddenly uncertain of her place. The mother superior had seemed so accommodating when they'd spoken earlier in the day, and her English was excellent, as was Sister Anna's. But then she remembered what Sister Anna had told her, that the mother superior was under a great deal of stress due to the ordered closing of the convent.

"*Madre, abbiamo portato del té,*" Sister Anna said, placing the teapot on the desk. Then she started toward the open window, saying, "*Almeno lasciatemi chiudere la finestra. O vi prenderete un malanno—*"

"*Lasciatemi* immediatamente *e chiudete la porta!*"

Her harshness startled Piper. She stopped where she was in the doorway, having no idea what the mother superior was saying, but there was no mistaking her tone. Sister Anna's eyes widened, then she whirled from the room. Piper grasped the doorknob, and in the flash of time it took to pull closed the door, she saw the scuffed black leather boots in the shadows behind it.

And on one toe, the cut shaped like a cross clear through to the metal.

The oaken door clicked shut. Sister Anna was already down the hallway, and Piper hurried to catch up to her, taking her hand and pulling her into the kitchen. The moment they entered, Piper grabbed the first thing she reached, a cast-iron skillet.

"What on earth—"

"Call the police, Sister Anna. The man at the *vaporetto* stop. I saw his boot. He's hiding in Mother Superior's office."

Piper was not about to let these kind women suffer because of her presence, and she started down the hall, stepping softly, until she heard a loud crash inside the office. She ran, threw open the door, then stood there, wielding the skillet with both hands, searching the room. At first she saw nothing but the broken shards of the teapot on the floor in front of the desk, the tea splattered across the tiles. And then on the other side of the desk, the man hovering over something on the floor. Mother Superior, she realized. Her eyes were closed and she was bleeding from her head. Piper raised the skillet. "Leave her alone!"

He looked up at Piper, his gaze widening. "*L'Americana!*"

He dove at her. She swung the skillet, but he ripped it from her grasp. The heavy iron pan flew to the ground, striking the terra-cotta floor. Piper scrambled for the door, but he grabbed her arm, pulled her into the hallway.

"Sister! Hel—"

"*Silenzio!*" He clamped his hand over her mouth and dragged her out into the night.

26

Washington, D.C.

McNiel's warning lingered in Griffin's mind long after he left the facility, then met up with Donovan that evening at the coffee house that they were now using as their pseudo base. Donovan was waiting at a back table when Griffin arrived, and a waitress immediately appeared, poured him a coffee, then left. He was just about to brief Donovan on his conversation with McNiel when his cell phone vibrated in his pocket. When he saw the number on the screen, then calculated the time in Italy, midnight, a feeling of dread swept through him. "Giustino," he told Donovan, then answered it.

"I have some bad news," Giustino said. "The girl was kidnapped."

"What happened?"

"I'm not sure yet," he said. "I had only just arrived back in Rome when I received the call that someone had taken her. So count in flying time to Venice, it will be at least a couple hours before I know more. Dumas is on his way as well. What I can tell you is this: Someone broke into the convent.

They knew she was there. Knew right where to look for her. I do not yet have the details, but the local police are searching for her even as we speak."

"Do Lisette and Marc know yet?"

"Yes. Their flight from Heathrow unfortunately is delayed."

"Keep me informed." Once he disconnected, he updated Donovan on what had transpired.

"Talk about going to hell in a handbasket," Donovan said. "McNiel's sacrificing himself for the kid, but someone got her anyway?"

"Let's hope that Lisette and Marc get there in time to find her. In the meantime, we have a major issue here." Griffin informed him about the files and the hard drive McNiel had to leave behind in the office.

"Great," Donovan said. "You realize the security in that building is designed to keep spies like us out? And in case that's not enough, they've also manned the building with armed federal guards. One's stationed inside the lobby. He met me the moment I came out, so I have to assume he's working in the control room, watching the monitors."

"It's going to take more than the two of us to bypass that system if we have any hope of getting in there," Griffin said. "And that's assuming we can even figure out how to bypass our own alarm system—and hope they haven't thought about recovering the hard drive from the copy machine."

"What about Fitzpatrick? We can trust her."

"Pretty sure I've worn out my welcome."

"Hate to say it, but you're going to need to suck up bigtime and beg. We don't have a lot of choices, because the two of us can't do this alone, and we don't have enough time to wait for Tex to fly in from Mexico. We need a third person. It's tonight or not at all."

Of course, he was right. Griffin was going to have to ask Sydney for help.

The worst she could do was say no. Then again, as Carillo had warned him, she did carry a gun . . .

"You're the *last* person I expected to see on my doorstep," Sydney said, as she met him outside the lobby of her building. Griffin had a feeling that if he'd actually shown up on her doorstep, as it were, she would never have opened the door, which was why he had called her and asked her to meet him here.

"I know. I didn't want things to turn out this way."

"What is it you need this time?"

"Your help."

"*My* help?" she asked, her voice filled with sarcasm. "I've definitely given my fair share these past few months. Find someone else."

"We're in trouble."

"Hard to imagine why." She turned and started walking toward the glass doors.

He followed. "The Senate is about to take a vote on shutting us down and McNiel's close to being taken into custody on contempt charges."

"Probably with good reason," she said, not bothering to stop. "A few too many illegal search and seizures."

"Look," he said, catching up to her, walking by her side. "I wanted to tell you about what happened in Mexico."

"*Wanted* to tell me? While I appreciate that you let me live, the polite thing to do when someone has a kill order out on them, even if it was rescinded, is to mention it *before* you start dating."

"Will you stop and listen to me for a minute?"

She rounded on him, and he could see the tumult of emotions in her eyes. "Leave. Me. Alone. I have paid my dues. I don't owe you or ATLAS a thing. And frankly, if they shut you down, they have my blessing."

"Piper's been kidnapped. Half the government wants to kill her, the other half use her for what she's seen."

The anger in her eyes was replaced by a moment of worry, indecision, then wariness. "I thought she was going into witness protection?"

"So did we. Long story short, the sketch you did with Piper? She saw him on TV. It's Parker Kane."

Sydney stared in disbelief at Griffin. "You expect me to believe that the man responsible for that murder in South San Francisco is Parker Kane? The about-to-be deputy national security adviser?"

"You did the drawing. You have to realize it looks just like him."

"It also looks like hundreds of other gray-haired fifty-year-old men. Those drawings aren't supposed to be used for identification. They're a tool to *eliminate* suspects."

"And we can't eliminate him based on what you drew."

"Neither can we eliminate Harcourt, my gray-haired fiftysomething-year-old boss based on *that* theory."

"She pointed him out on the TV. The sound was off. She didn't even know who he was."

Sydney pulled her coat tighter, as though the chill in the air was suddenly getting to her. "Kane is too high on the food chain to be showing up at some murder scene, don't you think? Especially one all the way across the nation."

"Normally, I'd agree with you, but in this case, I think he was there to make sure he got his hands on those numbers the moment they were found. We assume he's behind the kidnap as well."

"The numbers? The list *I* recovered from Mexico?"

"Yes. What you recovered is the key to unlock a program designed to spy on computer systems and Internet traffic. I don't know if Kane's been running some prototype of that program to monitor our every move, or if he has somehow gotten access to our computers. Either way, the same people who were in South San Francisco knew where we had Piper and that witness protection was supposed to be coming for her."

"Does this have something to do with Wingman and Wingman?"

"I don't know of any connection between Kane and W2 yet, but then we've never looked before now."

She stared at him for several seconds as though warring with her sense of self-preservation versus her sense of duty. "What is it you want from me?"

"Put your leads with mine."

"You took my leads. Or Pearson did."

"You're saying you have done nothing since the search of your apartment? Somehow I doubt that."

"In case you've forgotten, I've had a few things on my plate since then. Like *who* was searching my apartment."

"I swear it wasn't us. But that's why McNiel and Pearson were so upset when they discovered you were looking into the matter. The people we've been investigating are dangerous."

"A little clarity would have been nice."

"So if they'd told you that you'd end up dead like everyone else, you would have backed off? Because it's never stopped you before. At least not as long as I've known you."

"Point taken. But if Pearson and McNiel have failed with the resources available to them, what is it you expect I'll be able to do?"

"A fresh perspective, I hope. I have the collection of McNiel's notes on the W2 investigation over the years."

"You're actually going to let *me* see them?"

"With a slight catch. They're currently located behind the copy machine in the office. McNiel was attempting to remove the hard drive when the building was taken over. We need to recover that as well, and we're a bit short-handed."

And just when he thought she was going to decline, she said, "Fine. Let me get a few things from my apartment. How hard can it be?"

Apparently a lot harder than any of them had anticipated, at least according to Donovan, when she met up with him and Griffin at the coffee shop. The place had a vast dining room, and they were able to sit well away from the few patrons present, allowing them much-needed privacy. "It's like Griffin said," Donovan told her. "One guard inside, one outside. I didn't go around the rear, but I'd hazard a guess there's one or two there, too. What I did do was play dumb, and ask if I could go in and get the extra set of keys to my apartment. Frankly I was surprised they actually let me in."

Griffin picked up his coffee cup from the table. "I would've locked the doors the moment I saw you drive in the parking lot."

"Trust me," Donovan said. "It wasn't like they welcomed me with open arms. They escorted me the entire time. There is nothing going in or out that they're not watching. Reception area's deserted and there's a 'Closed' sign on the front door. The guard on the inside? He's monitoring the cameras and the security system."

"How'd you find that out?" Griffin asked.

"Because I made them think I left the keys in the security room. By the way," he said, holding up the key ring, "we now have the extra set to the surveillance van."

"A slim bit of good news." Griffin eyed his bagel, then pushed it away, having lost his appetite. "We need that file. Somehow we have to get in there."

"Can't you bypass the alarm?" Sydney asked. "God knows I've seen you do it on other buildings."

"It's not that easy here. We designed it specifically to avoid people like us getting in. We just never counted that our own government was going to be the one we were worried about."

"Actually," Donovan said, "there is a way. We can circumvent the video feed from the underground access."

"Video, yes," Griffin replied. "But not the alarm. We set them up on two different systems. For that very reason."

Donovan swirled the ice in his water glass, then lifted it in a mock toast. "But what if someone had too much to drink and caused a disturbance out front? An incident where, say, the inside guard came out?"

"One," Griffin said, "you're not drinking alcohol."

"An oversight on my part. That can be changed."

"Two, how are we going to know exactly when that disturbance is taking place and the guard exits? We're not going to have radio communication down in the tunnels, and we don't have phone communication inside. It's all blocked."

"Can't you unblock it?" Sydney asked.

"Jammer's in the security room," Griffin answered. "And I don't know about you, but hacking into that system from an external computer is beyond my abilities."

"You're pretty picky for someone who's desperate," Donovan said. "Why can't we just get Pete from IT? He could tap into the computer system for us, and handle everything."

"We contact him, we might as well hang out a red flag and alert them of our impending arrival. *And* he's a civilian."

"There's Izzy," Sydney said.

Izzy was a college-age kid with a knack for hacking beyond anything Griffin had ever seen. He'd assisted on the last case ATLAS had worked and was now running his own computer security company, and, thanks to a few recommendations from Tex and Carillo, was doing a fairly brisk business. "Another civilian. Too dangerous."

"Too bad," Donovan said. "He'd be a good choice. They're watching *our* IT guys. He's not even on their radar."

"Do we have a choice?" Sydney asked. "Who else can do what he does?"

"Exactly," Donovan said. "We need him."

They were right. They didn't have a choice, and Izzy at least was familiar with how they worked. "Call," Griffin said.

Twenty minutes later, Izzy met them at the grill. Griffin told him their mission.

"That's it?" Izzy asked. "I thought this was going to be something complicated. What is it you need? Video feed? Something that makes them think no one's in there when someone is?"

"You sure you can do all that?"

Izzy made a scoffing noise. "We're wasting valuable time, because I've got some firewalls to get through, and last time I was at your office, helping secure it from guys like me, we were installing some pretty mean security systems."

"I have remote access to my own computer, if that helps," Griffin said.

"See? I told your boss not to allow that. No one listens to me!"

"How fast can you get us in?"

"Anytime you're ready."

27

Lisette still felt nauseous over the news about Piper
after Giustino had called them during their stopover and significant delay at Heathrow. And now, as they stood in line
at customs, she began what-if scenarios. What if she had
insisted on giving Piper money and noticed her wallet missing sooner? What if she'd asked the alleged U.S. marshals
who had taken Piper for alternate forms of ID? What if their
plane hadn't been delayed due to weather? What if she'd
been able to answer Piper's voice mail? Piper had called Lisette's cell phone and left a message while they were on the
flight over, just to say she was safe and she was sorry. And
even though Lisette knew there was no way she could have
done anything, even if she had been there to answer it, the
guilt refused to go away.

Lisette leaned her head on Marc's shoulder. "She was
supposed to be safe . . . If our flight had not been delayed,
maybe—"

"It does us no good to second-guess."

"I know. It just helps to talk."

When they finally cleared customs, she was grateful to see Father Dumas waiting for them, and she searched his face, hoping for good news. "Have they found her?"

"Not yet," he said. He offered to take her bag for her, but she declined, thinking that it somehow seemed sacrilegious to have a priest playing bellhop, even if he was a spy.

"And Giustino?" Marc asked Dumas. "What has he said?"

"That the more time that passes without a lead . . ." He took a deep breath, let it out slowly. "I fear this is my fault. We have used this convent before. It should have been safe."

Marc reached out, put his hand on Dumas's shoulder as they walked toward the exit. "You are not to blame. None of us could have foreseen that she would fly to this country, or end up in Venice of all places."

"Agreed. But it concerns me how easily they found her. How quickly. As if they already had men in the country in anticipation."

"They probably did," Marc replied. "It is possible they have been monitoring our electronic traffic. They may have discovered our inquiry at Homeland Security under her name, then discovered Lisette's itinerary and, knowing Lisette was still in the U.S., made the proper deduction."

"Or," Lisette said, "they ran it before we did and were able to get a head start."

"Perhaps," Dumas said. "But how could they have made the connection to the convent?"

A question none of them could answer. They stepped outside, the cold brisk air temporarily reviving Lisette, but instead of walking toward the car park, Dumas directed them the opposite way.

"We're not driving?" she asked.

"No," Dumas said. "They may be watching the roads. Giustino is also worried about their seemingly prescient knowledge of all we are doing. Easier to slip into Venezia this way."

The walk to the pier took about ten minutes, and then he guided them onto a sleek watercraft, its wood gleaming beneath the lamplight.

"Extravagant," she said. "Surely not the pope's dime?"

"Giustino's cousin's fleet. The pope would have insisted on the car."

She climbed into the boat, sat next to Marc, and as it took off, the long day seemed to hit her. Yawning, she turned to Marc. "Wake me when La Serenissima comes into view. I love Venice at night."

He smiled, and in what seemed no time at all, she felt him gently shaking her awake as the boat slowed through the Arsenale Canal, then turned into the black waters of the lagoon. To her right were the bright lights of the bustling Piazza San Marco. Ahead to her left, a full moon, veiled by a thin mist, shone down onto two gleaming domes of the great white church of Santa Maria della Salute. On the opposite bank of the Grand Canal, the arched windows of great palaces lit the night in a golden blaze, their reflections shattering into myriad lights that danced across the dark water. "Where's a camera when you need one?" was all she could think to say.

"Photographs are wondrous things," Dumas said. "But they cannot replace the actual experience of seeing Venezia."

The boat pulled up past the La Salute, bobbing as the driver moored it to the dock. Dumas exited, then spoke to the driver, his Italian almost too fast for Lisette to keep up with. Marc helped Lisette disembark, and a moment later, the boat sped off, leaving them alone. Dumas led them down a dark *rio terra*. Their footsteps echoed down the filled-in canal as they approached a covered alley that opened up on to a very old building with arched windows on the edge of a small canal. A lantern with a bottled-glass shade shone on plaster that was peeling away from the ancient brick. "One of our convents that is now a bed-and-breakfast," Dumas said. "This one is from the thirteenth century, but you will find that we have modernized it in respect to the plumbing."

Marc smiled, since he well knew Lisette's preference for the modern amenities in life. "What more can a girl want?" he asked.

And Lisette replied, "A good cup of coffee come morning for when we begin our search?"

Father Dumas rang the bell on the front door, painted green, and it was opened shortly thereafter by a nun in a traditional black habit. She smiled. "Don Emilio, you have brought our guests."

"Honored ones, to be sure." He turned to Lisette and Marc. "I leave you in Suor Rosanna's very capable hands. I shall call for you both in the morning when Giustino arrives. Like you, he will be getting some much-needed rest tonight. It has been a long day for all of us."

He left. The sister held the door open for them, and they stepped into a small lobby, with a bare checkerboard floor of brown and white tiles. The nun led them down a long carpeted hall and unlocked an old-fashioned wooden door on the right, holding it open, indicating that the room was for Lisette, and that Marc's was down the hall. Lisette bid him good night, then entered the charming but sparely furnished room with two narrow beds, separated by a small table and a lamp. A crucifix on the wall above was intended to protect both occupants, had there been two. The only other furniture was a desk, a chair, and an old dresser topped by an even older mirror. As Lisette placed her bag on the chair, Sister Rosanna said, "The bathroom and *doccia* are through this door," and Lisette could see a gleaming tiled bathroom, very modern as promised by Father Dumas.

"Will you need anything else before I leave?"

"No, thank you."

She handed Lisette a key, saying, *"La piccola colazione—* the breakfast—is served between seven and nine-thirty."

"Grazie," said Lisette.

"Prego, signorina. Buona notte!"

"Good night, Sister."

Dead tired, Lisette dug out her toothbrush and toothpaste, nightshirt, and hit the bed in short order. Lulled by the lapping water that filtered in from behind the two curved arch windows, she slept soundly until the bedside phone rang.

She opened her eyes, disoriented by the unfamiliar surroundings, then reached for the phone, saying, "Perrault," belatedly realizing she wasn't at home, and it probably wasn't ATLAS calling.

A man's voice answered: *"Pronto, signorina."* It took her a second more to place her surroundings as he continued. "Father Dumas, he asks us to inform you that he will be here within the hour."

"Grazie."

She looked at the clock and saw it wasn't even five in the morning. Clearly something had happened for him to be waking them this early. Good news, she hoped. Forty minutes later she had showered, dressed, and was about to wander downstairs in search of Marc, when the clerk rang to inform her that Dumas had arrived. "I hope your room was sufficient?" Dumas asked, when she met him in the lobby.

"It was," she answered. "Who would guess that such a charming bed-and-breakfast is hidden behind the convent walls?"

"It helps pay the bills," he said, as Marc came down the stairs. And then one of the sisters came out, carrying a paper sack, followed by another with three paper cups of coffee with plastic lids. They handed them each a coffee, and Dumas the paper sack. *"Grazie,"* he said to the sisters. Then, to Marc and Lisette, "The good sisters have made us a few sandwiches. I hope you don't mind if we eat on the way, as we are in somewhat of a hurry."

"What happened?" Lisette asked, noting the tension in his face.

"Giustino has informed me that they have located the body of a young girl. She was found in the canal not too far from the convent where she was staying."

"The hair— They would know from that."

"Ah, but it is brown now. The sisters, they— I'm afraid you must make the identification."

28

Washington, D.C.

Sydney listened while Griffin went over the plan one
last time. Once Izzy disabled the jamming device covering
the ATLAS floors, they could communicate via cell phone
conference call and their Bluetooth earpieces. He would
also disable the landlines so if they were caught, the guards
couldn't use the landlines and call for help. It would at least
buy them some extra time.

Unfortunately, the enhanced security alarm to the ATLAS
floors was not connected to the same system. "It's a two-
step process," Izzy had said. "Someone needs to give me
the codes as they come up. If someone tries to bypass it and
gets a code wrong, that system's shutting down, the alarm's
going off, and I'm guessing they'll send the cavalry in. Or at
the very least, the goons they have guarding your building."

"How many codes are there?" Sydney asked.

"One for each floor," Griffin said. "I'll have to give them
to Izzy as they come up."

"Perfect," Izzy said. "That'll allow us to get someone into

the building via the tunnel entrance, once I override the video feed so they can't see."

Sydney picked up the sheet they'd mapped everything on. "One problem, guys," she said. "If Griffin's busy in the surveillance van helping Izzy with all the access codes, and Donovan's out front creating a distraction, *who* is going into the building?"

"You are," Griffin said.

"What happens if I get caught?"

"Assuming they don't shoot you?" Donovan replied. "You'll probably end up in a jail cell next to McNiel."

"Oh good. No worries then." She slid the map across the table. "Your plan sucks. Think of a new one."

"We don't have time," Griffin said. "We need to get that info if we want to get to the bottom of this investigation. It reaches far too high to just let matters be, and I, for one, do not want to work for Parker Kane."

Donovan laughed. "You really think he's going to let any of us *live* much less work for him once he gets ahold of those files? We're all a liability, and slowly but surely we'll either find ourselves in prison or dead. Just like every other person who's tried to investigate W2 and the theft of the Devil's Key. And that," he said, looking right at Sydney, "includes you. Because like it or not, your name is high on the list of people having been caught looking into it."

"This is why I don't like working with your group. Once again, I'm on a government hit list."

"If it makes you feel any better," Donovan said, "it was a national security threat list. There's a big difference."

"I'm sorry. How many bullet holes were in the hull of that boat I was driving?"

Griffin cleared his throat, clearly uncomfortable with the topic. "Can we move on before they get a chance to *act* on that list?"

She picked up her coffee cup, raised it in a mock toast. "Carry on."

Griffin and Donovan finalized what it was they'd be doing, and what she needed to do. They coordinated their watches and their phones. Everything hinged on them making their moves at the precise moment when Izzy gave the word. Sydney would have approximately three minutes to get up on McNiel's floor. Then she'd have that long to recover the files, then the hard drive from the copy machine.

Izzy accessed a blow-up of the copy machine from his laptop to show Sydney what it was she needed to do. "Fairly straightforward," he said, showing her where the panel was, and then the hard drive beneath that.

It looked easy enough, she thought as Griffin handed her a folding knife with a tool to loosen the screws on the plate securing the hard drive to the copy machine. She glanced at the schematic again. "One question," she said, slipping the knife into her pocket. "If we remove the hard drive, and you don't want anyone to know we were up there, won't it cause suspicion if they go looking for it and can't find it?"

"Yesterday, that would have been true. Today, I think it's a bit late to keep them from being suspicious. What we don't want is for them to have it. Or to know how much we know."

"And exactly how much do we know?" Donovan asked.

"Not enough. Otherwise it wouldn't have taken twenty years to find out Parker Kane was involved."

They waited until precisely twenty minutes after the hour, which was when Donovan said he would be making his approach. Griffin was in the surveillance van with Izzy and she had entered via the tunnels and was waiting by the elevator. "Now," Izzy called out.

She pressed the elevator button, then used the access code to get up to the second floor, which was as far as the elevator would go when the building was in lockdown mode. From there she was supposed to take the stairs. Each door would have to be accessed separately with a different code, which Griffin called to Izzy as Sydney announced her location.

"I'm at the stairs. Code?"

Griffin recited it. She heard a beep, pushed the door open.

"You have four minutes," Griffin told her.

That was one more than she'd been expecting. "Copy."

About one minute into it, she heard Izzy saying, "I've got access to the surveillance video inside on the first floor. You might want to go faster. I see them looking at the elevator . . . The inside guard's walking that way . . . He's in . . . looking inside . . . down the hall."

"Thanks, Izzy. I get it."

"Yeah, well now he's going to his room, and I really need you to hurry, because . . . ah crap."

"Ah crap, what?"

"In about a minute, I'm going to have to cut the power, because he's checking the feed to get up on that floor, and I really don't want him to see you."

"I'm there."

Sydney raced up the stairs to McNiel's floor, waited for Griffin to give the code, Izzy to unlock it, then pushed the door open. The copy machine was at the end of the hall, and she hurried toward it, removing the knife from her pocket as she approached. She rolled the machine away from the wall, found the accordion folder, then set it on top. The hard drive was all that was left, and she pushed the door, and had just started to loosen the first screw when the power went out.

"You have two minutes."

"Lights would have helped," she muttered, reaching up, feeling with her finger for the other screw. That one she got out. The third and fourth, not so easy, and she used the light of her cell phone to find the screw head.

"We're out of time. The power's going on. We're going out of lockdown mode and I'm sending the elevator up."

"I don't have the hard drive yet."

"You need to get out. If we run out of time, I'm not going to be able to get you down to the tunnels."

"What's more important. Recovering it or making sure they don't get it?"

She heard Griffin say, "The latter."

She got up, drew her weapon, and fired two shots at it. "No more hard drive."

"What the hell?" someone said. She couldn't tell who, her ears were ringing.

Then Izzy saying, "Get out of there."

She grabbed the files, ran down the hall, got onto the elevator, and then relaxed when it started down.

The elevator, however, stopped on the first floor. "Why isn't it going to the tunnel?" she asked. "What's wrong?"

"I don't know," Izzy said.

The door opened and she found herself staring into the lobby at the back of a security guard on the inside, and Donovan and a security guard on the outside. Donovan saw her, his momentary surprise as he swung his arms wide, pointing out to the parking lot, attempting to draw their attention that way.

The inside guard suddenly turned toward her. "Hey!"

At the same time, she heard sirens outside, and the strobe of emergency lights, red and blue, flashing in the parking lot.

The guard glanced outside, then back at Sydney as he drew his gun.

"Izzy!" she said, then pressed herself to the side, hoping the guard wouldn't fire.

"Working on it . . ."

She heard the guard's boots stomping across the floor. "Come on, come on . . ."

The doors whooshed shut, and she let out a breath, falling against the side. And then Donovan's voice in her earpiece, saying, "Oh shit."

29

"What the hell is going on?" Griffin asked. Donovan's
last transmission had him worried. He turned to Izzy, who
was clicking away on his keyboard.

"I don't know. I don't show any alarm going off . . ."

"Donovan?" Griffin said. No answer. He got out of the
van, ran across the street and into the parking lot of the *Recorder.*

And then in the background, he heard, "Put your hands up!"

"It's okay," Donovan said, though to whom, Griffin wasn't
sure since he didn't have visual of the front of the building.
"I work here."

"That right?"

"Reporter for the *Washington Recorder.*"

The first thing Griffin saw in the parking lot was the two
black sedans. The foremost one had red emergency lights
flashing. And then he saw Donovan talking to two men
wearing dark suits. One of them turned, saw him. "Keep
your hands where we can see them."

Since they were pointing weapons at Donovan, Griffin
complied. "Is there some problem?"

"Who are you?"

"I work here, too."

"That right?" one of the men said. "We received a call that there was an entry into the building. We're with the federal security." And he pulled his jacket aside, showing Griffin the badge on his belt positioned in front of his holster. The same crew as the uniformed guards.

Interesting, since Izzy had disabled the phone lines. So who called?

"There is someone," the uniformed guard said. "Inside. We saw her. We think they're working together."

"I don't know what you're talking about," Donovan said. "I was just as surprised as you."

"Who is she?" the man in the black suit asked.

"Not sure," Donovan replied. "It was dark."

And the uniformed guard, apparently feeling smug with his coworkers there, said, "These men need to be taken into custody."

"For what?" Griffin replied. "We haven't done anything."

Had they actually been cops, Griffin wouldn't have worried. But the guard was a little overzealous, and then the man in the suit said, "We'll take it from here. Mr. Griffin?" He wasn't surprised they knew his name. He was, however, bothered, especially when the next thing out of the man's mouth was, "You're under arrest for crimes against the federal government."

"What crimes?"

"Do you really want to go into this here? Now?"

He glanced at the guards, and if truth be told, was glad for their presence. "As a matter of fact, I do."

"Turn around, put your hands behind your back. The both of you. And do not reach for your weapons. We'd rather not have to deal with the paperwork from a shooting."

There were four men pointing guns at him and Donovan. The two uniformed guards and the two men in suits. With no choice, Griffin complied. The man grasped Griffin's wrist in a lock, reached beneath his jacket, and took his gun, handing it to the other agent. He cuffed him with a plastic tie, then led him toward one of the sedans, telling the guards they were no longer needed. The second agent cuffed Donovan with one of the ties.

"Where are you taking us?" Donovan asked as Griffin was placed in the backseat of the nearest car.

"Secure lockup."

"An address would be nice. So I can tell our lawyer where to meet us."

The first man placed one hand on the car roof, the other on the door, and leaned in close to Griffin. "Who was the woman inside the building? And what was she doing there?"

"I have no idea."

"You need me to speak a little slower?"

"I can hear you just fine."

"I'm talking about the people on the other end of your phone." He reached toward Griffin's face, pulled out the Bluetooth earpiece, and held it to his mouth. "Deliver the files you took from the building and turn yourself in—save us all the trouble of looking, and keep *anyone* from getting hurt." This last was said with his eye on Griffin.

"I doubt that whoever's on the other end of that phone will answer," Griffin said.

"Maybe this will help." He nodded to the other agent, who walked over to the two uniformed guards, who were both standing outside the glass door.

Which was when Griffin noticed the second agent was still carrying Griffin's gun. He raised it. Shot the first guard in the head, and before the second guard realized what was going on, shot him, too.

The first agent spoke into the Bluetooth, saying, "We'll give you a call when we're ready for a meet and greet so you can bring us those files you stole. In the meantime, we'll leave Mr. Archer here in the parking lot in case there are any questions. And bring a knife. He's going to need help getting out of his cuff ties."

He dropped the Bluetooth onto the ground, smashed it with his foot, then eyed Griffin. "Something to think about. It was *your* gun that killed those guards. Let's hope your friends don't do anything stupid."

And on that point, Griffin agreed.

30

Sydney raced through the tunnels, found the door that led up to the garage access, pressed in the code, unlocked it, then ran up the stairs. Another door to get through. This time, she hit the wrong code.

Last thing she needed was to lock herself out, because in this system, three chances was all you got. She took a breath, pressed in the code, making sure to hit each number separately, carefully, then placed her finger on the fingerprint scanner. It clicked and the door swung open.

The warehouse was empty, and she stood there a moment, trying to catch her breath. She called Donovan. No answer. They'd lost their connection when she was in the elevator, descending into the tunnels. They were supposed to swing by the moment she exited, except no one was counting on the police showing up.

She looked around, wondering how long she should wait. The place was set up to appear as a simple garage repair shop, only one that didn't have customers or cars being repaired. It was used solely as a way to access the ATLAS building without being seen. There were two other vehicles, and after several minutes, when she still couldn't get ahold of Donovan, she started a search for the spare keys.

She couldn't find any, figuring they must be kept at the ATLAS building.

And just when she was considering if she could hot-wire one of the cars, the bay door rumbled, then slowly lifted. The surveillance van was out front, Donovan at the wheel.

She got in, saw Izzy in the back.

"Where's Griffin?" she asked.

"They have him," Donovan said.

"The police—?"

"Not the police. These guys said they were federal guards. Just showed up out of the blue. Had to have been watching the place."

Her gut twisted. "Tell me they're legit?"

"Hope not. They shot the two security guards. And if they are, they're not playing by the rules. They want the files you recovered."

She looked down at the files in her lap. "They want it bad enough, it's got to be worth something. Griffin's life at least."

Donovan asked to see it.

She handed it to him. "There's also the sketch."

"I don't think they know about it. Where's the hard drive?"

"I shot it."

"Works for me." He opened the folder, quickly flipped through the pages. "Damned if I know what's what. McNiel was the keeper of this."

"Guys!" Izzy was still working at his computer. "Griffin's phone's still on. I'm tracking it on GPS."

"Where?" Sydney asked.

He turned the computer screen so she could see it. She was familiar with the area. The navy yard bordered by the Anacostia River was in a perpetual state of reconstruction as the district tried to reclaim the neighborhoods from crime and blight. There were far too many buildings and lots fenced off, allowing for someone to lie in wait as the unsuspecting drove through.

Donovan looked at the screen. "We have to go get him."

"What if it's an ambush?" Sydney asked. "Why else pick that area and just let you go?"

"It probably is. But we can't leave him there."

"We can't just show up. Not without a plan. Don't you have other agents who can come in for this? An extraction team?"

He glanced at her. "In case you haven't noticed, *we* are the extraction team."

"We're outnumbered."

"There's me," Izzy said.

Both Sydney and Donovan looked back at him and at the same time, said, "*No.*"

She glanced at the GPS map where Griffin's phone signal blinked. That area, it had to be a setup. They had to have left Griffin's phone active on purpose. But Donovan was right. What choice did they have? It was Griffin out there, and regardless of their shared history in Mexico, he had saved her life on more than one occasion and at risk to his own.

Donovan handed her the file as he started the van, and she recalled what Griffin had said about it. McNiel had twenty years of notes in there. "We could be handing over the only evidence that proves Kane is Brooks, and we don't even know what it is."

"You better look fast, because we're wasting time."

He backed out, hit the remote for the bay door, and when it was completely shut, drove off, while Sydney looked through the files. She removed the sketch of Parker and shoved it under the seat of the van. A few of the reports she'd seen on Scotty's files, but others she hadn't been aware of. "We'll never get the time to go through these."

"Not a lot we can do about that. Griffin's more important."

"And how do we know they're going to hand him over?"

"We don't." Donovan let out a frustrated breath as he stopped at a red light. "And now that I think about it, I'm pretty sure Griffin wouldn't want you to endanger yourself. He'd kill me if I let anything happen to you."

"Then it's a good thing he's not here to object."

"His phone's stopped moving," Izzy said. "It's been sitting in the same place for several minutes. It must be where they're setting up." He read off the address.

Sydney looked back at the screen, then at Donovan. "What are we going to do with him? It's not like he has a gun and can protect himself."

And Izzy said, "You know, I *can* help. I do have a computer connected to the Internet, so don't write me off yet."

Donovan glanced in his rearview mirror, then suddenly pulled over to the side of the road and into the parking lot of a coffee shop. "Sydney's right. You don't have a gun. And I'd feel a hell of a lot better if you weren't in the van when we make the trade. I hate to say it, but they're likely to put a bullet in our heads. Otherwise, why not just call us out in front of the ATLAS building and get the files there?"

"Which is why you need me," Izzy said.

"And what is it you think you're going to be able to do that we can't?"

"If these guys are government agents like you, except corrupt, they're not gonna want a bunch of civilians like me recording their every move. Sort of a bad publicity thing, wouldn't you say?"

"Which means they wouldn't think twice about putting a bullet in *your* head, Izzy. This isn't negotiable. Get out. We're in a hurry."

"You know," Izzy said. "It wouldn't hurt to think outside of the box every now and then." He grabbed his laptop, then opened the back of the van door. "Just because I'm a geek, doesn't mean I don't have a good idea or two."

"Here's an idea," Donovan said. "Out."

"I'm going." He slammed the door shut and stalked off to the coffee shop.

Sydney almost felt sorry for him. "So we don't get any brownie points for saving his life."

"Yeah, he'll get over it. We might not. I think you should get out, too."

"I might be mad at Griffin, but I owe him my life several times over. I'm not leaving."

He nodded, then took off.

Ten minutes later, they were driving toward the navy yard into a large lot next to a building under construction. The dark lot was surrounded by a chain-link fence with only one entrance, and a security chain was hanging down from the gate and the padlock on the ground. Not a good sign. She looked around, didn't see any cars, only a couple of tractors parked near the building currently under construction, and she wondered if Griffin was in the building, or if someone had simply placed his phone there in order to draw them in.

"There's no way out," Donovan said. "I think we should set up down the street."

And just as he turned the van to leave, two dark-colored sedans pulled in, stopping between them and the gate, effectively blocking their escape. They were completely isolated, and they were now positioned so that Donovan would have to drive around them to get out. Even worse, they could fire off an entire arsenal of rounds and no one would hear it, never mind respond.

She tried to see into the windows of the suspect vehicles, but they were tinted. "You think he's there?"

"Let's hope so. But I'm not liking this setup."

"Maybe we should call the police. At least have a little firepower en route."

"Trust me. I thought of that. But if these guys are working for Kane, they wouldn't hesitate to kill the cops right along with us. Look what they did to the guards. They'll probably use our guns, then kill us and be lauded as heroes for taking out the cop killers. I really don't want that on my shoulders." He looked out the window, was quiet a moment, then, after a deep breath, said, "I don't want your death on my conscience, either. Take the driver's seat. They want that folder, they don't get it until we know he's okay. If they don't have it, or anything happens to me, *you* drive the hell out of here."

"I'm not leaving you."

"If you're dead, who's going to bring us justice?"

"We'll discuss that after you bring Griffin home. Go."

He took the folder, then stepped out. She slipped into the driver's seat, drew her gun, and set it on her lap, rolled down the windows on both sides, then watched, her heart seeming to thump with every step Donovan took toward the two cars. He stopped about twenty-five yards away, and called out, his voice echoing off the abandoned buildings surrounding them.

"I've got the files. You don't get them until I get Griffin."

At first there was no response.

Then the passenger door on each car opened, and two men got out, one wearing a dark suit, the other in a leather jacket. The man in the suit nodded, and the other walked to the back of his car, opened the door, and Griffin stepped out, his hands secured behind his back.

She breathed a sigh of relief, and Donovan said, "Release him, and you get the files."

"Files first. We'd like to verify what's in it."

"How about you cut those plastic ties off his hands, send him this way."

"Tell you what. You're all fired up to get him back, you bring the folder, we'll send him your way. Nice and slow. Even trade. You do anything stupid, your friend gets a bullet in his back, you get one in your front, and we get the folder. Hand it over, your odds of leaving in one piece go up. And in case you've picked up a new weapon, leave it behind."

"Go!" Griffin yelled. "Don't do it!"

She saw Donovan's chest expand as he took a deep, calming breath, gathering his courage. Then, "Deal."

He returned to the van, opened up the sliding side door, reached beneath his jacket, pulled out his weapon, and set it on the floor of the vehicle. She wanted to yell at him to stop, that they couldn't be believed, but she knew he knew. And if truth be told, she wanted Griffin this side of that line. But not at the expense of Donovan's life. Because if Griffin was warning him off, it was with good reason.

The choice was made when the man holding Griffin pushed him. Still cuffed, he stumbled forward, nearly losing his balance. When he straightened, Donovan was walking toward them, holding out the file folder.

Her gut clenched. They had no way out of here.

"Toss it," the agent asked.

Donovan did as asked.

The agent raised his gun. Fired.

Donovan went stumbling back, then fell to the ground.

31

Shock, then adrenaline flooded through Sydney's veins, and her heart thudded triple time at the sight of Griffin in the middle of the parking lot as the gunman took aim.

She shifted into gear, stabbed at the gas pedal, then laid on the horn, driving straight toward them. Anything to cause a distraction, take their focus off Griffin and Donovan.

And just when she was wondering how the hell she could get Griffin, still handcuffed, into the van, then get Donovan and somehow get past the gunmen to exit the parking lot, the headlights of a car pulled behind the two sedans, silhouetting the gunmen. Several more cars followed. The gunmen turned to see who was entering, their attention diverted.

She didn't stop to look, instead driving between them and Donovan. And then through the open window, she heard the deep bass of a stereo shaking the air, and someone yelling, "Par-tay!" and then the flash of cell phone cameras.

Horns started honking as more cars poured into the lot, and in a matter of seconds it was nothing but people yelling, music playing, red plastic cups being tossed, and beer flying.

The gunmen seemed to falter as the area grew more crowded. And then Griffin was at her window. "Knife!" he yelled.

She jumped out of the van, dug the knife from her pocket, cut the plastic tie around his wrists.

"Get ready," he told her. "I'm going back for Donovan."

She nodded, climbed into the driver's seat, putting the van into gear, her foot on the brake. A moment later, Griffin was there, dragging Donovan into the van, and before he could even close the door, he was yelling at her to leave.

She slammed her foot on the gas pedal and gunned it straight toward the exit. Papers from the folder were flying across the lot beneath the tires of vehicles filled with kids and lighted cell phones as they snapped pictures of anyone and everyone, and she glimpsed the gunmen scrambling for the papers. She didn't slow until she was certain they weren't being followed, and even then she didn't stop, making sure they were well away from the area.

"Donnie boy," Griffin said. "Come on . . ."

She glanced in the rearview mirror, saw him leaning over Donovan.

"How bad is it?" she asked.

"Hit his shock plate."

"He was wearing a vest?"

Donovan moaned. "It hurts to breathe."

"Probably bruised a couple ribs," Griffin said. "And one killer lump on his head where he hit the ground."

"Oh my God," Sydney said, leaning back in her seat, feeling as if she could barely breathe herself. "How okay is he? Hospital?"

"He's fine," Griffin said.

And then Donovan, saying, "Hell. We need to get Izzy."

Sydney made a U-turn at the next signal, glancing over at Griffin when they stopped in traffic. "How are you?"

"Considering I thought we were all dead? Ecstatic. Definitely better than the guards. What the hell happened back there? Where'd all those cars come from?"

"Honestly?" Donovan said. "I don't have a clue. But thank God they arrived when they did."

"Oh no . . ." Sydney said, looking back at them. "You don't think . . . Izzy?"

Donovan laughed, then grabbed on to his chest.

She pulled into the coffee shop lot, and through the plate-glass window, they saw Izzy sitting at a table, a tall coffee in front of him as he worked away at his laptop, one foot bouncing as though he were fueled by way too much caffeine. When he noticed them, he closed the laptop and hurried out. "You're back."

Griffin opened the rear door to let him in. "Don't suppose you had anything to do with that interesting showing out there?"

He grinned. "Might've sent word that there was a wild party and the first hundred people to show would get free beer."

"That was extremely dangerous," Donovan said in a stern voice. "So don't do it again. But damn." He reached out, gave him a slight punch in the shoulder. "You saved our lives."

"So where we going?" Izzy asked.

"Good question," Griffin replied. "Whoever they were, they knew exactly where we were going and what we were doing."

"Which means," Donovan added, "someone's either very intuitive, or they've got a pulse on our actions *and* conversations."

"Guys . . ."

Everyone turned to hear what Izzy had to say.

"If they are government agents, they've probably got all the bells and whistles you guys do. Which means, cell phones? Any one of yours could now be a listening device. It's not like they don't know who you are."

To which they all promptly removed their batteries.

"We need a place to regroup," Griffin said.

"Where?" Donovan asked. "When they know every place we live? They have Lisette's home down, definitely Sydney's."

She didn't even want to think about going back there. "What about Scotty?"

"If anyone's associated with us," Griffin told her, "they're going to have them on their radar."

"I have one possibility," Sydney said. "A weekend retreat at a bed-and-breakfast that Scotty gave me. It was some promotional thing he won, which means it's not connected to the Internet in his name. Maybe they'll reconsider and take us on a weekday."

"One room?" Donovan said. "For all of us?"

"If you think of a better idea, let me know."

"Actually," Griffin said, "it could work. Small establishment like that makes it easier to stay off the grid."

"So what do we do? Just show up?"

"Unless someone's got a cell phone that they can guarantee isn't compromised."

"I do," Izzy said.

He handed it to Sydney. She made the call, hoping there'd be a room open, since she hadn't confirmed the reservation. She made up a story to the proprietor about a family reunion that lasted longer than they thought.

"You're in luck. Winter isn't exactly bustling. What was the name?"

"Scott Ryan."

"Of course. And your name?"

"Sydney Fitzpatrick."

"When might we expect you, Ms. Fitzpatrick?"

"I'm not sure. I have a few errands to run. But tonight."

"We'll have the room ready for you."

"Any chance you have another? I have friends who are interested."

"I do, but there will be a charge. It's not included in the promotional offer."

"That's okay. You do accept cash?"

"Oh. Of course," the woman said, her voice warming. "I'll see you in a while, Ms. Fitzpatrick."

The first thing they did before driving out there was stop off at the local Wal-Mart, buying prepaid cell phones and minutes to go with them, as well as a second laptop, since Izzy insisted that he'd need another to work with.

The inn, an old converted barn house, was located in the woods just the other side of the Potomac in McLean, Virginia. Had they not been there under such dire circumstances, Sydney might have enjoyed the old country charm. As it was, they were tense, tired, and feeling a bit out of sorts, especially, at least in Sydney's case, when faced with the notion that there were only two rooms.

The innkeeper, Betsy, a spritely woman in her sixties, was happy to see Griffin's cash as he paid for the extra room up front. She eyed the four of them. "I'm afraid it's going to be a bit cozy. There's only one queen-sized bed in each room."

Sydney about choked. "I— Are you sure there isn't another room available?"

"I'm sorry, dear." She slid two room keys across the counter. The keychain on each had a color written on it. One blue and one green. "But the blue room has a small couch if that helps."

Donovan grabbed the blue key, saying, "I'm injured. I need my own bed. Izzy can have the couch."

Sydney felt her face heat up slightly, realizing the position she was suddenly in. "How many rollaway beds do you have?"

"None. I do apologize."

"We'll manage," Griffin said, all business. "I don't suppose you have anything to eat or drink this late?" He set down a hundred-dollar bill.

She smiled. "I'm sure we can find something."

Once they were settled in their rooms, which were down the hall from each other, they met up in the blue room's private dining area. Betsy served them dinner, left them the wine and brandy, then excused herself to bed after telling them to leave the dishes there and she'd get them in the morning.

As they ate, they went over plans. Izzy was busy setting up his new computer. Donovan was nursing a glass of brandy.

"Let's have a look at that chest," Griffin said.

Donovan lifted his shirt. There was an L-shaped purple bruise where the shock plate had pressed against the ballistic vest when the round hit. "As long as I don't laugh, I'm fine."

"Damned lucky you suited up."

"Like I was going to go rescuing you *without* wearing gear?"

"Thanks, by the way." Griffin lifted his glass. "To all of you. For not leaving me out there."

They all lifted their glasses, drank, and after the conversation died, Sydney decided that her best option was to be in bed *before* Griffin got there. She stood, told everyone good night, then left.

Of course one thing she hadn't thought of was that she had nothing to sleep in. And when she was standing there, trying to decide what to do, Griffin walked in, closing the door behind him, and with their near-death escape, and the brandy coursing through her veins, she was having one hell of a time trying to remember that she was furious over his actions in Mexico, and his failure to tell her about them. "I'm still mad at you," she said.

"I realize that." He locked the door, and she was certain she heard her heart thumping through the wall of her chest as he turned, looked at her, then crossed the room, not stopping until he was directly in front of her. He reached out, ran his finger along her cheek. "And you have every right to be. There's no excuse, except . . . I knew I'd lose you."

That's exactly how she'd felt tonight, when she saw him running from the gunmen, believing he'd be shot along with Donovan.

"Answer one thing for me," he said, "and I'll do whatever it is you want. There's a couch downstairs. I can sleep on that."

"What?" she said, noting he hadn't moved, was still standing entirely too close to her.

"Tell me you haven't thought about the first time we kissed on those stairs in Rome. That you haven't asked yourself what might have been."

"It doesn't matter what I wanted then."

"It does. Remove our jobs from the equation. If we'd met anywhere else, we'd be together."

"It doesn't work that way."

"Close your eyes, Sydney."

She shook her head.

He moved closer. "Do it."

She hesitated, knew she should just order him out, but then, without knowing why, did as he asked.

He lowered his head toward her, whispered in her ear, and she could feel the heat of his breath on her skin. "Think about that time in Rome when we were standing on the stairs at the safe house."

"Nothing happened."

"But you remember that moment. As much as I do."

The very realization that *he* remembered was intoxicating in itself. She'd been so certain that he would kiss her, but he hadn't. It left her wanting him more. Just as he said, imagining what might have been.

"And that night in Amsterdam," he continued, his voice lowering as he moved even closer. "At the museum . . ."

"We kissed . . ." She wasn't even sure if he heard her, the words catching in her throat. They'd pretended they were lovers as part of their cover. It had been snowing and she remembered the chill of the cold stone wall behind her and the warmth of him against her . . .

"And Paris . . ." he whispered. "The hotel . . . I can still feel you in my arms, taste the brandy on your lips . . . Tell me you remember . . ."

She nodded, the memories as vivid now as they were then. They flooded her senses. She remembered his kiss, the way he slipped his hand inside the shoulder of her pajamas, his skin against hers, and then just when she was sure her knees would give out, he carried her to the bed. She'd thought about each of those nights, how close they came, how much she'd wanted him.

He reached out, tucked a strand of hair behind her ear, trailed his finger along her collar, then downward, lingering at the vee. He kissed her neck, scraped his teeth softly against her skin. A shiver went through her, and the nerves and muscles in her stomach quivered. He wrapped his arms around her, pulled her close, his mouth against hers.

She *had* wanted this. From the very beginning. Right now it didn't matter that she hated herself for giving in to her baser desires. The only thing she cared about at that moment was getting as close to him as she could, feeling her skin against his, his hands on her body. God help her, because she couldn't stop herself.

And before she knew it, they were on the bed, tearing at each other's clothes, at their own, their breathing becoming ragged, faster, harder . . .

32

Venice, Italy

Her capacity for memorizing aside, Piper didn't know whether it had been the blow to her head as a child that had made her a quick learner, or the fact that life had usually dealt her a poor hand, starting with nearly every foster home she'd ever lived in.

It didn't matter how book smart you were, she thought, watching her kidnapper in the next room through the partially open door. One didn't survive in the U.S. foster system without some form of street smarts, at least not in the types of homes in which she'd been placed. Lying on her side on a narrow, unmade bed, she struggled to loosen the duct tape binding her wrists behind her back. Her ankles were also bound together, and she could do little more than lie there.

Her captor, Vittorio, looked over at her every now and then, undoubtedly checking to make sure she didn't move. He was talking on the phone in Italian, and she wished she'd been hit in the part of the head that allowed her to pick up languages instead. Had she been smart, she would have bought a book on Italian and read it on the plane trip over. Then again, memorizing a word in another language was a far cry from hearing it spoken. Besides, the books she'd flipped through all discussed how to order at a restaurant or book a room in a hotel. In retrospect, she wasn't sure what she'd planned on doing in this country, except perhaps eating her way across it on a stolen credit card.

Next time she picked a foreign country to run away to, it was so going to be an English-speaking one. If she didn't escape, though, she wasn't going to get that chance.

"Hey!" she said. "I have to go to the bathroom."

He ignored her, continued talking on the phone, and she heard him saying, " . . . *istruzioni a casa nostra* . . ."

She might not know Italian, but she knew enough Spanish to figure out he was about to give directions to his house. Undoubtedly so someone could come get her, and she closed her eyes, trying to take in what he was saying. Unfortunately it was too fast and all she heard was " . . . *sempre diritto* . . . *accanto la farmacia*." Then, "*Sì un'ora*."

That she understood. An hour. She had an hour to get out of here.

"Hey! I have to go to the bathroom!"

The man looked at her. "*Che cazzo! Sta zita!*"

From the way he bellowed it, she figured he was swearing at her. Well, screw him. "Look. I have to go to the bathroom and if you don't let me, I'm going to pee right here on this bed. *Pee. Comprendo!*" she said, hoping the Spanish translated over. "Right here on this bed. I hope it's not yours."

This time he got up, stopping in the doorway. He concluded his phone call, snapped the phone onto his belt, looking annoyed.

And just when she thought he was going to turn around, leave, he walked in, pulled her up. "This way."

"Thank you," she said, as he held her by one arm to keep

her from falling as she hopped beside him. The bathroom was down a short hallway. The white tiles on the floor and walls magnified the cold as she stood there looking down at the toilet. And then she craned her neck around. "I can't go like this."

"Why not?"

"I'm a girl. I need my hands."

He regarded her, his dark eyes filled with suspicion. "Do not do anything stupid."

Wouldn't dream of it, she thought, as he took a folding knife from his belt and cut the tape at her wrists. And then he stood there in the doorway.

She glared at him, crossing her arms across her chest. "You are *seriously* going to watch me? Where am I going to go? There isn't even a window."

He looked up at the blank wall as if a window might magically appear and apparently decided she was correct. But only after he pushed past her, grabbed the razor blade from a mug in the sink. "I will be *here*," he said, waving the razor in her face.

She reached over, closed and locked the door, then turned the faucet to a trickle so that she could search through the cupboard beneath it. She found a travel-sized bottle of shampoo and conditioner, extra toilet paper and towels. After using the toilet, she took the small bottles, then slid them into the back of her underwear, flushed the toilet, washed her hands, then opened the door.

He peered inside, looked around, and apparently satisfied nothing was missing, tossed the razor back in the cup, then took hold of her arm, holding tight while she hopped beside him back to the bedroom.

"Can you slow down?" she said. "I'm going to fall."

Instead, he pulled her faster toward the table where the roll of duct tape sat. She tripped, grabbing at him, trying to slip his phone from his belt. It went flying from her hand to the floor, when he turned at the last second, and she misjudged her distance.

He pushed her toward the bed so that he could retrieve his phone. Piper fell forward, her knees striking the tiled floor. Pain shot through her and it was several seconds before she could pull herself up, onto the bed.

He drew his knife, and she froze, worried that he'd seen right through her fake fall against him. But then he used the knife to simply cut a length of tape from the roll, to bind her hands once more. He walked toward her, carrying the tape, and she held up both her hands in front of her. He wasn't going for it, instead pulling her hands behind her back, taping them there.

And then he returned to his chair in the other room to watch his TV, leaving the door partially open. Not what she was hoping for.

She shifted on the mattress, staring up at the ceiling, her hands at her back making it difficult to get comfortable. Instead, she concentrated on the pain in her knees. But she was used to pain, she'd been hit before, and so she thought of her friend, Bo.

It wasn't just that he'd been shot, but that he'd given her up, told them where to find her.

That was enough to send her over, and she allowed the tears to come, sobbing loudly.

"*Silenzio!*"

"It hurts! My knee! I think it's broken!"

"It's a good thing you won't be walking. No?" And then he got up and slammed the door closed.

She sat there in the dark for several seconds, stunned at how easily the tears had worked.

Smiling, she hiked up the back of her skirt, pulled the small bottles out, opened the first, and did her best to direct the contents onto her wrists. If she could work it into the tape, she might be able to slip her wrists out.

It took longer to loosen her bonds than she'd anticipated, and when she finally was able to free herself, she worried that it might be too late. She listened at the door, heard the TV droning in the background, as well as some soft snoring. At least something was going her way.

She ripped the sheets from the bed, moved to the window, unlatched and opened it, then opened the wood shutters to a blast of cold air. But when she looked down, her heart sank. No paving stones below, or even a narrow walkway. Just the black water swishing against the building's base. A *rio*, the sisters had called it. Not that the name mattered.

She couldn't swim.

Somehow she'd overlooked that small detail. She'd become used to the sound of the water, had stopped hearing it—or maybe she was too intent on listening to the man in the other room. Either way she was screwed, and she dropped the sheets right there, since they'd do her little good. She turned back, looking around for something she might use for a weapon. A twin bed against the wall, a wardrobe by the door . . . Maybe something in there. She moved softly, opened the door, felt around. Clothes hanging within. Nothing else.

A muffled knock sent her pulse racing. She froze. It sounded again, and she realized it must be coming from the front door of the house. The snoring stopped, and she heard some mumbling, followed by the sound of someone shuffling across the tiled floor, then down the stairs.

What she wouldn't give right now to be able to swim.

She looked around, wishing for rafters as in Bo's kitchen. Wishing for the man who had helped her escape. Zachary Griffin.

Right now all she had was the narrow bed, which they'd be able to see under the moment they walked into the room.

The wardrobe, on the other hand, was right next to the door. They were bound to be looking at the bed first thing . . .

She scrambled toward the window, grabbed the sheets, knotted them together. Then, tying one end to the iron balustrade at the base of the window, she threw the length over the side.

Please let this work, she thought, then opened the wardrobe, climbed inside, hid behind the clothes.

She heard talking from the other room. Italian first, then English. "The girl?"

"In there."

"You did not talk to her?"

"About what?"

The sound of footsteps, then the door opening.

Piper's heart pounded hard and fast.

"Where is she?"

"Tied up. On the bed."

"You see anything on that bed?"

Silence, then, "The window!"

"Vittorio, you idiot! She went out the window!"

"She was tied up. I swear."

"Yeah? How long ago?"

"All night. I was right outside the door the whole time."

"Gianni, go out and look around."

"I don't even know what she looks like."

"I'm guessing she looks like a wet nun, you idiot. Go!"

Footsteps leaving, then the sound of the front door slamming closed, Gianni apparently not happy he had to go search.

"What should I do, Paolo?" Vittorio asked.

"Nothing. We're done with you."

"Paolo. No—" A gasping noise followed by the sound of something soft but heavy hitting the floor.

Piper held her breath, praying they'd leave. When she heard footsteps retreating, fading, she peered out between the clothes to see Vittorio's body on the floor, and a growing puddle of blood beneath him.

Piper eyed the open window. So close . . .

And then she looked back at the man on the floor, Vittorio. His face pointed in her direction, his jaw slack, his gaze unseeing . . .

His phone . . . Still on his belt.

What to do?

Closing her eyes, she listened to the sounds. The TV playing in the background. The icy air making her shiver. Worried that her chattering teeth would give her away, she tried to pull the clothes around her, like a makeshift blanket. Several minutes went by, the room growing colder. She tried not to think about that. Instead, she needed the courage to slip out and get that phone. If she skirted the room by the window, she could maybe avoid being seen from the doorway. And he wouldn't necessarily be watching in here, since he thought she was gone. And Vittorio was dead. She hoped.

Now or never. She parted the clothes, was just slipping her foot out, when she heard the creak of springs from the chair in the front room. She pulled her foot in, stilled, unable to move the clothes closer together, and watched in horror as Paolo reentered the room, standing there as he looked around, like he was thinking.

About her.

Please don't let him turn around.

He didn't. He walked over to the window, and was just about to reach out, close it, but stopped to pull up the sheets hanging over the side. He tried to untie the length from the balustrade, but couldn't get the knot loose, so he simply dropped the tangle of sheets outside in a pile, then pulled the window shut. When he turned to leave, she relaxed slightly, figuring that he was probably just cold.

But then Paolo stopped next to the body. Nudged it with his foot, bent down, and panic gripped her as he reached for Vittorio's belt. But he didn't grab the phone. Instead, he used the belt to turn the body to its stomach so he could slip the wallet out of the back pocket.

Paolo opened it, pulled out some money, tossed the wallet onto the floor, took one last look around the room, his eye catching on the open wardrobe.

He walked toward it. Terror coursed through her veins. He reached for the wardrobe door, pulled it all the way open.

And somehow over the pounding of her heart, she heard the low vibration of his cell phone. He stopped, pulled it from his pocket, answered it. "You find her . . . ?" he said, then eyed the wardrobe's interior. He reached inside, grabbed a coat, and thankfully turned as he pulled it from the hanger. "Where the hell's Pietro? He was supposed to be watching this place until we got here. Get ahold of him and get back to me. We're not leaving until she's found. And hurry the hell up," he added, as he walked out. "It's like a goddamned refrigerator in here."

He walked out of the bedroom and slammed the door closed. And still she didn't move. Fear paralyzed her, and it seemed forever before she could even think, much less force her body into action.

She needed to do something. They were coming back.

The phone was her only option. She slipped out of the wardrobe, tiptoed toward the body, careful not to step in the puddle of blood growing beneath it. And just as this Paolo did, she tugged at the belt, having to reach beneath his waist as she blindly felt for the phone. She found it, then retreated back to the wardrobe. Before she climbed in, she took a folded sweater from the shelf at the top and slipped it on, hoping that would keep her teeth from chattering. She scooted all the way into the corner, pulled the door closest to her slightly shut, hoping no one would notice it wasn't exactly the same should they reenter the bedroom.

The first thing she did was set the phone to silent. Then she thought about texting Lisette's number, but had no idea

if she was even in Venice yet. The *carabinieri* officer, Giustino, would probably be the better option. Closer. He'd given
her his business card. She closed her eyes, pictured the card,
saw the number in her mind, and sent him a text: "Don't
know where I am. They killed the man who took me. I'm
hiding in the wardrobe upstairs."

33

Sydney woke up in an empty bed, her head aching, probably from the late night brandy and not enough rest, and was trying to justify how it was she'd let herself sleep with Griffin. She told herself it was to eradicate him from her system, and that the only reason she wanted him to begin with was that he was the forbidden fruit. But the vivid memory of their lovemaking was potent, the craving for more far too strong. Had he walked in at that moment, she would have dragged him back to bed.

That was something she couldn't do. They had issues. Big issues.

She needed a clear head, definitely a cold shower, and she forced herself to get up, then walked into the bathroom and saw the steam on the mirror. Apparently he'd already showered before he'd left, whether to avoid seeing her or to give her a few minutes to herself, she wasn't sure. By the time she got out, he was back, holding two steaming mugs of coffee.

There was an awkward moment of silence as she stood in

the bathroom doorway, neither of them knowing quite what to say. "Coffee," was what came out of her mouth, while her brain was thinking something completely different, and entirely sexual.

He set her mug on the dresser. "I'd have brought you something to eat, but I wasn't sure what you'd want. There's food in the sitting room."

"My head is pounding."

"The coffee should help. I can check downstairs for aspirin."

"I have some."

He nodded, his gaze flicking to the bed, then back to her. And as if he sensed her discomfort, he moved to the door. "I should go. They're waiting for us in the sitting room."

"How's Donovan?" she asked.

"Bruised, but he'll survive. Bring your coffee, we have some planning to do before we leave this morning."

She grabbed the yellow pad she'd brought from home, along with the coffee mug, then followed Griffin into the sitting room where Donovan and Izzy were waiting. There was a basket of cranberry orange muffins on the table, and she took one, pleased to discover they were still warm, the tops delicately crisp with a crust of sugar, and the inside moist and fragrant with orange zest.

"They're great," Izzy said, opening his laptop and setting it on the table. "The couch was even pretty comfortable. Slept like a baby. How about you?"

Sydney, her mouth full of muffin, looked up, realized he was talking to her, and the only thing she could think of was sex. With Griffin. The temperature of the room seemed to rise several degrees and she was certain her cheeks had turned a deep red.

"Fine," she said, the word coming out more like a croak as the muffin seized in her throat. She grabbed her coffee, took a sip, trying not to notice Donovan's amused gaze bouncing from her to Griffin, who seemed fascinated with the wood grain on the tabletop. Izzy, at least, appeared clueless, his attention now on his computer. "The bed was fine," she added, once she could speak again.

"Let's get started," Griffin said, drawing everyone's attention to more important matters.

Donovan gave a slight cough. "Good idea. Since we no longer have the file, we're going to have to start from scratch with what we do know."

Izzy turned the laptop around so they could see the headlines on the Web site. "Looks like someone broke into the *Washington Recorder* last night and murdered two guards."

Sydney read the article, her stomach knotting with each word, expecting to see her name as well as Griffin's and Donovan's. But none of them was mentioned. "They used your gun," she said to Griffin. "I thought for sure they'd list you as a suspect—"

"They can't come out and say it was us without saying what *they* were doing there. The ballistics will come back to my weapon soon enough, which I'm sure is what they're counting on."

Izzy's foot started tapping. "Maybe we were a little too thorough in eliminating that video surveillance."

"Can't be helped," Griffin said. "Our best bet is exposing Parker Kane before that happens. And anyone else he's working with."

"Which would be who?" Donovan asked. "Every time we eliminate one of these guys, there's another one taking his place. It wasn't quite the job security I was thinking of when I signed up."

Sydney brushed the crumbs from the table in front of her to clear the spot for her pad of paper. "We need to be logical about this. What we know—at least what I know is that this all started when Orozco and my father stole this list, code, whatever it is, presumably from Wingman and Wingman."

And she wrote: "#1. Theft. W2."

Then, poising her pen over the paper, said, "Anyone else?"

"The Devil's Key," Donovan said.

"The what?"

"That," Griffin said, "is the name of the code your father and Orozco stole. What Orozco gave to you when you found him in Mexico."

"Oh." She looked down at the paper, thinking the name rather apropos, considering. "And what does it do?"

Griffin looked at Donovan, but neither man said anything.

"For God's sake," she said. "They're already trying to kill us over the thing. I think the rules go out the window at this point, don't you?"

"Izzy's here."

Izzy looked up from his computer screen. "Huh? Are you serious? Who *doesn't* know what it does. One of the greatest conspiracy theories of . . . I don't know. The last couple decades, I guess. It's a case management software called SINS commissioned by the government, stolen, actually, because they never paid the developers. Only it was enhanced with a back door so that anyone running it can be spied on."

"That's it?"

"Isn't that enough?" Griffin asked her.

"No. Even I've heard of that. Wasn't Canada involved? The whole thing blew up when they started investigating that they were being spied on. It just sort of died, didn't it?"

"It died because the government did everything in its power to make sure it was relegated to conspiracy theory. They sent out a security patch to close the back door to any countries using the software, and made sure that any remaining keys were destroyed."

The thought that her father had been involved in the theft of this Devil's Key sickened her. And though she wanted to believe that maybe he and Orozco had stolen it to keep it safe, protect the government, she knew it wasn't true.

Orozco had told her otherwise, and everything she'd learned about her father since had confirmed it.

She leaned back in her chair, trying to remember all that Orozco had talked about when she'd found him in Ensenada, because there was still some element about this she felt she was missing. "Orozco told me the government was trying to whitewash it. But there has to be something more to this."

"What more do you want?" Griffin replied. "Enemy countries learning that the U.S. sold them software so they could be spied on? Seems pretty cut and dried to me."

"Why not just have them remove the program? That's what I would do. Why run around and kill a bunch of people? We're missing something. I know it."

"What else did Orozco tell you?" Griffin asked.

"Mostly he thought it was related to the BICTT banking scandal, and BICTT's Black Network having ties to the government . . . And the information from those numbers would literally cripple corporate America and end treaties with a number of countries."

"Which fits with what we know about it. No one likes spies in their midst."

"He also said it was the tip of the iceberg. That about covers it."

"So write down BICTT, the Network, and corporate America."

"Which tells us the Network and W2 have to be related." She added Orozco's information to the list.

"Except," Donovan said, "BICTT was closed down."

"The investors' money," Sydney replied, "was never recovered. Millions upon millions of dollars still out there."

Griffin eyed the list Sydney was making. "The BICTT money is finite. Hard to believe it didn't end up in the Network's coffers anyway."

"Again my point in why are they so hot to get this thing?" She stared at the pad, trying to think what she was missing, what he wasn't telling her about the program, when her gaze caught on the torn edge at the top. That was the page of notes she'd ripped off the day her apartment was searched.

They hadn't taken the pad during the search—the pad she'd just written all over.

Twice after she'd completed a sketch for Griffin, he'd confiscated her entire sketchbook, on the off chance someone could re-create the sketch by using the sheet below . . .

How had she not remembered that?

Because she wasn't thinking of sketches.

"I need a pencil."

Izzy tossed her his, and she held it so the lead was flat against the paper, lightly rubbing it across the surface.

"What . . ." Griffin leaned forward to see what she was doing.

"This is the pad of paper I used to write the list of names from those files Scotty gave me, and that Pearson confiscated." Within a short time she had the column of names covered. Unfortunately she had written across half of them, but she thought she still could make some out. "Some of these people we know about. My father, Orozco. But some of them I have no idea who they are."

"We look them up," Donovan said. "Never too late to reopen an investigation. Just gotta figure a way to do it without an electronic trail. Maybe through old phone books and microfiched news articles at the main library. One that isn't connected to the Internet."

"That will take forever to go through. The Internet would be much faster."

"There's four of us," Izzy said. "Divide and conquer. The library in Washington, D.C., still has a large microfiche file of past newspaper articles. It's electronic, but not on the Internet. I have a feeling most of what we want to look up is not going to be recent stuff."

He was right about that. They spent the next couple of

hours at the library, reading archived newspaper articles on the names. It wasn't too long before Sydney noticed a pattern with each name she'd written down. Every one of them had died an unnatural death.

Between the suicides, car accidents, and small planes going down, there wasn't one person on there who was alive.

"Now what?" Sydney asked, feeling close to defeat.

"Easy," Donovan said. "We do what Orozco did. Move to Mexico."

Griffin was sitting across the table from her and Donovan, and he looked up from the article he was reading. "Maybe not. I remember this case." He slid it across the table toward them. "John Hettinger. Investigative journalist who committed suicide about eighteen years ago. He, apparently, was looking into the suicide of White House deputy counsel Gannon Ferris, and thought there was some sort of conspiracy with tentacles reaching deep into the government."

"How does this help us?" Sydney asked. "He's dead."

"He left behind a wife."

"What's she going to tell us that she hasn't told someone else?"

"Hard to say unless we ask. But there's an interesting quote at the end of this article. Hettinger was allegedly on antidepressants, and at first his wife denied that was true."

"At first?"

"Apparently she changed her mind."

"Someone got to her."

"Exactly. And if we're lucky, nearly two decades of being left alone might get her to tell us why she recanted."

34

Lydia Hettinger was not listed in the phone book, nor was she still living in the home she'd shared with her late husband. They were able, however, to track her down by contacting the neighbors, one of whom had kept in touch with her over the years and provided an address as well as her new name, Lydia Hettinger Walton. Sydney and Griffin went to interview her, while Izzy and Donovan continued the research to see what else they might find.

As Griffin was pulling up in front of the house, Lydia Hettinger Walton was backing out of her driveway. She was younger than Sydney expected, late forties, which meant she'd been a young woman at the time of her husband's death. Griffin followed her car, a gray Mercedes, to a school about two miles away. He parked in the slot next to hers. "Might be less intimidating if you approach her," he said.

Sydney got out, followed the woman toward the school office doors, where two preteen girls, both blond like Lydia, exited and walked toward her. It appeared as though school had been out for a while, since there were very few cars in the lot.

"Lydia?"

The blond woman looked back, saw Sydney, and gave a polite but vacant smile.

"Sorry to bother you, but do you have a moment?"

"I'm heading into town. What's this in regards to?"

"A case from almost twenty years ago."

Lydia's gaze flicked to her children, then back to Sydney. "Who are you?"

"I'm with the FBI."

"ID?"

Sydney pulled out her credentials from her pants pocket, noticing that Lydia stood firmly between her and the girls as they walked toward her, making sure they couldn't see.

She examined the identification, seemed to think about it for a moment, then handed her keys to one of her daughters. "Go wait in the car. I'll be right there." When they left, she said, "I need to drop them off at tutoring. I can give you five minutes."

"Thank you." Griffin joined them. "He's with me," Sydney said, when Lydia turned suddenly wary at his presence.

"Is this really necessary after all this time? My daughters know nothing about my first husband's suicide and I'd like to keep it that way."

"Are you sure it was a suicide?" Griffin asked.

Lydia stared at them for several seconds. "You can't be serious?"

"We are."

"After all the evidence your agency bombarded me with to convince me it was?"

Sydney had to decide what to tell her, and settled on the truth, even if it meant it would shut down any chance of learning her side of the story. "We're not investigating officially."

"Then what are you doing?"

"I think your husband was writing about a case that my

father was involved in. And when I read that he'd committed suicide, I realized I needed to know if that's what really happened."

"John had a very fanciful imagination. I think when he was finally faced with the realities, that all these things he had conjured up led nowhere, it was too much for him."

"What if they were true?"

Lydia's mouth parted, but then she clamped it shut, and turned away. When she looked back at Sydney, she said, "I've remarried. I have a family that I don't want involved in this. I've moved on. You should, too."

"I can't. I believe there's more to this than what's been released to the public."

"You work for the government. You do realize that?"

"Yes. And I believe in the government I work for. I just don't always trust it."

Lydia held her gaze for several seconds. "I'm sorry. I can't help you."

Sydney nodded. Then, handing her a business card, said, "If you change your mind, leave a message on my voice mail."

She and Griffin turned away, started walking toward the car, when Lydia called out to them. "Why would my late husband have been interested in your father?"

"My father stole something that the government wanted back."

"And what are you looking for?"

"Answers."

Lydia's eyes shimmered, as though she knew what that meant, the need, the desire to find out why something bad had happened. "I can meet for coffee."

Sydney nodded. "When?"

She gave the cross streets of a coffee shop, saying, "In half an hour."

"I'll be there. Thank you."

Forty minutes later, Lydia still hadn't shown up and Sydney told herself that was to be expected. After all, who would want to relive one's husband's suicide? "How long do you think we should wait?" she asked Griffin.

"I'd say as long as it takes, but given the lethal outcomes of everyone else involved in this case, and the fact we've been followed before, I'd be more comfortable knowing she's safe."

"What do you want to do?"

He looked at his watch. "You stay here. I'm going to drive past her house, just to make sure nothing's amiss."

He left. Twenty minutes later, Sydney walked out, tossing her coffee into the trash, wondering where Griffin was, and disappointed that Lydia had failed to show. Lydia was the last link. There were no other names, she thought, as a vehicle pulled up alongside her.

"Ms. Fitzpatrick?"

Sydney turned, saw Lydia Hettinger Walton behind the wheel. A different car, she noted. This one a white Ford. "Hi."

"I thought we could go for a drive? Alone."

Sydney eyed the vehicle, then looked around the lot, trying to decide if this was a wise course of action. Where the hell was Griffin? Getting into a stranger's car was not something she usually did. But in this case, her desire for answers outweighed her reticence.

And her gun at her side helped tip the scales.

"Sure." Sydney walked over to Lydia's vehicle, getting in.

"I'm sorry about being late, but I had to be sure that you were alone."

"I am."

"Never mind I changed my mind. Several times in fact."

"Why?"

Lydia glanced over at her, then back at the road. "It's been nearly twenty years. I've remarried, put that part of my life away. It's not something I wanted to revisit."

And that Sydney understood. "Where are we going?"

"There's a park I want you to see. My husband—first husband—felt that there were a lot of inconsistencies in a story he was investigating, and this park is where it all started."

Sydney's curiosity was piqued. She wasn't aware of what particular case John Hettinger had been looking into at the time of his death that had to do with a park. "I appreciate you taking the time."

"So why now? No one's contacted me in forever. After the official statements came out, the newspaper articles, the magazines searching for sensationalistic conspiracies that never materialized, why now?"

Since Sydney wasn't prepared for a cross-examination, she wasn't even sure what to say. There was so much she *couldn't* say, but she knew she had to tell this woman something, especially if she wanted her cooperation.

Partial truths were better than lies, and so she decided to mention the only thing she knew was in the public domain. "My father was murdered around the same time that your husband died. I started looking into it and found that he was involved with some people who may have crossed paths with your late husband. Every time I turn around, there are more questions than answers, and I'm just not sure what to believe anymore." She glanced out the window, trying not to think about her own father, the things she remembered, the hurt and confusion when she discovered he was not the man she thought she knew. For so long she wanted to discover he had been wrongly accused, and yet the deeper she dug, the guiltier he became. "I found your name, saw what your husband was looking into before he allegedly committed suicide, and I had to wonder if any of what I've been told is true."

"Who was your father?"

"Kevin Fitzpatrick. I think he may have been more on the fringes of whatever this was that your husband was looking into. Honestly, though, I don't know."

Lydia took the freeway, eventually crossed the Potomac into Virginia, then drove for several minutes along the George Washington Memorial Parkway, eventually exiting into an area known as Fort Marcy Park. "This is where it started."

"Where what started?"

"Another suicide. The one that got my husband involved. He believed it was a murder and started investigating. I'll show you where."

They got out, and Lydia led her along a path through a heavily wooded area of the park. She stopped, pointed down a low hill. "That's where Gannon Ferris killed himself."

"Ferris?" she prodded, as though unfamiliar with the case.

"Deputy White House counsel. You would have been too young to remember." She looked over at Sydney. "What are you? Early thirties? Well, twenty years ago, Gannon Ferris allegedly drove into this park, leaving his vehicle where mine is now, walked down that hill, and shot himself. The only problem is that nothing added up. When they found him, his car keys were not in his pocket. His car was up here, but the keys weren't in it, either, because the people who killed him forgot that tiny little detail. And yet the keys mysteriously showed up in his pocket at the morgue after a couple of White House employees paid a visit. That never sat well with my husband, and so he started looking into it."

"Did he say why he thought Ferris was killed?"

"Because he knew too much."

"About what?"

"*That* is the question, isn't it? My husband didn't share with me what he was looking into, I think because he knew the dangers. And in the end, he told me that if anyone asked me what I knew, it was important for me to say I knew nothing. Honestly, I thought he was blowing this all up." She crossed her arms as a breeze picked up, her blond hair blowing about her face. "The day before my husband died, he was supposed to be meeting with someone who had the answers. He said that there were tentacles reaching deep into the government, and this witness was going to blow it wide open. He was excited. He said it would make Watergate look like petty crimes in comparison."

She gave a cynical laugh. "He was sure that this was worthy of a Pulitzer. As did every journalist after him who started looking into *his* suicide." When she turned toward Sydney, her eyes were cold, determined. "After he died, I was like you with your father. I wanted answers. I knew he wouldn't kill himself. Someone that excited about a story doesn't just sit down in his motel room the next day, pull out a razor, and slice his wrists. I've since abandoned the notion of ever getting answers, and I have refused all requests for interviews since."

"Why?"

"Because the law enforcement officials have wrapped it up so tightly, there is no other explanation but suicide. And the few who dared venture further into it? Their careers were ruined, and as far as I know, they're all dead." She reached out, touched Sydney's arm. "If you want my advice? Do what I did. Walk away while you still can. Tuck that part of your life away and never revisit. It will only bring pain."

"I'm not sure I can do that."

"I wasn't sure, either. But now that I've remarried, and have children, I find it much easier. I have them to think of."

She looked up at the sky, at a bird flying past beneath a canopy of gray clouds. After several seconds of silence, she turned back to Sydney. "We should go. I promised the girls I'd take them for ice cream after their tutoring is over."

The drive back was made in silence, and just as Sydney got out of the car, Lydia handed her an envelope. "As painful as it was to make the decision, I've moved on. Please don't contact me again."

She drove off before Sydney had a chance to thank her, or even look inside the envelope. Griffin pulled into the lot after she left.

"Where were you?" Sydney asked.

"Following Lydia. I was curious when she switched vehicles, then sat in some parking lot up the road for a while. What happened?"

"She said her husband was investigating the suicide of Gannon Ferris at that park. And then she gave me this." Sydney opened it and found a newspaper article about a civil lawsuit against Wingman and Wingman and the U.S. government. Apparently a small IT company called CalDorTek in California allegedly designed a computer program for a law firm also located in California. The program was sold to the U.S. government as a case management system by a former employee of the law firm, who coincidentally ended up working for Wingman and Wingman, resulting in a civil suit, because the IT company believed they were owed royalties.

She gave the article to Griffin to read. "It certainly looks related to me," she said when he'd finished. "They're clearly talking about the SINS program."

"Yes. Just not that Gannon's alleged suicide was connected to the civil suit."

"Obviously we need to contact this IT company."

"First, we make sure it's still in business. Last thing we need is for someone to know we're running the name, then have the owner end up dead. Or us. But neither do I want to fly all the way out to California if they're no longer there."

"I'll call Doc. If anyone knows a way to find this out without running it on a computer, he will."

Michael "Doc" Schermer was an FBI agent who worked out of the San Francisco field office. Like Carillo, he was one of the few people who actually knew about ATLAS and the cases they worked. What made Doc the go-to man was his specialty in digging up obscure information culled from the Internet. This time, though, they'd need it searched the old-fashioned way, by hand.

Doc, of course, commented on the unknown number Sydney was calling from.

"Prepaid phone," she said. "Worried about being monitored." In fact, Doc was one of the first people who told her she should stay off the Internet when it came to this case.

"That bad?"

"That bad. Any chance you've ever heard of an IT company called CalDorTek?"

"In California? There's got to be a million IT companies."

"This one may be one of the missing puzzle pieces in my quest that started with my trip to Mexico. I'm going to snap a picture of this article and send it to your cell phone. Since it's a California case, you might have a better chance of finding something."

"I'm assuming you want to avoid any electronic or paper records of a search?"

"Preferably."

"Send the article. I'll see what I can dig up."

It didn't take him long. Less than thirty minutes later, in fact, he was calling her back. "I'm not so sure it's the owner of the IT company you want to interview. The case has been around. If he knew anything, he'd probably be dead. Which tells me he probably wasn't involved or doesn't know enough about the program in question to be a threat, beyond what you know. Which begs the question, why was this article kept all these years? Hence, you two might want to find a couple IDs that pass muster and fly out here to California for this."

"Why is that?" Sydney asked.

"Aside from the IT company connection, the person you're going to want to talk to is in Sacramento. An editor for the *Sacramento Weekly Review*. It's one of those papers that usually lean to the left, unless they're leaning to the right. Supported by massage parlor ads and single white somebody or other looking for someone of various sexual persuasions."

"That's a bit off the beaten track."

"That's because the reporter, Tim Ronson, who wrote that article you sent me ended up there. I found a former colleague of the reporter, who said he was fired from a major San Jose newspaper for writing a series of articles, including the one you sent, without verifying his sources. That he essentially made up his stories, some of which have to do with governmental improprieties."

"And how does that lead to Sacramento?"

"That's where Ronson was working when he committed suicide. Only in this case, I'd call it a case of assisted suicide, like a botched job. It took two bullets. The first shot when he allegedly tried to blow his brains out via his open mouth apparently missed the mark, taking out his jaw and face, which could easily happen if, say, one were struggling with the gun, or someone was holding it, thereby causing it to miss the brain stem. It was the second shot point blank to the head that did him in. Which, in most death investigations, sort of discounts the whole he-shot-himself theory, mostly because it's really hard to pull the trigger the second time when you're missing half your head. Especially when physics come into play and you know the kick from that first shot probably flung the gun out of his hand."

"Suspicious to be sure, but how's his editor going to help us?"

"Because the editor never bought the suicide theory and

had the foresight to hide the guy's case notes in the advertising files, single white male seeking single white male. Guess they weren't comfortable searching that section when they served the search warrant. He's expecting your visit."

"We're on the next plane out."

35

Venice, Italy

Lisette was still reeling, long after she'd realized that the body had not been Piper's. She recalled the moment they arrived at the building that morning, the morgue, and Giustino walking them over to a figure draped by a sheet, lying in a puddle that flooded the porcelain table. They'd fished her from the canal, and the room smelled of the dank water. Her heart had skipped a beat at the size, so similar, but when she saw the face, she knew without a doubt it was not Piper.

And so, after finding out that she might still be alive, they sat down at a café, drinking more hot coffee, while detailing the areas they would be searching. Giustino suggested that Dumas take Lisette and Marc to the convent, where, he hoped, they might learn something that could help them.

Dumas led them through a maze of alleys and over bridges, through several large squares, *campi*. After several minutes, they ended up on the Grand Canal. "Hurry," Dumas said. "We can catch the *vaporetto* and save some time if we don't have to wait." The water bus was just pulling up to the pier. "Let's get out of the cold," said Dumas, opening the door to the cabin, which held surprisingly few passengers. Undoubtedly Venetians, since they were oblivious to the beauty around them. The three took a seat near the back. The boat moved leisurely from stop to stop, and after her and Marc's long trip to get here, the hum of the motors, the cries of the terns all seemed remote, even dreamlike. The weather closed in. The dark waters of the Grand Canal reflected the steel gray of the clouded sky. The great waterside palaces seemed tinged with melancholy. Had they been there for a leisurely visit, it would have been the perfect spot to while away the hours with Marc.

Unfortunately it was not, and Dumas broke into her reverie. "Ours is the next stop." The boat bumped against the pier, and the attendant secured the mooring, then slid back the steel barrier, letting the passengers disembark.

Dumas led them through another complex maze of narrow *salizade*, and through a short dark wooden passageway, this *sotoportego* splitting the ground floor of a Renaissance house, the tunnel dark and smelling of damp wood.

At the end of it, the three traversed another bridge, this one bringing into view the very old, rather plain redbrick church with a leaning campanile. Surrounded by water on two sides, it stood to one side of an L-shaped *campo*. The doors of the church were closed; the *campo* seemed to be deserted. A long, high wall studded with glass at the top stretched out behind the church, the closed double doors set into the wall, and the convent where Piper had been kidnapped adjoined it. They were apparently expected, because as soon as the priest knocked, a nun admitted them to what proved to be a large kitchen garden.

Silently, she led them down a path to another set of doors, which opened into a columned cloister, which enclosed a smaller furrowed garden. Lisette imagined that in the springtime it would be blooming with flowers. Turning the corner, the sister stopped, and knocked on the door of a small office.

"*Avanti!*" a woman's voice invited them to enter.

A younger nun was seated in a chair next to the desk, behind which was seated a nun who appeared to be in her early seventies, undoubtedly the mother superior. There was a butterfly bandage on her forehead with a few stitches visible, and purple bruising. "Don Emilio," she said, rising. "You are prompt as usual." She turned her gaze to Lisette and Marc. "These are the agents who will be helping to search for young Piper?"

"They are. Lisette Perrault and Marc di Luca, this is the Reverend Mother Angelica."

The reverend mother appeared distraught. "I must apologize to you for our failure to protect the child."

"No," Lisette said. "The fault lies with me. I was responsible."

Dumas cleared his throat. "Perhaps we should get started?"

"Of course," she said. "Don Emilio tells me that you would probably want to inspect the premises and look for . . . leads, I believe he called them."

"If we could," Marc said.

Dumas took them around.

Marc and Lisette examined the courtyard outside the mother superior's office, Marc saying to Dumas, "I am still having a hard time understanding how it is they found her so easily."

"We believe she was traced to the convent after she called the States."

Marc, however, was not happy. "How did she get to a phone when it was specified that she would not have access?"

"It was not done intentionally," Dumas said. "She is, however, somewhat more resourceful than the . . . *usual* guest?

To this end, the good sisters are praying that her less than stellar talents will serve her well in her time of need."

"Let's hope so," Marc said. "So they traced her call? From which end?"

Lisette's throat tightened. "She called my cell phone and left a message. To apologize. Do you think they traced that?"

"It's possible," Father Dumas said. "And something to keep in mind as we search," he said. Not finding anything, they returned inside to inspect the mother superior's office in hopes that a piece of evidence might have escaped notice there. They were interrupted a few minutes later when one of the sisters knocked on the open door, announcing that Giustino of the *carabinieri* had arrived.

"Good. You're all here," he said. "I was hoping that would be so, since I have a small bit of good news." He held up his cell phone. "She managed a text to me. Assuming this truly is her, she is still in Venice. Trapped in a wardrobe, if her message is to be believed."

"*Where* in Venice?"

"The phone is now turned off, so to find a more accurate location via GPS is not possible."

Marc read the text. "Have you tried to contact her back?"

"Of course. I asked her to turn on the GPS. No answer, *sfortunatamente*. I have a handful of trusted men searching, but we are worried that someone is monitoring and we don't dare put out that we have been in contact."

"Monitoring the *carabinieri*?"

"Us, the local police. As it stands now, we're not sure. If they are, imagine what would happen if they discover she is there still. As you can see, that limits our resources, which is why I came to deliver this other news personally. We have only just now received a report of a suspicious incident in the area we will be searching."

"What sort of incident?" Lisette asked, feeling a spark of hope.

"A couple returning from a party very late recalled seeing a man carrying a young woman out of a boat, one whom he claimed had too much to drink. They also had been drinking, so at the time it seemed plausible. It was only after they sobered, and were discussing it with others in their travel party much later, that they were told they might want to report it. The man, he resembles the suspect who was seen in the convent." He took out a map, pointing to a location, circled. "This is where he was seen getting out of the boat with the girl. Where we will be searching. Marco, since you are native Italian, you will not stand out so much. You, Lisette, can be a tourist, shopping or some such. The more eyes and ears we have out there, the better."

"And how," Lisette asked, "are we communicating? Especially if we suspect our transmissions are being monitored?"

Giustino pulled several prepaid phones from his satchel. "These and Bluetooth. In light of the possible monitoring, I do not suggest using any electronic communication that is assigned to you." He handed them each a phone. "Let us get started."

The area they were searching was Campo San Polo, one of the larger squares—if a roughly clam-shaped architectural space can be called such. It was, in Lisette's opinion, an unusually pleasant place to do a stakeout, since it boasted numerous cafés, a large magazine kiosk, and the customary marble well-head, surrounded by numerous pigeons and a handful of comfortable park benches.

Marc blended with the local residents who bought their daily newspapers, dropped into a café or trattoria, while Lisette wandered among the tourists. As the winter sun disappeared over the stovepipe chimneys, though, Lisette, who in other circumstances might have appreciated the beauty of her surroundings, was ready to give up hope.

There were ten of them searching altogether, and they had yet to find anything that might tell them where in the square their suspect had taken the girl. Eventually Giustino had half the team break off for dinner, while the other half would continue the search.

A thin winter fog began creeping into the narrow *calle* as Lisette and Marc approached the Rio di San Trovaso. As they rounded the corner on to the narrow *fondamenta*, the fog had become quite dense, muffling the lap of the waters against the decaying bricks of the quay. They could just make out the welcoming windows of the Taverna San Trovaso at its dead end, and were soon seated and ordering. Just as the waiter was serving the *primo piatto—spaghetti alla carbonara* for Lisette and a more Venetian spaghetti with squid in its own ink for Marc, his cell phone rang, upsetting the tranquillity of some locals at the next table, who shot him a withering look. It was Giustino.

Marc listened, then said, "We're on our way."

"What?" Lisette asked.

He stood, pulled several euro notes from his pocket, then placed them on the table. "Giustino said they have located the fruit we have been searching for."

36

Giustino pointed. "There. I have a man watching the location. It is on the *piano nobile* of that gothic *palazzo*. The third arched window from the left."

Marc looked that direction, saw a blue wavering light, as if from a television. "How are we expecting to get in there?"

"We storm the door," Giustino replied.

"And hope," Lisette said, "that Piper isn't caught in the crossfire?"

"Unfortunately, yes. That is our only option with our limited manpower. Unless you can think of another solution."

Marc looked at the map Giustino had drawn. "There's no way in via the side entrance?"

"The *rio* prevents this. I would call my cousin with his fleet of boats, but that would only get us in the *rio* and not up to the window in question. We would need more time and that we do not have."

"How sure are you that someone is monitoring police traffic?"

"We're not," Giustino replied. "It is only a suspicion at this point. But are you willing to risk it?"

Lisette turned around and faced the two of them. "Why not find out? Set a trap. If they fall into it, we know for certain there is a leak. And it may even confirm if she is in this area. If they don't . . ."

"What do you have in mind, *amica mia*?"

"They think Piper has escaped. So we announce that we have her and that she is going to point out to us the house where she was held captive. We just fail to give our location."

"*Probabilmente . . .*" Giustino tapped at his chin, while he eyed the apartment. "*Sì . . .* I do believe it will work. But we must have a position of advantage. Both sides of the *campo*."

"The *sotoportego*," Marc said, nodding toward the far side. "Lisette and I can set up there."

"If it works, we will need to make sure they are drawn out. And someone would need to make entry."

"Lisette and I can make entry. In that position, we can get the closest without drawing attention."

"*Sì*. Like lovers. When you are in place, I will make the call."

Marc put his arm around Lisette. "We'll make it work," he replied. "I just need to know what our contingency plan is if it turns out otherwise."

"If police communication has been compromised? Then we must storm the place and hope she is not harmed." And then, in a voice too low for Lisette to hear, he said something to Marc in rapid Italian, finishing with, "*Non è vero?*"

Marc nodded, then took Lisette by the arm. "Let's go."

She looked at Marc as they walked away. "What was it he just told you?"

"Nothing."

"Nothing? That was a pretty spirited conversation for nothing. Why not have this nothing discussion in front of me?"

He sighed. "I did not want to worry you, *cara mia*. Giustino has informed me that his men have the same order to kill—"

"Did I miss something? McNiel lost his job protecting her location. They're trying to shut down ATLAS because *we* are protecting her. I thought we all agreed. We are *not* going through with this kill order."

"Giustino did not say he was planning to go through with it. It was more a warning that we need to be careful if we are to save her, because the order is out there."

Somewhat relieved, she glanced back at Giustino, who seemed to understand her concern. He gave a slight nod, as if to say he was still on their side, and she breathed easier. It still didn't lessen the guilt of knowing that it was her fault that Piper had been kidnapped. The girl had trusted her, and Lisette had betrayed that trust by allowing her to be taken by two men posing as U.S. marshals.

Marc led her beneath the arch. The blackness of the *sotoportego* enshrouded them, the dim wire-caged bulb doing little to dispel the dark. For several minutes she and Marco pretended to be a couple whose mutual desire kept the cold at bay. The rather enjoyable pretense was interrupted when Giustino called both of them, so that their cell phones were connected via conference call. "We are waiting for two more of my men to arrive, and then I will make the call on my police phone, announcing that we have her and she is showing us where she was being held."

"*Sì.* Copy."

He and Lisette waited in the shadows. The water moving against the buildings in the *rio* behind them was the only sound, until Giustino's voice in her Bluetooth broke the silence. "Someone is entering the *campo* and walking your direction."

"I have visual," Marc said. "Did you make the call?"

"*Affermitiva.*"

They waited in silence, and after a couple of minutes, the

sound of footsteps echoed across the paving stones. As Lisette, her arms around Marc, looked over his shoulder, she saw a man approaching a nearby *palazzo*. "I see him," she said.

The man walked straight toward the *palazzo*, retrieved a large key from his pocket, opened one half of a tall double door, and disappeared into the depths of its unlit ground floor.

"Two are leaving," Marc said quietly. "Still no contact with our . . . fruit?"

"I sent a text," Giustino said. "There is no answer."

The half moon slid behind a cloud, offering some cover, and she and Marc stepped out from beneath the *soto-portego*, in order to cross over. Just as the two men were about to turn a corner, one of the two looked back. Marc quickly moved Lisette into the shadows, and for a moment she thought they'd been spotted. False alarm. The man's face glowed momentarily as he cupped his hands to light a cigarette. A moment later, he was on his way again, following his partner.

"We're moving in," Marc said.

He and Lisette crossed the *campo*, Marc's arm around her as though they were a couple, returning home from the Vivaldi concert, which had just ended at the Church of San Polo. They worried about not hearing from Piper, especially when she had been in touch that one time. But all they could do was continue on, and when they reached the double green door, Marc looked around, surveying the *campo*. "We're here," he said into the Bluetooth.

"The two men have not reached position one."

Marc hesitated. They should have reached that point. He looked at the door. They were so close. "We're going in."

"*Non ancora!* My men, they are not here. What if—"

"We're too close. Just let us know when the suspects come into view."

"*Sì.*"

He reached out, tried the door, found it unlocked. They took that as a sign. Marc aimed his gun, and Lisette swung the door open. The downstairs entry was dark, and they stood there a moment, listening. Marc pointed upward, where the sound of a TV droned. After a quick check of the entry, they took the stairs up. This appeared to be the main living area, lit only by a television. They cleared the room, then entered the hall, passing the bathroom. They stood in front of the only other door, which was closed. Marc turned the knob, pushed it open with his foot, standing to one side. When Lisette looked in, she saw the body on the floor, the puddle of blood reflecting the moonlight. Too big to be Piper. Relief swept through her.

Lisette whispered the girl's name.

There was no answer.

They entered, swept their weapons across the room looking for threats, then turned toward the wardrobe. "I am here. Lisette."

The wardrobe door flew open, and Piper burst out, running right into her. Lisette held her gun up and away as Piper hugged her tight.

"We have her," Lisette said.

But instead of congratulations, what she heard from Giustino was "The men. They are both returning. There are five now and I think they have automatic weapons. You need to get out."

Lisette led Piper to the hallway, Marc on their heels.

The three ran down to the bottom of the stairwell, across the entry, then stopped at the door. The *campo* was still empty—for all of about sixty seconds. And then five men emerged from an alley.

"Whatever we do," Marc said, "we'd better do it fast."

He was right. They hadn't been spotted yet, and right now, distance was their friend. He grabbed Piper's hand, exited the building, then led the three of them across the square to the *sotoportego* where they had hidden earlier. A shout alerted them that they'd been seen, then the sound of their pursuers running after them, their footsteps echoing across the *campo* like sharp, staccato shots. Marc didn't slow down, just led them through the short tunnel, then around the corner and on down a narrow walkway that bordered the water. A wrought-iron gate blocked their path to freedom. A rusted chain hung from the gate, the lock just out of reach on the other side. A spiked brick arch over the top kept anyone from hopping over.

Piper stared at the brackish water. "I can't swim."

"Hopefully you won't have to." He looked up at the arch over the gate. It was too high for them to jump, and Lisette was wondering what he had in mind, when he said, "You think you can pull Piper up?"

"Worth a try."

He boosted Lisette, and she climbed onto the bricks, avoiding the spikes intended to foil thieves, then waited there for him to lift Piper, who was about a foot shorter. Lisette leaned down, grasped the girl's hand, helped her climb over, then onto the other side, using a niche in the wall on their way down.

Marc unholstered his weapon, then handed it to Lisette through the gate.

"What am I supposed to do with this?" she asked.

He didn't answer. Just looked at her.

She tried to hand the gun back. "You have to come with us."

"We're outgunned and outmanned. I'm hoping they'll follow me, not you. But if they don't—"

"Do *not* get hurt."

He reached through the bar, shoved his cell phone and Bluetooth at her. "I'm going to do my best to keep it from happening." When she hesitated, he said, "This will only work if you're out of sight."

"Be careful." She put the phone and Bluetooth in her pocket, turned, took Piper's hand, then ran down the path, discovering that they were trapped in a courtyard. If spotted, they'd have nowhere to run, and she looked around for a place to hide. A potted topiary next to the wall was the best she could find. She and Piper pressed their backs to the brick wall, and she prayed they wouldn't be noticed.

A moment later, she heard what sounded like several men running, followed by a loud splash as Marc leaped into the canal toward the other side.

"Over there!" someone shouted.

"I saw three. Where are the other two?"

"Well, where else would they go? They definitely turned this corner, and that gate's locked."

"They could have gone over it."

Lisette felt Piper tense. "Don't move," she whispered in the girl's ear, hoping she'd listen.

"Over? Then who was that in the water? Goddamned mermaid? Follow them."

"In there?"

"Unless you want to call Brooks and tell them you lost his prize."

A moment of silence, then a loud splash, followed by another. "Bloody cold."

"Then swim faster. It'll warm you up. I'm going to find a boat."

Lisette held her arm in front of Piper, making sure she stayed in the shadows. She dared a peek through the topiary's leaves, saw three men still standing at the water's edge, looking out. Piper's teeth started chattering, and Lisette moved in closer to her, trying to transfer her warmth to the shivering girl. They waited several minutes, and then Lisette leaned out. Seeing nothing, she ventured toward the wrought-iron gate. The path was clear. "Time to go."

She helped Piper back over the wall, and they ran through

the passage. Eventually they turned into a narrow *calle* that led over a bridge, ending up in a small open space surrounded by modest *palazzi*, most with plaster peeling from their decaying bricks. The hour was late, though, and the windows beneath their pointed gothic arches were dark, the residents having long been abed. This was to their advantage, since light was their enemy.

A wooden door stood ajar to the right, and Lisette saw that it led down a narrow alley between two buildings. Another door, this one closed, was at the far end, but fortunately was not locked. Lisette pulled it slightly ajar and looked out, discovering that they had traveled in a circle, because the alley led back into the Campo San Polo, not too far from where she and Marc had hid earlier that night.

They stayed in the shadows, skirting the edges of the *campo*.

This was not what Lisette had intended, and she was concerned about their proximity to the *palazzo* where Piper had been held. Still, she said nothing, not wanting to worry the girl.

"Are you mad at me?"

Lisette looked over at her, surprised by the question. "For what?"

"For stealing your passport and credit card?"

"No. Yes. I am, but—we'll talk about it later."

She pressed the button on her Bluetooth, to call Giustino. "I have her," she said.

"Where are you?"

"In Campo San Polo, near . . ." She looked out, trying to describe the area. "Near the bulge of that funny old church. Not too far from where Marc and I were hiding."

"Ah. Behind the apse of San Polo. I am very nearby. I have men with me, in uniform, so don't be alarmed."

Several men, all uniformed, crossed the square, and Lisette was glad he had warned her. She wouldn't have dared to show herself, not knowing who could or could not be trusted.

Giustino looked around. "Where is Marc?"

"Leading them on a wild-goose chase. We were trapped. He dove into the canal."

He nodded, then ordered two of his men to search in the direction Lisette indicated, then sent two others up into the *palazzo* where the body was located.

It wasn't until his men had been dispatched that Giustino seemed to notice Piper, who was shivering. He removed his jacket and put it around her shoulders. "This way. We will take you someplace safe for the night."

"How will Marc find us?" Lisette asked.

"He already knows to meet at the safe house."

And Piper asked, "Is that where we're going?"

"Yes. The sooner we get you off the streets, the better. I worry that we are being watched, even now."

37

Once Giustino determined that they were not being
followed, he dismissed all but one of his men, then hurried
Lisette and Piper through a dark narrow street, their footsteps echoing across the paving stones, making it sound like
an army was marching with them. The street seemed to wind
on for the longest time—in what direction, she couldn't tell,
except that it was well out of the area frequented by tourists. No shop windows lighted their way, but every now and
then a crook-backed bridge would suddenly loom up before
them. After several minutes, they walked under another *sotoportego*, where they were confronted with the vast turbu-
lence of the Giudecca Canal.

"It's not far now," Giustino said, then ushered them down
a dark street that led away from the busy waterway into what
seemed to Lisette to be a rather depressed working-class
area of the city.

Eventually, they arrived at their destination, a rather pecu-
liar brick corner building, which faced onto the *rio* and the
deserted *campo* of a large church with an imposing square

campanile that somehow seemed out of proportion with the rest of the church.

"Up one floor," Giustino said. Lisette's heels clicked on the tiled stairs, which led her to what, in a better class of Venetian house, would have been the *piano nobile*. There was little that could be called noble about this unprepossessing house. She and Piper walked into what passed for a sitting room, with windows overlooking both the *rio* and the *campo* of the ugly brick church.

Marc arrived shortly thereafter, his hair and clothes dripping, and smelling of canal water. "A man who sacrifices himself deserves a hug, don't you agree?"

Lisette eyed the growing puddle around him as he stood in the tiled entryway. "Undoubtedly. But not from me. Giustino? He's *your* friend."

"I'll be glad to give him a hug. *After* he showers."

She smiled at Marc, then looked around. "And in which room will Piper and I be sleeping?"

"This way," Giustino said.

He led them to a room upstairs, and Lisette was pleased to see that it had an en suite bathroom. The furnishings seemed decent enough. There was a dark wood dresser with a marble top. Its mirror reflected the two single beds with high, dark wood headboards. And, as in the convent, a crucifix had been set on the wall to protect any sleepers. Lisette took the bed closer to the door, trying to ignore the lumps in the hard mattress as she sprawled across it. Piper bounced once on the bed, then got up, announcing she was going to take a shower. It seemed to last forever. Had they not been on the upper floor overlooking the *rio*, Lisette might have suspected her of turning on the water, then slipping out through the bathroom window. She emerged eventually, trailing a swath of steam, a towel wrapped around her hair, wearing a nightgown that Giustino had supplied, and carrying her clothes in a wrinkled bundle. "Sorry it took me so long. I just needed . . . I don't know. To chill, I guess."

"Are you okay?"

Piper nodded. "Just glad to be out of there. The things you don't think about when you steal someone's passport and fly off to another country."

She tossed the clothes onto a chair, and a phone bounced out and onto the floor. "Vittorio's phone. I took it after that man, Paolo, killed him. That's what I used to text Giustino." She picked it up and placed it on the end table. "I suppose right now it'll be evidence?"

"Possibly," Lisette said, removing the battery. "They'll be able to use it to find out who was in touch with him, maybe even who was behind your kidnapping. We'll give it to Marc in the morning."

"I hope they catch them," she replied.

Lisette, deciding not to take any chances even though Piper was supposedly reformed, locked her bag in the bathroom while she showered and changed. When she emerged, Piper was in bed, eyes closed, lying on her side, her hands tucked beneath the pillow. Lisette left the bathroom light on, and only partially closed the door, allowing a sliver of light through, then tiptoed to her bed.

Piper's eyes opened, and she looked right at Lisette.

"What's wrong?" Lisette asked.

"Did you hear something?"

"No. We'll be safe here. Don't worry."

After a few seconds, Piper said, "Are you sure they're not going to arrest me?"

"For what?"

"For stealing your passport and credit card. That's identity theft."

"If nothing else, I hope you have learned some valuable lessons."

"I have," she said, her voice quiet. ". . . Thanks."

Lisette tossed and turned all night, her dreams chaotic, confusing, as she raced through the streets of Venice, never sure if she was actually awake or dreaming. At one point her gaze caught on the phone that Piper had stolen from her captor. It glowed with an incoming call. She wasn't even aware it was on, and reached over, picked it up, and saw the caller ID showed "*privato*" on the screen. And then she was racing through a pitch black *sotoportego*, chased by someone as one thought swirled through her head.

Who would be calling a dead man's phone?

But when she got up to find Marc, to ask him, he was sinking to the bottom of the canal.

She awoke with a start, her heart pounding. Still dark out; she glanced over, couldn't even see the phone on the bedside table. Had someone called it? Or had she dreamed it?

Too tired to think, she reached out, felt it beneath her fingertips, and picked it up. She fumbled with it, but managed to pull the battery, then returned it to the table, trying to decide if she was even still dreaming—because surely she'd already removed the battery—all while knowing there was something about that phone she needed to tell Marc, something important . . .

38

Washington, D.C.

Parker Kane looked around the crowded hotel ball-
room, until he found Trenton Stiles, a top Network man who
ran Wingman and Wingman. He weaved his way through
the formally dressed guests to get to him. "We have a serious problem." Parker Kane took Trenton Stiles by the arm
and led him well away from the others gathered at the party.

"What sort of problem can't wait until morning?" Stiles
asked.

"Let me put it this way. If this gets out, the president might
as well just hang up his hat. There won't be a second term."

Stiles pasted a false smile on his face, for anyone who
might be looking. "Why not?" he asked through his teeth,
nodding at a passing couple on their way into the banquet
room.

"Because the matter *you* wanted to erase, the political
contribution that can be tied into Wingman—well, let's just
say that if ATLAS recovers the key before we do, we're
screwed." Which was the smallest of Parker Kane's prob-

lems if they didn't find the key. He could give a rat's ass about the political contribution. There were much bigger issues he needed to deal with.

"I thought you had this matter handled."

"I did when I thought we'd have the program up and running. Unfortunately there have been a few setbacks along the way."

"The Network pays you well to make sure we do *not* have setbacks. So what seems to be the problem?"

"ATLAS is still operational."

"The building was shut down. How can they be operational?"

"Someone broke in. The files we'd hoped to find weren't there."

A waiter walked up, offered both men champagne flutes. They each took one, nodded their thanks, then moved even farther away. "Do you realize how hard it is to get the proper people elected to office these days? Especially with the Internet. You're with the goddamned CIA. About to be deputy national security adviser. Are you telling me you can't handle this job?"

Kane's grip on his glass tightened. "Of course not. But—"

"You said you would have this Satan's key—"

"Devil's Key—"

"Whatever. What you need to remember, Mr. Kane, is that your appointment is not yet confirmed. I'd hate to see something come up in a background check that might prevent it. My suggestion to you? Fix this or there won't be an appointment. Am I clear?"

"Of course."

"I hope to hear a more positive report from you soon." He handed his untouched glass to Kane. "Enjoy the party," he said, then walked off, leaving Kane standing there alone, feeling like an idiot with two champagne glasses in his hand.

He found a waiter, deposited both on the tray, then left, doing his best to look calm, unconcerned, when he was seething inside.

Trenton Stiles and his ilk were all about getting the right men in office, men they could control, while people like Kane worked behind the scenes, making it all so easy for them.

He hadn't spent the last twenty years clawing his way to the top to be dismissed that easily, and he wasn't about to let it happen now, he thought, waiting out front for his car. When it arrived, he told the driver to take him back to his office. Time to see what the night crew had accomplished.

When he got there, the lights were on in the command center. "Update," he said, loosening his tie.

"The girl is back with ATLAS," Alan Madison said.

"Where?"

"Venice still. A radio transmission was intercepted. She apparently brought the police to where she was being held captive."

Alive . . . Thank God, he thought. "Any word on where they have her?"

"No, sir. But we also intercepted a digital transmission from Vittorio's phone."

"Vittorio?"

"The man who took her from the convent."

"I thought he was dead."

"He is. Or so Paolo reported. Of course, that does not explain why there would be a text message from his phone *after* he was killed."

"Going to where?"

"California, sir."

He walked over, looked at the computer screen. "The hell . . . Whose number is that?"

"In California? We're not sure. Right now we're trying to pinpoint its location in Venice."

"Good. In the meantime I want to know who in California this other phone belongs to. Find out."

A half hour later, he had his answer.

"It's Kendall Lawrence. Brother. Foster care. Sixteen, still in the system."

"How did we miss this?"

"They haven't lived together in over ten years."

"That would be normal for foster care?"

"Undoubtedly."

He nodded, then paced the room, thinking. "The Mexico team? Are they back?"

"I expect so."

Which meant he did not, unfortunately, have anyone on the West Coast. At least not who he trusted with such a sensitive issue. "Get them on the phone. I want them in California by morning. I want this kid picked up the moment we locate him."

Madison hesitated.

"Don't just sit there! Get moving!"

"Yes, sir."

39

Venice, Italy

Marc was already up when Lisette emerged from the bedroom.

He was talking to Dumas and looked upset. "What the hell is going on that we can't even hide a witness?"

"I worry about her being here," Dumas said. "I don't think we have the means to protect her. Not when we don't know who is hunting her. Who are these other people?"

"I'm not sure. They spoke English."

"The problem is how to get her on a plane without being stopped before she gets through the airport."

"Or killed before she gets there."

"It would be nice to know whom we can trust." Dumas looked up, saw Lisette. "Coffee?"

"Please." She held out the phone and battery, pulled apart, knowing Marc was not going to be happy with what she had to say. "It's the one Piper used to text Giustino. From the kidnapper. There might be an issue with it."

Dumas eyed both pieces. "But how? If the battery is out?"

"I have a feeling Piper may have put it back in. A call came in, which was when I noticed it and removed the battery a second time. I'm afraid I was a little too out of it to realize—well, the damage is done."

"A call?" Dumas said. "Who calls a dead man?"

"No one," Marc said. "Unless you didn't know he was dead, or you realized the phone was missing and wanted to track it."

"I fear it is the latter," Dumas said. "But perhaps we can use it to our advantage?"

"How?" Lisette asked.

"A decoy. We will send the phone in the opposite direction, hoping they follow it instead of you."

Marc opened a cupboard that contained an assortment of tools and equipment. He intended to clone the phone, and after a glance at the monitors, seeing it was still clear outside, he got to work.

Piper emerged a few minutes later, just as he managed to bring up the numbers on his computer screen.

"The incoming calls," Marc said, pointing to the screen, and scrolling through the numbers. Most were blocked, but a few were not. "Now the outgoing . . ."

Marc tapped the screen that showed a U.S. area code for the Bay Area. "San Mateo County?"

Piper gave an apologetic sigh. "South City. My brother, Kenny's, phone. Why should it matter? This phone doesn't even belong to me."

Marc swore in Italian.

"What?" Piper asked. "I didn't think I was ever going to see him again. I mean, what would you do? I wanted him to be able to call me."

Whoever these people were, they'd already monitored Lisette's phone, thereby locating Piper at the convent. If, for some reason, they were monitoring the kidnapper's phone, then it might be an issue. Lisette hoped it wasn't, that they were giving too much credit where it wasn't due. It did not, however, answer the bigger question. Who exactly was looking for Piper? Kane's men? Or someone else?

It was Marc, however, who pointed out the real danger. "Let us hope they are not monitoring your brother's number as well."

"But it was just a text, and not even from the same phone I used to call Lisette when— Oh my God . . . This is all my fault." Her face paled as she turned to Lisette. "He'll be okay, won't he?"

"I hope so," Lisette said.

"Are his foster parents in any danger? Can we protect them, too? They have other kids there."

This was snowballing, and she worried that if they weren't able to give Piper the answers she wanted to hear, she'd do something foolish, jeopardizing their safety. That was something she hoped to avoid. For the girl's sake and theirs. "I think," Lisette said, "that as long as he is not near them, they are safe. What I do worry about is that they might try to use him to get to you. Our friends will look into it. I promise you."

"But we have to warn them!"

"Where does he live?"

She gave Lisette the address, adding, "If he's not at home, he'll be at school. He goes to South City High."

Marc abruptly left his chair, undoubtedly to pass on this information to Giustino. When he returned, he said, "Our immediate concern is coming up with a solid plan to get you safely out of this country. It's clear they know you're here. If we want to get you out of Venice alive, it's got to be completely off the grid."

"He's right," Lisette said, then asked Dumas, "About using a decoy? What's your plan with that?"

Dumas picked up Piper's stolen phone. "We send three people to the Marco Polo Airport, with tickets in your true name on a return flight. They carry this phone, which we will turn on at key places to send key texts. *If* they are monitoring the phone as we suspect, they should follow it and our decoys to the airport, while you three are leaving by a different route."

Marc went back to pacing the room, while everyone watched him. "I like it."

"I don't," Piper said. "How will that help my brother?"

"Our friends in the States will be helping him," he said, stopping at the window, and staring out across the *rio* at the *campo* and the pseudo-Palladian marble archway above the entrance to the church. "Giustino is contacting them now. Let us work on the more immediate plan. So we must carefully compose a text to your brother to let our enemies know what route to take. One that won't be as suspicious."

Lisette thought about how close they'd been to being caught, all because of that damned cell phone, and the temptation of one young girl to contact her brother . . . The question now was if they were going to be able to get out of the country at all.

Lisette and Dumas had stayed behind at the safe house with Piper. Giustino left to make the arrangements with his men to set up the travel plans and the decoys who would be leading a false trail to the Marco Polo Airport, where three air tickets back to Washington, D.C., were waiting under their real names. Marc, on the other hand, was picking up the forged passports that Giustino had arranged under their new assumed names. They'd been gone several hours, which was to be expected, considering the number of documents and plans that had to be finalized. Still, if all went well, Lisette thought, looking out the window, they'd be on their way to Rome within the hour. Dumas was watching the monitors, and Lisette kept watch from the windows, since the cameras did not cover the entire square. Despite the ungainly proportions of the church and campanile in respect to the *campo*, she savored the view. Too bad she was here to work, she thought, envying a couple of idlers sitting on one of the benches, enjoying a sliver of sun as they read their newspapers. A glance at the sky, however, foretold the sun would not last, as dark clouds moved in, threatening rain.

Piper walked up beside her. "It's like stepping back in time," she said. "You can almost imagine what life would have been like centuries ago."

The shrill ring of someone's phone echoed across the empty space, the acoustics of the building intensifying the sound. Dumas laughed. "So much for the illusion of stepping back in time, no?"

A moment later, the roar of a motorboat cut through as it pulled up to a dock on their left. It idled there, the three men content to sit in their boat, not seeming to care that the engine noise was disturbing anyone, or that their boat's fumes were polluting the clear Venetian air.

"Suddenly a popular location," Lisette said, then saw a man standing in the shadow of the church doorway talking on his cell. He turned his gaze toward the *rio*, where the boat was docked. She glanced that way, saw another man on the boat talking on his cell.

Talking to each other?

Her instincts went on high alert, and though she didn't think anyone could see in through the partially closed dark green wooden shutters, she stood off to one side. "Those men are watching our direction and talking to each other."

Dumas cracked open the shutter of the far left window about a quarter of an inch, allowing just enough room to peer out without being seen from the outside. "On the boat?"

"I think he's communicating with the man in the church doorway. I could be wrong." One of the men from the boat walked over to join him. "If you have any suggestions, Father, this is the time."

He turned to the monitors. "I'd say we make our exit via the boat dock at the rear. That is, assuming it is not also covered."

"And?"

"The monitor is showing nothing unusual. Where's Piper?"

"Here," she said, standing not too far away, looking alarmed.

Poor girl, Lisette thought. "It may be nothing. But stay close."

Lisette turned her attention back to the window, and just when she was thinking that it could all very well be something innocent, one of them looked toward the safe house and nodded. She stepped back, even though she knew she couldn't be seen. "We're definitely being watched."

"I'll check the back exit," Dumas said. "The monitors don't allow a view far enough down."

Piper watched him leave, then asked, "Are we still going home today?"

Lisette looked over at her, saw the worry in her eyes. "Of course."

She seemed relieved to know she wasn't being left behind.

"Have a seat," Lisette told her. "It could be a long wait."

Father Dumas confirmed as much on his return. "We are being watched from the back as well. They are just outside the view of the cameras."

Lisette focused out the window and saw someone across the *campo* quickly duck into the shadows of the church. "Tell me you have something more than a prayer book to throw at these guys?"

"Unfortunately no. My work is more of the intelligence type."

Great. One gun between them. Hers.

Piper stood next to her. "We need to call the police."

"We can't," Dumas said. "We have no idea if it was your phone that led them here or someone is monitoring our traffic in another way. Giustino was careful, but perhaps they saw through our ruse last night when we rescued you from that wardrobe."

Lisette called Marc's number, listened to it ring, and was relieved when he answered. "We have a bit of a situation," she said.

40

San Mateo, California

Carillo glanced at the clock, saw it was just after seven, and was tempted to let the call go to voice mail, knowing that whatever it was this early couldn't be good. He did not, however, because the area code was from Italy, which was where the girl, Piper, had fled to. "Carillo," he said.

"Giustino here. Is Tex with you?"

"Asleep in the other room."

"Good. If you could be so kind as to take him your phone. It is possible his is compromised."

"That would have been nice to know a lot earlier. Some reason mine isn't?"

"The possibility exists, but the margin is greater for his. Therefore . . ."

"Great. I'll just drag my ass out of bed and get him. Long day."

"*Grazie.*"

Tex was asleep on the couch, facedown, when Carillo walked in.

"Yo. Tex. One of the Italians on the phone for you."

Tex stirred. "Tell him to call back in the morning."

"News flash, Sparky. It's morning."

Tex shifted on the couch, reached out blindly, and Carillo stuck the phone in his hand. "What . . ." His tone was anything but pleasant. Then again, he and Carillo had spent the last couple of days running round Mexico. They flew home, arriving a little after nine last night, and both had been too tired to do much more than drink several beers, then go straight to bed.

And though that was where Carillo wanted to return to, he knew that the moment he did, Tex would be back, informing him about something he didn't want to hear. Or do. Which was why he plopped down on the chair and waited, while Tex conversed in Italian, impressing Carillo that he could do it in his near-comatose state.

After several minutes, Tex held out the phone for Carillo. "Here."

"What was that lively discourse about?"

"The girl they picked up apparently has a brother. Kenny."

"And that means what to us?"

"Welfare check. Low-key."

"The location being . . . ?"

Tex finally sat up, looking around, as though it finally hit him that there was still work to be done. "He's texting you the kid's address. But figures the high school might be a better option. Something called South City."

"That'd be South San Francisco High," Carillo said.

"Guess we'll need to set the alarm. Don't want to miss the first bell."

Carillo looked at the wall clock. "Yeah. Probably gonna miss that. Maybe the tardy bell."

And so it was they ended up at the boy's school that morning. While Tex waited in the car, Carillo stood in line behind a slew of kids apparently turning in notes for being sick, late, or wanting to go home. Budget cuts. The office was short staffed, and the secretary overwhelmed by a phone that rang constantly. Her two student aides were busy fielding the notes, and since he wasn't about to announce who he was with about a dozen witnesses, he stepped back, standing in the doorway of an empty counselor's office waiting for the crowd at the counter to thin, and the secretary to get off the phone.

A good thing, it turned out, because two men walked up, cut in front of the kids so that they were first in line at the counter. Both were dressed in dark suits, and one held up a black credential case, flashing some sort of ID at the student aide, then asking for the kid by name. Kendall Lawrence.

Carillo didn't recognize either man, but he certainly knew the government-spook type when he saw them.

Or rather, the creepy government-spook type. These two gave him a bad feeling, and he decided now was not a good time to be spotted. Stepping back into the empty office, he pulled off his tie, tossed it on the chair by the door. Then, after unbuttoning his top shirt button, he grabbed a sheaf of copy paper from the shelf by the desk, acted like he was looking through the papers, then walked out into the main office, hoping he looked more scholarly than he felt. One of the aides, a brown-haired girl with a long ponytail, nodded at the two men, then glanced over at the secretary, who looked up the kid's room number on her computer. The woman covered the mouthpiece of the phone, said, "Mr. Albertos. Room 143."

"I'll get him for you," the girl told the men, then headed toward the door.

Carillo stepped aside, allowing her to go first, then followed her to the classroom. After she went in, notified the teacher, then exited, he stopped her just outside. "You're one of the TAs in the office this period?"

"Who are you?"

"New sub. Any chance you can take this paper to the athletic office? They need it to make flyers."

"Sure."

"Thanks."

She took off in the opposite direction and Carillo waited for the kid to exit the classroom. He walked out about sixty seconds later, carrying a backpack.

"You're Piper's brother? Kenny?"

The kid looked wary. "How do you know her?"

"She's, uh, in a bit of trouble. Asked us to look you up, make sure you're okay."

"Who are you?"

"Tony Carillo, FBI," he said as he flipped open his credentials, then guided the kid away from the classroom door. The last thing he needed was to have the teacher walk out and be able to identify him later on should there be an inquiry. Sort of ruined the whole under-the-radar thing. "Don't suppose you know of any way to get out to the parking lot without going past the office?"

"Why?"

"There's two guys waiting there for you, and I guarantee they're not on your sister's side. Or yours. Piper was pretty adamant about getting you out of here."

"No offense, but she's like, not here, so how do I know you're really who you say you are?"

"You don't, but it's me or the two waiting for you in the office, and I have no idea who they are, so take your pick."

"Why are they looking for me?" Kenny asked.

"Your sister witnessed a crime. She's in trouble."

The kid stopped in his tracks.

"We need to hurry."

"What do you mean she's in trouble?"

And no sooner had the words left his mouth than the two suits came walking around the corner in the hallway.

"That would be them," Carillo said softly.

The men looked up, saw Carillo and Kenny, their focus sharpening, and he figured they had about twenty seconds to come up with a Plan B, since getting out undiscovered at this point was long gone. Before he could even think of something, Kenny slung his backpack onto his shoulder, then walked straight toward the men. "Oh my God, Dad," he said. "You're *such* a jerk! I didn't hit him first. He hit me."

The two men eyed Kenny as he headed straight toward them. "Hey," the taller of the two said. "Are you Kendall Lawrence?"

The kid gave them a withering look. "I wish. Maybe then I wouldn't be grounded. *God* I hate my life."

"Yeah?" Carillo said, thoroughly impressed, while doing his best to keep up with the kid. "You hate it now? Wait until your mother finds out." He ignored the two men, walking past them, as he followed Kenny around the corner toward the office. Just before he turned, he saw them reach the classroom, one of them pulling open the door. Carillo quickened his pace. "There's a blue Crown Victoria parked out front with my partner at the wheel. Head for that."

Before they reached the car, the two men burst out of the office door. "Police! Stop!"

Kenny looked toward them. "Police?"

"Trust me," Carillo said. "They're not."

The kid hesitated.

Carillo opened the back door, shoving him into the car, then got in the front passenger seat. "Time to go," he told Tex.

"Hey!" The goons ran toward them.

Tex started the car, hit the gas, and raced out of the parking lot, his tires screeching. And the one thing on Carillo's mind was that if they were law enforcement, or government agents, he sure as hell hoped they didn't copy his license number. FBI or not, kidnapping minors from school grounds was still very illegal. "Buckle up, kid. I have a feeling this is going to be a wild ride."

41

Venice, Italy

Lisette explained the situation to Marc, about the men outside the safe house, watching them.

Marc was apparently now with Giustino at his office near the *ferrovia* at Santa Lucia. "You're safe?" he asked her, when she finished.

"For the moment. They seem to be waiting. Whether it's for us to leave, or for reinforcements, I don't know. I think we're fairly defensible for a short period . . . but there is only the one weapon here."

"Hold on. Giustino is bringing the area up on satellite." She heard the sound of a keyboard clicking in the background. It was not a live feed, since he was not at an ATLAS office, but at least it would give them a decent idea of what they were dealing with. Not that it was much different from what she could see from their windows now. The safe house was surrounded by water on two sides, a narrow *rio* ran the length from front to back, and at the rear of the building. A large public square was situated at the front of the building, through which they would have to pass on foot if leaving that way.

She heard Giustino asking, "There is still access to exit by boat in the rear?"

"Tell him no," she said. "Dumas believes that they are watching the back. There is a gate at the front, which opens into a courtyard, through which one walks to the main entrance. The men are positioned across the square watching us, both to the left in a boat at the dock, and to the right, where we would have to walk. There is no exit that way."

"What about a distraction here?" she heard him asking Giustino.

"No," Giustino said. "If they are watching the back, it will be useless."

"Bait and switch," Marc told him. "Your cousin? How many boats does he have in his fleet?"

"Four."

"And men he can trust?"

"Four brothers. We can trust them all. Why?"

And then she heard Marc say, "Here's what I propose . . ."

Lisette peered out the window into the *campo*. It had been nearly a half hour since she'd called Marc, and it was starting to rain. "I count at least three men. I'm not sure why they're waiting."

"Thanks be to God that they are," Dumas said.

Piper paced the room, then stopped when Dumas's phone rang. Lisette stepped back from the window, listening, hoping for a break. He lowered the phone and looked at her. "Giustino's cousin, Antonio, has enlisted a couple of his taxi friends to take fares past the canals to get a view of the area. They have confirmed that the safe house is being watched from the canal entrance beyond the views of the cameras. It will be impossible to leave that way."

Lisette peered out the window again, hoping for a miracle. It wasn't forthcoming as a fourth suspect joined the others, two on each side of the square. "They have the front covered."

And Piper said once again, "We should call the police."

Dumas shook his head, then held up his finger, indicating he needed quiet, while he listened to whatever Antonio was telling him. "*Sì.*" He looked up at Lisette, saying, "We have a new plan." He took a piece of paper and drew a map. "They are here in the square, and here, to the rear of the safe house, according to Antonio, waiting across the canal watching the dock. But they do not believe anyone is watching here." He tapped the paper.

Lisette eyed the map showing the narrow water passage that ran along the left of the safe house. "The only way into that boat is through a window that, if I'm not mistaken, has bars over it."

"Which is why we are going out the upper story window."

"Rappelling down the side of a building isn't exactly a specialty of mine."

"Fire escape ladder," he said, nodding to a box in the corner. "Giustino informed me it is in good working order."

"Okay. Let's say we all make it safely out. How are they proposing we get past the sentries they've posted? The boat has to pass by one or the other end of the canal and both are being watched. I'm guessing they may be armed."

Dumas relayed her concerns to Antonio, listened, then covered the phone, saying to Lisette, "His first thought was to provide a funeral boat. We would hide in the coffins."

Lisette shook her head. "Rappelling down the side of a building is one thing. Hiding in a coffin? Tell me he has a Plan B?"

To which he told Antonio, "Lisette is not fond of the funeral boat idea . . ."

A movement at the window caught her eye, and she glanced out. She saw one of the men talking on a cell phone, and he walked from his spot against the side of a marble column, sauntering toward the *rio*, as though out for a casual stroll. To the untrained eye, sure. To Lisette, he was casing the *palazzo*, surveying the area to see where it was she and Piper might escape from. If he stayed there for any length of time, they were in trouble, because he now had a clear view down the narrow waterway from which they'd have to make their escape. She estimated they'd need at least three minutes to get from the window down to the boat without being seen. "Tell Antonio that we're going to need some sort of distraction when that boat gets here, or we'll never make it out. One of the sentries has moved so that he can see down the *rio*."

Father Dumas repeated the info, then said, "*Sì*, she may like it better. *Ciao*." He disconnected. "He thinks he has a Plan B."

Lisette turned her attention back to the square. "He did say he'd provide a distraction?"

"Yes," he said, walking over to the fire ladder. He bent down, grabbed a handle on the box, and slid it toward the green-shuttered window overlooking the smaller *rio*. He un-latched the windows, pulling both open, and any heat within was lost, dropping the temperature of the room by several degrees, and allowing rain to spatter in. At least the deluge had not yet started, the heavier storm not expected for at least an hour.

The waiting was the hardest part, as was the unknown. How exactly did Antonio plan to spirit them out of there beneath the noses of the sentries? It was getting dark fast, which should help. A few minutes later she heard the low rumble of a motorboat, from the open window, followed by raucous laughter and singing. She looked out, saw a taxi boat with at least five passengers steering down the *rio* past the *campo*, then stopping very near the sentry posted at the water's edge. Someone leaned over the side of the boat, an-other person shouting, and then a second boat followed, this also containing a number of people, who looked as though they were in the same group.

Dumas's phone rang. He answered, listened, then said, "*Sì.*" He watched the people in the square. "*Tutto finirà bene.*" Then to Lisette said, "Our ride is here, as is your distraction."

Two more boats pulled in, one of them continuing down the *rio*, while the other docked, letting off several passengers who staggered from the boat, singing and waving bottles of champagne around. They stood on the dock, helping other passengers from the boat, and Lisette realized they were there not only to distract the sentry, but to block his view down the *rio* and the side of the *palazzo* where she and Piper would be climbing down.

"Help me with the ladder," Dumas told Piper.

Together they lowered the ladder, slowly, trying not to let it swing in the wind, so as not to bring attention to it. When the ladder was locked in place, he assisted Piper, then called Lisette over. One last look at the men in the *campo* told her their focus was on the group of revelers. So far, so good, and she crossed the room, threw one leg over the sill, then waited until Piper made it to the bottom and watched as a couple of men helped her into the idling boat that bobbed below.

"Now," Dumas said. She gripped the ledge, feeling with her toe for footing, then lowered herself down, rung by rung, rain hitting her back. When she neared the bottom, she felt someone grasp her, then assist her into the boat.

"Put this on, signora," a man said, handing her a bright yellow raincoat, then a matching hat. Piper was dressed similarly, and the moment Dumas touched deck, they were outfitting him the same, as the driver started the boat toward the canal. And just when Lisette wondered if anyone had bothered counting passengers, there already being three yellow-clad men in the boat, the men dropped to the bottom and were covered by a tarp. "The rain, she is timely!" the boat's driver said, as it splattered down. "Better than the coffins, *sì*?"

"Are you Antonio, then?"

"*Sì*. And you, Marco's Lisette. *Ombrello—al reparo da pioggia*."

Lisette translated for Piper, "When his driver turns the *motoscafo*, the boat, into the canal, you raise the umbrella. As a cover. I suggest we act the giddy tourist."

"Giddy?"

"Drunk. Preferably too drunk to get out of the rain."

Piper smiled. "I can work with that."

And as the motorboat putted slowly under the first bridge, past the sentries standing guard across from the back of the safe house, she thought they might get away with it. They were just making a right turn under the second guarded bridge when the boat picked up speed, and a gust of wind tore the umbrella from Piper's hand. She turned reflexively, trying to catch it.

A shout from the sentries, then the start of an engine.

"They've seen us!" Lisette shouted.

Antonio ordered them down, and Lisette fell back into her seat as the boat shot forward. She grabbed the side, hanging on as the cold wind whipped her hair about, and rain splashed on her face.

Dumas shouted something, but his words were lost in the wind. She heard the sharp crack of a gunshot, then another, and she yanked Piper to the bottom of the boat. Antonio maneuvered the craft with precision, and then suddenly slowed, made a left into a narrow passage. Antonio picked up speed in the widening *rio*. Soon they would reach the safety of the Giudecca Canal with its continuous traffic, and the patrolling boats of the Guardia di Finanza. And for a moment she thought they'd lost the other boat, and she breathed a sigh of relief. Short-lived. The revving engine warned them they'd been found. She watched in horror as the boat gained on them. But Antonio's taxi sped under the Zattere bridge and burst into the waters of the Giudecca, slowing down enough not to bring undue attention to their boat. Although their pursuers were gaining speed, they must have realized the danger for them, for they veered left into the Rio di San Nicolo.

Relieved, she glanced over, saw Father Dumas sending up thanks. Eventually they arrived at the train station, and Antonio brought the boat up to the dock, as the three tugged their rain slickers off, then threw them in the bottom before disembarking.

"*Bon giorno!*" Antonio cried, as the boat sped away with the three men in their yellow slickers taking their places.

They didn't stop to say good-bye, just ran up the platform, then hid until they felt the danger was past. When the suspect boat failed to appear, they emerged and started toward the train station. "I hope they're okay," Lisette said.

"I expect he will draw them out to the Canal Grande," Dumas said. "I don't think much will happen to us here, in so public a place. Now let us get you home."

Marc and Giustino met up with them at the Santa Lucia train station, once they finally received word that the plans were finalized, and decoys were ready with the compromised cell phone, waiting to be activated at the right time en route to Venice's Marco Polo Airport. They, however, would be boarding the train to Rome.

Piper was under orders not to speak, thereby alerting anyone to her nationality, while Marc and Giustino carried on a lively Italian conversation on either side of her, discussing the latest Lazio-Roma football rivalry as a cover. Lisette sat off by herself, since the Network operatives were looking for a group of three, two women, one man. And just before

Father Dumas left them, he took Piper's hand in hers, telling her, "Be careful my child. There's a reason God has commanded, 'Thou shalt not steal.' In your case, so that thou shalt not get killed. Keep your hands in your pockets."

"I promise."

Lisette watched the platform for any sign they were being followed, but all appeared clear as the train left the station. Soon the last signs of Venice disappeared, and she told herself she, frankly, was glad to see it go. She stared out the window, paying little attention as the darkened fields and hill towns of Etruria rather suddenly gave way to the brightly lit apartments as the train finally pulled into Rome's Stazione Termini. One of Giustino's fellow officers was waiting for them on the *binario*. As they made their way through the crowd of other arriving passengers down the long platform, the two men spoke rapidly, in urgent voices, but were too far away for Lisette to hear. Not that she needed to. It was undoubtedly bad news, and as soon as his colleague left, Giustino confirmed it. "I think it is best if you split up once again," Giustino said in Italian, clearly concerned that Piper might overhear.

"Why?" she asked, looking around. They still had to take a train to the airport.

"There are government agents watching the trains. Leo has just informed me that they are searching for a group. Two women, one man. We think they took the names from the passenger list at the Venice airport. Yours, Lisette's, and Piper's."

"What about me?" Piper said, hearing her name.

Marc ignored her, and in Italian asked Giustino, "The U.S.? Any particular branch?"

"The military."

Lisette glanced at Marc, saw the worry in his eyes. The military was the one instructed to carry out the kill order.

Which meant there were two groups after Piper, and she

glanced at the girl, suddenly wondering if this capacity for memorizing things carried over to languages. But Piper, thank God, did not seem to understand Italian, as Marc said, "The military wants her dead, and the Network wants her alive. Either way, this is not good. Maybe we should come up with a different plan."

"Perhaps not," Giustino said. "Your flight leaves before the Venice flight. They can't possibly have discovered the names *you* are traveling under, since they've never been used before. No one outside the four of us knows of them." In fact, their passports were brand-new, the names clean, the photos only added that morning by a trusted specialist that Giustino regularly used. No electronic data had ever been passed. And, as an extra precaution, Lisette's plane ticket had been purchased separately from Marc's and Piper's, in case they were searching for groups of three.

Marc surveyed the terminal as he handed two of the train tickets over to Giustino. "You take Lisette. I'll take Piper. When we get to the airport, stay behind us, watch for anything unusual. We meet on the plane."

Giustino nodded, then drew Lisette with him. Neither spoke until they were on the train to Fiumicino, in a different car from Marc and Piper. Finally Lisette leaned toward him. "What if we don't make it?"

"You must not think like that. You will."

42

San Francisco, California

The long night was wearing on Griffin. Though they could have flown directly into Sacramento, he and Sydney took a late flight into San Francisco.

After spending the night at Doc's, they were on the road to Sacramento by eight that morning and pulling up in front of the *Sacramento Weekly Review* by eleven.

The editor, Bob Michaels, a man in his sixties, with a crown of white hair and a craggy face, wore gray slacks and a white dress shirt, but no tie. He asked them back to his office, a room with a window that overlooked the freeway.

"Sorry about the mess," he said, pushing aside a stack of papers on his desk, along with a half-eaten bagel. "Deadlines. Gets a little hectic around here. Coffee?"

"No thanks," Griffin said. Sydney also declined, and after they were seated in the two chairs opposite his desk, Griffin thanked him for seeing them on such short notice.

"Least I could do. Tim Ronson was a good guy. I never liked the way they threw him to the wolves in San Jose."

"So what happened?" Griffin asked.

"He was blackballed, plain and simple. When his story about the government funding their ops with drug money broke, it was huge news." He leaned back in his chair, looking out the window a moment as though trying to recall the events of so long ago. "What I do remember is that his editor publicly lambasted him in the paper, saying he was unable to prove his allegations. And then the CIA mouthpieces made certain that the other major newspapers, *L.A. Times*, New York, Washington followed suit. You can imagine. His career was over. A year before, he could've written a ticket to any paper in the country. After? He had two choices. Wal-Mart or here."

"That had to have shaken him," Griffin said, thinking it could be a good cause for suicide.

"Not just him. A lot of starry-eyed journalists woke up when they saw him hit rock bottom. It ain't all Clark Kent out there, dig for a story, then have everyone cheering you on as you win a Pulitzer exposing the evil ways of the world. They forget those big corporate papers are usually part of major holdings. And those businesses didn't get that big without a few backroom deals made by political types. In other words, don't step on the wrong toes, especially when they're attached to a sleeping tiger."

"He ever talk to you about it?" Griffin asked. "What he was investigating? Whose toes he stepped on?"

"Not much more than what I've told you. All he wanted was something to pay the bills, so he could continue investigating, earn his name back. Thing is, we don't have the budget those big papers have. I told him if he wanted to work on that on the side, he was welcome to it, but on his time and his dime."

"And what was it?"

He didn't answer right away, as though trying to decide at this late date if perhaps he'd said too much. "Where's this going, anyway?"

Griffin looked at Sydney, gave her a slight nod. She was good at garnering sympathy for the cause, so to speak. And she didn't disappoint.

"My father was murdered around the same time, and we think the cases might be connected. That his case and Mr. Ronson's might have been involved somehow."

"But you're with the FBI?"

"I am. But I'm not investigating it for the FBI."

"Who was your father?"

"Kevin Fitzpatrick."

And before either of them could say anything about it, he typed the name into his computer to see what would come up.

Sydney took a breath, probably wondering the same thing as Griffin. Would anyone be monitoring her father's name? God knew they had back when she'd been looking into the case. But perhaps Kane's focus would now be elsewhere. "Santa Arleta . . ." Michaels apparently read what was on the screen, then nodded. "You'll have to forgive me, but when I got the call you'd be coming out, I started thinking, you know, maybe it wasn't a good idea to say anything. Pretty powerful people when they can get an entire police department and the coroner's office to say he committed suicide. There is no way that man killed himself."

"But he *was* depressed."

"Yeah, he was depressed about not getting a decent press job. What do you expect? Pulitzer Prize winner forced to write copy for a two-bit paper funded by single white male ads? After the suicide ruling, well, first thing I did was hide his calendar and case notes, and they've sat there ever since."

"Can we see them?" Sydney asked.

"Sure. They're in the basement. Archived in the old classifieds."

They took the stairs down, the dull, industrial, once-white linoleum tiles now worn clear through to the cement in some spots. As they passed through the hallway, a line of fluorescent lights flickered overhead, the ballasts apparently close to giving out. Michaels led them into a room at the end of the hall, which held dozens of file cabinets. And though he'd apparently hidden the thing there eighteen years or so ago, he knew right where to go for it. Second drawer from the bottom, about midway back, he pulled out a file folder with a lot of carbon-copy type forms people must have filled out for whatever advertisements they'd bought.

He handed it to Griffin, saying, "I think this is one of the reasons I've never bothered to clean out the place. In the back of my mind, I knew this was here. I just didn't know what to do with it."

"Is there someplace we can sit down to read this?"

"Hell. Take it. I never did feel safe having it here, but it wasn't like I knew who to call."

"Thanks."

"Sure thing. Just do me a favor. Vindicate him."

Once outside the building, Griffin looked at the packet, about an inch thick. "Where to?"

"Working lunch? There's a Japanese restaurant on the other side of the freeway. Kamon's on Sixteenth. I used to eat there back when I was a cop."

He gave her the keys, since she knew the area. Once in the car, he checked his voice mail, found out that Carillo had called. Griffin called him back.

"I'm assuming you want the update on Piper's brother?" Carillo said.

"Yes. You found him?"

"We weren't the only ones. There were two goons at the kid's school when I got there. I'm guessing they were Kane's men." Carillo briefed him on what happened.

A mixture of relief and worry went through Griffin's

mind. Kane seemed to have a handle on every step they were taking. "Where is he?"

"With a mutual friend. Safe for now," he said, undoubtedly in case anyone was listening in. "Not that the kid can't take care of himself to some extent. If not for his quick thinking, we wouldn't have made it out of there."

"Runs in the family," Griffin said, recalling Piper's actions the night he met her. "We'll touch base later."

Sydney pulled into the restaurant parking lot, a gray-blue building in a rundown strip mall. The interior, however, was pleasant, although a bit dark. Sydney asked for a table at the back, which would offer them a touch of privacy, and once seated, ordered an assortment of appetizers—gyoza, something called a firecracker roll, and stuffed mushrooms— which would allow them to easily eat while they worked.

Griffin broke open the manila envelope, which was still sealed, curious as to what, if anything worthwhile, they might find. It appeared to be mostly pages torn from a spiral notebook, the majority handwritten, though there seemed to be several copies of newspaper articles. He handed half the stack to Sydney, then started sorting through the other half.

"Any idea what we're even looking for?" she asked after several minutes of reading.

"I'm hoping it'll jump out at us," he said as the waitress brought the firecracker roll, which turned out to be seared tuna in some sort of panko-covered *inari* wrapper, then deep-fried and covered with a spicy sauce. Griffin popped one in his mouth, was surprised at how good it was, and when the waitress returned with the other two appetizers, he said, "Add another firecracker to the order."

Sydney looked up from a letter she was reading. "That's usually the reaction when someone tries it for the first time."

He was about to quip that she should have ordered two to begin with, but his eye caught on a blue piece of paper with writing that did not look like Ronson's. He picked it up, saw it was written on both the front and the back, and realized by the signature it was from Lydia Hettinger, the journalist's widow Sydney had spoken with at Fort Marcy Park.

Dear Mr. Ronson,

I apologize for the brevity of the phone call. I no longer trust that I'm not being listened to or watched.

The night my husband was killed, he met with an informant who promised to give him the information he needed to prove that Deputy White House Counsel Gannon Ferris was murdered. He called me that night, excited about the meeting, which is why I don't believe he would go back to his room and kill himself. When the authorities found him, all his files were missing, or I would have gladly sent them to you along with his appointment book. They were not in his car or his motel room although he had them when he left.

Unfortunately I have little else to offer. He did not discuss his work with me. The only thing I know for certain is that he received a call the morning before he left to meet with this informant, and I overheard part of it. He said something about meeting with Brooks about someone's sins.

I wish I could be of further help.

Sincerely,
Lydia Hettinger

He gave the letter to Sydney to read. "Brooks?" she asked once she'd finished. "You think it was Parker Kane who met up with him that night?"

"Assuming Kane is Brooks."

"Sins? I'm assuming it's the program Izzy was talking about?"

"Probably."

"Which stands for . . . ?"

"Strategic Integrated Network Case Management System. SINCMS, shortened to SINS."

"SINS? Devil's Key? Who thinks of this stuff?"

"The official name for the version that was sold to the various countries was simply called the product key. We didn't hear about the Devil's Key until rumors started to surface that there was a back door built into the SINS program."

"Well, you now have Brooks mentioned in the same sentence as SINS. If you're looking for further proof, here it is."

"A nearly twenty-year-old letter isn't going to do it."

Sydney pulled out another sheet. "How about a list of the major points that allegedly prove why Gannon Ferris was murdered? Looks like Ronson was on to something. Number one," she read. "Intended to expose SINS. Number two, no gun found at scene. Number three, broken driver's window on his car, blood on seat, seat in wrong position. Number four, Fort Marcy Park Police assigned homicide investigation have never worked homicide. Number five, no shot heard, even though there were houses located less than five hundred feet away . . ." She scanned the list. "It just gets worse from here. How's it possible anyone could ignore— Did you know this? They fired the head of the FBI the day before Gannon Ferris's alleged suicide . . . ?"

"Are you starting to see a pattern here? That's what they did to McNiel. You eliminate anyone who is getting too close to the issue. Whether it's by removing them from power or killing them. Either method works. One's just more permanent than the other."

Sydney stared at the document, then turned an accusing glance his way. "If Gannon Ferris was killed by government agents, because of the SINS program—"

"We don't know that."

"Let's say that's the case. We just assume they're working for the dark side. The point being, how is that different from a government-sanctioned kill order? Going after me, for instance? Or Orozco? You get the government's blessing, it's okay?"

"Is anything I say going to make a difference in what you think?"

She leaned back in her chair, crossed her arms. "Probably not. Let's just say I have a vested interest in your answer."

"The reasons behind a kill order are for national security. The safety of our nation and the people who live in it. One life to protect many lives. What Kane is doing by killing anyone getting in his way is strictly to benefit a small group of individuals. A personal agenda. When Orozco stole the Devil's Key, the possibility existed that he could turn it over to the enemy, that it could be used against us. Against our country. The kill order followed the key and who had possession."

"That just doesn't make sense."

"Sydney. I—"

"This whole Devil's Key being the precursor to the next war, just because a handful of nasty countries discover we're spying on them. That's utter and complete bullshit. For God's sake, we've been spying on them since the dawn of time. There has to be something we're missing. Something bigger than a case management program that opens the back door into someone else's computer . . ."

It took him a moment to realize she had switched gears— and frankly, he was grateful. "There is. The program, the back door, it's present in hundreds of thousands of computer chips that are already in circulation."

"I'm not sure I'm following you."

"There were some computer chips that were manufactured in China for the U.S. and European markets which contain the back door. It's not that we can spy on a few countries running this program, it's that this program can spy on *everyone* whose computer contains a chip with the back door. And you'd be hard-pressed to find a computer that *isn't* running on one of those chips. Everyone from our government and our military to the local dry cleaners."

Sydney stared in disbelief. "That's insane," she said after a few seconds.

"What's insane are the countries who aren't aware of it—and that's the majority of them. They're running power plants and nuclear reactors. I'd like to think that ours is one step ahead, but to replace every single chip . . ."

"How can our government let something like that happen?"

"Sometimes we don't find things out until after the fact and then it's a matter of damage control. If Kane gets the key, and he is part of the Network . . ."

"Maybe he's just in it for the money."

"God, I hope so, because simple greed is far more preferable. Until we find out otherwise, keep looking."

Several minutes later, Griffin was almost through his stack of papers, thinking they were once again striking out. It was nearing two o'clock and the waitress had long ago cleared the table, the majority of lunch diners gone. "I'm not seeing anything," he said. "You?"

She shook her head. "The only thing I have left are a few pages that look like they were from an appointment book. Unfortunately we don't know whose, and none of the names on here mean anything. To me at least."

"Appointment book? Didn't Lydia Hettinger mention something about an appointment book?" He dug through the pile of papers, looking for the blue sheet of notepaper.

"I thought she said it was missing along with her husband's case notes."

"Unless we read it wrong . . ." He found the note. " 'I would have gladly sent them to you along with his appointment book.' "

"There is no book. Just a page torn from one." She shook her head. "Can't be from Lydia Hettinger. Look at the year. Her husband was dead by then."

"Then who?"

"Everything ends in December. Isn't that when Ronson allegedly killed himself?" She slid it across the tabletop. "Not much. Last entry December 5. 'FCC Tuc. RC 2:00.' Whatever that means."

"Federal Correctional Complex," Griffin said. "In Tucson. But RC . . . ?"

"The initials written on the back of my business card Tex and Carillo brought back from Mexico. What if RC is Ronson's informant incarcerated at the federal prison?"

"Good question. I think we need to contact McNiel."

"And if they're listening?"

"We're going to have to take that chance. It'll be quicker than calling the FCC to ask them for the name of everyone incarcerated there with those initials. We're at a dead end, until we can figure out who RC is."

Griffin didn't want to burn his own number by calling McNiel directly, and so used the restaurant phone, going through the operator to make a collect call.

McNiel answered, accepting the charges. "Where are you?"

"Sacramento." He gave McNiel the restaurant phone number.

"Give me five minutes. I'll call you right back."

Griffin waited by the phone, which was located at the bar, an area of the restaurant not used during the lunch hour. It rang and he picked it up.

"Sorry," McNiel said. "I needed to get to a secure landline. How are things?"

"Progressing. We've run across a set of initials twice now, that we think is related to the case. Orozco wrote 'RC has 112' on the back of Sydney's card, intending that she be notified. Sydney and I just found the initials of RC on a datebook from a dead investigative reporter in Sacramento. Something about Tucson Federal Correctional Complex with the time of two o'clock."

"The only name that comes to mind is Rico Chapman. Part of the W2 investigation. One of those names that keeps popping up, but is always discounted. Allegedly he was involved in the original computer program, or rather the design of the back door to it. He was picked up about twenty years ago on drug charges. None of his stories ever checked out."

"Maybe they haven't checked out because there was always someone making sure they didn't. I'd say it's high time to go see what he has to say."

"The sooner the better. There have been some significant developments. Kane's asked that ATLAS be absorbed into his unit at the National Counterterrorism Center. He's about to issue warrants for the entire team, if he hasn't already. He said that preliminary ballistics are showing that your gun killed the guard at the *Recorder*."

"My gun, yes. His man pulled the trigger."

"And there's conveniently no video. The good news is that Pearson's stalling him as far as Fitzpatrick and Carillo, saying that the FBI can handle their own. Kane doesn't have anything on them, but there's a rumor he's going to try to bring Carillo in for kidnapping Piper's brother from the school. The FBI has sent a couple of agents out to the school to interview the witnesses. Apparently there's a video showing Carillo pushing the boy into a car, which they construed to mean he was being forced."

"How long do you think we have?"

"You and Tex? Less time than you think. Carillo likewise. Sydney . . . Look, Griffin. This could get ugly. Kane is threatened, and he's going to do everything in his power to make sure he wins. Izzy may be the only one right now *not* on Kane's radar. Thank God, because he's actually got a halfway decent plan. Implement the program."

"*The* program?"

"We have the key. Well, we will as soon as Lisette and Marc's flight gets in from Venice. Izzy's champing at the bit to get those numbers."

"Do you think that's wise? All these years trying to block the program from being implemented . . ."

"Kane's running a half-assed version of it now, which is how he's managing to stay on top of us. We need it to beat him at his own game. And if anyone can get it up and running, Izzy can. Izzy informs me that once he connects to the Internet and runs that code, you'll have about forty-eight hours to get the evidence against Kane before Kane tracks Izzy. That's not very long, Griffin."

"If Rico doesn't have the evidence on Kane, we'll find out who does."

43

Lisette didn't relax until she, Marc, and Piper were halfway across the Atlantic, each of them having boarded with their forged passports. They kept their conversation to a minimum until Piper finally nodded off, and even then, Lisette was careful about what she said, conscious that others around them could possibly hear. Piper stirred in her seat, and Marc pulled out his copy of the in-flight magazine. The poor girl didn't need any more drama in her life. Not after the nightmare in Venice. Neither she nor Marc had mentioned the two strange men posing as law enforcement officers who had shown up at her brother's school, trying to pick him up.

Some things were best left unmentioned, Lisette thought as they finally landed at Dulles, and the three cleared customs, their false passports easily passing scrutiny. Marc took Piper's from her the moment the agent handed it back.

"Don't trust me?" the girl asked.

"And this surprises you?" he replied.

She gave him a look laced with sarcasm and annoyance, as she matched her stride to his. "So now where are we going?"

"A safe house."

"I thought I was going into witness protection with my brother. You promised."

"You are. But not until we can make the arrangements to ensure your safety and his."

"How long will that take?"

"As long as necessary."

Another look of annoyance, but this time she didn't question him. Lisette was going to get the car, then follow them to the new safe house. Donovan would be picking up Marc and Piper, again in case anyone was watching for a group of two women and one man. When the elevator door opened on their floor, Piper surprised her with a quick embrace. "Thanks for helping me."

"You're welcome. But you know I'm going to be right behind you in my car?"

"I know. I just . . . wanted to say so."

Once in the parking garage Lisette took the elevator to her level, which felt very empty after the hustle and bustle of the terminal. Her footsteps echoed across the concrete floor, and she felt strangely alone. The sound of a car engine rumbled to life, and then the squeak of wheels as it pulled out of its parking space a couple of rows over. She glanced that way, then quickened her pace, a feeling of unease coming over her. When she reached her car, she hit the key, expecting to hear a beep-beep as it unlocked.

Apparently the angle was wrong, and she held the key higher, heard the first beep, then *bang!*

Lisette jumped between the cars, ducking down. Her heart pounded in her chest as she looked out, tried to determine where the sound originated, but it echoed. And then she saw the car that had pulled out of its space heading toward the exit. Not at any high rate of speed, but slow, cruising through the parking lot. *Bang!*

A backfire.

She took a deep breath, had to lean against the vehicle, waiting for her heartbeat to slow. Finally she got into her car, locked the door, then sat there for several seconds. She turned the key in the ignition, then pulled out, thinking that the first thing she wanted to do when she got home was take a hot bath. And then have several drinks. And not necessarily in that order.

Except she couldn't go home. Not as long as Piper was with them. In fact she had no idea where they were going to go. Where did one hide when being hunted by the government?

When she drove around to the passenger pickup and spotted Donovan's car as he pulled away from the curb after picking up Marc and Piper, she called Marc. He noticed right away that something was wrong, hearing it in her voice.

"I'm fine," she said. "A car backfired. I think I'm just tired."

"We all are."

"Where to?"

He gave Lisette the address of the new safe house in case they were separated, and she was immediately relieved to know that they had a place to go.

It was not the nicest building they'd stayed at, but it certainly wasn't the worst, she thought, when they pulled up in the Washington, D.C., neighborhood. The unit was about ten stories high and located in an area that was partly under construction.

"Not my first choice," Donovan explained when they arrived. "We didn't have a lot of options, and this was one of the few apartments we had that wasn't listed on any computers. In case Kane has access to our files, we figured we were better off not using anything we've used before."

"At least it has three bedrooms," Lisette said. "Always a plus when you have a crowded house."

Izzy got up from the table where he was working on his laptop. "You're Piper?"

She nodded.

"Man, you might have the coolest head in the world. Brain. I'd give anything to have it."

"Most people think I'm a freak."

"Freakin' awesome," he said, and Lisette was rather amused to see that Piper was actually blushing. "So, when do we get started?"

"Started on what?" Marc asked.

"The program. She's the key, and I'm gonna turn it." He looked at Piper, his face turning as red as hers had a moment ago. "Guess I should go back to work . . ."

He returned to the table and his laptop.

Piper walked over to watch him work. "Doesn't it bother you that you have to stay in here? That you can't go anywhere?"

Izzy shrugged. "It's kind of fun working with these guys. They're sort of all about protocol and crap. Like how they won't let your brother come here until this is over, because he might be in danger."

"My brother?" Her expression quickly turned serious. "What do you mean in danger? He's coming into witness protection with me, right?"

Izzy stared at his keyboard, as Marc hesitated, then pulled out a chair and sat. "He's safe. But they found him. They would have tried using him to get to you."

"How?"

"They would have asked that we give up the key."

"Then let's give it to them."

"We can't."

"Yes. We *can*."

"Piper," Lisette said, taking her hand and holding it. "First of all, *you* are now the key. I am not willing to give you to them. Under any circumstances. And I don't believe your brother would want this for you, either. You must think of how many lives will be lost if these numbers, this key, falls into their hands. That is what we are faced with."

"So my brother has to live in fear for the rest of his life? Just because this is in my head? What if they come after him again?" She pulled her hand from Lisette's. "You have to fix this. That's what you all do, right? You think of a way to get around this. You can't just sacrifice his life like that."

"Piper."

"No," she said, backing away from them, tears running down her face. "I'm so tired of this." And then she turned, ran into the bedroom, and slammed the door.

No one spoke for several seconds.

"Sorry," Izzy said. "I thought she knew about her brother."

"At least he's safe," Lisette said. "She's tired is all. We all are."

"Well, I need the numbers from her so I can implement the program."

"Implement?" Lisette said. "Slow down and please fill us in. We're a bit jet-lagged and out of the loop."

It was Donovan who explained. "McNiel wants to get it up and running. Fight fire with fire. Only he's hoping our flame will end up being bigger than Kane's."

"Are we sure this can't wait until morning?"

"We wish it could."

"Then at least after we eat dinner." Once dinner was served, they broached the subject with Piper. She actually looked happy to be doing something for the cause.

Lisette, however, was fading fast; she glanced at the alarm panel, saw it was set. "Donovan, you'll be up with them?" He nodded. She retired to her room and was asleep the moment her head hit the pillow.

She awoke the next morning and found Izzy asleep in one armchair, Donovan in the other. Piper was on the couch. Apparently they'd worked all night, and when she started the coffee, Donovan awoke. "Long night," he said.

"Progress?"

"No. It didn't work. Our only shot, and it didn't go off."

"Meaning what?"

"Meaning this code everyone's been chasing her around for isn't worth a damn. At least not the versions she's carrying in her head."

Lisette glanced toward the computer. "If he tried to make it work, won't that come up on Kane's system? Isn't that how Kane found Piper's friend? When he started running those numbers?"

"One, her friend didn't know what he was doing. Two, Izzy took precautions. It's not infallible, but he says it'll take them a while before they can trace it. The problem is they *can* trace it, and the more he runs it, the bigger chance he has of getting caught."

Piper stirred on the couch, and Lisette walked over, shook her. "Hey. Go to bed, okay?"

The girl nodded, got up and walked to the bedrooms, then stood there a moment, rubbing the sleep from her eyes. "Which one?"

"The one with the open door."

Once it closed behind her, Lisette continued the conversation. "Exactly how long do we have before they figure out we're here?"

"Izzy? Wake up."

Izzy stared at them, clearly out of it.

Lisette turned back to Donovan. "And if they *do* find us?"

"You don't want to know. At least not before your coffee."

Izzy finally stirred and looked up at the clock. "You might want to have that coffee soon. I started running that at midnight . . . Eight hours ago . . . Forty hours max and they'll be knocking on our door."

44

Tucson, Arizona

Sydney and Griffin drove to Arizona, deciding it was the safest route, and would allow them the freedom of carrying their weapons, something they couldn't do if they flew, now that Griffin was likely to have a warrant for his arrest. The trip took about thirteen hours, and they pulled into a hotel that night a little after three in the morning.

Which, of course, meant there was the whole sleeping arrangement thing, something Sydney hadn't really even thought of until the clerk, a dark-haired woman in her twenties, asked, "Just the two of you?"

"Yes," Griffin said. "There should be a paid-for reservation under my name." He slid his fake ID across the counter. The clerk barely looked, then typed something into the computer. Doc had paid for it online with his credit card.

"One night, two occupants. Here you go." She handed Griffin a small folder with two plastic card keys. "Breakfast is served between six and nine just off the lobby."

"Thank you."

Their room was on the fourth floor overlooking the parking lot and the freeway. There were two double beds, and Sydney dropped her bag on the farther, then walked toward the window, looking out, wondering what, if anything, she should say. It wasn't like they hadn't slept platonically in the same room before. They had. It was more that she hadn't expected to be hit with the very vivid memories—and her body's reaction to them—of the first and only time they'd slept together in the same bed. She was beginning to think he was like a drug, and apparently two days' time was not enough to get him from her system. Why else was she hyperaware that they were here, alone, and no one around to disturb them?

Another point was that there was still a very deep chasm between them. Even knowing about the kill order, she trusted him with her life. But this was a different sort of trust. Maybe it was more that she realized how very little she knew of him. They'd worked together, slept together, but they didn't really know each other.

That awkward silence that had filled the room the morning after at the bed-and-breakfast was back. And suddenly she was aware that he was standing behind her.

"Sydney. If you're more comfortable, maybe we should get separate rooms."

"I'll be fine."

"You want the shower first?"

"Sure." She started to slip past him as he stepped away, and then she remembered her bag on the bed, turned, reached for it, brushing against him, losing her balance as she tried to pull back.

He caught her, and they stood there for a few seconds, his breathing as ragged as hers. Neither spoke. She realized that he was waiting. He'd let her make the first move.

Listen to her body or her head?

"Things are *not* settled between us," she said.

"I know."

And then she pulled him down to the bed.

They arrived at the Tucson facility a little after ten. Sydney used her real ID for this, thinking they'd get more mileage with an FBI credential than their fake identifications, which had no law enforcement affiliation.

First, however, she called the warden to set up the visit, and he was waiting for them in his office.

"I wasn't aware there'd be two of you."

"Yeah," Sydney said. "He's, uh . . ." She turned to Griffin, waiting for him to fill in the blank.

Griffin held out his hand. "*International Journal of World Peace.* Special interest section. We're doing a cover story."

Sydney smiled at the warden. "As you can see, I'm not really here in an official capacity, so I hope that's not an issue."

"Not with me," the warden said. "Mr. Chapman will have to be the one to decide. He's allowed visitors like any other prisoner. That being said, I'm curious why the interest in this guy? Typical drug bust. Don't think he's had a visitor other than his ex-wife in at least a decade, and even she hasn't come the last couple years."

Sydney owed the guy some explanation, if nothing else than to satisfy his curiosity so that the matter wouldn't be looked at too hard. "Old conspiracy case. He-said, she-said sort of thing. A rumor he was set up on the drug charges."

"Not likely," the warden said. "Right after you called, I looked at his file. The guy's a career criminal. Arrested on drug charges starting when he was twenty-five, manufacturing meth. Not a big stretch to think he was manufacturing it twenty years later when he was arrested on his current conviction."

He opened the folder. "We're in the process of going digital. Not quite up to two decades ago, so you're in luck, or these wouldn't be here."

"Anyone else making inquiries on this guy?"

"Like I said, you're the first in about forever." Sydney eyed the prisoner folder on his desk. "You wouldn't mind if I had a look at that, would you?"

"Don't see why not, seeing as how you're FBI."

He slid it across the desk toward her. The first thing she examined was the custody log, which followed a prisoner wherever he went. In this case, it showed Rico Chapman had been incarcerated in this facility about the entire time. Considering he'd been in here close to twenty years, there weren't that many visitors. The ex-wife, a couple of FBI agents whose names she didn't recognize, and the reporter, Ronson.

That wasn't the most damning thing in her mind. It was the printout of the conviction record. And after she returned the file to the warden, and he had a guard take them back to the visiting room, where they waited a few minutes alone, she asked Griffin, "Did you see his crim hist?"

"The case he was convicted on? Unremarkable—unless one counts that there are murderers who don't get as many years."

"Exactly what I was thinking. How is it they're keeping this guy locked up for so long?"

The guard brought Rico Chapman in, then, surprising Sydney, said, "Good thing you guys came when you did. Any later, he'd be gone."

"Gone where?" Griffin asked.

"Being transferred back East is all I know." He looked at his watch. "In about two hours."

And once again it was like someone knew the next steps they'd be taking.

Rico Chapman did not look like a computer geek or a scientist. If anything, he looked like a beer-drinking redneck. He had shoulder-length graying hair that was receding at the temples, crow's-feet around his eyes, and a gut that said he didn't spend much time in the prison gym.

He eyed Syd and Griffin with suspicion as he took a seat across from them. "You're not my attorney."

"Not sure how that mistake was made," Sydney said. "Then again, we didn't go to law school. I would, however, suggest you check your attorney's credentials."

"What's that supposed to mean?"

"I've seen murderers get less time than you. What the hell'd you do? Sell methamphetamine to kindergarteners?"

"I guess you can call me the guy who knows too much. I just can't get anyone to listen."

"Which," Griffin said, "in your case, could be a good thing."

"How's that?"

"Just about everyone else involved in this case is dead—you being the anomaly."

"And all this time I figured I was here because I pissed off all the wrong government officials."

Sydney took a seat opposite him, while Griffin stood off to one side. "You think the government's involved?"

Rico's brows went up. "You're kidding, right?"

"Yes, I'm kidding," Sydney said. "Even so, I'm going to admit, I know next to nothing about your case."

"Then what the hell you doing here? You're another one of those reporters?"

"I'm not," Sydney replied, then nodded toward Griffin. "But he is."

"Who are you, then?"

"FBI."

"Not interested. Last time I talked to the FBI—and that was *over* a decade ago, I got stuck in solitary confinement."

"I'm not like other agents. In fact, I'm not even here officially."

"Another white hat, gonna save the world? Little late, don't you think?"

"We sort of stumbled across your name pertaining to a case we're working on."

Griffin added, "Something to do with some numbers smuggled into Mexico."

He didn't seem surprised. "The Devil's Key."

"See?" Sydney said to Griffin. "Here's where it helps to talk to someone in the know. All this time I thought they were offshore accounts or maybe all the missing money from when BICTT went under."

Rico looked amused. "Assuming you're talking about the list of numbers stolen from Wingman and Wingman?"

"Wingman and Wingman?" Griffin said. "What about them?"

"What do I get if I talk?" he asked Griffin.

"Has it gotten you anything in the past?"

"Besides the fact no one believes me? Another stint in solitary."

Sydney leaned forward across the metal tabletop. "Are you starting to see a pattern here, Mr. Chapman? There's people out there who don't want what you know to get out."

"Question is," Griffin said, "why haven't they killed you yet?"

"Because *I* wrote the code. They *need* me. Something happens to it, they're screwed. They got screwed when the key was stolen from Wingman Squared."

"Why?" Griffin asked, even though Sydney was certain he knew the answer.

"Unlike the first nine keys the government destroyed, *this* one happens to be a key to every program sold to foreign countries. Canada, Israel, Iraq, Russia . . . Need I go on?"

"Slow down, Rico," Sydney said. "Pretend like I'm clueless in all this—because I am—and start from the beginning."

Rico cocked his head, smiled slightly. "The beginning? You've heard of the SINS software? A case management system the government purchased from a small software company in California. They liked it so much, they decided to implement it nationwide. Next thing I know, the DA of our county is taking *my* system and claiming it's his, and using it as his ticket to make a bid on Washington. You might recognize him as one of the Wingman Squared crew, now that he's left Congress. Trenton Stiles? He's probably running Wingman Squared."

"So you wrote a code for a case management system for the software company?"

"Right."

"And the government is now using it."

"The *entire* government. Every federal office, in fact. And the software developer sued the U.S. government. The developer lost, but what do you expect when you take on the Feds?"

"Hard to believe they're killing this many people over royalties. What's a few million or even a billion dollars to a government that's trillions in debt?"

"Because it's not about the royalties. It's about the back door the CIA paid me to write into the program."

"The CIA?" Sydney asked. "You're sure they were behind it?"

"Well, someone connected to them. It was all very hush-hush."

Griffin said, "Like a Trojan horse back door?"

"He catches on quick."

"Sometimes," Sydney said. "In this case, he has insider knowledge that I don't have. You're talking about a case management system that's in *every* federal office in the U.S.?"

"No. I'm talking about a case management system that's in nearly every country in the world."

"So," Griffin said, "the U.S. is using it to spy on other countries. We've heard the spiel."

Sydney crossed her arms over her chest. "Not buying it. You don't kill this many people over that. After all, they're doing a pretty good job making anyone who *suggests* this scandal sound like a lunatic—those who live. Case in point, look at you."

Rico laughed. "You don't *really* think it's all about national security, do you?"

"What else is there?" Griffin asked.

"What do you think? Money."

"The royalties?" Sydney said. "Thought we'd established that wouldn't do it."

"Not royalties. Money. All of it."

"Not sure I understand."

"It's about the handful of billionaires and major corporations running the world. Them and their representative sitting on Capitol Hill, making sure that the bills they need passed get passed to keep their kingdoms intact. It's about their tentacles reaching into every major conspiracy you can think of. You mentioned the late, great BICTT? The bank the CIA was running? Yeah, it's part of that. But it goes beyond that. It reaches into the government, the military, and the federal law enforcement agencies charged with investigating it. It's about having the ability to track every dollar being moved and to move every dollar being tracked."

Sydney glanced at Griffin, who nodded. This was nothing he didn't already know, but clearly he was hoping to find out something more. "You're gonna have to be clearer than that," Sydney said.

"Banks. Back doors. Control of the world's money."

"The world?"

"As in the *chips* that have been imported to the entire

world. If money is being moved electronically, yes. But it's more than that. The program is doing it seamlessly. *Without* a trace. And it's not just money. You can go in, change things around, and no one will ever know you're there. Or you can add something. A Trojan horse with a specific task, search for and set off a nuclear warhead with no one the wiser on how it was done. Sabotage something? No problem. As long as you have the key. Because the program's already out there. The Devil's Key accesses those chips. The SINS program was just the start. The Devil's Key is the end. It's just knowing how it works that's the hard part."

"It can do all that?"

"If you can think of it, it can do it. It's the closest thing to artificial intelligence out there. And trust me. You go back with what I tell you, you'll find yourself transferred to some outpost, or discredited, or brought up on false charges. Or dead. So have at it. The global elite have already set it in motion, and once they get the Devil's Key, the world is theirs."

She was beginning to wonder if this was a dead end, that Rico wasn't going to tell them anything they could use. "The global elite? So the world is being run by a bunch of billionaire Bilderbergs or something?"

"Bilderbergs?" Rico said. "The conspiracy theory that those guys are running Europe?"

"So they say."

"Yeah. Well the group here? In charge of running the world from Capitol Hill? They go by a different name. The Network."

And that was a name Sydney and Griffin *had* heard of.

It certainly explained why Parker Kane was so hot to shut down ATLAS. Who wouldn't want that sort of knowledge and access to not only the world's money supply but all its computers?

Sydney glanced at her watch. They had a little over an

hour to wrap up this interview and get out of here before they were found out. "You have any questions you want to ask?" she said to Griffin. "Pretty sure this is all way over my head."

Griffin moved closer, leaning toward Rico. "Why are they keeping you alive?"

"Because they need me."

"There's a lot about this that doesn't make sense. The money, being able to move it seamlessly, maybe. But you obviously don't have the key and couldn't re-create it, or they'd have forced that from you a long time ago. And they've spent countless resources trying to recover the key . . ." He looked at Sydney, then back at him. "There's something you're not telling us. Something they know that we don't."

Rico shrugged.

"You realize *we* have the key? *We* recovered it. Maybe that's why you're suddenly being transferred."

There was a flicker of something in Rico's eye. Fear? she wondered. "That's impossible," he said.

"No, it's not," Griffin said. "Robert Orozco found it. In fact, he's the one who sent us to *you*."

"You're lying. Robert left the country. I'm the one who helped him. Helped erase his tracks."

"Well, you forgot to erase her father's tracks. He's the one who helped Robert steal the key."

Rico glanced in her direction. "Who was your father?"

"Kevin Fitzpatrick."

His brows went up a slight fraction. "Doesn't mean anything."

"Doesn't matter," she said. "What does is that I went down to Robert's villa just north of Ensenada, and he gave me the key, which was tucked in a bank bag, and he told me it was the tip of an iceberg so large, they didn't dare let the American public know the truth. Sound about right?"

He gave a dismissive shrug, but she could tell he was

shaken. Which meant they were close. Carillo had said that Orozco had written something on the back of that business card, which he couldn't decipher. That RC had one, one, two. One hundred and twelve . . . What the hell had he been trying to say about the Devil's Key? One one two . . .

Not one one two. One *slash* two. "Oh my God. You have half."

"I don't know what you're talking about."

"Bullshit. Orozco only had half the code. That's why they needed you. Doesn't do them any good if they only have half. They *had* to keep you alive, because you were smart enough never to allow the entire key together. That would be suicide. Where is it?"

A bead of sweat appeared on his upper lip, and his nostrils flared as he looked from her to Griffin, then back. "They'll kill me."

"They probably will," Sydney said. "They killed Orozco. And that was when they thought he might still have his copy. The way I see it, though, you've been granted a twenty-year reprieve. You should have been dead a long time ago, like every other player in this game."

"If I give it to you, I'm going to need protection."

"We can't make any promises," Griffin said.

"But you'll try?"

"We'll try. But your best bet is going to be to get us the other half before they do. And I'd avoid mentioning that we were here."

"They're going to find out. They always do. They're paying someone on the inside. They have to be."

She glanced at Griffin, wondering if the warden was the one, especially since he failed to mention the impending transfer.

Griffin, however, blazed right past that. Probably figuring there was no sense spooking him any more than he was. "And where does one find this program key?"

"It won't do you any good, unless you got someone who knows a lot about computers."

"Pretend we do."

"Stored in an underground bunker out near Pocito, a little town between here and the border." He gave them the address. "It's locked up in a safe."

"That's it?"

"Yep. But good luck getting to it."

"Why is that?"

"You know those methamphetamine charges I was convicted on? Well, the people who were actually making it, that's their land. They tend to take a dim view of trespassers."

"Who lives there now?"

"Besides my wife? She's on the other side. Dirt road divides the place. Like a little compound in the valley. Hatfield and McCoys." He laughed.

"You were saying about who lived there?"

"Right." He closed his eyes. "New guy, my wife told me. Moved in a couple years ago . . . Quin, Quint? Something like that."

"Quindlen?" Griffin asked.

"Yeah. That could be it. You know him?"

"His name's come up a time or two."

"Undoubtedly. The guy's running the largest meth operation this side of the Mexican border. Heard there was a big gun bust not too far from there. Some federal operation. You can guarantee he had his hands in that, too."

Griffin had actually been involved with the case, even if only peripherally. Quindlen was implicated, but they weren't able to make him on it. If Quindlen was connected to this, Griffin wanted to take him down. He looked at his watch. "Hate to break up the reminiscing here, but we're running out of time."

"Time? For what?" Rico asked.

"We'd rather not run into whoever is picking you up."

"You *are* going to stop them, right? From transferring me?"

"We don't have a lot of say in that. But once we take care of business, we'll see what we can do."

Griffin moved to the door, hit the call button to get the guard to let them out.

It wasn't until they were several miles away that Sydney thought about what Rico had said about the property and trespassers. "That name he mentioned. Quindlen? As in the Quindlen that was mentioned when you and I were in Pocito? Ex-CIA, current drug runner?"

"Too much of a coincidence to think otherwise."

"Assuming he was connected with the dirty cops in Pocito, and he's one of Parker Kane's men, we might want to call in a little help."

"How fast do you think Carillo and Tex can drive down here?"

"It took us what . . . thirteen, fourteen hours? I think if we want their help, they're going to have to risk a plane trip. Maybe Doc can set them up with some suitable undercover IDs."

45

The air was brisk, cold, and so dry that it hurt Griffin's eyes. Tex and Carillo had arrived sometime close to dawn, and after lunch, they drove out to Pocito.

They were parked on a hill, a dirt road overlooking the land where Rico's old trailer sat, where he'd lived with his wife before his arrest. They had circled the complex, which was located in a shallow valley between two hillsides, and discovered a little-used dirt road adjacent to one of the abandoned mines in the area that ran into the back of the property. Apparently the small complex where Rico and his wife had made their home used to be part of the mining operation.

The mine had been abandoned long ago, and the road they'd taken rough from non-use. It ended on the west side of the complex, giving them a decent view. Griffin and Tex left the car higher up the road out of sight, where Carillo and Sydney were acting as lookouts, while he and Tex moved farther down the hillside on foot. They crouched down behind some shrubbery and a large boulder about five hundred feet west of the compound.

Just as Rico had described the place, the complex was divided in two by the main road, which appeared to be gravel. On the right was a small ranch house, and next to that a dilapidated old bunkhouse, probably left over from when the mine was open, but now little more than a gray shell of wood that looked about to fall down at any time. Next to that was a corrugated metal building large enough to house a car or two, or even some ranch equipment, though it didn't look like anyone was doing any ranching, unless you counted the half-dozen goats in the pen and the chicken coop located behind the ranch house.

On the right of the gravel road was the trailer, presumably where Rico's wife, Charlene, lived. And just behind her trailer was the bunker Rico described, the cinder-block structure where the safe was supposed to be located.

Tex handed Griffin the binoculars. "Couple dogs on the porch of the ranch house. That could be an issue."

Griffin surveyed the property. "Never mind getting down there without being seen by anyone in the house. I don't like this. Too risky."

"What about a distraction on the right side where the ranch house is, so the bunker side is out of the limelight?"

"And how would you do that?"

"We set up there," Tex said, pointing to a curve in the dirt road. "Carillo and I can skirt along the hillside to the right. Of course, that's assuming you and Sydney can now get along."

"We're fine."

Tex looked over at him. "Just an observation, but she seems . . . tense around you."

"Let's just say we're a work in progress."

"You might try working on something besides the sex."

Griffin would have denied it, but Tex had already turned his attention back to the compound, saying, "I think we can get past the dogs. I can head down the hill behind the ranch house. A few hamburgers or something, get the dogs' attention off you, while you come down to Rico's place, get in, get the code, and when you're clear, we all leave."

"And what if those animals are trained not to eat meat thrown down?"

"Look at that place," Tex said. "Does it scream highly trained canines?"

"Don't forget that Quindlen allegedly lives there."

"Yeah, well what I remember most about him when he was with the CIA was that he was an ass."

"A highly trained ass."

"Agreed. But let's say he did train the dogs, they're still going to be back there, barking. At me. Not you. So unless you can find any other agents who want to go in on an illegal search, we're it. Let's just hope the Pocito Police Department isn't as corrupt as it was on your last mission in this area. I'd rather be arrested than shot."

"That makes two of us."

46

About an hour before dusk, they drove to the edge of
the valley, waiting for the sun to drop toward the horizon,
casting their shadows across the red dirt in the direction of
the compound. When the sun was just over the hilltops, they
started out, the vehicle idling until they reached the slope,
and then Griffin put it in neutral and shut the engine off, allowing it to roll down the hill, slow enough not to kick up too
much dust or make any noise. As Griffin let the car roll into
the same spot he'd parked before, it bottomed out. Sydney
heard metal hitting rock. "Careful," she said. "This car's on
Doc's credit card."

And Carillo, sitting next to her in the back, laughed.
"Doc's aiding and abetting federal fugitives, *and* harbor-
ing Piper's brother who is currently listed as missing in
every police department in America. I'm thinking Doc's got
bigger issues to worry about."

"I'm trying to think positive here. That we're going to
make it and return the car in one piece."

"I'll be happy if *we* return in one piece."

They all got out and walked to the crest, where they could

see the ranch below. Griffin went over the plan one more time.

"Which one's Quindlen?" Sydney asked.

"Denim jacket. The man on the right." He eyed the two men on the porch, both sitting on chairs. The other, wearing a long-sleeved plaid shirt, he didn't recognize. Both men were drinking beer, but the one in the plaid shirt was also smoking a joint.

Carillo and Tex started off to the right, while Griffin and Sydney waited, watching the front of the house. Griffin glanced over at Sydney, thinking about what Tex had said. Sleeping with her wasn't the answer, but right now he was at a loss. And when he tried to think of something profound, that it wasn't all about the sex, the front door opened, and a woman with long black hair stepped out. Wearing jeans and a sweatshirt, she was carrying two plates. She handed one to Quindlen, but when the man in the plaid shirt seemed to take offense at something she said, she dumped the plate onto his lap. He got up, backhanded her across the face, then dragged her in the house. Quindlen just sat there eating, like it was commonplace.

"Seems to be a fight," Griffin radioed to Tex. "Plaid Shirt and woman inside. Quindlen alone on the porch with the dogs."

"There's half your distraction," Tex said.

Griffin adjusted his radio's earpiece as he watched Tex and then Carillo traverse across the side of the hill. There was just enough shrubbery to offer concealment and the two men kept low.

"I can actually hear the two in the house arguing," Tex said. "The other guy is named Lee . . . Apparently he's been cooking all day . . . and the least she can do is have his dinner ready on time."

"Which means," Griffin said, "one of those buildings is where they're cooking their meth. Something to keep in mind. A lot of chemicals, never mind someone might still be in there."

"If I had to pick one," Tex replied, "it'd be the old bunk-house. All that missing siding gives it better air circulation. Safer."

"Yeah," came Carillo's voice. "Always high priority with meth cookers. My money's on the nice shiny warehouse, where they can lock it up."

"From whom?" Tex asked. "Not like they have to worry about some passersby seeing it."

"Boys," Griffin said. "Can we get back on task?"

"Almost there," Tex said. "It's a bit steeper than I thought." A minute later he landed at the bottom of the hill.

Griffin could no longer see him, because of the chicken coop. That did not mean anyone else couldn't, and Tex still had another fifteen feet of open ground to cross to get to the goat pen. He looked at his watch. The sun had disappeared behind the hill. The only source of light came from inside the house and spilled out onto the porch where Quindlen sat eating his dinner, the two dogs at his feet, one a pit bull mix, the other a German shepherd.

"This is insane," Sydney whispered. "We shouldn't be here."

"You think of a better way to get this code?"

"For all we know, there isn't one. He's setting us up."

"A chance we have to take, unless you're looking forward to sitting in prison or worse." Griffin lowered his binoculars, unable to see Tex or Carillo anymore. "Status," he radioed.

Carillo answered, "Looks good from up here."

Tex said, "I'm moving in."

"Get ready," Griffin told Sydney. He figured they had about one minute to slide down the hill and get to the far side of Rico's trailer, and what he called the bunker house, a cinder-block structure that looked as if it was partially dug into the hillside. Griffin eyed it, wondering if there had been some purpose to building it that way. Rico didn't seem the type to prepare for nuclear fallout. Who knew? Right now the only thing he cared about was getting in there, finding the code, and getting out.

"Tex is at the pen," Sydney said.

He could just make Tex out, figured he was opening the gate. The goats brayed, shifted around, but stayed within the confines of the barbed wire.

"They're not cooperating," Tex said.

"Can't you get behind them? Scare them into running out?"

"Not without coming into view of the ranch house window. Lee's still going at it with the woman. I can see them in the window. If we weren't busy with this, someone needs to go in there and pound some goddamned sense into him, like he thinks he's doing to her."

"Goats, Tex."

"Yeah, yeah." Tex reached down to the ground, grabbed something and threw it into the pen. Griffin guessed it was a handful of pebbles. Whatever it was, it had the desired effect, and the goats scurried toward the gate, even faster when Tex repeated the process.

The dogs' ears perked up, and suddenly both animals were on their feet, barking, then racing around the trailer.

"Dogs coming your way," Griffin reported. Quindlen got up, went inside, then came out a moment later. "Quindlen's got a gun."

"Copy. I'm outta here. Hoping the dogs chase after the goats not me."

"Let's go," Griffin said to Sydney, the moment the front was clear.

They started down the hill toward Rico's trailer, crouching down below the windows, as they stopped at the back of it. Griffin glanced across the dirt road, didn't see anyone outside, then motioned for Sydney to wait. He ran toward the bunker, seeing the door was secured with a standard padlock. He didn't see any alarms, and, using the pick in his wallet, it took him about thirty seconds to open the door. He hung the lock on the hasp, hoping that if anyone glanced that way, they wouldn't notice. He opened the door, signaled Sydney over, and she followed him in.

The bunker was larger than he expected and seemed to be used primarily for storage of old computer equipment and boxes of zip drives and floppy disks. Even if any computers still read that type of data storage, it would take weeks to go through it all.

There was a thick coating of dust on everything. Apparently no one had been in here in who knew how long.

He walked toward the back of the room, opening a door that led deep into the hillside. Definitely deceptively small from the outside. More importantly, he found the safe, and hoped it wasn't the sort that required explosives.

Sydney searched the battered metal desk first, something that looked like a military castoff. It contained little of interest, a few pens, paper clips, and a drawer full of blank envelopes, and she moved on to the file cabinets, going straight to the one that was locked. It took about ten seconds to pick it with a paper clip, and she pulled open the top drawer, which held a number of hanging file folders. They were neatly tabbed, and she thumbed through a few, seeing several filled with odd diagrams and hand-drawn notes, many of which looked like they were outlines for projects Rico had started detailing. Not seeing anything that stood out, she opened the next drawer down and saw a tab marked "SINS."

"Bingo." She pulled it out, saw a hand-drawn chart for the program. A circle was drawn in the center, where the word *SINS* was written. Then emanating from the circle, like spokes on a wheel, were lines leading to various points he'd written listing what the program could do. It was very much like an octopus, she realized, and she thought of what Ronson, the investigative journalist, had said prior to his murder. That the tentacles reached far into the government. Scary to think that someone could get that much information about your life, banking, utilities, phone records; essentially anything that passed through the Internet could be viewed. Or manipulated.

The next chart seemed to outline the back door and show how it worked in concert with the computer chips that had been designed specifically to allow SINS to work undetected. There had been a deal with China to mass-produce the chips, and the U.S. had purchased the majority of them.

They were everywhere, she realized.

Griffin walked in, looking defeated.

"There's no code," he said. "The only thing in there was money. Maybe a few hundred K. The bills are all from over twenty years ago, I'm guessing payment for services rendered."

She looked around the room. "Maybe it's somewhere else. One of these disks or something."

"We'll never find it in time."

"If nothing else, we have the early workings of the SINS, detailing the back door. Sort of in the planning stages, including the deal with China to manufacture the computer chips. Why the hell would someone like Parker Kane allow this sort of incriminating evidence out where anyone could find it?"

"He wouldn't. That's mine."

They both turned, saw a woman, late fifties, standing in the doorway, pointing a shotgun at them. Too old to be the woman they'd seen earlier, Sydney figured this was undoubtedly Rico's wife.

"Get your hands up. The both of you." She aimed the barrel at Griffin. "You. Hands. Now."

"We're federal agents."

Her gaze was on the file Sydney held, but the gun was still pointed at them. When she looked up, she said, "They must've lowered their standards over the years. Ain't none ever come with less than ten, fifteen men. You're in here with what? Four?"

"Budget cuts."

"Yeah. See, that's why I don't bother to vote. Just a bunch of nitwits sitting in Washington. Crooks, too." She angled her shotgun at his hands. "Keep 'em up. Away from your weapon. Who sent you?"

"Rico."

A look of disbelief swept across her face. "He wouldn't do that. *Who* are you?"

"FBI," Sydney said. "I have ID if you want to see it."

"FBI? You got a death wish?"

"Not really," Griffin said. "So if you wouldn't mind lowering the weapon."

"Why?"

"Because I don't want to get shot."

"No. I mean why now? Why are you interested in *that* file. There's gotta be a million dollars of meth on this property, and several hundred thousand in cash in that safe you just opened—I got a video in my house. You didn't touch none of it. Not a lot of folks would leave the money. What I want to know is why now and not back when Rico tried to tell the FBI about what was going on?"

"We weren't around back then," Sydney said. "And it seems like anyone who's looked into it has had singularly bad luck."

That snort again. "Ya think? And here you two are, not looking real lucky, either."

"Except you haven't shot us."

"Don't think I won't." She moved the barrel, pointing for them to step away from the file. "You got about fifteen seconds to tell me why I shouldn't."

"You know who Parker Kane is, right?"

"You being funny?"

"No."

"Because if you're trying to say he sent you, then you're full of shit. You realize he owns this property?"

"The records state otherwise."

"He's not that stupid to put his name on the deed. Who do you think is running all that meth?"

"You're saying Parker Kane is?"

"Weren't you the one talking budget cuts? How do you think he funds all his operations? The illegal ones, that is. Uncle Sam?"

Not the first time someone from the government used drug trading to fund their ventures, Sydney thought. "What sort of operations?"

"Anything the Network sees fit. Just depends on which way the wind's blowin'. But if you're looking for evidence of that, you're on the wrong side of the road. And seeing as how this little valley will soon be filled with Parker Kane's men, I'm thinking don't bother buying a lotto ticket. It ain't your lucky day."

Griffin looked as calm as ever, but Sydney saw him eyeing the door, then the gun, knew he was probably working out how to disarm her. "You called Parker?" he asked.

"Me? Hardly. Id and Yut did."

"Who?"

"The two IdYuts across the road. One of your guys must have tripped the alarm in the meth lab sometime after he let the goats out. Saw one of your guys snooping around in there. Might want to warn him, not a good place to hide. All those chemicals and propane, one well-placed bullet and boom!"

"How long have you been watching us?"

"Since you first showed up to check out the place. I was coming back from the store, saw you pull into the old service road. Knew right away something was up. Right now though, we're running out of time. So I'll ask you once more? Why that file?"

"The other half of the code," Griffin said, surprising Sydney that he'd come right out and admit it. "We're trying to get it before Parker does. Rico said it was in the safe."

"And what are you planning to do with it?"

"Use it against Parker."

For the first time she smiled. It wasn't a nice one, either, but she did lower the gun at the same time. "I'd pay good money to see that. You got a pen?"

"Pen?" Griffin asked.

"You want the damned code, don't you?"

"Yes, ma'am."

She stared at him for a moment, then to Sydney. "Not too bright, this one. The desk, numbskull. Top drawer."

Griffin found a pen, then grabbed one of the envelopes, having to scribble circles to get the ink to work. When she finished reciting the numbers, she asked him to turn the envelope so she could see it. She nodded. "Ten little numbers . . . Hard to imagine they could be worth so much. So what do you need to do? Call them in somewhere?"

47

Lisette stood at the window and kept an eye on the parking lot and the road beyond, the darkness occasionally broken by a vehicle's headlamps as it drove past. Donovan was watching the monitors, while Izzy was working the code Sydney had called in to him. On the one hand, Lisette thought, at least they had now confirmed that Piper did not know the whole code, which was one reason they kept her from the computers, not letting her see anything that was visible. Maybe that would be a bargaining point with the military, assuming they could escape Parker's men as well.

Piper walked over to the window to stand next to Lisette, and in a low voice, asked, "What if he doesn't get it up and running in time?"

"He will." But Lisette glanced back, saw tenseness around Marc's eyes, and knew he was worried. "And if he doesn't, we'll just move again."

Piper sighed. Then, after a moment, she asked, "You think any of this would have happened if I'd gotten into witness protection? I mean, if I hadn't run off to Venice and you got me to the right people?"

"Perhaps," Lisette said, trying to instill some peace into the girl. "Then again, maybe you saved your life by doing that very thing."

"This is beautiful," Izzy said. "Like a candy store, with something everywhere you turn and you don't know what to buy."

Marc said, "Buy me anything with Parker Kane's name on it."

"You're assuming what you want has his name on it. He was CIA. Don't you think he'd be smart enough to make sure that isn't an issue?"

"Let's just say I'm hoping he made a mistake."

"Kid's got a point," Donovan said. "Look for anything related to Brooks or Trenton Stiles from W2 or that can connect Kane to them."

Izzy was opening and closing files so fast that they couldn't keep up with what he was doing. After a moment, he said, "You guys realize you're asking me to do the impossible? Twenty years of investigation in what? A couple hours?"

"Yeah, yeah," Donovan said. "Just find us something we can use."

Izzy glanced at the other monitor. "Not going to do us any good if they find us before I find—well, whatever it is I'm trying to find. It'd be nice if I had a hint."

"Same here," Donovan replied. "Something that looks like proof ought to do it."

"*That* narrows it down," Izzy said.

Several minutes later, Lisette noticed Marc pacing the room. "You should sit. It's bad enough we have one person who can't keep still," she said, nodding toward Izzy.

"How can I when it's taking so long?"

"Sorry," Izzy said. "I have to keep moving our location, while they're probing the Internet. Last thing we want is for them to come knocking on our door." Izzy pulled the other computer keyboard toward him, bringing up a different screen. "This," he said, pointing to the monitor and a map, "is where we are. *This* is where they see us. The problem is they're moving. Hate to say it. They found us."

"How long do we have?"

"Driving time from there to here." He went back to the computer, read something on the monitor. "*Yes*. You want proof? How's this?"

He kept them in suspense while he typed, then stopped, turned in his chair and faced them. "Guess who chartered a jet to California, landing at a private airport a few hours before Bo Brewer was murdered? That is Parker Kane's name on that manifest. The location was listed elsewhere, but once they got in the air, bingo . . ."

Donovan leaned over to see the monitor. "Do you show when it returned?"

Izzy brought up a different screen. "Next morning. But I'll do you one better. Bring up the video surveillance at the airport parking lot . . . and voilà!" He typed something else, leaned back so they could see. "His car. Bingo! That's the beauty of this thing . . . If it travels through the Internet, we can find it."

"It's still not proof," Donovan said. "Find me the connection between Parker Kane and W2."

"What was the W2 name again?"

"Trenton Stiles."

"Easy enough . . . We put in Kane's name, search for phone records that match up to Stiles or Wingman's . . . Nothing's coming up for any number associated with W2."

Lisette thought about that. "As you said, a man like Parker Kane is *not* going to let any numbers he's using be connected to W2."

"He wouldn't," Izzy said. "But . . ." He typed, waited a second, then said, "Maybe Mr. Stiles is not as careful. Maybe he's thinking that the Parker Kane's phone is a throwaway, and can't be traced to either of them."

"Which helps us how?"

"I look up the calls to Stiles's phone the few days before . . . and the few days after . . . Looking for patterns, any repeat numbers, and, more importantly, any that show calls made both here and in South San Francisco . . ."

A list of numbers popped up on the screen. He filtered out those that didn't match his criteria, then ended up with one. "Here you go. Your smoking gun."

"Not quite," Donovan said. "We still need to know who is on the other end of that phone."

"Right. I knew that . . . Now we just need to turn it into a microphone. We catch Kane using it, and hopefully in the midst of some very incriminating conversations . . ."

"You know how to do that?" Lisette asked.

"Are you kidding me? Ever since I heard the freaking FBI use this technique all the time to spy on the Mafia, it was like— It's not hard, if you know what you're doing."

"How much time do you need?" Donovan asked, his attention back to the other monitor.

Izzy looked at it. "Yeah . . . We're going to need a *serious* distraction. I'm going to need more than ten minutes. They are so on their way here . . ."

"Me," Piper said.

"No." Lisette shook her head. "Absolutely not."

"I'm the one they want. So why not? I run out there, they chase after me, and Izzy can keep doing what he needs to do."

Lisette turned to Marc, hoping for a little support. But what he said was "Actually, I think we can make it work."

Piper smiled.

Lisette narrowed her gaze. "Are you insane? This is way too dangerous."

"Hear me out, *cara mia*. This may be the perfect plan. For

one, they aren't about to harm the girl they believe is their most valuable asset on the face of the planet right now."

"And what about the military? Where are they?"

Izzy brought them up. "About two minutes behind Parker's guys."

"See?" Lisette said. "Because if I'm not mistaken, *they* consider her the most dangerous *threat* on the planet right now. Or are you forgetting the other group that was searching for us at the airport in Rome?"

"We'll cross that bridge—"

"When they start firing?"

"Not to worry. I have a plan."

"I already don't like it."

"When you hear it, I'm sure you won't. But it is the only way I see of buying us time."

She looked out the window, saw the cars pulling in, the headlamps bouncing off the parked vehicles. "Well, whatever it is, we need to do it now. They're here. So what is the plan?"

"Since we know Parker Kane is not going to shoot Piper, we send her out as a decoy."

48

Pocito, Arizona

Griffin and Sydney were with Rico's wife, Charlene, in her trailer, when Griffin happened to look out the window and see the headlights at the top of the hill coming down the main road. Not one, but two vehicles. "We have less time than we thought."

Charlene looked that direction. "I'd say five minutes. Curvy road. Gotta take it slow."

Crack!

Griffin drew his gun, ran to the door. Sydney tossed the files she'd found onto the table, drew her gun, and joined him. They heard another shot.

"Status?" Griffin commanded.

"Okay, but trapped." It was Tex. "On the chicken coop. Weapon down."

"Carillo?" he radioed.

"Fine," Carillo said. "Up on the hill. Can't get to Tex, and can't get to our vehicle without breaking cover. Got a shooter on the west side of the house. Can't tell if it's the wife beater or Quindlen."

"We're on our way," Griffin said.

But as he and Sydney started out the door, Charlene put her hand on Griffin's arm. "Don't underestimate them. They're both dangerous."

He nodded, then slid out the back door, Sydney right behind him.

They edged around the west side of the trailer. And just as Carillo had said, the gunman was across the road, on the front porch of the house. It was too dark to see if it was Lee or Quindlen. Whoever it was, he was leaning out, aiming his weapon toward the goat pen—whether at Tex or Carillo, he didn't know.

Griffin fired two rounds, and the man jumped back, then ran into the house. Every light was off, the windows pitch black. The full moon, high over the south side of the house, cast shadows across the ground, which might offer some concealment if Griffin could get across the road. What he couldn't see was the second gunman, and he wondered if the man knew Tex was unarmed, and intended to press the advantage. "If I can cross over, I can get into that bunkhouse doorway. Have a chance of saving Tex."

"What do you want me to do?"

"Cover me. Fire a couple shots to make sure the gunman in the house doesn't come out. And then I want you and Carillo to get to the car."

"We're not leaving you."

"If something happens, you get that file to McNiel. If nothing else, it'll clear you and Carillo, and the rest of the ATLAS crew."

She nodded, then maintained her position at that corner of the trailer. Griffin worked his way back to the other side, knowing she wasn't happy, but there was little he could do about it. He didn't know this other man, but he knew Quindlen and what sort of training he had, what he would do or have his partner do. Head to the east side to take Tex out, because that direction would shield him from Carillo up on the hill.

When Griffin reached the front of the trailer, he radioed, "Now."

Sydney fired a volley of shots.

Griffin ran. He made it to the front of the bunkhouse across the road. Now all he had to do was work his way toward Tex. That wouldn't be easy, since he didn't know where the second gunman was. He soon found out when he saw the man's moonlit shadow on the ground, elongated, making him look like a ten-foot Frankenstein, not an ordinary human.

But it also told him that this was Lee, not Quindlen. Quindlen would have been cognizant of his shadow telegraphing his position. This man might be dangerous, but not in the same way, and the last thing Griffin wanted to do was announce to Quindlen exactly where he was. He needed the element of surprise. Take out this man without Quindlen knowing. In other words, no gunfire.

He pressed himself into the siding of the bunkhouse, feeling the rough wood against his back, then heard the slow, deliberate steps of someone attempting to mask the sound, but not being successful. Griffin hoped that meant the guy had enough alcohol and pot in his system to slow his reaction times. He could use a break.

The shadow man stopped. Whether because he sensed Griffin's presence, Griffin didn't know. But soon it was creeping forward again, like a specter on the ground, gliding over every rock, every pebble, and Griffin watched as a shadow knife appeared on the ground, swordlike. It swung toward Griffin. But Griffin waited until Lee cleared the building before he jumped out, threw his arm up to block the thrust of the knife.

Lee was quick on his feet. He slashed his knife at Griffin, the blade glinting in the moonlight. Griffin blocked the blow with the gun barrel, metal hitting metal. The knife went flying, skittered across the coarse ground.

If this guy was good at anything, it was hand-to-hand combat. Lee got a couple of decent blows in and one kick. But the alcohol had dulled his senses, and Griffin managed to sidestep the next blow. Lee stumbled forward. Griffin grabbed him by the shoulder, hit him across the face with the gun butt, then slammed his head into the ground.

He wasn't dead, but he wasn't moving, either.

Close enough, Griffin thought, then stopped short as the woman came running out of the house, toward them. She dropped to the ground. "Lee. Oh my God! What'd you do to him?"

The next thing he knew, she was drawing a gun on *him*.

And then Charlene came out of her trailer across the way. "Jesus, Hilary. The guy's a piece of shit. Had this man killed him, he woulda done you a favor. Now put the gun down."

"But—"

"*Put* the gun down. We got bigger problems." Then to Griffin, she said, "Yut is on the other side. Got your friend at gunpoint."

Griffin ran between the buildings. Sure enough, Quindlen was standing there with a gun pointed toward the chicken coop, where Griffin could just make out the top of Tex's head. Quindlen must have been hoping Tex would make a break for it.

"What are you waiting for?" Griffin called out, his gun pointed at Quindlen.

"For my boys to come down the hill. Should be here any second."

"Tell you what. You lower your gun, and I'll let you live."

"You kill me," Quindlen said, "and you'll never survive what Brooks brings down on you."

"Brooks or Parker Kane?"

"They're one and the same," Quindlen said.

"Why are you doing this?"

"Same reason as Parker. For the good of the nation. The thing is, I'm willing to die for my country. Are you?" he asked, aiming at Griffin.

Griffin fired. "Not today," he said as Quindlen dropped to the ground.

A few goats brayed. Then came the sound of car tires rolling across the graveled road as Parker Kane's men arrived on the scene.

49

Washington, D.C.

Charles Gilroy telephoned Parker Kane the moment he arrived at the ATLAS safe house. "We're here," he said, then waited to hear what Kane wanted him to do.

After a long stretch of silence on the other end of the phone, Kane finally spoke. "You're sure this is the right place? The girl is there?"

Gilroy looked at the apartment building through the binoculars. "We believe so. I assume the orders are the same?"

"There's been a change of plans," Kane said. "The president has rescinded the kill order."

Gilroy could have told him that would happen. Election year. Last thing you want out is that you're killing U.S. citizens. Especially young ones. "That makes it easier for us, then. We have the same goal as the military."

"Actually it changes things. I can't take the risk that the military finds her first. Kill her before they get to her."

"What about Stiles? And the program?"

"If I'm arrested, Stiles is going down. I'll make sure of it. Don't call me until she's in a body bag."

Gilroy rubbed at the bridge of his nose, tired from the long day's surveillance and constantly looking through the binoculars. If he had his way, he'd force entry into the building. It was a ten-story structure, bordered by an alley along the back, and on the sides, a mix of old office buildings that were being gutted and converted to condos and lofts, at least according to the billboard advertising the possibility of future sales. The target building was accessed with a security key in the front, which opened a set of glass double doors, and a side door. There was an entrance in the back at the alley, a wrought-iron rolling gate, accessed by remote, but apparently it wasn't used except on Thursdays when the trash was picked up. Right now he had visual of the front and a partial view of the side. Enough streetlights kept the area lit up so that they didn't need night vision goggles.

"They're leaving the apartment." The transmission was from Jeffries. He was parked down the street opposite Gilroy and had a better line of sight to the front doors, where a delivery van was currently parked, blocking Gilroy's view.

"As in all of them?" Gilroy asked.

"The two agents."

Gilroy adjusted his binoculars. Damned delivery van. "Is the girl with them?" he asked.

"Doesn't look like it. Should we make entry?"

He was parked about four hundred feet away, just down the street, and when the vehicle came into view, he watched the pair through his binoculars, trying to decide what steps to take. "Doesn't make sense . . . Has to be someone there with her."

"Who?" Jeffries asked. "The two agents leaving the building look like the ones in the surveillance photos from Venice. Unless it's a trap."

The possibility certainly existed, but he doubted that they'd leave her alone. She was too valuable an asset. "Jeffries, follow the car. Halford, likewise. I want to know where they're going. Make sure the girl's not in the car with them. Do *not* lose them."

"Copy."

The vehicle pulled out, then drove south. A moment later, Jeffries's car followed, then Halford's. Unfortunately that left only Shipley, who was on the opposite corner.

The apartment was on the third story, the windows facing the front. What if she wasn't in there? The curtains were pulled, and he couldn't see a thing, he thought as a familiar-looking SUV drove past, then on into the apartment parking lot. "Shit. Tell me that vehicle doesn't belong to one of General Woodson's men?"

"What vehicle?"

"Black SUV, just pulled in the drive." He focused on the plates. Government issued, military. "Definitely one of Woodson's guys."

"Military? Here?"

Gilroy ran his hands through his hair. "Shit!"

"You said that already."

"That's because they're under orders to bring her in. Our op has changed. We are no longer bringing her in alive. *We* have the kill order."

"Sir? The military vehicles?"

He focused in on the vehicle, saw it contained two men. He thought he recognized the passenger. Their presence all but confirmed that the girl was there. At least they were acting on the same intelligence. "Engage them," he told Shipley. "Go up, pretend you live there, whatever the hell it takes."

Halford came on the radio. "They're driving into a shopping center. Parking . . ."

It took him a moment to switch gears. Halford. Following the two agents. "Stay on them."

"They're both getting out of their car, walking into the store."

"Check the car," he said, keeping his eye on the SUV, wondering what the hell they were up to.

"She's not in there."

A movement from the third floor window caught his eye, and he aimed his binoculars that way, only to see the curtains dropping, as though someone had been looking out. When he turned his attention back to the SUV, he realized one of the men had gotten out, was pointing up.

Shit. They were going to get her first.

"Shipley. Get on that SUV. Ask for directions, bump it, do whatever it takes."

A burst of static hit the radio as though Shipley's transmission was cut short. But a moment later, he was back on the air again. "Someone's coming out the side door."

Gilroy turned his binoculars that way, catching Shipley's car as he drove to the front of the building. Gilroy didn't have visual of the door, since it was inset. There was a narrow cement walkway that led through the landscaping of rocks and low shrubs and a few patches of gray snow where the sun never hit. But a moment later, he saw a hooded figure exiting. Female. Every nerve in his body screamed that she was the one. "I'll check it out. Get on that SUV."

"Copy."

He pulled forward, slowly, watched the girl looking around as though waiting for someone. A bit of dark hair was just visible beneath the hood—short, dark hair, and when a gust of wind blew, catching at her hood, he saw a flash of pink. It was everything he could do not to hit the gas and race over there, spooking her, alerting the military and anyone else in the area. She stood there a moment, then started walking toward the alley. Finally, something working in his favor.

"It's her," he said.

Shipley radioed back. "You want me over there?"

"Negative. You keep them engaged. I do not want them coming this direction."

"Copy."

"Halford, Jeffries, forget the two agents. Get back here. Now!"

He watched as she strolled toward the alley, her hands in her pockets. And then he glanced toward the front of the building, where Shipley was pulling up to the SUV, hopefully drawing their attention. Last thing he needed was for them to discover the girl. Or discover him. He'd be dead, and she'd be in custody.

He wasn't about to let that happen.

A car approached from the street adjacent to the alley as he was about to make a right turn, and he wondered for an instant if someone else was on the hunt. Didn't look like a military vehicle. Green compact sedan. When it kept going, the driver, a blond woman, not even noticing the girl, he relaxed, made the turn, cruised slowly toward the alley.

The girl turned into the alley, and he pulled his foot off the gas pedal, letting the car idle.

This was going to be beautiful. There was no one back here. He reached over, unsnapped his holster, then steered in. She looked back, saw him, her eyes going wide, and then she bolted.

Gilroy stepped on the gas, was nearly to her when she darted to the right, through a catwalk between two brick warehouses under construction. "In the alley," he called on the radio. He hit the brakes, screeching to a stop, threw the door open, ran after her. Damn, she was fast. When she reached the end of the catwalk, she turned left. Out of his view. Her footsteps echoed between the buildings, then suddenly it was quiet.

Gun drawn, he emerged from the catwalk, and realized why the sound had stopped. There was a chain-link fence blocking her from going farther.

Gilroy stopped where he was, a mere twenty-five feet away from the prize. She stood there like a cornered rabbit—no, like a cornered little punk rocker, her back to the fence, waiting for the inevitable.

He smiled, aimed his weapon at her. "I'm not going to hurt you," he said.

"Then why do you have a gun?"

"There're some other people around here I don't trust. They do want to hurt you. Kill you, in fact. Trust me. We want you alive."

She took a step back. "I don't care. I'm not going with you."

"Not an option. You're trapped."

"And what if I start screaming?"

"You scream, or make any noise in general, and they're gonna spray this area with bullets and kill you. Me? I'm wearing a ballistic vest, so I might survive. It's a chance I'm gonna have to take. You? Not a good option."

She glanced behind her, then up, probably assessing if she could make it over the chain-link fence. "I think I'll take my chances."

The last thing he wanted was for her to make any noise, or the military would be killing him. "Not a good choice."

She simply stared at him.

He didn't like that look in her eye. The deadly calm. And for a moment, he was actually worried. "You think you're some badass, because you're all dressed in black? I'm really going to enjoy this."

Her hand came up quicker than he realized, and just when his mind registered that it was moving, that he should do something, he felt a sharp pain in his shoulder. He stumbled back, dropped the gun, vaguely aware that she was approaching him.

"I might not be a badass," she said as she walked over, picked up his gun, aimed it at him. "But I'm good with a knife."

And it was only then that he realized this girl was much older than the one he was looking for.

Not the same girl at all.

50

Lisette kept the gun trained on her would-be killer as he gripped at the knife wound in his arm, the blood seeping through his fingers.

"I wasn't really going to shoot you," he said.

"Then you shouldn't have pointed your gun at me," she replied as she dug her Bluetooth out of her pocket and tucked it on her ear. "Did you copy all that?" she asked Marc. The Bluetooth had been on the entire time.

"A bit muffled, but yeah. Where are you?"

"Took the catwalk to the construction site."

"Why there?"

"He got here a little faster than I was counting."

"We're on our way."

She eyed the man on the ground, recognized him as one of the fake U.S. marshals. "What's your real name?"

"Charles Gilroy."

"You're the guy who pretended to be WitSec."

"I'm bleeding all over the place. An ambulance would be nice."

She looked down at his arm. "Hold it tight. It's not arterial."

"You a medical doctor, too?"

"If I wanted to kill you I would have aimed for the throat."

"Aren't you just the super-duper agent."

"Don't make me regret restraining myself," she said as Marc drove up. He got out of the car, walked over. "What took you so long?"

"Had to take care of the tail. We better hurry. Those operatives from the military are about to make entry into the apartment. Pretty sure we don't want to be around when they figure out she's gone. And boy wonder's working his magic from a new spot."

Marc leaned over, grabbed Gilroy by the arm, pulling him to his feet. Lisette kept her weapon aimed on him as Marc patted him down, then walked him back to the car, using his keys to pop open the trunk. "Get in."

"You serious?"

"About not getting blood on my upholstery? Yes. There's a rubber mat in the trunk. So much easier to hose off."

Gilroy stood there, not moving. Marc leaned in closer. "Either get in or I'll put you in. And unlike my partner, I am not likely to restrain myself."

Gilroy climbed into the trunk.

"You should put some pressure on that wound."

"Go fu—"

Marc slammed the lid closed. "Your funeral."

Lisette slid into the passenger seat as Marc got behind the wheel, started the car, made a three-point turn, then drove out. She looked over at him. "Everything else go okay?"

"So far, so good."

"What are we going to do with him?"

"Get him patched up for starters. Why the knife?"

"He was pointing a gun at me."

"I mean why didn't you shoot him? You had a gun."

"He said he was wearing a vest. And I thought we didn't want any noise."

Marc sped off in the opposite direction as the apartment building, putting plenty of distance between them and Gilroy's men.

"What happened to the tail he put on you?" she asked.

"The car they were driving in was reported stolen. Apparently there was a computer glitch at the Department of Motor Vehicles."

"It happens."

"As do anonymous calls to the police."

She leaned back in her seat, smiling, wondering what else Izzy had up his sleeve. Finally, something was going right.

51

Pocito, Arizona

Griffin and Tex were trapped. The two vehicles with
Parker's men had pulled up to the west of the house, cutting
off their escape to the hill and the car that was hidden up on
the dirt road.

Griffin and Tex barely managed to escape to the back of
the bunkhouse as they heard the car doors opening and closing, then someone asking, "Where are they?"

And Rico's wife, Charlene, saying, "They killed Mr.
Quindlen, then ran off. I didn't see what direction."

"What about you?"

Then Hilary, sobbing. "I don't know."

"Come on, Hil," Charlene said. "Let's get you inside.
Where are the dogs?"

"In the house."

"Good. Safe there. You'll be fine."

Griffin turned to Tex, whispering, "What the hell were
you doing on the chicken coop?"

"Damned dogs came after me."

"Don't suppose there's any goats left in that pen we can use for a distraction."

"Griffin?" Sydney's voice on the radio. "What's your location?"

"By the bunkhouse."

"Copy. You need to move away from there. Get to the other side of the road."

"Repeat?"

"Move *away* from the bunkhouse."

"What the—"

"There'll be a small explosion to cover you two running across the back of the bunkhouse. Meet me on the east side of Charlene's trailer in five, four, three, two, one. Now!"

A boom sounded, like an acetylene bomb going off, and sure enough, Parker's men ran toward the back of the property, toward the sound.

Griffin and Tex raced across the road and found Sydney standing by the trailer. "Carillo," she radioed. "Let me know when you're ready."

"Ready."

"Let's do it."

The rev of the engine, then Carillo racing down the hill. And when Parker's men ran alongside the bunkhouse, Sydney stepped out slightly, taking aim at the open door of the old, dilapidated building. She fired. The bunkhouse exploded, flames shot up, and wood went flying. Griffin felt the heat on his face as the force of the explosion carried the hot air.

And then Carillo pulled up, and the three of them raced to the car.

The moment they were in, he hit the gas and drove out the main road, gravel and dust kicking up behind their vehicle.

Griffin glanced back, saw Charlene on her porch, watching the flames.

"Meth cookers," Sydney said. "Leaving so many volatile chemicals in one location. Not safe."

"You and Carillo were supposed to go to the car to wait."

"Yeah," Carillo said, glancing over at him as he sped up the road away from the complex. "We did meet up. But we saw those headlights, knew they'd get here before you and Tex could get out. And when it comes right down to it, Sydney's just not that good at following orders anymore."

52

Washington, D.C.

There were certain things in life that McNiel enjoyed immensely. Working a good case successfully and seeing the fruits of their labor were high on his list. In this instance, Lisette, Marc, Donovan, and Piper were sitting around the table of their latest hotel room, listening to the final moments of Izzy's manipulation of the SINS program. McNiel, however, was walking into the National Security Council meeting, as he had finally agreed to provide the whereabouts of Piper, but only to the entire council. And as expected, Parker Kane was present. Unbeknownst to the council, Lisette, Marc, and Donovan had audio via McNiel's phone.

"Gentlemen," McNiel said, watching Kane, who sat next to General Woodson, as though he hadn't just lost a handful of men on a failed mission. "First, my apologies. There was a reason I couldn't tell you about where the witness Piper Lawrence was located, due to what I suspected was a leak in this council. Fearing for her safety, I wasn't about to release her location until I knew it could be done safely. That time has come."

"About time," Woodson said.

"First, however, there is something I'd like you to listen to. It's a recording of a conversation made this morning by one of my team."

He placed a digital recorder on the table, hit play.

"Quindlen's dead. They got away with the files."

Parker Kane jumped up from his seat, saying, "This is an illegal wiretap."

Woodson grabbed him by his arm, pulling him back into his seat, saying, "Shut up, Parker."

The voice on the recording continued. "The ATLAS agents blew up Quindlen's meth lab. And all your product, too. They got away."

And then Parker Kane's voice clearly saying, "You find them and kill them. No matter what it takes. I've got a god-damned National Security Council meeting to get to."

"But—"

"Just get it done."

McNiel switched off the recorder, then addressed the council, saying, "Are there any questions?"

53

That evening, over celebratory pizza and soda for Piper, but beer for everyone else, Lisette informed her that she and her brother would be placed in witness protection together.

"I know it's not what you want."

Piper gave an exaggerated sigh. "After what I've been through, I think it will be a welcome change."

"The good news is that it's only temporary, until we finish ferreting out everyone involved in this affair. Izzy is fairly sure that he can manipulate the SINS program so that even if someone were to torture you, you would be useless."

Marc raised his brows. "You can talk torture, but I can't? How is torturing her good news?"

"What I mean is that she is no longer on the most wanted list. One day if she wants to go to Venice on her *own* dime, she can."

Piper smiled, then held up her soda for a toast. "To all of you. Thanks."

They raised their glasses, but then Lisette noticed Piper's expression turning somber. "What's wrong?"

"Mr. McNiel. He was in trouble because of me. What's going to happen to him now? And the rest of you?"

"Not to worry," Lisette told her. "ATLAS is once again in the good graces of the president, and McNiel back in charge."

Donovan waved for them to be quiet. "Kane's picture's on the news."

He turned up the volume, as the newscaster said, ". . . Soon-to-be appointed deputy national security adviser Parker Kane was found dead in his home of a single gunshot wound to the head. According to a police department source, who spoke on condition of anonymity, Parker Kane's maid reported that he'd gone into his office, closed the door, and a few moments later, she heard a gunshot and called the police. A political source states that Kane, a former CIA department head, had recently learned of some allegations made against him while he worked for the CIA. Although all evidence points to a suicide, the police are investigating.

"And in other news . . ."

54

Sydney had slept most of the way home, grateful when the plane finally landed.

Tomorrow she, Griffin, and Tex were expected to report for a full debriefing. Tonight, the only thing she wanted to do was take a hot bath, then go to bed.

As they walked out of the airport, the three heading to the parking garage, Tex said, "I have no idea where I even parked."

Which reminded Syd that Griffin had driven her to the airport. "You know, I think I'll just take a cab home."

"I can drive you," Griffin said.

She thought about it for a second, then shook her head. "What I need right now is some alone time."

"Can we talk about this?"

And Tex said, "I'll just step over here. Out of the way . . . Not listening."

Sydney watched him walk off, then turned to Griffin. "What happened the last few nights . . . I'm sorry, Griffin. I'm just not ready to forget."

"I know we need to talk."

She eyed the baggage carousel as it started up and everyone gathered around, waiting for their luggage. "This goes a bit beyond personality differences or things you can work around. I just . . . I don't know how long it's going to take me. How do you fix something that I'm not sure is fixable?"

He looked at her, and she could tell he didn't have a clue what to say. And that was the problem.

"Friends tell each other things," she continued. "Important things. We start there and work our way up."

"I can live with that."

"Good. See you around." She started to walk off, stopped, then retraced her steps. "Friends also do things together. Dinner, movies, that sort of thing . . ."

"Dinner?"

"Perfect. Tomorrow. Seven. Don't be late."

Fact or Fiction?

Unsolved mysteries, cyber terrorism, dead journalists, intersecting cases, including many that involved the BCCI, the black ops bank used by the CIA and my inspiration for BICTT, the Black Network bank first introduced in *Face of a Killer*. We're talking conspiracy theory at its finest. So what's true and what isn't? In this case, there's more fact than fiction.

In 1991, Danny Casolaro, an investigative journalist, was allegedly investigating government corruption and the Inslaw Affair (detailed below), intending to write a book on the subject. In August of that year, the day after Casolaro had met with an informant who was going to break the case open for him, he was found dead in his West Virginia motel, having cut his wrists numerous times with a knife. His notes were never found. His death was ruled a suicide.

There are far too many unanswered questions about Casolaro's death for it to be anything but suspicious, and so I based my first fictional journalist on him. For further reading, try *The Last Circle: Danny Casolaro's Investigation into the Octopus and the PROMIS Software Scandal* by

Cheri Seymour. And for a more academic take on the subject, try *Conspiracy Theories: Secrecy and Power in American Culture* by Mark Fenster.

Of course one can't look at the Casolaro case without examining the mysterious death of David Webb several years later. Webb, a Pulitzer Prize–winning investigative journalist for the *San Jose Mercury News*, wrote a series of articles detailing the CIA's involvement in drug running that was connected to their Iran-Contra ventures. Webb was exiled from journalism as a result of the series. He later turned the series into a book and had allegedly found new evidence of further exploits involving the CIA, which he was beginning to put together for publication. On December 10, 2004, Webb was found dead in his home of not one, but two gunshot wounds to the head. The coroner ruled it a suicide. Even with two shots, the conclusion appears to be accurate. For the purposes of my story and my second journalist, I decided otherwise. Webb's series of articles can be found on the Internet under the title *The Dark Alliance*. He also wrote a book by the same name.

In my current book, I combine two premises. One, that the U.S. developed a case management software that they used to spy on other countries, and two, that there are computer chips found in computers around the world that could compromise our nation's entire infrastructure and safety, *if* someone had the key to open the secret back door built into it.

Both premises are true.

In the 1970s, the U.S. government contracted with Inslaw Corporation, a small IT company, to develop a software program called Prosecutors Management Information System, or PROMIS. This was a cutting-edge program for case management that could process and integrate information from a vast number of different computer programs and databases. It could be used to track anything from terrorists to credit card spending, depending on how one used the software. It was developed by former National Security Agency (NSA) programmer and engineer Bill Hamilton, owner of Inslaw. The program was sold to at least eighty countries, both legally and through the black market. Unbeknownst to the rest of the world, and even Mr. Hamilton, a back door was allegedly built into the program by computer prodigy Michael Riconosciuto—at the request of U.S. intelligence, so as to allow widespread computer espionage against other countries.

And there the tale might have ended, if not for the U.S. deciding that it did not owe Inslaw or the Hamiltons millions of dollars for their program. In 1991, Riconosciuto was arrested on illegal drug charges. He states it was because he provided information to the Hamiltons for a civil suit against the U.S. More than twenty years later, when I began to research this book, Riconosciuto was *still* imprisoned on those drug charges. He's gotten more years than the average meth cooker gets, which makes me wonder why his sentence seemed a bit excessive (not that I don't think illegal drug manufacturers should be imprisoned for lengthy terms).

The PROMIS/Inslaw Affair was instantly relegated to the annals of conspiracy theory and was dismissed by our government—at least as far as the spying was concerned. Anyone who believed it obviously believed in Santa Claus and the Tooth Fairy. Would the U.S. really commission a computer program that could be used to spy on other countries, allowing it to be sold on the black market, so that those other countries would install it, use it, then become vulnerable? Would they really kill journalists who found out what they were doing?

I knew right away that this would be the premise behind those missing numbers Sydney recovered in *Face of a Killer*. But I also knew that computer technology had advanced significantly since then. Would a program like that hold up if installed today? Allegedly it's been improved, enhanced, the closest thing to artificial intelligence out there, and that back door isn't just for spying. It's also used for manipulating data or moving money seamlessly in and out of the most secure bank accounts, which also operate a similar but parallel PROMIS program based on Hamilton's original program.

When it comes to espionage, however, the biggest weakness of the PROMIS program is that its software must be physically installed on computers. That leaves too much to chance. A much more efficient workaround is to infect hardware, the chips and flash drives or memory cards that everyone *must use* to run a computer or store data.

More importantly there is no current means to protect hardware against such threats.

That means that some manufacturer can create and compromise hardware that is destined to be installed on certain types of computers such as those used in weapons or nuclear power plants. By the time the computers are up and running, even fresh out of the box, they're already infected, the back door is already in place, and all one needs is the key to unlock it.

The stuff of legends? Conspiracy theory? Unfortunately not. It's apparently already been done. A computer chip manufactured in China that is used in U.S. weapons systems, nuclear power plants, and public transportation allegedly has a secret back door built into it. A team at the University of Cambridge's computer laboratory developed a silicon chip scanner that discovered the back door that had allegedly been inserted by the manufacturer. They extracted the key, which can be used to disable or reprogram the chip—even if locked by the users' own key.

According to the Cambridge researchers, the vulnerability could allow such a system to be turned into an "advanced Stuxnet weapon to attack potentially millions of systems." And if you aren't aware of Stuxnet, look up the episode of the CBS news show *60 Minutes* that aired in July 2010 (conveniently viewable on the Internet). Stuxnet is a computer worm. It quietly and invisibly bides its time on an innocent-looking flash drive or computer system, waiting to move to the next one, in search of a specific target, in this case, Iran's nuclear facilities. And before you say, well, it *was* Iran, and we really don't want them operating nukes, so what's the big deal?—think about this: It can be used against us. According to experts interviewed by CBS, it can attack our country's *entire* infrastructure, "from the heat you have in your home to the money in your bank account." And that's the little stuff. A few but not all systems it can attack include our traffic lights, water treatment facilities, electricity, and of course our weapons and nuclear facilities.

So who opened Pandora's Box by sending Stuxnet to Iran? The FBI is currently investigating where the attack originated.

In the meantime, lawmakers are in the process of reviewing our country's preparedness when it comes to cyber threats. To quote U.S. representative and chairman of the House Permanent Select Committee on Intelligence, Mike Rogers (R): "We *will* suffer a catastrophic cyber attack. The clock is ticking."

Maybe that's why I still prefer paper statements from my bank. It's always good to have a backup record beyond computers.

Covert agent Zachary Griffin is a man of dark secrets, and there was one occasion in the past in which he'd requested Special Agent Sydney Fitzpatrick's assistance on a supposedly simple mission—specifically to give him the opportunity to disclose what he'd kept from her ever since they began working together. But circumstances dictated otherwise . . .

Continue reading

The Last Second

A prequel novella by Robin Burcell

Available now from Harper Impulse

Zachary Griffin glanced over at his passenger, then
back at the road. He had his reasons for asking Sydney Fitzpatrick to assist him with this case. They worked for two
separate agencies. He was a covert operative for ATLAS,
an intelligence agency that handled national security threats
both domestically and internationally. She was an FBI agent.
Typically the FBI would not be working with ATLAS. Very
few people even knew his agency existed. But he'd crossed
paths with Sydney on more than one case, and, since she was
also a forensic artist, her clearance had been raised when
they'd needed her assistance.

This investigation, however, was not one that needed a
sketch, forensic or otherwise. He'd asked her to come with
him as a pretext to discuss a past case he'd worked. One
might even say it was a confession. A secret he'd held on to,
even though he should have told her before they'd started
dating.

Now it was time to clear the air.

What better way to do it than when they were stuck in

some small town, two thousand miles away, where she couldn't simply drive home? Maybe then she'd listen long enough to see things from his point of view.

One could only hope, he thought, checking his rearview mirror, then glancing over at her as she finished reading the case she'd started on the plane. They were now on the road, heading south from Tucson, Arizona. Unlike the gray January skies they'd left behind that morning in D.C., here it was blue and cloudless.

"This guy looks guilty," Sydney said, turning the page. It was a thick file, but she was nearly finished.

"He probably is."

"So why are we going out on it then? The guy skipped bail. You really think he's going to talk to us?"

"Assuming we can find him. If he can give us Quindlen, it'll be more than worth our while to offer him a deal."

According to the report, Calvin Walker, a Pocito police officer, was suspected of working with the Mexican cartels. He'd been seen talking with a known gunrunner and ex–CIA agent, Garrett Quindlen, who was under suspicion of running the entire operation. When Walker was stopped on his way home, the Pocito police found a number of guns in his trunk, along with a large amount of cash and drugs. He was arrested, and, for reasons Griffin had yet to determine, was granted bail before any other agencies had a chance to go out and interview him.

Their only hope now was getting to Walker through his sister, Trish, who they hoped might still be in touch with him.

They met Trish Walker at a coffee shop in the next town over. She had short, wind-tousled blond hair. Her blue eyes were rimmed with dark circles, and her skin looked gaunt, as though she hadn't slept or eaten much the past several days. The restaurant was empty save for two people sitting at the counter, one scanning the paper, the other the waitress, who was reading a book. The three took a seat at a table near the window, and the waitress got up to pour them coffee, took their order, then went back to her reading.

"We're hoping to offer your brother a deal," Griffin said to Trish. "Information on who's actually behind the operation in exchange for a lighter sentence."

"He's innocent."

"The evidence speaks otherwise."

"He's one of the most honest guys I know. A good cop. Always has been. He would've taken this all the way to court to prove his innocence."

Not wanting to alienate her, he decided to let her pursue her brother's innocence. "Did he tell you what's going on? What he thought was happening?"

She shook her head. "He said he couldn't talk on the phone, but that he didn't do what they said. His lawyer thinks he's lucky they even allowed bail."

"And after you posted his bail, what did he tell you?"

"That they set him up, and he was going to find out what was really going on. He was sure that this man Garrett Quindlen was behind everything. That he's the one who's actually calling the shots at Pocito PD. But no one can prove it. He told me he had his suspicions, but warned me about talking to anyone at the PD. He said they'd find out, and I'd end up in a body bag."

"When's the last time you saw your brother?"

"He was heading out to the old McMahon place. It's an abandoned house on the edge of town, where he thought he might find some sort of evidence. That's the last time I heard from him."

"How long ago was that?"

"Three days ago."

She looked down at her coffee cup for a second or two, tracing her finger along the rim. When she looked back up again, her eyes shimmered with tears. "You have to help me.

They killed him. I'm sure of it. He would *never* have jumped bail. Never."

Unfortunately, Griffin thought, they were only here to gather information. But he couldn't leave her like this. "What sort of help are you looking for?"

"I want to clear his name. If I can prove he was killed, I think the townspeople will take a stand and do the right thing. *Someone* in that police department's dirty, but it's not my brother. Right now no one in town will talk to me. They're all afraid."

"And how do you plan to prove he was murdered?"

"By finding his body. He was killed at the McMahon place. I'm sure of it. That's where he was going, and it also happens to be where the police department found that large cache of explosives they say belonged to him. It's not his. I know it."

"What makes you think it happened there?"

"Because I've finally found the one witness who *isn't* afraid to step forward. The only problem is that I seem to be the only person who believes him."

Now this was possibly something he could use. "And who is this mystery witness?"

"His name is Max."

"Where can I find him?"

She took a deep breath, clearly uncomfortable with what she was about to tell him. "The thing is . . . he doesn't speak English."

"I speak fluent Spanish."

"Actually," Trish said, "he doesn't speak Spanish, either."

"What language does he speak?"

She gave a hesitant smile. "This is the part you *might* have trouble with."

"Try."

"My witness is a dog."

"A dog?" He wasn't even sure how to react to that. Even Sydney looked stunned. "A *dog*?" he said again.

Trish handed him two photos. The first was of a once-white Victorian mansion on a low hilltop, which, judging from the peeling paint and missing sideboards, had seen better days. The second photo focused on a low wall made of large rocks that surrounded the bottom of the hill around the old Victorian's perimeter, then extended out about thirty feet.

And there, lying in front of the broken section of the wall, was a brown and black German shepherd, its head on the ground between its front paws.

He showed the photos to Sydney, and she asked, "Whose dog is it?"

"My brother's dog. Max. He's been there every day since Calvin went missing. Come tomorrow morning, the police department plans on detonating that cache of explosives they found in the basement of the McMahon house, and they don't seem too concerned if the dog's there or not."

"Why not remove the dog?"

"There's a high fence around the entire property," Trish said. "The gates are locked. And now that that dynamite's been discovered, the police won't let anyone near it. I've tried calling Max out, but he won't come. That's what makes me think my brother is buried there beneath those stones. Right where the wall's broken."

Griffin focused on the broken section, particularly the rocks in front of it. "Some of those weeds growing around the rocks look more than a week old. The bush growing next to it looks pretty intact."

Sydney leaned over to get a closer look at the photo. "I read a news article once about this dog that found its way to the cemetery and stayed by its master's grave for *months* after the man died. I'm with Trish. The dog must sense he's buried there, or why stay?"

"Truthfully?" Griffin said. "They blow up that cache, I think the dog is far enough away where it won't be hurt. We can check the rock pile afterward."

Sydney picked up the photo and held it in front of him. "Look at his face, Griffin. It's like he *knows*. We need to help Trish find the body and get it out. But if the police blow up that place, you can't guarantee debris from the house won't hit the dog. He could get hurt."

"And," Trish said, "those people need to know what happened to my brother. They need a hero, even a dead hero. Only then will things change around here."

Griffin eyed the photo. McNiel, his boss, would never allow him to run a rescue mission for a German shepherd. And he seriously doubted McNiel would make an exception to recover a suspected gun smuggler's body. The moment Griffin gave notification of his intent to help, he'd be shut down.

Black ops agents did *not* run rescue missions for pets.

But like Sydney, Griffin was a sucker for the underdog, especially when it was a real dog. He slid the photo into his notebook. "Maybe we can get in there posing as the press. I think it's time the *Washington Recorder* interviewed the police chief on what is clearly a human interest story."

"*Washington Recorder?*" Trish asked him.

"A newspaper we use for our nonofficial cover."

"I'll warn you," Trish said. "He doesn't like the press. Last thing he wants is news coverage."

Sydney smiled as she poured some cream in her coffee. "I'm pretty sure if he had a choice, he'd take the press over us any day."

Pocito, population twenty-three hundred, an old mining town, was not the flat, cactus-covered desert Griffin would have imagined. Set in the rolling hills at the foot of the Mule Mountains in southern Arizona, Pocito looked as though time had simply passed it over, stopping in the late 1800s. One almost expected to see the head lawman stepping out of the brick-fronted building with a six-shooter on his hip and a gold star on his chest. He did not, and the past disappeared into the present as Griffin and Sydney pulled open the door of the police department, stepping into a fluorescent-lit lobby where a woman sat behind the counter, typing away at a computer.

Judging from the equipment on her desk, Griffin figured she was receptionist, dispatcher, *and* phone operator. She smiled expectantly at the two of them.

"May I help you?"

Griffin adjusted his tortoiseshell glasses on his nose, then nodded in greeting. "Zachary Griffin, *Washington Recorder*, and Sydney Fitz, my photographer. We were hoping to have an interview with the chief."

"If you let me know what this is in regards to, I'll see if he's in."

Griffin glanced up at the plaque on the door behind her, the one that read "Chief of Police" on it. "Apparently," Griffin said, loud enough to be heard through the door, "there's a dog whose owner abandoned it. Out on some property that's about to be leveled."

"The McMahon place," she said. "I'm afraid Chief Parks is not taking any interviews on that until tomorrow." She gave Griffin a patronizing smile. "At least not until *after* the detonation."

"Too bad," he said. "Big special interest story. This place will be a zoo once it gets out. Of course, if I can get an exclusive, I'd be inclined to keep it under wraps until tomorrow."

The door behind the woman suddenly opened and out stepped a tall man, early fifties, wearing a khaki uniform, with a gold badge on his chest and stars on his collar. "It's okay, Irene. I've got time for a quick interview."

"Yes, sir."

Griffin followed Sydney back to the chief's office, where he directed them to the two chairs in front of his desk. "Sorry about that little bit of misunderstanding," Chief Parks said. "Got me a whopper of a case here, and I told Irene to—well, I've been on the phone all morning with the ATF and the DEA over it. Haven't even had a chance to break for coffee." He took a seat himself, then looked directly at Griffin. "Afraid I missed the name of your paper?"

"*Washington Recorder.*"

"Washington. You don't say? State or D.C.?"

"D.C."

"Dang. Over a dog?"

"The world's always looking for a feel-good story."

"Hard to feel good about a dirty cop working with the Mexican cartels. Guess I shoulda suspected something was up when Officer Walker was suddenly interested in cultivating his so-called informant."

"Any idea who this informant was?" Griffin asked him, wondering if it might be Quindlen or someone who could lead them to Quindlen.

"No clue. But we did try to find out. Followed Walker on multiple occasions out to the property where we found all that evidence. Then again, if you really want proof, maybe you'd like to see the photos of the dynamite Officer Walker had stored in the basement? And the guns?"

"You have photos?"

"Damned straight we do. Of course, the DEA's got the guns, but we kept a record." He pressed a button on his phone, then leaned over the speaker. "Irene, can you bring in the evidence book on Calvin Walker's case . . . Thanks." He hung up.

A moment later, Irene walked in, carrying a large black binder. "Anything else?"

"If you got any coffee made, I'd love a cup. For our guests, too."

"None for me," Sydney said.

"Already had my cup today," Griffin replied.

"Just one, Irene."

She smiled, then left. The chief opened the book, turned it so that it was facing the right way for Griffin, then slid it toward him across the desk. "You know much about guns, son?"

"Enough to know I never want to be on the wrong end of one," Griffin said, looking up at the chief through the rim of his glasses.

"Expect you reporters don't get around them much. These here? Extremely deadly." He tapped a photo of a metal long box containing an assortment of weapons. Off the top, Griffin recognized a couple of AR–15s and some semiautomatic AK-pattern rifles. Below that were at least two dozen more long guns, most of which, due to bad lighting, Griffin couldn't see clearly enough to identify. The chief tapped the page. "You hear of that bungled operation the Feds were running? Made all the news recently, letting all them guns cross the border into Mexico? Straw buyers and gun walkers?"

"Vaguely. I usually cover the human interest side of things."

"Well, this here cache of guns, every serial number traced back to that operation. Every one of them was found in the trunk of my officer, Calvin Walker. I'd say that makes him guilty."

"Allegedly," Sydney pointed out. "If I'm not mistaken, there hasn't been a trial yet."

The chief scoffed. "See, that's what's wrong with the media these days. Always so warm and fuzzy." He glanced at Sydney, then leaned back in his chair and pinned his gaze on Griffin. "There wasn't nothing *alleged* about it. What *happened* is that Officer Walker was moving them guns from his house here in town out to the McMahon property so he could hide 'em. Or he would've if we hadn't caught him. And if that wasn't bad enough, Walker jumped bail, missed court, and that tells me he probably headed straight to Mexico where his cartel friends are hiding him. Which makes him Mexico's problem, not mine."

Griffin turned the page in the book, curious to see what other evidence there might be. One was a picture of the Victorian mansion he'd seen in Trish's photograph. "This the McMahon place?"

Sydney leaned in for a look. "Impressive."

"It was," the chief said. "Back in the day. McMahon and Sons Mining. Old McMahon sold it and moved out of state some years ago. The new owners went bankrupt and the house was repossessed. Been empty so long, had to fence it off as a public nuisance. Of course, you turn to the next page, you'll see why it's being detonated in the morning." Griffin did as asked, and the chief said, "Either of you know anything about explosives?"

Sydney looked wide-eyed, and Griffin replied, "Let's just say they don't cover that in journalism school."

"That," Chief Parks said, tapping the photo, "is dynamite. Old mining towns, we expect to find this. But not there, in the McMahon basement."

Sydney moved closer for a better look. "Could it have been left behind by the past owners? For their mining operations?"

"No, ma'am. Because that there basement was empty when the last owners abandoned it. We know, because we rousted a few kids out of there over the years, which is why we had to erect the fence around the property. Too dangerous," he said, as Irene walked in with his cup of coffee. "Thanks." He turned his attention back to the binder. "We found that dynamite in a search of the property after Calvin jumped bail. Most officers I know don't keep cases of explosives around unless they're up to no good. And now we gotta blow up the place."

"Blow it up?" Sydney asked, playing the ingénue to perfection. "Why?"

"Wouldn't take much to set it off. Nitroglycerin's degraded. Couple of them sticks even rub together and boom!" He slammed his hand on the desk.

Sydney's brows went up, and Griffin asked, "But what about Officer Walker's dog? Can't we at least get in there and take it out?"

"Like I said, too dangerous. Right now, my officers are under orders to arrest anyone who shows up. Afraid I can't make any exceptions."

"Even for photographs?" Sydney asked. "For our article?"

"Tell you what," he said, steepling his fingers together. "You can take all the photos you want. As long as it's *outside* the fence line. That's the best I can do." He made a show of looking at his watch, then standing. "You two got any other questions? I got a town council meeting I gotta get to."

"Actually," Griffin said, "there is one thing. Now, mind you, I'm not the investigative expert here or anything, but we heard rumors that maybe that dog's waiting on that property because there's a body buried there somewhere."

"A body?" He shook his head. "Said it was beneath that rock pile by the broken wall?"

"Yes, sir."

"I take it you been talking to Walker's sister? Well, dog or no dog, I assure you there's no *dead* body beneath *that* rock pile or anywhere else on the property." He turned to his computer. "Who knows why the damned dog is there. Now this," he said, typing something on the keyboard, "is a photo taken a couple years ago, when we decided to fence the house off, due to it being a public nuisance. Last thing we wanted was to be sued 'cause some drunk-ass kid fell in one of them old mine shafts that litter the area, never mind falling down the stairs in the abandoned house." He waited while the article loaded, then turned the screen so Griffin and Sydney could see it. "You can see the fence crews working in the background. That puts it about two years ago. And there? Same broken wall. Same location. Same configuration. So unless someone went to the trouble of piling it up in exactly the same way, ain't no way they moved 'em to bury a body there."

"Is it possible to take a look ourselves? At least to retrieve the dog?"

"Can't let you do that. Ain't no reason that dog'll get hurt where it's at. Dynamite's in the basement. Dog's a few dozen yards away. Trust me. We got experts out there overseeing the whole thing, and they assure me that house is going straight down, not out. Ain't no one gonna get hurt, as long as they stay *outside* the fence line." He walked over to the door and opened it. "But tell you what. You want to be here in the morning when we blow up the place? I'll give you front-row seats. In the meantime, you leave the explosives to the guys who know what they're doing and we'll leave the article writing to you."

"Well?" Trish asked Griffin, once they were back at the car where she was waiting.

He removed his glasses and tucked them in his pocket. "Guess we're going to save a dog."

Sydney reached out, hugged him, and he forced himself to let go when she did. "Thank you," she said softly, and he hoped she'd remember that there was a good side to him, when they finally did get that chance to sit down and discuss his past. "What made you decide?"

"He's lying through his teeth. At least about the dynamite."

"I'm not the expert you are," Sydney said. "But I was under the impression that nitroglycerin *is* very unstable once it degrades."

"It is. And like he said, I'd expect to find long-forgotten dynamite in an old mining town like this. But what I saw in that photo happened to be military-grade explosives, which is made *without* nitroglycerin. The military designed it specifically for its stability. So either there's another dirty cop who fed Chief Parks a line of bull about what sort of explosives are down in that basement, and he's clueless, or he knows *exactly* what it is, and he believes *we're* clueless." He looked over at Sydney as she slid into the passenger seat. "Guess which scenario I'm banking on."

Sydney smiled. "Score one for the mild-mannered reporter."

Griffin started the car, then pulled away from the curb.

"So," Trish asked. "Where do we go from here?"

"The old McMahon place," Griffin said. "Seems to me if the chief's so hell-bent on keeping us out, that's the first place we need to check."

Assuming no one was hurt in the operation, the worst thing that could happen *if* he and Sydney got caught was that they'd be punished for using government resources in a non-sanctioned, nonvital operation. They could be suspended without pay for such a move.

Then again, they could both be fired.

Least of his worries right now.

Ten minutes later outside the fence line, as Griffin eyed the dog through his binoculars, he told himself that he didn't care if what he was doing went against the rules. In his mind, this was one case where it was better to ask for forgiveness than ask for permission. And if they took down a corrupt local government while they were doing it, all the better. "Exactly how did you plan on getting in there past the patrol officers guarding the place?" he asked Trish.

"There's a gate on the perimeter fencing around the back. It's locked. But there's also a hole near the gate where the dog got through. I think it's big enough for us."

"What sort of patrols do we have?" Griffin asked.

"A uniformed officer drives the outer circumference, checking on the property about every thirty minutes, making sure the gates are locked. Ever since they discovered the explosives, they haven't varied their schedule."

"Beyond the chief, you think the officers are in on this?" he asked her.

"I don't know. I never got the chance to ask my brother."

"And the agents who they turned the guns over to? Could they be in bed with the corrupt police?"

"I don't think so. The biggest problem with them is they're too by the book. At least according to my brother."

Of course, Griffin thought, there was one thing neither he nor Sydney considered when they set out on this mission. "What happens *if* we find your brother's body? Any chance the police chief's going to let us waltz out of here with it?"

Sydney gave him a sardonic look, but any quip she might have uttered died at the sight of a dust cloud in the distance.

Apparently the road coming from the south wasn't paved. "That's probably the patrol." He checked his watch. "Now we know their schedule. Nice of them to make it easy for us."

A minute later, the vehicle drove past the gulch where they hid. It stopped, the red dust settling as the officer got out, checked the chain on the gate, then stood there a moment, looking in their direction. Although they were hidden in the brush, Griffin felt Sydney tensing next to him. But then the officer turned away, got back into his vehicle, and drove off.

They waited until the trail of dust was long gone before they got up, moved to the gate. Trish showed them where the dog had gotten through, a hole beneath the chain link. Griffin lifted it, allowing first Sydney, then Trish in, before sliding under it himself. Sydney and Trish climbed the hill toward the house to have a look around, while Griffin, using the shrubs for cover, worked his way to the end of the broken wall, where the dog rested.

When he reached the break in the wall, the dog turned toward him, his sad eyes looking suddenly hopeful as he raised his head, then wagged his tail hesitantly. In that moment, had all the forces of Washington, D.C., ordered him off, Griffin knew without a doubt that he couldn't walk away.

"Hey, Max," he said quietly, not wanting to scare the dog. "C'mere."

Max stood, but didn't move, watching with a wary expression as Griffin neared. He looked thin, his coat dull from the dust.

"Max." Griffin took a few more steps, held out his hand, then clicked his tongue. "C'mere, boy. Come."

The dog remained steadfast.

At least he wasn't growling. Griffin took that as a good sign, talking softly, moving forward, slow, steady, until he was just two steps away.

"Good dog." He reached out, allowed the dog to smell the back of his hand. "Where's Calvin?" The dog's ears perked up. "Where's Calvin? C'mon, boy. Show me."

Max gave a slight whine, then jumped down and started digging in the hard, sandy soil, right beneath the foremost rock.

Griffin might still have doubts about Trish's theory on the location of Calvin Walker's body—he saw no signs of a fresh grave, nor smelled the stench of decaying flesh that in this climate was a sure sign. But this dog was trying to tell him that *something* was beneath there.

He crouched down next to the dog, looking at the rocks, and the dog pushed his nose against Griffin's arm, as though urging him forward. Max jumped so that his forepaws were on the rock. He barked twice, and Griffin wondered if perhaps there was a murder weapon, or something that belonged to his master that would explain why the dog had steadfastly remained in this one spot of all places. He leaned forward to peer into the shadows cast by the bush growing right against the break in the wall.

What he didn't expect was to feel air moving against his face. Or a sound coming from beneath the rocks. Like the noise a seashell makes when you hold it to your ear.

The rocks weren't there to cover up a grave. They were there to cover up an old mining shaft.

"Anyone down there?"

No answer.

Griffin pulled one of the rocks off and it rolled down the pile. Then another, until he partially exposed a metal grate covering the shaft. He cleared the remainder of the rocks from it and saw it was a little over a half meter in diameter. The bush growing next to it blocked the sunlight and he couldn't see how deep it went. Someone certainly could have dropped a body down there, but after three days, there would have been some smell of decay—unless it was too deep. "Calvin Walker? Are you there?"

He couldn't tell if what he heard was a raspy faint response or an echo of his last word. The dog, however, whined. That was proof enough for Griffin, and he started to lift the grille when Sydney called out to him. He looked up to see her and Trish on the porch.

Sydney pointed toward the service road. "The patrol car's coming back around." Sure enough, there was a growing cloud of dust, which suddenly settled, indicating the car had stopped a couple of hundred yards out.

Sydney turned her binoculars back to the road. "Getting out of the car . . . Gun!" She pulled Trish down onto the porch a second before the first shot rang out. Bits of rock and dust went flying past Griffin's face.

Griffin dove to the ground, on the far side of the rocks. A second shot rang out. Max gave a sharp cry.

Unsure if he was hit or simply scared, Griffin called him. "Max! Come!"

The dog obeyed. Griffin grabbed him by the collar, so he couldn't run off. Although Griffin couldn't see the officer, he wasn't about to poke his head up over the low wall to look, so he held the dog to the ground next to him. From that distance, it had to be a long-range rifle. "Sydney! Visual?"

"Clear! . . . Run!"

Gripping Max's collar, he sprinted up the hill to the house, onto the porch where Sydney and Trish hid. Sydney was standing behind the trellis, the thick, leafless vines giving her cover as she watched.

"What's he doing?"

"Backing up, I'm assuming so he can call in reinforcements."

"We could use some big guns of our own," he said, pulling out his cell phone. Tucson's FBI field office was the closest. Only one problem. "No signal."

In fact, no one had a signal, and Trish said, "Come to think of it, every time I've come, I haven't been able to get service on this hill. I just thought it was my phone."

"They must have a jamming device," he said.

"What does that do?" Trish asked.

"Used by the military to block radio or phone signals that might detonate a remote-controlled improvised explosive device. A good idea if you've got something wired to blow."

"That," Sydney added, "is a mighty sophisticated piece of equipment for a two-bit town like this. So where do you think they have it?"

Griffin looked around the property, eventually spying an old wooden shed about fifty yards down the hill. "Probably in there."

"We could always shoot it. The wood looks like it's ready to fall off anyway."

"Not a good idea when you're sitting on top of who knows how much explosives. Right now, the jamming device is a good thing."

"One of us could leave and call for help," Sydney suggested, and he knew she meant Trish, hoping to keep her safe.

Unfortunately there was not enough cover between there and the gate. "Too risky."

"I don't understand," Trish said. "Why would they need a jammer if no one's coming in until tomorrow to set up the detonation?"

"A very good point," Griffin replied. "I think it's time we find out." He turned to examine the door.

Trish looked aghast. "Do you really think it's safe to go in there?"

"No choice. I can't tell where the biggest threat comes from. The cop shooting at us or in the basement. Any chance you can keep watch out here while Sydney and I check?"

"Sure," Trish said.

Sydney reached out, touched her shoulder. "Stay out of sight and let us know when anyone else arrives or they start moving this way."

Trish nodded, then focused on the officer. "He's just standing behind his door, the rifle pointed this way."

Figuring they had about ten minutes before reinforcements arrived from town, Griffin examined the door, hoping no one had thought to booby-trap it. Seeing nothing that alarmed him, he gave it a good kick. It flew open, hit the interior wall, then bounced back.

He pushed it wide, took a look in. The place appeared as though someone had started gutting the house, but stopped midway. Walls were torn down, jagged piles of Sheetrock remnants filled one corner, and an extension ladder leaned against the wall in the other. The wood-planked floor was warped, but felt solid beneath his feet. To the right, stairs ascended to the second floor. And to the right of that, there was a partially open door. Before he could determine where it led, the dog bolted forward, pushed through the door, then on down another staircase.

"Max!" Griffin called out.

The last thing they needed was a dog loose in a basement filled with explosives.

He relaxed slightly when he discovered that the door at the bottom was closed tight. Max scratched at it, whining.

"Guess we start there."

"Right behind you," Sydney said.

The stairwell wasn't the brightest, but they weren't about to see if there was any electrical power in the house. One did not turn on light switches or any other power source in proximity to explosive devices. When he reached the bottom, Max scratched at the door again, then looked up at Griffin.

"Sit."

The dog obeyed.

Griffin grabbed his collar, held tight, and after a cursory check of the door, turned the knob and opened it. He was glad to see that there was enough light from outside filtering in through the basement windows, and he took a look around before making a move. It appeared they were storing some of their building supplies down here, possibly doing some work. There was a stack of plywood sheets leaning against the wall to his left, and about an inch of sawdust on the ground in front of it.

More importantly, there were four cases of military-grade explosives stacked in the very center of the basement on the concrete floor, between two support beams. To Griffin, it seemed an odd choice for someone involved in illegal trafficking of any kind to store their explosives right where someone could see if they happened to look into any of the basement windows.

"Sydney. Grab Max's collar and don't let him move from the doorway."

She took the dog and he stepped into the room, walked to his right, surveying the floor first, making sure there were no trip wires.

Even though the outsides of the boxes indicated that they were military explosives, he wasn't about to assume that's what they contained. The first thing he looked for was signs of crystallization that would indicate any nitroglycerin had degraded.

"Clearly they lied by reporting it as too unstable to move."

"And you're surprised by this?" Sydney asked.

"Just stating a fact," he said, slowly walking the perimeter of the basement. The anticipated timer and detonation device was on the far side, and he stopped short at the sight of bright red coming from the timer. It took a moment before he realized that it was just the sun angling in from the window reflecting on the LED light.

He knelt down. Used his cell phone to take a picture of it and the serial numbers on the closest box of explosives. The serial numbers could be traced back to where it originated, and as long as Griffin's phone wasn't blown to bits, and him with it, he'd have some proof of where it came from.

"Can you disconnect it?"

"Too soon to say. There's a secondary wire on the timer and detonator, running straight down to the floor. It looks like it's running back underneath all the boxes."

"Booby trap in case you move them?"

"Maybe." He got up, continued his path around the room, and realized the wire continued on past the boxes across the floor to the left of the stairwell, then straight underneath the sheets of plywood leaning against the wall. He hadn't noticed the wire earlier, because of all the sawdust covering it, undoubtedly to conceal it from the casual observer.

He knelt down beside the plywood, noting the space between the bottom of each sheet. No pressure device. "Where the hell is the wire running to?"

"Can't you just cut it?"

"Not until I know its purpose." He only hoped it was straightforward, a matter of simply disconnecting the wires, but this setup had him stumped. Careful not to disturb the wire, he lifted the sheets of plywood one by one and stacked them against the wall a few feet away. He moved the last piece and saw a wooden cupboard door about four feet high, barred from the outside and secured with a padlock. The wire ran beneath it. "I'd say something's in there. The wire isn't thrilling me, though."

Max whined quietly, and Sydney reached down to pet him.

Griffin found a hammer in a toolbox in the corner and gave the lock a solid hit. It popped off. "You might want to move inside the stairwell."

"Seriously, Griff? If that stuff blows, this flimsy wall isn't doing either of us any good."

"Stubborn as ever," he said, then pulled open the cupboard.

The moment he did, the dog tried to escape from Sydney's grasp.

"Easy, boy," she said.

"There's a tunnel," he told her, when she tried to angle over to see. "Meter wide by a meter high." Griffin hated dark, tight spaces, and this was definitely dark and bordering on tight.

Max pulled Sydney forward.

"Don't let him go."

"I'm trying not to," she said as the dog's claws scratched at the concrete.

He leaned down, peered inside. The area was dark, and he could just make out the rough-hewn walls of the tunnel. The wire snaked along the bottom off to one side, and he pulled out his phone, turned on the flashlight feature. "Another box of explosives farther in."

"Why would you blow up a tunnel that is hidden from view?"

"You wouldn't, unless there was something down there you didn't want anyone to find."

The sound of metal hitting metal startled them. It came from outside, somewhere near the gate, Griffin thought.

Max barked, broke free, then scrambled for the tunnel. Griffin dove for the dog.

Max darted to the side, raced past him down the long passageway, right toward the box of explosives.

"Max!"

The dog never stopped. Griffin tensed. But the dog jumped over the explosives, then on past it, disappearing around a corner.

And then Trish called out from upstairs.

"You better get up here!" Trish said. "Some cop just crashed his car through the gate. He's parked at the bottom of the hill. There's another car right behind his."

Sydney looked toward Griffin.

"I need to see what this wire's for," he said.

"Be careful, Zachary."

He wasn't sure he'd ever heard her use his first name before. "You too."

"Aren't I always?" And then the sound of her footsteps as she raced up the stairs.

Griffin, phone in hand as his only source of light, entered the tunnel. He took a deep breath, and then another before starting forward. He'd had to train himself to get past the tight spaces, relax enough to let the claustrophobic feelings pass. The tunnel was not going to come down on him, and he kept his eye on the wire to the right, careful not to disturb it. At the same time, there was the box of explosives up ahead, and with the phone angled that way, the light bouncing as he moved, he half imagined there was another source of light shining on the dirt wall near the box in front of him.

He stilled.

It wasn't his imagination. Nor was his phone *the* source of the light.

Even worse, the light he saw reflecting off the rocky wall looked suspiciously like it was some sort of digital device flashing in countdown mode.

He doubled his pace, dirt and rocks digging into his palms and knees, and he wondered if the dog had somehow set off a detonator on this secondary device. The box of explosives was nearly in the middle of the tunnel, and he leaned over it to view the timer.

Two minutes, thirty-nine seconds. And counting down fast. A mercury switch. The dog must have brushed against it and set it off.

He heard something. Panting.

Max, he realized, but turned his attention to the detonator, vaguely aware that the air here smelled. Of urine.

Dead men didn't urinate. Men who were trapped in tunnels did.

Trish's brother was going to have to wait. He had a bomb to disarm. Using his phone as a flashlight, he examined the device on all sides. Whoever had set this up had used a simple connection. Finally, something going his way. He dug out his pocketknife, then cut the wire. The timer stopped. But then came that millisecond of worry, until nothing more happened. He took a deep breath, sat back, and was about to start down the tunnel again, when he eyed the mercury switch, suddenly getting a bad feeling. Why have a mercury switch *and* a wire connecting it to the other detonator? The mercury switch on this detonator would have set it off just from the vibration when the main cache exploded . . .

The answer suddenly became clear—fail-secure—and he hurried back through the tunnel toward the basement, jumping out, then racing over to the four boxes of explosives sitting in the middle of the floor. Sure enough, the LED timer flashed down the seconds at warp speed. He cut the wire, grateful it was such a simple device, then stood there, his heart racing at the close call.

Not quite a dead man's switch. More like a delayed dead man's switch.

Just when the adrenaline started to leave, he heard Max barking.

Time to see what the dog found.

He reentered the tunnel, noticing that it widened at the curve just before he saw a thin stream of light filtering in through the grille overhead. Undoubtedly where the rocks covered the grille opening he'd seen from above. The shaft, slightly more than a half-meter wide, allowed enough light to see the dog at the feet of a man who sat with his back against the tunnel wall. The dog looked up, his tail wagging. The man merely watched him, perhaps trying to decide if he was there to help or hurt.

"Calvin Walker?"

"Yes—" He cleared his throat. "Who . . . ?"

"A friend of your sister's."

"Any—" He stopped. "Sorry. Laryngitis . . . Shouting." And indeed his voice was raspy. He held up his handcuffed wrist, the silver marred with his dried blood from trying to pull out of it. A long chain snaked from the handcuff to a large eye hook anchored in the rock wall of the cave. "Key?"

Griffin examined the locking mechanism. Standard handcuff, double locked, which made it more difficult to open, but not impossible. "No. But I have the next best thing." He pocketed his phone, took out his wallet, removing the money clip, which, had anyone examined, was noticeably slimmer than what came with the wallet. About the thickness of a large paper clip, its end turned up slightly. In his line of work, it wasn't a good idea to carry around a handcuff key, especially when working undercover. Too often identified with law enforcement, whereas a lock pick designed as a money clip was usually overlooked.

"How'd you end up here?" Griffin asked, inserting the tool into the lock, fishing it around to get a feel inside.

"Politics." Calvin gave a weak smile. "I refused to join the chief's party."

Griffin found the double-lock mechanism, turned the tool, and heard a click. Now for the main lock. "Who's behind this?"

"A guy named Quindlen."

"You know him?"

"Met him a few times. He's a friend of the chief. I think they got to my informant, killed him. Haven't seen him since my arrest."

"So why keep you alive down here?"

"Quindlen's idea. Harder to explain a bullet hole in an autopsy. Hence the water," he said, holding up an empty bottle. "Don't want your body—if it's found—dying of dehydration. But an explosion? It fits the scenario they cooked up."

"Quindlen's behind this?"

"He's behind everything here. But someone's behind him. Someone big. Don't know who." The lock popped open, and Calvin rubbed at his wrist. "Thanks."

Griffin replaced the pick into his wallet. "So this big investigation they have on you?"

"Set up by Chief Parks and Quindlen." He reached out, scratched Max behind his ears. "Never saw it coming."

"Any idea where Quindlen's operation is based out of?"

"Unfortunately no. But it can't be too far from here, because I see him in town a lot."

"Can you crawl out, or will you need help?"

"I can do it. Perhaps not quickly . . ."

The sharp crack of gunfire echoed down the air shaft. The patrol officers were taking shots at Sydney. "Sorry. Gotta go."

Calvin, one arm resting on the dog's back, nodded. "We'll get there."

Griffin ducked back into the passageway, hurried through the tunnel. Just as he emerged from the basement, he heard several rapid shots coming from outside.

Sydney . . .

Griffin took the stairs two at a time. The ground floor was empty. Sydney had propped the extension ladder against the front door, undoubtedly to serve as a warning should someone try to enter—she'd hear the ladder falling and know the entry was breached. Knowing she'd go for high ground, he raced to the second floor, found her in a front bedroom, her weapon gripped in her right hand. She stood next to the window, peering out through tattered curtains, yellowed with age.

"What's going on?" he asked, taking the position opposite her and drawing his own gun.

"They're aiming at the ground down by the wall. Three officers, fully automatic weapons. Considering they thought we were reporters, and don't even know we're armed, why not just shoot us? Spray the house with gunfire? There's not a lot to stop it."

"Good question." He thought about what Calvin said, about no bullets being found at an autopsy. "If I had to guess, they want to blow us with the house. Make it look like an accident."

The two of them stood like that for several seconds, watching, waiting, when she suddenly turned to him. "I wasn't planning on dying this weekend."

"Same here."

"Any last words in case we don't make it? You said you wanted to talk about—"

He heard Max and Calvin enter the room, and was grateful for the timely interruption. Calvin ordered Max to stay, then he crouched down next to him in the doorway, keeping his head below the level of the window.

"That would be Calvin," Griffin said. "Trish's brother."

Sydney turned, stared at the man for a full second. "Oh my God . . . *Trish?* Get in here."

A moment later, Trish was barreling down the hallway.

"What's wrong? Did——?" Her face crumpled when she saw her brother, and she dove into his arms. "I thought you were dead . . ." She started crying. "Why didn't you call me?"

"I'm sorry."

A smile lit Sydney's face and she looked over at Griffin. "Nice job, Griff."

More gunfire erupted.

Griffin saw the dirt flying up at the base of the hill. Sydney was correct. They were purposefully shooting low.

She pressed herself against the wall, away from the window. "This might be a good time to brainstorm, because I'm out of ideas."

"I could give myself up," Calvin said. "I'm the one they want dead."

"No," Trish said, burying her face in her brother's shoulder.

"If I did, they might let you all go."

"I doubt it," Griffin said, "since they're expecting to blow the house sky-high and us with it. I'd just like to know what they're waiting for."

"Just be grateful they *are* waiting," Sydney said, then eyed Griffin. "You *did* disarm the bombs?"

"Twice."

Her brows went up.

"Technical glitch. Right now, we may have a bigger problem."

"Like what?" she asked, turning her attention back to the window.

"Anger issues. Like what happens when they shut off the jamming device and the bombs won't detonate."

"Oh good. Because death by long-range automatic weapon is much preferred. In case you haven't noticed, we're outgunned *and* outmanned." She glanced down at his Glock. "With thirty-two rounds between us, I don't think we're going to last that long, even if they did move into range."

"You have a better idea?"

"Get the phones working and call in the damned cavalry."

"It would have been nice to know we needed the damned cavalry *before* we got here," he quipped.

"Like they would have come?"

She had a point. Their only evidence had been a dog sitting by a broken wall.

He glanced out, eyed the wall where he'd first seen the dog, then his gaze moved to the shed where the jamming device was probably located, far enough away to prevent injury if the explosives were detonated, and close enough for him or Sydney to shoot, if the men approached. But they hadn't approached. And Griffin was certain it had nothing to do with them thinking that he or Sydney was armed, or they'd be taking better cover than they were. Undoubtedly they still considered the two of them as reporters. And yet, had any of the officers wanted to, they could still move closer, probably shoot right through the walls . . .

"They can't switch off the jamming device until right before they detonate," Griffin said. "Or they risk us calling for help. That means they're waiting."

"We've established that," Sydney replied.

"But not *what* they're waiting for."

Calvin extricated himself from his sister's arms, then joined them at the window, looking out. "The chief's not there. They won't make a move without him."

"Maybe he really did have a meeting," Sydney said. "That's what he told us when we left his office."

"Town council?" Calvin asked.

"That's what he said."

Calvin actually laughed as he peered through the curtains. "No wonder. After the meeting, Parks usually heads to the massage parlor for the chief's special. I understand it involves handcuffs, leather, and a safety word, *and* he turns his police radio off."

"This wouldn't constitute an emergency?" Griffin asked. "Wouldn't they call him on his cell phone?"

"Trust me. You do *not* want to be the guy who interrupts *that*. See the officer in the middle? He did that once. Lucky to still have a job. Probably wouldn't, except it's hard to find good sheep in cops' uniforms these days."

Griffin parted the curtain slightly, surveying the area. "So how long does Parks's little interlude last?"

Calvin looked at his watch. "He keeps a pretty regular schedule, which means he's probably on his way here."

"Sydney?"

"God knows there's enough explosives down there. Can't we use that to blow the cops up?"

"No way to get a bomb from here to there, without them sweeping us with gunfire."

"So how do we draw them closer without making us targets? At least then we could shoot them."

"Just a thought," Calvin said. "But couldn't we let them blow up the house, then let them *think* we're dead?"

"How?" Griffin asked.

"Use fewer explosives than they had wired up. We hide in the tunnel, the house goes down, they leave. We emerge unscathed."

"Too risky. The blast will carry into the tunnel." He peered out the window, his gaze following the length of the wall to the end, where he'd first seen the dog waiting . . . "What we need to do is get closer."

"How?" Sydney asked.

"The tunnel. We use the ladder you found to climb out."

"Will the ladder reach?"

Two eight-foot extensions . . . Unfortunately he hadn't paid too much attention to the height of the tunnel, but he didn't think it was much more than fifteen feet. "I think so."

They agreed. Sydney stood guard at the front door, while the three of them and the dog retreated below.

Griffin carried the ladder, but it wasn't until he slid it into the tunnel that it occurred to him the thing might be too long to get around the curve near the air shaft. One way to find out. He grabbed one end, Calvin the other, both trying not to let it hit the ground or make noise. When they reached the curve, Griffin turned, pulling the ladder with him.

It fit. Barely.

Extending it, however, was another issue altogether. The ratchet mechanism rattled the aluminum and the sound echoed up the chamber.

"Slow," Griffin said. "One click at a time, then wait."

Calvin nodded. The dog wagged his tail.

"I'm going to get Sydney."

He left Calvin and his sister to finish extending the ladder, then crawled out the tunnel, through the basement, before calling up the stairs to her.

She hurried down.

"Any sign of the chief yet?"

"No."

Turning back, he eyed the boxes of explosives sitting in the middle of the basement. "Shame to waste it," he said, then proceeded to gather the detonator and the length of wire from beneath the boxes.

"What are you doing?"

"Contingency plan, Sydney," he said, rolling the wire as he moved toward the tunnel entrance. "Grab a few sticks on your way."

"How many?"

"Four to six should do it."

The others were waiting in the chamber, the ladder fully extended.

Max sat, his tail thumping, undoubtedly glad to be with Calvin.

Griffin wrapped the wire around the sticks as well as the detonator, outlining his plan to the others when a high-pitched squeal followed by the sound of tires on gravel echoed down the chamber from the ground above.

Everyone froze.

"Chief's here," Calvin whispered. "That's his car."

Griffin placed the bomb onto the ground, then took hold of the ladder. "Everyone know what to do?"

At their collective yes, he started up the ladder, with Sydney following. Calvin and Trish held the ladder steady. At the top, Griffin lifted the heavy grate, metal hitting rock as he set it to one side.

"You hear that?" someone from outside said.

Griffin's heart pounded. He reached for his gun, listening for a sign that someone was walking toward them.

After what seemed an eternity, he heard Parks say, "Probably that damned dog of Walker's that's been hanging around. If I didn't think the town would lynch me for putting a bullet in its head, I'd a done it a long time ago. Now what the hell's going on in that house?"

"Those reporters showed up here snooping around. We've got them cornered inside. No one shot, just like you said."

"That right? Where are they?"

"Saw them upstairs a few minutes ago."

"Apparently they didn't believe me when I told 'em there weren't any dead bodies. Boys? I think it's time to move up that detonation from tomorrow to now. Guess that *dynamite's* a lot more unstable than we thought." Some laughter, then, "Richie, shut off the IED jammer."

"Yes, sir."

"The rest of you boys take cover. Don't want any debris to hit you."

Griffin heard gravel crunching beneath booted feet, the sound moving away from them. He climbed out, grateful that the broken wall shielded them from view. Sydney handed him the wired explosive device. After he helped Sydney climb out, they dropped down behind the broken wall and Griffin peered through the bush, seeing an officer walking toward the shed, his AR–15 slung across his back. The chief, his attention on the house, stood by his car, holding a remote in his hand, his sidearm still holstered. One officer was crouching behind the trunk of the chief's car, the other behind the car nearest Griffin. Both had their rifles aimed toward the house.

Perfect.

Griffin signaled to Sydney, then pointed at the nearest officer.

She nodded, and together they approached, careful not to disturb the gravel.

By the time the man realized they were on top of him, it was too late. His eyes widened as Sydney shoved the nose of her gun to the back of his neck. "You talk, you die," she said quietly. "Now stand, slowly."

As the officer complied, she reached around him, grabbed the AR–15, and slung it over her shoulder, while Griffin removed the man's sidearm from his holster.

"Back up slowly," Sydney said.

The moment he did, Griffin slapped the sticks of explosive against the man's chest. "Hold tight. Because if you let go, boom!"

The officer looked down, would have dropped to his knees had Griffin not been holding him.

He walked the uniformed man toward Parks, who was fingering the control in his hand. Parks looked up, saw Griffin. "What the—"

"I wouldn't press that remote if I were you."

"Except you're not. So I think I will."

"Your funeral." Griffin pushed the officer forward, and he stumbled toward the chief, still holding tight to the makeshift bomb.

Parks took a step back. "What the hell . . . ?"

"You know anything about explosives?" Griffin asked him.

It was a moment before Parks drew his gaze from the officer and what he was carrying. "You're asking me? Who the hell you think wired that rig down there?"

"Then you undoubtedly recognize the remote timer that used to be connected to the initiator on those four cases of military-grade explosives."

"I'm just trying to figure out how you got it off without getting blown up. What the hell kind of reporters are you?"

"The kind that work for the U.S. government."

Sydney raised the AR–15 and pointed it at the chief. "Actually, the impatient kind. Drop your weapons to the ground. Everyone!" The other two officers hesitated, until Sydney aimed right at them. Both AR–15s went down, followed by their handguns.

"You know what I think?" Parks said, making no move to unholster his gun. "I think you're not stupid enough to connect that firing switch to the detonator. I think that wire is wrapped around it just for show."

"Feel free to take a closer look. But like I said. *Your* funeral."

Sydney gave a frustrated sigh. "I've got plans for the weekend. How about I just shoot him?"

"Remote on the ground," Griffin ordered again.

Parks glanced at Sydney, as though wondering if she might actually pull the trigger. When she lifted the rifle higher, he held the remote out, slowly placing it on the ground.

"Now the gun," Griffin said. "On the ground, then kick it forward."

Sydney leaned in, probably wishing the chief would make a wrong move, but he tossed the handgun to the ground, then kicked it toward them.

Griffin removed the makeshift bomb from the first officer's arms, then set it on the ground. In short order, they had all three officers and the chief cuffed. Once they were secured, Griffin sat each man on the wall. "So which one of you men wants to tell me where we can find Garrett Quindlen?"

The three officers stared at their feet. Chief Parks spit on the ground, then glared at Griffin. "You're insane if you think any of us will talk. We'd be dead in a heartbeat."

"Even if we made a deal?"

"Especially if we made a deal. It's his boss that pulls the strings, and even I don't know who that is."

"Somebody really high up," one of the officers said. "Brooks."

"Shut your trap, boy," Parks told him. "You're gonna get us all killed."

Brooks was a name Griffin had heard before, an aka. What they needed to know was the identity of the man behind it. All Griffin knew was that he was rumored to be a very large player in the Network, the criminal organization suspected of running the drugs and guns. And that made a lot more sense than someone like Quindlen, a low-level ex–CIA agent, pulling the strings. Quindlen was obviously running one arm of the operation from here, not the whole show. But now they had a link between the two names. A step in the right direction, he thought as Calvin Walker and Max emerged from the house, followed by Trish. Calvin was talking on Griffin's phone as he and Max walked down the long drive, then over to the wall where the officers waited.

The three officers looked down, as though ashamed for their part in what happened. The chief continued glaring as Griffin asked Calvin, "You get ahold of my partner?"

"I did," Calvin said, holding out the phone. "He wants to talk to you."

Griffin took it. "Tex. I take it you heard the news?"

"I did. Border Patrol's sending a helicopter to pick up the prisoners. You get the information on Quindlen?"

"Just that he's involved." He stepped a few feet away, not wanting to be overheard by Parks or his men. "One of the officers said that Quindlen was working for Brooks. The chief shut him up. Said they'd all be dead if they talked."

He heard Tex talking to someone else, probably their boss. A moment later, he was back on the line. "McNiel wants you and Sydney back here at once. If this is Brooks's operation, he's bound to find out even before you get to Quindlen."

"My understanding is he lives nearby. We should at least—"

"Sorry, Griff. The boss says back here for debriefing. If there's any chance we can get Brooks, last thing we need to do is spook him by going after Quindlen. You'll get him later."

He disconnected, walked up to Sydney, saying, "We're heading back. Today."

If she was bothered, she didn't show it. Or maybe it was more that her attention was focused on Max as he stopped suddenly, refusing to move forward, when Calvin was walking past the officers on the wall. The dog eyed Parks, lowered his head, then growled.

Parks inched back. "Should've shot it when I had the chance."

Calvin grabbed Parks by his arm, pulled him to his feet, his free hand clenched, shaking.

"What're you going to do, boy? Hit me? While I'm cuffed?"

"I should."

"You always were a coward. And you smell like piss."

Griffin reached out, grasped Calvin by his shoulder. "Not worth it."

Calvin hesitated, then lowered his fist. He walked Parks to the patrol car, pushed him into the backseat, then slammed the door shut.

Unfortunately the window was rolled down and Parks leaned out, apparently not knowing when to shut up. "Pissed your pants like a coward! I should've killed you *and* your dog. You stink, boy!"

Sydney slung the AR–15 onto her back, then picked up the remote and the bomb Griffin had made. "Calvin? Get Trish and the dog and leave out the gate. *Now.*" And then she walked over to the patrol car where Parks sat. She set the bomb on the front dash with the timer facing toward him. When she was certain he saw it, she held up the remote so he had no choice but to look. "What was that you said about cowards?"

His eyes widened, but then the bluster returned to his face. "If that thing were real, you wouldn't be standing here."

"Guess you'll find out at the last second," she said, then looked toward the officers sitting on the wall. "You might want to hit the ground."

"Sydney . . . ?" Griffin called out, as he backed up with the others. "*Don't.*"

"He deserves it, Griff." She shoved the remote right up to Parks's face, pressed the button, then ran toward Griffin. The timer flashed red, counting down the seconds.

Parks went wild, throwing himself against the car door. It held fast. The three officers looked on in disbelief, then dove to the ground.

Crack!

The tire blew.

The ensuing silence was almost as deafening as the gunshot from Sydney's AR–15. Parks stilled in his seat, looking shocked that he was alive.

Sydney walked up, leaned toward the window. "Huh. Guess you were right. Detonator *wasn't* connected." And then she gave a pointed look at the growing wet stain on his khaki pants. "But who smells like piss now?"

The Border Patrol arrived to take custody of the officers, and were soon joined by the various alphabet agencies, all interested in the gunrunning that Parks was involved in.

Griffin and Sydney gave a brief statement of their involvement. And contrary to Chief Parks's accusation, no one was trying to kill him. The discharge of the weapon that took out the patrol car tire? Purely accidental.

Finally they were allowed to leave. As Griffin and Sydney walked toward the car still parked out by the gulch, she reached out, gave him a quick hug. "That was actually fun."

"Not bad for a day's work."

"Too bad we have to fly back for debriefing. I was looking forward to a nice quiet weekend. Just you and me . . ."

"Same here," he said, though he wasn't being entirely truthful. He looked over at her, wishing he could just come right out and say what he had to say. Some secrets were never meant to be divulged, and this was one. Even so, until he told her, there could never be anything between them. And if he did tell her? He knew without a doubt she'd leave. Never look back.

The laughter left her eyes as she studied his face, apparently sensing his struggle. "So . . . what was it you wanted to talk to me about? We've got a few minutes before that helicopter gets here."

"It can wait," he said, hoping he wasn't making the mistake of his life.

They walked in silence a few minutes, and then she linked her arm through his, her face lighting up once more. "God, I wish I had a photo of his face when I shot out that tire."

He looked over at her and smiled. "Priceless."

AWARD-WINNING AUTHOR
ROBIN BURCELL

THE DARK HOUR
978-0-06-213347-2

A high-profile killing has brought FBI Special Agent and forensic artist Sydney Fitzpatrick to Amsterdam—even as the assassination of a prominent U.S. senator rocks the political world. Two seemingly unrelated murders are leading Sydney to the threshold of a shocking conspiracy to spread a plague of death across the globe. Now Sydney must race against the clock to prevent a biological nightmare of astronomical proportions.

THE BLACK LIST
978-0-06-213354-0

FBI Special Agent Sydney Fitzpatrick is called in to lend her expertise in an increasingly troubling murder case. The investigation reveals that a popular relief charity's funds have been siphoned off to bankroll terrorist cells in black list countries. Unless Sydney and her partner, Zachary Griffin, can get to the root of a monstrous conspiracy, untold thousands will die in a nuclear catastrophe, and a nation will be reduced to untold chaos.

THE KILL ORDER
978-0-06-227371-0

FBI Special Agent Sydney Fitzpatrick knows nothing about The Devil's Key, except that her father was involved in its theft and murdered as a result. Anyone caught with the code in their possession is terminated with extreme prejudice. Sydney, unaware of the standing kill order, has just recovered it.

RBU1 0913